WHAT SLEEPS BENEATH

JOHN QUICK

BLOODSHOT BOOKS

READ UNTIL YOU BLEED!

WHAT SLEEPS BENEATH

JOHN QUICK

CHAPTER ONE

"**Y**ou gonna do it, or just stand there like some chickenshit all night?"

Ryan didn't bother reacting to the comment. Maybe if Matt doled such homilies out a little less often, potential insults like that would bother him. Since they comprised the majority of the things Matt had said to him during the years they'd been in school together, Ryan was able to ignore it easily enough. It also helped him to ignore the snickers from the older boys who were hanging out with Matt tonight, though if he'd heard Hunter start in as well, it might have succeeded in getting under his skin. Friends could make fun of each other all they wanted, but when it came to things like this, they had each other's backs, no matter what.

He kept his attention fixed on the sagging chain-link fence and the dilapidated building across the courtyard beyond it. The John Spector Mental Hospital had closed down decades ago, back in the eighties, and in all that time no one had bothered to do anything with the building or the land it sat on. Maybe it was because it was too far outside of town to be convenient, or maybe it was because of the legends of the place being haunted. Ryan seriously doubted it was that last one, though. It served to scare kids his age or younger, but he couldn't imagine any adults actually caring about ghosts or whatever running around a place—if you could find any that would even admit they believed in such things at all.

Haunted or not, the place was creepy, there was no question of that. If the rumors were to be believed, it had a right to be. Supposedly the place had been shut down after the patients staged a revolt against the doctors, turning the tables and performing the same procedures on them that the doctors had been using on their wards. The way Ryan heard it, the doctors had been doing stuff that was better suited for the times when using leeches on someone was the height of medical science. Whatever had happened, the place now carried a thick air of menace around it and had become a popular spot for kids to go and try to scare the living shit out of one another.

Or, as was the case tonight, to use the place as a way to see who was worthy of being in with the "cool" kids.

Still nine months and counting until his sixteenth birthday and the days where he could get his drivers' license in order to seem cool, Ryan didn't see many other choices. He didn't want to do this at all, but Hunter had pointed out that this was quite possibly the only way they had of keeping from being bullied for another two years (actually two years and three months, as Ryan had insisted). Begrudgingly, he'd agreed with Hunter. The other boy had been his best friend since they were barely old enough to form any type of relationship with someone that wasn't family, and while he thought Hunter could stand to be a bit more conservative in how he acted at times, he usually had the right idea about things, even if he went about it the wrong way.

It wasn't that Ryan was all that afraid of running into the ghost of a former patient at the hospital, or even one of the doctors who'd fallen prey to those he was supposedly trying to help. What had Ryan so hesitant about going through with this was the idea of stepping onto a rotted section of floor or having a worn chunk of ceiling fall onto either his or Hunter's heads while they were exploring the place with nothing more powerful than a cigarette lighter pilfered from Hunter's mom's purse to light their way. Old buildings could be dangerous, monolithic structures like this even more so. By going in there, they were just asking for trouble.

Of course, by not going in there they were still asking for trouble, albeit of a completely different kind.

"Well?" Matt asked, his voice growing more annoyed by the second.

"Dude," Hunter said, leaning close and speaking quietly. "If we don't get on with this, they're just going to beat us up and bail. You know that, right?"

Ryan spared a glance over his shoulder and saw Matt, cigarette dangling from the corner of his mouth, a look of angry irritation forming on his face. His ever-present companions looked like they were ready to go ahead and start with the pummeling rather than wait for the two younger boys to grow a pair and do what they'd agreed to come here and do. Zach and Brandon were too subservient to Matt to do anything on their own, but the instant Matt gave the go-ahead, it was a one-way trip to pain city for both Ryan and Hunter. They'd run out of time and options, and Ryan wished for what might be the hundredth time tonight that he hadn't let Hunter talk him into this.

"We just go in, grab something to prove we were in there, and then we're good, right?" Ryan asked. "That's all?"

"Yeah, that's all," Matt agreed, blowing a plume of smoke that hadn't even been inhaled right into Ryan's face. "Just has to take you a half-an-hour. And the clock don't start until you walk through the doors. None of that starting the timer when you go through the fence shit. Anything less than that, and I'm going to be convinced you're just a scared little pussy and get on with my life. Now, last chance, get the fuck in there, or the door of opportunity gets slammed in your face."

Brandon only chuckled at that, but Zach laughed like it was the funniest thing he'd ever heard in his life. For all Ryan knew, it was. He doubted Zach was a connoisseur of wit, and suspected he was only in possession of half what most people had.

Ryan sighed and started walking toward the fence, Hunter right beside him. There was a spot almost directly in front of him where others had done the same thing he was about to do and had managed to fold the thin metal wire over to provide access to the courtyard grounds beyond. Hunter got to it first, pushing down with one foot while he lifted the broken fence higher to allow Ryan to pass underneath it without having to duck-walk the whole way. Ryan shook his head, wondering how he ended up being the one to go first on an idea that was Hunter's to start with, and made his way through, taking care to not snag either his clothes or his skin on any of the sharp, jagged metal edges. Once he was on the other side, he turned to help Hunter through as well, but the other boy was already crawling in unaided, barely missing a particularly painful looking barb as he passed.

"Remind me again why we're doing this," Ryan said, once they'd passed far enough across the courtyard that he could be reasonably sure Matt and his cronies couldn't hear them. "I didn't think you even liked those guys."

Hunter looked over his shoulder to make sure the other boys weren't following and shook his head. "Matt's a dick, no question there. And Zach's not much better. Brandon's okay, though. And, he turns sixteen next month. Already got a car and everything. That means we can look cooler when we go places, if we can catch a ride with him instead of using our bikes."

"Why is it so important to look cool, anyway?" Ryan insisted. "We've done okay on our own so far."

Hunter snorted. "Yeah, and how many girls have you hooked up with?"

"None. Same as you, I should point out."

"That's what I'm saying!" Hunter said. "Obviously what we're doing isn't enough to attract any female companionship, but those asshats always have hot chicks hanging around them. Don't you want to be in on that?"

"It'll happen when it happens," Ryan said by rote. "That's what Kyle said, anyway."

"Yeah, but not all of us have older brothers in the Army to give us bullshit advice."

Hunter went silent for a moment, and Ryan had just begun to think he was letting the matter drop when he finally gave him an evil grin.

"I know," Hunter said. "I just figured it out. You don't care about a bunch of girls, do you? You just care about one of them. One named Kayla, right?"

Ryan stopped walking and stared at his friend, amazed that he would even think of playing that particular card right now. Kayla Monroe was one of the prettiest girls in school and had been for as long as Ryan could remember. He didn't know when it started, but he'd developed more than a healthy crush on her in the last couple of years. In truth, he'd damn near become obsessed with her. He'd confessed as much to Hunter during a sleep-over this past summer, and Hunter had sworn he'd keep the secret.

Apparently, keeping the secret didn't preclude him from using it as leverage against Ryan whenever he felt the need to.

"What's your point?" Ryan asked.

Hunter shrugged. "I'm just saying. Aside from that time you accidentally stepped on her foot in the hallway and she accepted your apology, have you even talked to her? Does she even know you exist?"

Ryan sighed. "I don't know."

"Exactly!" Hunter said, pointing a finger at him for emphasis. "And right now, why should she? Let's face facts, the two of us haven't exactly done anything to make ourselves stand out, now have we? But if we start hanging out with those guys? We'll be part of the cool group. That's leverage, something you can use as an excuse to start talking to her."

Ryan barked a laugh and started walking again. "Yeah, that's real effective. What am I supposed to say? 'Oh, hi, Kayla! See who I'm hanging out with? Want to go catch a movie sometime?' I'll sound like a pretentious asshole."

"I see what you mean," Hunter said. "Won't be much of a difference, will it?"

Ryan made as if he was going to punch him, and Hunter backed away, hands raised, laughing.

"Maybe you don't say exactly that," Hunter said. "But think about it. Think who she hangs out with. Some of those chicks also hang out with Matt and Brandon and Zach. That means there would be some common ground, something you can use to break the ice. See what I'm getting at?"

As much as he didn't want to admit it, Hunter did have something resembling a point there. "Maybe."

Hunter laughed and clapped him on the back. "It's not much, but I'll take it! Let's do this!"

* * *

As he feared, the inside of the place was nearly pitch-black in places, with only faint traces of moonlight trickling in through the broken windows in the entry hall to guide their way. Ryan fingered the lighter through his pocket, debating on whether or not it was time to pull it out yet, and decided there was no rush. They had just walked through the door, which meant they had thirty whole minutes to kill before they had to find their way back out again. He knew that realistically all they had to do was hang out over by the abandoned reception desk for a while, then snag some small thing that had been here before the place closed down and head back out, but now that he was actually here, his curiosity was starting to get the better of him.

"So where should we go?" Hunter asked, his voice quiet and surprisingly almost reverent, as if he didn't want to intrude on the eerie stillness of this place by speaking at a normal volume.

Ryan considered as he looked around. The building didn't look to be in bad shape, other than the normal deterioration that came from sitting abandoned and neglected for so long. Well, that and the assorted debris from countless parties and make-out sessions that had probably occurred here over the years since it closed down.

Which was strange to consider, actually. Ryan couldn't think of a less romantic place than an abandoned insane asylum. Still, it was secluded, and private, and he supposed if he had the chance to make out with Kayla here, he wouldn't turn it down.

"Let's try to stick to this floor," he said, his voice instinctively matching Hunter's in volume and tone. "If we can't find anything to take back pretty soon, then we can figure something else out."

Hunter nodded and pointed toward a long hallway barely visible through a set of half-closed doors. "That way, then?"

The doors were almost directly ahead of them, just past the crumbling remains of the desk and right next to a set of wide stairs leading to the upper floors of the building. There were no other ways in or out of this room aside from the one they'd come in through, so it was as good a place to start as any.

It was even darker in the hallway than Ryan expected, forcing him to pull the lighter from his pocket and consider striking it. He hesitated, wondering how much fluid it had left. The last thing he wanted was for them to end up deep in the bowels of this place and then run out of fuel, leaving them unable to find their way back out again. He wasn't afraid of the place being haunted, but that didn't mean he wanted to spend the night here, trapped in the dark with only Hunter for company. He supposed it was better than being trapped in the dark in here alone, but not by much.

He found that after a moment his eyes adjusted to the dark somewhat, the faint grey glow coming from the reception area still giving them enough to see the basic shapes before them, even if they weren't able to make out any details. He decided to keep the lighter ready, but to only use it when they either couldn't see at all or needed to look at something more closely.

They had barely gone a dozen steps down the hallway when Hunter grabbed his arm and pulled him to a stop. Ryan turned, and saw his friend was facing an open doorway along the side of the hall. Something was crisscrossing the doorway, something that fluttered gently from the wind of their passage. He sighed, wondering for the first time how much Matt and his asshole friends had prepared this place before bringing them out here. He had a feeling that if he struck that lighter and held it to the door, he would see bands of yellow police tape barring their way. Once upon a time, that might have been believable, but after so many years and so many previous visitors, he just couldn't accept that something like that would still be here, much less intact. Surely it would've been stolen a long time ago, by some adventurous kid hoping for a really neat souvenir of their visit here.

He went ahead and lit the lighter anyway, more to appease Hunter's apparent interest than anything else, and saw that while he wasn't exactly correct about it being police tape, he was still close in his assumption.

Two thick bands of yellow tape were stretched across the door, the word "caution" standing out in thick, black letters at regular intervals along the tape's length. Surprisingly, though, there was a piece of paper stuck at the intersection of the tape, bearing what looked like some kind of official letterhead. He leaned closer and saw that it was from the

Asbury Heights Police Department, but it wasn't notification of this being a crime scene. Instead, it was a warning that the floors in this area had sustained severe water damage and had begun to rot in places, and that they had the potential of giving way at any time, resulting in possible bodily harm.

Just before he had to let the lighter go out before it burned his thumb, he saw the look of excitement on his friend's face, plain as day. Ryan shook his head, and then realized how foolish that was since it was unlikely that Hunter could see it.

"Uh-uh," he said. "No way. That is exactly what I was worried about to start with."

"Think about it, though," Hunter said. "If that tape's still up, maybe nobody's been in that room. We could find something to show Matt, then just hang out back in the entryway until our thirty minutes are up. If we go in here, it might make this whole trip safer in the long run."

"That tape is pretty new," Ryan said. He had no idea if he was correct or not, but at the moment it didn't matter. He just wanted to try and stop Hunter from doing something that could end up getting one or both of them hurt. "That means the cops probably know about kids coming in here and put that up once they learned there was a problem."

"That doesn't make any sense," Hunter said. "By putting it up, they almost guarantee that someone's going to go in there."

It was Hunter-logic, which meant that on the surface it didn't make any sense, but if you looked deeper, it made perfect sense. He'd stated exactly how kids thought, and simply assumed the cops would know that as well. That the cops probably didn't give a shit one way or the other and had just put that warning up as a way to keep the state or whoever still owned this land from getting sued when some dumbass went in there and fell through the floor was beside the point.

And sadly, in keeping with the insanity of both Hunter-logic and the place they were in, it did make a kind of sense to try and get their prize quickly, so they didn't put themselves through any undue risk. Ryan sighed, and heard Hunter give a soft hoot of victory.

Ryan flicked the lighter again, using the flame to try and get a look at the floor beyond the caution tape. It was obviously wood, which made him wonder exactly when this place had been built, and why it hadn't been upgraded to have concrete floors in the time since. Whatever the reason, the floor looked sturdy enough, and he could see the open cabinets and drawers on the other side of what had apparently been an exam room back when the place was open. He let the lighter go out, took a deep breath, and ducked under the caution tape.

No sooner than he stood up straight inside the room, the floor gave a loud, groaning creak. Ryan froze in place, on the verge of panic at the sound. Hunter, apparently not realizing that Ryan had stopped, slammed into his abdomen, knocking him off-balance and sending him staggering a couple more steps into the room. Before Hunter had the chance to apologize, the floor gave another loud groan, and then Ryan heard a crack and felt his feet go out from under him as his fears came to reality and he fell through the rotten beams.

CHAPTER TWO

It took a few seconds for Ryan to realize that while he had fallen through the floor and into the basement, he wasn't injured beyond a few bumps and scrapes. How that happened, he couldn't begin to figure out, but at the same time he was thankful that nothing had really been hurt worse than his pride. He felt around beneath him and found that he was lying amidst a tangle of broken wood atop something soft, something he couldn't immediately identify. He let his fingers trail across the cloth, and suddenly realized he must have landed in an abandoned pile of sheets that probably once were put on the beds upstairs. He doubted very seriously that they were the least bit clean, but since they'd broken his fall and spared him breaking anything else, he was thankful for them all the same.

Then he felt something skitter across the back of his hand, something that had more legs than he cared to think about, something that was followed by dozens more of its friends, and he had to bite back a scream of revulsion. He scrambled from his resting place, wincing as his back protested the sudden movement, and shook his hands before slapping wildly at himself in the hopes of dislodging whatever it was that had been disturbed by his landing and was currently clinging to him.

"Holy shit!" Hunter called from somewhere up above him. "Are you okay?"

Ryan looked up and was just able to make out his friend's face peeking over the edge of the hole he'd fallen through. He couldn't make out any details, but from the edge of panic in his voice, he knew Hunter was probably more freaked out than he was.

"Yeah," he called back. "Just knocked the wind out of myself."

He looked around again. "And trapped myself in the basement."

"Shit, man," Hunter said. "I should've listened to you. This is all my fault."

"I'm the one who was stupid enough to go in first," Ryan replied. "Don't worry about it."

"How are you getting out of there?"

That was the question of the moment, it seemed. His hands were empty, which meant he'd dropped the lighter when he landed. As much as the idea made his skin crawl, he needed to feel around on that pile of whatever-it-was to try and find it. He tensed as he reached out, groaning softly as his hands pushed aside the insects that had swarmed him, searching for the lighter. He wished he'd thought to grab a flashlight before coming out here, but he'd been in such a rush and so reluctant to come in the first place that it had slipped his mind until he was nearly here.

Finally his fingers brushed against something hard, and he felt his breath catch as he took hold of it. The shape was familiar, and he let out a long, relieved sigh as he picked the lighter up and flicked the dial atop it. It sprang to light, the flame flickering wildly but still giving him his first real look at where he'd ended up.

As he'd suspected, he was in an old laundry room, the massive drum shapes of the washing machines lined up against the far wall like gigantic alien soldiers standing in formation. He tried to ignore the small black shapes that rushed to find shelter from the sudden glare and looked down at the pile of discolored sheets that had been his salvation. The bugs were bad enough; he didn't even want to begin to consider what all those dark stains were. He shuddered and looked away.

The lighter was starting to burn his thumb, but Ryan did his best to ignore it as his gaze fell on something laying on the concrete floor several paces away. It was a shadowed cylinder, a little larger on one end than the other. He hissed out a breath as the pain in his thumb caused him to let go of the lighter, barely managing to hold onto it as he fought the urge to jerk his hand away.

"Well?" Hunter asked, no longer sounding panicked, and instead beginning to allow a hint of frustration to creep into his voice. Ryan didn't know what he was so irritated about since he was the one trapped in a dark basement.

"Hold on a second," he said. The lighter's dial was still hot to the touch, too much to make re-lighting it possible yet, so he shuffled slowly in the direction he'd seen the thing on the floor, hoping that it was what he thought it was, and that it actually still worked. He stopped when he felt his toes bump into something and cause it to shift and clatter across the floor. He reached down and grabbed it, relieved to discover that his guess had been correct: he'd managed to find a flashlight.

He held his breath and clicked the switch on the side. The light that emerged wasn't bright, or at least nowhere near as bright as it probably should have been, but it was better than what he'd had, and wouldn't burn his fingers. He smacked the side of it, the way he'd seen his dad do countless times before, and the beam brightened slightly. Hopefully, the batteries would last long enough for him to get the hell out of here, or until he got to a place where he could manage with just the lighter again.

He turned slowly, finally able to get a good look at the room he was in. There was an elevator not too far away, its doors standing open to reveal a hole filled with what looked like grease and mechanical parts. He had no idea where the elevator car was, but it obviously wasn't in the basement. He had a quick mental image of the car plummeting from the top of the building, slamming into the ground and turning the people inside it into something that resembled strawberry jam, but then shook it away. That hadn't happened—at least there was no debris or wreckage to show that it had—and was more a product of watching too many movies than anything based on reality.

A door sat crooked and partially open in the wall opposite where he was standing. The hallway beyond was dark, the faint light from his recovered flashlight not enough to let him see what might be beyond the door. If there was an elevator, it was a safe bet there were stairs around somewhere as well leading back up to the main floor. Since they weren't in this room, they had to be somewhere beyond that door. So long as it wasn't jammed in its frame and could be opened, he should be able to find them easily enough.

"Stay there," he called up to Hunter. "I found a light, now I'm going to try and find the stairs so I can get back up there. Hopefully this will last until I can get back to you. If not, I do still have the lighter. I'll get there, it just might take me a minute."

"Or," Hunter said, his voice starting to take on an edge of panic that Ryan didn't think he was even aware of. "You can toss the lighter up to me and I can start working my way around to try and figure out where the stairs down are."

"And what happens if this flashlight goes out?" Ryan replied. "You've at least got a little light up there. I'm underground, pretty much. It's going to really suck if I get stuck down here without any way to see where I'm going."

"Yeah, okay," Hunter grumbled. "I guess you've got a point there."

"I'll be as quick as I can be," Ryan said. "I swear."

"You better," Hunter said. "Don't make me have to kick your ass."

Ryan smiled despite the situation he was in and headed toward the door. It took a bit of juggling to make sure he didn't drop the flashlight as he lifted the door so he could swing it the rest of the way open because of how it was hanging by one of the hinges, but it didn't give him any real trouble. As he'd expected, the hallway beyond was pitch black, which meant that even the little bit of light his flashlight gave off was able to go a long way toward making it where he could see where he was going.

Several doors sat along the walls, all closed. When he tried the first one, it didn't budge, the lock long since frozen through combined rust from the elements that had trickled in over the years and pure, simple neglect. He didn't immediately see any stairs, though, so he was forced to keep going, trying the occasional door to see if any were unlocked, but not expecting to find one. When one finally pushed open, he was so shocked he very nearly ended up falling again. He managed to catch his balance and started to turn and leave, then figured that since he was here, he might as well go ahead and see if he could find anything interesting to take, so he could kill two birds with one stone and finish this stupid dare Matt and the asshole brigade had sent him on.

The room he found himself in was much larger than it had looked based on the spacing of the doors outside in the hall, and when he looked over he saw the reason for it. Another door sat several paces down, leading back out into the same hallway as the one he'd come through. That at least explained the room's size. With two entry points, it could take up more space and still be unobtrusive from the hall.

As best he could tell, this was a storage room of some sort, with rows and rows of shelves creating an almost maze-like feeling to the room. Several of them were knocked over, their contents dumped on the floor, and others were bare, possible victims to looting in the early days after this place had closed down. Either way, he was sure he would be able to find a prize of some sort here.

Ryan made his way deeper into the room, taking care to not trip and fall over the detritus scattered across the floor. Most of what he could see appeared to be maintenance equipment: assorted tools, broken light bulbs, spare faucets for sinks, and other things that would be needed to keep a place like this running efficiently. None of it looked remarkable or interesting, though. He knew Matt was going to want something particularly awesome in order for him to say it counted.

When Ryan reached the end of the row he'd been walking down and saw what lay in the center of the room, it was all he could do to not scream like a little girl.

There was a body there, a human body, and it didn't take much for Ryan to know that whoever this person had been, they were far beyond dead now. His hand trembled, making the light jump as it played across the shriveled skin, the sunken cheeks, and the hair that looked like it belonged on a broom and not a person's head. He trailed the light lower, down the dead man's chest, and stopped at the chunk of wood that rose from the corpse's pectoral region. Ryan hadn't ever taken any anatomy classes, but he was smart enough to know that the heart lay just beneath the left breast, slightly off center from the sternum.

A wooden stake driven through a corpse's heart. Ryan knew good and well what that sounded like, but it was impossible. There was no such thing as vampires, not in the real world. They were fictional creatures, legends told to scare people, and nothing more. He became acutely aware that he was standing in the basement storeroom of an abandoned insane asylum and wondered if this was the result of one of the patients having delusions and the cops never finding the body, or something else entirely that he didn't even want to begin to consider.

He was going to have to call the cops—there was no question of that. He'd just found a dead body down here, and even if Matt never spoke to him again except to threaten him before kicking his ass on a daily basis, it was just the right thing to do.

Hoping to get as much information as he could before he made that call, he crept closer to the body, looking for some sign as to who they had been in life. He couldn't tell much with the way the clothing had worn away, and from how badly decayed the body was, but he thought it was a man—at least based on the style of clothing they were wearing—but anything else was lost to the ravages of time.

Ryan let out a low breath and started to turn away, realizing there was no information to be had here, but his feet tangled and jammed up against an upended tool box, the heavy hammer wedged into the handles and creating an effective block to catch his ankles and cause him to fall for the second time tonight. He threw his hands out in a vain attempt to catch himself and succeeded only in knocking the stake free from the corpse before he landed sprawled out on top of it, knocking up a dust so thick it felt like it coated the inside of his nose and mouth.

This time, he did scream. Long, loud, and just as high-pitched as he feared it would be when he was capable of caring. He scrambled to his feet, wincing as his hand slid across the corpse's face in the process, and turned tail to run. Miraculously, he avoided the debris and made it to the door without incident, catching the frame with one hand and using it to spin himself in what he hoped was the right direction.

He found the stairs on pure accident, slamming his ankles and then his shins into them hard enough to make himself fall yet again, crashing against them and leaving a burning line of pain across his belly and chest. He would probably have a bruise there tomorrow, but right now he couldn't care less. He was driven by the simple desire to the get the hell away. He didn't even bother trying to stand up again, simply crawled up the stairs on all fours, finally getting to his feet when he reached the first-floor landing. He turned and slammed the door open, rushing through it and sprinting down the hallway, somehow instinctively keeping the flashlight pointed in front of him to avoid running into anything else.

Hunter appeared from seemingly nowhere, suddenly just there, right in front of his face. Ryan didn't even pause, just ran right past his startled friend, intent on reaching the door, the exit—freedom—as fast as he possibly could. He was dimly aware of Hunter swearing and running after him, and then he was through the door, out the entrance hall, and back in the soft moonlight of the courtyard outside. Still, he kept running, not stopping until his only choice was to either halt or slam into the chain-link fence they'd come through to get here in the first place.

Unsurprisingly, Matt and his friends were gone, the only bikes remaining outside the fence those belonging to him and Hunter. He couldn't give less of a shit. He was out, he'd gotten away, and for right now, that was the only thing that mattered to him. He would have to deal with Matt's teasing later on—he knew that as sure as he knew he needed to breathe to live—but for now, he was safe.

CHAPTER THREE

Sleep was nothing more than wishful thinking. The image of that body replayed over and over in Ryan's mind every time he closed his eyes. Not how it looked, but the sick realization that he knew how it had felt, too. The rough, dry skin and brittle bones beneath, the complete lack of fat or musculature from where decay and heat and time had mummified it into something that he wished he thought was nothing more than a Halloween prop, but which he was all too aware was realer than real. Lying here in bed, after two showers where he'd scrubbed himself so hard his skin looked pink and swollen afterward, he could still feel it on his skin, could still almost taste it from the dust that had gotten into his mouth when he fell on it.

He'd been determined to call the cops, to alert them to what he had discovered in the basement of that old building, but Hunter had somehow managed to talk him out of it. He'd pointed out—perhaps correctly, perhaps not—that they would end up in trouble for having been trespassing and might even be accused of worse. He'd reminded Ryan that when he fell on the corpse, he'd knocked the stake out of it, so it was possible the cops might say they'd tampered with a body, or been responsible for pulling a prank and putting it there to start with, or one of a thousand other potential scenarios that would result in the pair of them winding up in deep, deep shit.

Ryan didn't know if any of that was true, and had strong suspicions that none of it was, but he was too freaked out at the time to make a coherent argument against the insanity of Hunter-logic. He'd debated with himself on the way home, and by the time he got there and in the shower—which was the first order of business, no matter what else he finally decided to do—he'd convinced himself that it would be better for him to just try and forget it had ever happened at all. He doubted he would be the last person to set foot in that place, and it was obvious from the warning across the door he and Hunter saw that the cops did go inside on occasion, so he would just leave it to them to find the body and deal with it.

And if they didn't? Well, then it really wouldn't matter anyway, would it?

It wasn't like he'd seen any missing persons reports or unsolved cases that might tell him that it was the body of someone who'd been killed recently. And if it was an older case, he was sure it would've been a rumor or legend he'd have at least heard about by now. He'd go on Google tomorrow and see if he could find anything out.

If he ever managed to get any sleep, that was.

Ryan sighed and rolled over for the hundredth time or so, kicking his covers down as he did to try and cool himself off. He lay on his side, staring out the window at the gentle breeze blowing the tree limbs in strange patterns across the pane. Fall wasn't quite in full swing yet, only at the beginning when the leaves first began to change colors, but there were still enough missing from the tree to make those limbs look almost skeletal as they danced across the night sky. It reminded him too much of that corpse, of its shriveled and spindly arms lying helplessly at its sides. He shuddered and rolled over onto his back, staring up at the ceiling and wishing his mind would just shut itself off so he could rest.

This was no better, so he rolled to the other side and stared at the wall, across the scattering of empty potato chip bags, half-drunk glasses of water and juice and cola sitting on his nightstand, and at the flashing LED lights screaming over and over that it was three-fifteen in the morning. It was a Friday night—well, Saturday morning, now—so he didn't have school the next day, but his dad had been clear that tomorrow was when the last yard work of the season was to take place, and Ryan knew he wouldn't accept not sleeping well as an excuse get out of it. The irony was that Dad would also be upset if Ryan started dozing off while mowing and either missed a spot or ran down one of Mom's flowers that she kept forgetting to put garden bricks around for protection.

The longer he lay there staring at it, the more it seemed the clock was taunting him, mocking him for his inability to close his eyes and drift off into whatever dreams were in store for him tonight. Even if they were nothing more than a constant stream of nightmares, it would be better than lying here awake and miserable all night. The clock didn't care. Ryan could almost imagine it going off suddenly, the normal blaring alarm replaced by manic laughter.

Which was a testament to how tired he really was if such a thing actually seemed plausible.

After one final attempt at lying on his back, Ryan gave up and got out of bed. He tried to convince himself that the reason he couldn't sleep had nothing to do with his discovery in the asylum's basement and everything to do with how freaking hot it was in his room. He held a hand up to try and feel the air coming from the vent in the ceiling, but what little there was felt room temperature or colder. It should have been cooling the room off nicely, but for some reason, it wasn't. He debated on going out to the thermostat and turning the temperature down but knew Dad would throw a fit over that come morning if he saw it. Instead, Ryan pulled a chair over and stood on it so he could close the vent completely. That done, he went to the window and raised it slightly, allowing some of the cooler night air to drift in. He started to feel better almost at once, savoring the way the breeze drifted over the exposed skin of his bare legs and arms. He pulled his t-shirt over his head and allowed it to caress his chest as well for a moment, then returned to his bed and lay down on top of the covers, propping his pillows up behind him so he could lean back in a half sitting position.

Finally, something seemed to be working. He could feel his eyes starting to droop within minutes, his body relaxing as he began to drift. His mind wandered, images of the asylum flickering across the screen of his subconscious. He tried to force them away, attempting to pull a picture of Kayla into his thoughts to counteract it, but her smiling face dissipated before it could even fully form.

Suddenly, it was as if he was in the asylum again, only with some differences from how it had really been. It was still dark and abandoned, but for some reason he was able to see things clearly, like he was wearing those night vision goggles they always used on the spy and military shows his dad watched on television. He was in the storeroom again, hiding amongst the shadows, listening as footsteps outside drew closer and closer. He felt fear, but only a little. Mainly he felt irritation and annoyance that someone had come so close to finding him. They had succeeded in cutting off any avenue for escape, and he knew it was only a matter of time before they discovered him here and did something even worse.

The doors flew open on either side, the bright beams of flashlights piercing the darkness and making him wince as it demolished whatever dark vision he'd been using. He heard raised, angry voices, but couldn't make out what was being said. The fear increased as he felt the walls against his back push harder, and it took a moment for Ryan to realize that they hadn't moved—he was trying to push himself as far into the shadows as he could, hoping in vain it would be enough to keep him hidden.

It wasn't. The lights passed over him and then shot back, illuminating him fully for those who had entered the room. As best he could tell, it looked like five of them were now racing toward him, but he had the sense that there were more outside, waiting for the word to come and join their companions.

He somehow knew that he was perfectly capable of fighting, of defending himself, but he was not as strong as normal. While his dream-self knew the reason why, Ryan couldn't manage to recall it. For now, it was just a surety born of the dream he was trapped in. Before he had time to consider this, two of the men who'd come for him leapt, one grabbing at him while the other waved something at him while mumbling some prayer under his breath. Ryan saw with no real surprise that the object was a crucifix, and while it didn't bother him all that much, the insanity that the man wielding it would think it would was enough to distract him.

The other man landed on him, grabbing him by the throat and jerking him from his hiding place. The man turned and shoved him, sending him stumbling backward across the room. Something slammed into his shoulders and then into the backs of his knees, buckling them and causing him to collapse to the floor in a heap. As soon as he hit the ground, the other men were moving, grabbing his arms and legs, the man who'd thrown him planting one knee on his forehead to try and hold him in place.

Before he had the chance to try and beg for mercy, another man appeared, bigger than the others, his eyes filled with righteous fury. The man held a long wooden shaft in one hand and a heavy mallet in the other. With no warning whatsoever, the man dropped to his knees, straddling him, and placed the wooden shaft against his chest.

He knew what was coming, wanted more than anything to prevent it, but he was too weak to fight back against so many at once. Before he could do anything else, the mallet fell, striking the wooden stake and driving it deep into his chest. He felt it nick his heart and knew the end was almost here, then the mallet fell again, and the world went dark, lost in a sea of the most unimaginable pain he could remember feeling.

Ryan jerked awake, sweat drenching his body, eyes wide and searching the room as his hands flew to his chest, searching for the stake he knew had to be there. Sunlight was trickling in through his open window, giving him a clear view of his smooth, uninjured chest. He looked over at the clock wildly and was shocked to see that it was now just after eight in the morning. Only then did he realize it had all been a dream, an insane little horror movie brought on by his discovery of the corpse and the strange manner in which it had apparently died.

Slowly, his breathing began to even out and he was able to relax. He didn't feel as rested as he hoped, but he did feel better than he expected to a few hours ago. He would be making an early night of it tonight, that was for damn sure, but at least he should be able to make it through the day without too many issues.

As he rose and began to get dressed, he found himself remembering bits of that dream, or nightmare, or whatever it had been. Even in the light of day it lingered, feeling more like recalled memories than a simple dream. Even as he put gas in the lawn mower and pulled the cord to start it up, he still found himself dwelling on it. Each time he circled the yard, a trail of cut grass flying out beside him, he caught himself looking for the men who'd come for him in the dream, expecting to see them at any moment leaping from the bushes with crosses, stakes, and mallets in their hands. They didn't, of course, but Ryan couldn't stop thinking that it was going to happen at any second, probably when he least expected it.

The strange feelings finally began to fade as he traded the mower for a weed-eater, but he still couldn't manage to shake the thought that, for some strange reason, this was only the beginning of something much, much bigger.

CHAPTER FOUR

Even though he'd managed to get some sleep, it hardly counted as restful sleep, so Ryan was starting to zone out while he was finishing up mowing the yard. He barely noticed Hunter standing there watching him until he'd nearly run his friend over. He stopped just before he mistook Hunter's legs for especially thick weeds, jumping a little as he saw someone where he hadn't noticed anyone before, then let go of the little trigger on the weed-eater's handle, killing the motor. He pulled his cell phone out and hit pause on the playlist of heavy rock music that had been intended to help keep him awake but was succeeding only in helping him nearly drift off again, then took one of the ear buds out of his ear and let it fall, slapping lightly against his chest.

"Dude," Hunter said. "You look like shit."

"Aw, thanks," Ryan replied. "How sweet of you. Did you need something, or are you just here to flirt?"

Hunter snorted a laugh and smiled. If he'd experienced any lack of sleep after the events of last night, it certainly wasn't showing. "Just wanted to see how you felt after all those falls you took."

"Sore," Ryan said. He was surprised that the bruises he'd expected to see hadn't materialized, and truthfully he felt about the same as if he'd played a strenuous game of football or baseball or something the day before after not doing it for a long time. It was about the only thing that was going his way today. "Not bad, though."

He narrowed his eyes when he saw the look on his friend's face. There was more to it than just checking on his well-being, and it was plain for anyone who'd known him for any real length of time. "Okay, stop bullshitting me. What do you really want?"

"I was thinking," Hunter said. "We didn't come up with anything to show Matt and the asshole twins, did we?"

"The flashlight I found in the basement," Ryan answered. "I kept it. Other than that, no, we didn't."

Hunter gave him a look of mock-innocence that was so blatantly fake it made Ryan want to reach out and slap him. "Do you really think they're going to accept that?"

"I don't know," Ryan said, running a hand over his face. "Probably not. Why does it matter, anyway? They ditched us, in case you forgot."

"You could see it that way," Hunter replied, nodding. "Or, you could see it as that being a part of the game in the first place."

Ryan stared back at him, deadpan. "Get us out there, wait till we go in, then split and leave us to figure it out from there? That doesn't make any...."

He caught himself before he could finish the statement, the truth of the matter popping into his head a bit slower than if he'd been completely with it today. "Okay, that actually does sound like something they'd do, but it still doesn't explain why you care whether or not we got a souvenir from that place. If they split on us, it's not very likely that they intended on following through with letting us into their little club to start with."

"That could be," Hunter agreed. "But do you really want to take that chance, to have gone in there and gone through all that for nothing?"

Ryan laughed without humor and shook his head. "You want us to go back, don't you?"

Apparently, Hunter took the laughter to mean that he was winning Ryan over instead of the opposite. "I figure we go back tomorrow morning. Half the town's going to be in church, and the other half's going to be sleeping off a hangover from whatever trouble they get up to tonight. It'll be perfect! We stash our bikes in that drainage ditch not far from the fence and walk the rest of the way in. I doubt anyone will see us, so we get in while it's still light outside, find something cool, then get back out and be home in no time."

Ryan shook his head some more. He had no intention of going back in there, not tomorrow, not ever, but he knew his friend well enough to know that if he just came right out and said that, he would end up butt-hurt for a few days. He'd get over it—he always had in the past when Ryan shot down one of his crazy ideas, anyway—but Ryan really didn't want to deal with the headache in the meantime. Better to let him down slowly, so he could get used to the idea of his plan not happening.

"Okay, so how do we explain coming home with whatever we found? You know we'll get asked where we've been."

Hunter smiled broadly. "Actually, we probably won't. Your dad's going to be kicked back in front of the game, your mom's going to be tinkering with fall decorations, and my mom's going to be so hung over she won't even notice I was missing to start with."

"And your sister?"

"If she doesn't end up staying the night with that dickhead she's been fucking, she'll be in the bad shape as Mom will be. She won't notice shit."

"Watch your mouth," Ryan said absently, trying to think of his next argument. "My Dad's outside."

"Sorry," Hunter mumbled, sounding anything but. "So are you in or not?"

Ryan sighed. It looked like there was going to be no easy way to do this. He could only hope that Hunter stopped moping about it sooner than he normally did. "Not."

Hunter's smile froze for a brief instant before it slowly faded to a scowl. "Not? You're kidding, right?"

"No," Ryan said, rubbing a hand across his face. "I'm not. The last thing I want to do, especially feeling like I do right now, is to go back into that deathtrap and risk doing worse damage to myself than I did last night."

"So we did that for nothing," Hunter said, nodding once. "Put up with those guys' shit for a week, then get dragged out to the middle of nowhere, risk breaking our damned necks, all so we can come back with a flashlight they're going to say we just went to the store and bought on our own."

"They weren't going to be our friends anyway," Ryan insisted, mounting one last attempt at convincing Hunter that the plan had been flawed from the start. "Those guys don't care anything about us, except for when they can beat our asses next. There's nothing in this for them, so why would they do it?"

"I don't know," Hunter said, his voice rising a bit as he started to let his anger and irritation show. "But it was a shot, wasn't it? It was a chance to finally stop being the low men on the damn totem pole and finally start getting some respect. But that's fine. You don't want that. You don't care about getting in with that group, about stopping the beatings and the teasing, or about getting Kayla to notice you for once. Fine. You just keep daydreaming about her and never do anything to try and make it actually happen. My life's been shit for so long, what's another couple of years going to matter, you know?"

Ryan sighed again. "Hunter...."

"No," Hunter said, raising a hand and turning to leave. "It's fine. You don't want to do it. Whatever. I need to get home. I've still got that report to do for English class."

"You want me to come by later and help you with it?" Ryan asked.

"Nah, don't bother," Hunter replied without turning around. "I'll manage on my own. I'm kind of used to it."

Ryan stood and watched his friend storm away, stopping at the edge of the yard just long enough to pick up his bike from where he'd laid it over on its side before coming to talk to him. Hunter didn't even bother with so much as a glance in his direction as he got on and rode away down the street. This was one of the worst moods Ryan had seen develop from being shot down on some scheme in a long time and was probably going to be one that held out for longer than normal, too.

He shook his head one last time as Hunter rounded the corner and disappeared from sight, and then he tucked the ear bud back in, and hit play on his phone. As the music blared directly into his brain, he got the weed-eater started again and got back to work, trying to forget about his friend's bad mood as well as the nagging feeling that, despite knowing better, he almost thought he'd been right in wanting to go back to the asylum.

* * *

The thought wouldn't go away. The longer the day wore on, the more Ryan felt his urge to go back to the asylum grow. At first he thought it was just his subconscious mind trying to appease Hunter, trying to make peace and stave off the inevitable pouting annoyance that would follow, but it seemed to be more than that. As he tried to wind down and get ready for bed—early, but after the day he'd put in doing yard work, neither of his parents said much of anything about it—the more he realized his desire to return to the abandoned hospital had less to do with his friend's feelings and more to do with that body he'd seen in the basement, and the dream he'd had about it last night.

It was ridiculous when you got right down to it. If he did anything because of that body, it should be call the cops and report it, even anonymously, not go back to get a second look at it. The only reason the thing had gotten into his brain the way it had was because of how freaked out he'd been when he first saw it and then fell on top of it. That was all. There was nothing more to it.

Unless there actually was, but what that could be was so far beyond Ryan's ability to fathom that there was no point even trying.

He sat down at his desk and powered on his laptop, figuring that he could do some research on the place, maybe find out the truth about why it closed, but by the time the system came up and he opened his web browser, the idea wasn't as interesting to him as it had been only minutes before. He loaded up Facebook instead and spent a few minutes idly clicking "like" on some of things his few friends and family posted, but that quickly lost its appeal as well. He glanced down at the clock in the lower corner of his screen and saw it was barely past nine. Any of the people he cared about interacting with on social media or anywhere else would be out doing fun, normal teenage things, not sitting at home in their boxers and a faded t-shirt messing around on the internet.

After another couple of minutes aimlessly clicking on links and watching mindless videos, he closed the browser and shut down the computer. His body was exhausted, but his mind was racing, in dire need of something to help it shut down so he could go to bed and hopefully get some decent sleep tonight. He glanced over at his bookshelves, filled to overflowing with used horror and fantasy paperbacks, but nothing looked appealing. He'd read them all countless times already, and he wouldn't be making his monthly trip to the used bookstore in town until next weekend, so there wasn't even anything sitting in the spot normally reserved for his "to-be-read" pile. He let his eyes drift to the next shelf down, where a small collection of comic book trade paperbacks sat, but none of those held any interest for him, either. It seemed he was destined to be bored as hell until he finally just fell asleep because there was simply nothing else to do.

So thinking, he went to his bed and lay down on top of the covers, crossing his hands behind his head and staring up at the ceiling. It had the opposite effect from the one he'd intended, though. The longer he lay there, the more the desire to go back to the asylum felt like a compulsion, a need that could not be ignored for much longer. He glanced to his closed bedroom door and saw the light trickling in beneath it from the hallway beyond. His parents were still up, and if he got dressed and started to leave the house now, they would give him the third degree and tell him it was too late to be going out, and to go back to bed. Whatever he finally decided to do, he was going to have to wait. If he was lucky, he'd fall asleep before he did anything too stupid.

His thoughts turned to Kayla, and he began replaying a few of his favorite fantasies about her through his head. While Hunter was convinced these "daydreams" were extremely pornographic in nature—and to be fair, there were a few of those stored in Ryan's imagination, too—the ones he enjoyed the most were considerably more innocent. He and Kayla going to the movies, or to the park for a picnic, or even just going to parties together where they tended to forget there was anyone else there in favor of staring lovingly into each other's eyes.

It was silly and childish stuff, he knew that. The very idea that two people as young as they were could fall so deeply in love that they would end up spending their lives together, or even more than a month or two, was insane. Still, he was so infatuated with her that he hoped for exactly that, and to Hell with what anyone else thought.

When the last of the fantasies finally came to its conclusion, with Kayla kissing first him and then their child, who had just been born—and don't bother asking why she was up and walking around less than an hour after giving birth; fantasies didn't have to make sense—he looked at the clock and was a little surprised to see it was now closing in on midnight. Much too late to go out, though from the darkness beyond his door, he knew his parents were in bed and he was free to sneak out and do just that should he so desire. He may as well just give it up for the night, close his eyes, roll over, and go to sleep.

Only he couldn't do that. His mind was racing just as much as it had been before, the momentary distraction now passed and his focus back on that body and the abandoned storeroom where he'd found it. Ryan sighed. He knew there was only one way he was going to be able to get this out of his mind long enough for him to get to sleep, even if doing it was the last thing he really wanted to do.

He got out of bed and crossed to his dresser, quickly pulling on a pair of jeans and a sweatshirt over the top of his t-shirt before picking up his shoes and creeping to the door. He made his way downstairs, pausing to glance back at his parents' door, expecting it to fly open at any minute and his father to ask him just where the hell he thought he was headed to this late. It remained closed, however, and the house remained silent.

When he got to the living room, he turned and headed into the kitchen instead of going out the front door. His dad would have set the alarm before going up to bed, but Ryan knew he tended to leave the door to the garage on bypass, meaning it wouldn't trigger if it was used in the middle of the night. It was a hold-over from the days when they'd had a cat that tended to wander and come back late at night. He and Mom had convinced Dad to leave the garage door itself cracked a little so Sammy could at least come back in out of the elements when it was raining. Sammy was two years gone, but the habit remained, and the only way to set the alarm with the garage door open was to bypass that zone entirely.

Ryan had begun to use it to his own advantage only recently, but it was a definite way out without alerting anyone that he was leaving. It was also a plus tonight because he knew Dad had a bunch of flashlights and the like out there in the garage for emergencies.

He waited until he was out of the kitchen and actually in the garage before pulling on his shoes and going over to the storage cabinet where Dad kept the flashlights. He grabbed two: a normal-sized one and a larger one that had a beam so bright it could almost count as a hand-held floodlight. He considered how he was going to carry both of them and ride his bike at the same time, then dug through a box of old clothes and managed to find a backpack he'd last worn to school when he started the seventh grade. It was pretty ragged, one shoulder strap torn free, its frayed ends dangling loose, but it would suffice for what he had in mind. He dropped the lights into the backpack, slung the single strap over his shoulder, and then carefully lifted the rolling door to the garage enough that he could slip both himself and his bicycle out without causing a ruckus.

The trip to the asylum seemed to take hours, but when he checked his phone after storing his bike in the same drainage ditch where Hunter had suggested they put them tomorrow, he was surprised to see he'd made the trip in just under ten minutes—a personal best for him, and he hadn't even been trying.

He found the hole in the fence quickly and—barely five minutes after arriving—he was back inside the abandoned hospital, heading down the hallway to the basement stairs. He made sure to use the smaller flashlight while he was on the ground floor, not wanting the brighter beam to draw any attention from a cop who might happen to drive past and make sure no one was up to anything out here, and then switched to the larger one once he was standing on the basement landing.

Surprisingly, considering the speed with which he'd left the room last night, he found the storeroom with ease, creeping slowly through the still-open door and paying close attention to where he stepped to make sure he didn't do something stupid like knock a bunch of heavy stuff over on himself when there was no one else around to help him should he get into any trouble. He moved down the narrow aisle formed by a pair of shelves, then took a deep breath and turned when he reached the end.

His mind raced, and his heart started beating faster in his chest as he played the beam across the empty floor ahead of him. He saw the wooden shaft he'd knocked free lying amidst an area of disturbed dust, but what he expected to see wasn't there.

The corpse was gone.

CHAPTER FIVE

Shock kept Ryan rooted to the spot, shock and a wild fear that made his hair want to stand on end and tightened his bowels and bladder until they were almost too uncomfortable to deal with. The beam from the powerful flashlight jittered across the bare patch of floor where the corpse had been last night, and Ryan's mind swam with confusion as he tried to figure out what had happened here. He knew he hadn't imagined it—the wooden shaft lying there amidst the dust verified that, at least to some degree— and there was no chance that the person had only been unconscious. While people's skin did start to wrinkle as they got older, it didn't shrivel up and pull away from their teeth until they were well into the process of decay.

At least that was what he thought. He hadn't seen anyone who'd been dead for that long outside of movies, and then it was all makeup effects and visual trickery.

Ryan closed his eyes and counted to ten, then opened them again, sure that his mind was only playing tricks on him, but nothing was changed. The body was still gone. He turned slowly, searching the floor nearby, wondering if maybe he'd just started looking at the wrong spot in spite of the obvious indication that he wasn't, but the other areas of the floor looked much the same: dust and debris scattered here and there, but no body.

"This isn't happening," Ryan muttered, wincing as his voice echoed even at low volume in the immense room. He turned and looked behind him, searching for signs that someone else had been here during the day, someone who might have found and removed the corpse, but there was no indication that anything had been disturbed. There was no police tape over the door—and wouldn't he have seen that when he first came in?—nor was there anything that seemed out of place from last night, aside from the missing body in the middle of the damn floor.

Something drew his attention to the far corner of the room, some whispery sound that probably would've gone unnoticed under most circumstances, but which was almost over-loud in the otherwise still silence of this place. Ryan took an involuntary step backward as he shone his light in the direction he thought the sound had come from, fully prepared to break and run even if all he saw was a mouse or rat or something scurrying across the floor. He saw nothing of the sort, however. The light landed on a bare, shriveled foot beneath the cuffs of filthy, ragged slacks. His mind scrambled to come up with some reason why someone had moved the body way over there, and then the foot moved, shifting in his direction.

Ryan screamed as he raised the light to reveal the horrid, half-decayed countenance of the corpse he'd seen the night before, now standing, eyes open and staring back at him with primal desperation flickering across them. The thing's withered lips twitched as though it was snarling at him, and then it was moving, racing toward him, closing the distance between them in long, quick strides.

This time, Ryan was too terrified to scream, to make any sound at all other than a weak and ineffectual squeaking sound that didn't even sound like it came from a human being. His bladder let go as he scrambled backward, trying to get away, but stopped when his back slammed against one of the shelves, knocking God-only-knew-what onto the ground in a clatter that was loud enough to nearly drown out the world. He tried to turn and run, but the thing was already on him, sandpapery hands closing over his shoulders and jerking him toward it with a strength that belied its withered state. Ryan didn't try to fight, actually went along with the motion, ducking down at the last instance and landing painfully on his knees before trying to crawl between the thing's legs.

The creature never missed a beat, simply reached down and grabbed Ryan by the back of his sweatshirt and jerked him back to his feet hard enough that Ryan heard the fabric tear. While everything in his brain screamed at him to either get away or just stand still and let whatever was about to happen, happen, Ryan chose a third option: he swung the flashlight in his hand as hard as he could, hoping that he didn't end up breaking it in the process of defending himself. It smacked into the side of the corpse's face, knocking it sideways and nearly driving it to its knees as well. It turned toward him, eyes blazing, and Ryan hit it again, this time bringing the light up in an arc, so it connected with the underside of the thing's chin. He heard the corpse's teeth click together as it let out a massive grunt and went sprawling onto its back.

Ryan was moving on pure instinct and adrenaline, racing to where he'd last seen the wooden stake lying on the floor. He had no idea if this would work, nor whether he even had enough strength to drive the thing home, but since it had been lying docile last night with the stake in its chest, it was the only thing Ryan could think of to buy himself the time to escape. He hit the floor and slid, much like a baseball player stealing third, and came up with the stake in his free hand. He turned toward where he'd last seen the thing that attacked him, shining the light ahead of him, and found it huddled against the wall, rubbing its chin with one gnarled hand.

It looked over to him, and the fury in its eyes quickly turned to fear when it saw what he was holding in his hand. The thing raised one trembling hand toward him, weakly trying to fend him off even though he'd done nothing more than pick it up so far. His guess was apparently correct, that the stake was somehow tied to the corpse's former docility, but rather than be elated that he was on the right track to saving himself, he found himself feeling sorry for the thing. The scariness was gone—aside from what was caused by a walking corpse, at least—leaving only a pathetic helplessness in its wake.

Ryan wanted to scream, knowing what a walking corpse that could only be stopped by a wooden stake to the heart almost had to be, but he refused to let himself even think the word, much less admit to such a thing being real.

The creature must have seen something in his face, because it slowly lowered its hand, finally seeming to actually see the person holding it for the first time. His eyes flicked across Ryan's face, down his arm to the stake, then back again. While the thing's skin was too tight to tell for sure, Ryan thought a wistful smile had crept onto its face.

"You're a kid," the thing said, its voice raspy and weak, as though it hadn't been used in a while—or the vocal chords had deteriorated so far that normal speech was impossible to achieve. "Not only did I nearly kill a kid, I got my ass handed to me by one. Oh, how far we can fall."

In the wake of such a casual pronouncement from something that had been planning to kill him, Ryan had no idea what to say, so he chose to say nothing.

The thing started at him a little more intently, but Ryan had the sense that it wasn't seeing him with its eyes so much as with its mind, with something deeper than normal sight. Finally the thing made a noise that was probably intended to be a snort but ended up sounding like a wheeze instead.

"You're the one who freed me," the thing said. Ryan didn't think it was actually talking to him, despite the fact that it was addressing him. "Unbelievable."

It made a rasping, panting sound that Ryan finally realized was supposed to be a laugh.

"Okay, kid," it rasped. "You haven't come after me with that thing yet, and it looks like I owe you one, so I'm all for calling a truce here."

Ryan blinked. Of all the things that could have happened tonight, this was nowhere on the list. He knew he should ignore anything this creature said to him, should hurry and plant the stake back in its chest where he'd found it last night before it had a chance to react, but his curiosity was starting to override his common sense. He actually wanted to know what this thing was going to say or do next, insane though that thought was.

"What do you want?" Ryan asked, unable to believe the direction this night had suddenly gone.

"Simple," the thing said. "Help me."

"Help you with what?"

The thing made another rasping sound, a sigh, this time. "You are not this stupid, kid, I can see it in your face. But, we can play the game out. I need you to bring me something to feed on."

"I don't have any money," Ryan replied without even considering what the thing was really asking for. He knew, the creature was right about that, but he was in no way ready to admit it to himself, much less out loud. "I suppose I could run home and get you a sandwich or something."

The thing shook its head, and Ryan could swear he heard the tendons in its neck creak from the motion. "You know better, but let me guess: you want me to say it, right? Fine. 'Even if a sandwich would do me any good, I couldn't eat it.' To which you'll ask why, and then I have to tell you what I am, right?"

"Well," Ryan said. "What are you then?"

The thing made another rasping chuckle and offered him a cadaverous grin—thought to be fair, at the moment it was the only kind of grin it could manage. "And here we go. What am I, you ask?"

The thing leaned forward into the light, casting a horrific and bemused look of mock-aggression at Ryan. When it spoke, its voice practically dripped with sarcasm. "I'm a thing of the dark, a being damned, a creature from the bowels of Hell."

It threw its arms wide, presenting itself as though it were some majestic being instead of a rotting husk in human form.

"I," it said grandly. "Am a vampire."

CHAPTER SIX

I t was going on three in the morning by the time Ryan finally snuck back into his room and started changing for bed, his mind racing from the shocks of the previous few hours. He still wasn't sure if he wanted to do what the vampire had asked of him, but that was a problem for tomorrow. It was much too late to even try to do anything right now, even if he decided he was going to.

Actually, some of that wasn't entirely true. He knew good and well he was going to end up helping the vampire, even if the thought of what he'd been asked to do turned his stomach.

Finding a stray wasn't going to be that difficult. There were always dogs and cats wandering around the neighborhood without collars, their fur matted and tangled from many nights spent out in the elements. Convincing the stray to follow him shouldn't be too hard either. The part that he had a hard time coming to terms with was what the vampire would end up doing to the thing once it got ahold of it.

It could be worse, though: at first Ryan thought the vampire wanted to feed from him, or another human being. While it had joked about both, it had apparently seen the look of terror that came over Ryan's face and backtracked quickly. It explained that while human blood would be the most effective in helping it to heal, it did understand how impractical it would be to send a "kid" to procure a victim for it. As for feeding from Ryan himself, the thing explained that with as far gone as it was, there would be no stopping once it started, and it didn't want the death of a kid on its conscience.

That was the most surprising bit for Ryan, that such a creature even had a conscience, much less cared about things that could affect it. Still, the thing seemed sincere—not that Ryan had much experience in seeing through such things— and it hadn't attacked him since the first time, so he was inclined to take it at its word.

He was curious whether it was male or female, and what its name was, but for now it was easier to just see it as some "thing" rather than something close to a living, thinking person. It made it easier to deal with for some reason. He was sure he would find out in time, if he really wanted to, but he was leaning toward simply bringing it what it asked for and then forgetting that anything had ever happened at all. It would certainly make his life easier.

Ryan wasn't entirely sure why he was so willing to help that thing in the first place. Everything that he'd ever read, or seen, or heard about vampires indicated that they were evil, soulless creatures bent on destroying humanity or treating them as nothing more than cattle to be fed upon whenever the vampire so desired. The one tonight had seemed that way at some points, but its insistence that any living creature would suffice, that it didn't have to be a human being, seemed contradictory to what he'd expected. Granted, the only information he had to base is assumptions on came from movies or television—some fictional source, in other words—so he shouldn't be that surprised that the truth might be something different.

Not that any of that reasoning explained why he was so willing to help the vampire. While he liked to think of himself as open and welcoming, he never thought it would apply to this degree with a stranger, especially not one who had attacked him only minutes before. And how had the thing known that Ryan had been the one who had removed the stake? It had been accidental, but the vampire hadn't focused on that, had only been concerned about the fact that Ryan was the one who "freed" it. Again, how could it have possibly known that?

If it had psychically bonded with him somehow, it would explain that strange dream he'd had last night. Ryan wasn't at all comfortable with the idea since it could also mean that his agreement to help was the result of some kind of mind control, and that he wasn't in control of his actions. That was more disturbing than the realization vampires existed in the first place.

He lay back on his bed and considered calling Hunter when he woke up, to fill him on this new development. Finally, he decided against it. First, with the mood his friend was in, Ryan really didn't want to deal with the attitude that would ensue during the conversation. Second, he didn't know if he would be able to convince Hunter that he was telling the truth. He supposed he could take him back to the asylum, show him in person that there really was a vampire in the basement, but something told him that would be a bad idea. He didn't know why and thought it might be something trickling through whatever mental link there was between him and the vampire, but it was enough to keep him from going through with it. Hunter might be pissed if he ever found out, but that was okay, too. Better that he was pissed but alive than accepting and dead.

Sleep claimed him on the heels of those thoughts, coming on so quickly that it was more like losing consciousness than drifting off into slumber. Blissfully, he slept without dreams this time, his eyes opening at just past nine and causing him a moment of confusion when he saw the sun was up and beaming through his bedroom window. He felt as though he'd only just closed them a moment before, yet when he sat up he felt more refreshed than he had in months. Since summer, at least, when he'd been able to sleep as long as he wanted while his parents were at work and he had no school to occupy his time.

In addition to feeling rested, his mind was considerably clearer than it had been the night before. His concerns about being manipulated had faded in the light of day. He still felt a desire to help the vampire, but now it had more to do with the fact that he'd made a promise and felt obligated to see it through than some unknowable and mysterious reason. He could just ignore it—after all, what kind of guilt would he really feel about not helping some creature that by its own admission was damned—but if there was even the barest chance that it truly did have some sort of powers and could reach out to him over long distances, it was better not to risk it.

He still felt that his decision not to involve Hunter in any of this was the right one, but his resolve slipped when he looked out his window and saw his friend pulling into the driveway on his bicycle. Ryan truly had no idea what he was doing here. it was definitely strange, considering how upset he'd been when he left yesterday afternoon. Maybe Hunter was starting to realize how insane his plans really were and had come to apologize. Ryan waited until Hunter glanced up and noticed him in the window, and then raised a finger, indicating that he should wait and not knock on the door. Hunter nodded, and Ryan moved back into his bedroom to get dressed.

Hunter was standing next to his bike, idly kicking at a broken hunk of concrete in the driveway as Ryan approached. His face was blank, his expression unreadable, and Ryan had to wonder if he was here to make peace or resume the argument. He didn't say anything as Ryan stopped in front of him, didn't even look up to acknowledge him. It wasn't a good sign, but there was still no way to tell what it meant.

"You're out early," Ryan said after several more minutes passed with Hunter paying more attention to the cracked driveway than to him.

Hunter shrugged. "Have to be, if I'm going to get to the hospital and back without risking anyone seeing me."

Ryan's stomach fell at his words. He wasn't here to apologize, he was here to try and convince Ryan that he should join him on this stupid-ass quest. Now, though, Ryan was even more convinced that Hunter had no business going back out to the asylum. Not with that thing in the basement looking for a meal.

"You're still going to do it," Ryan said. "Even though it's probably not worth the risk."

"I have to try," Hunter said. He raised his head and finally looked up, and Ryan hissed out a breath when he finally saw what his friend had been hiding. One of his eyes was black and swollen, unable to open more than a slit. A small cut circled just below his eyebrow, already scabbing over, but obviously painful. In the other eye, Ryan could see the tell-tale signs of desperation leaking through.

"Dude," Ryan nearly whispered. "What the hell?"

"Mom's newest overnight guest," Hunter said, but didn't elaborate further. Ryan had heard enough stories that he didn't have to.

Ryan shuddered, mentally thanking God or whoever was listening that his parents were still together and not at all abusive, beyond his occasionally over-dramatic thoughts that they could be too strict at times. "That truly sucks, but I'm not seeing how one connects to the other."

Hunter raised one shoulder in a half-shrug. "I've already got enough shit in my life, I can't pass up the chance to improve at least one part of it, even if you're right like you probably are about it being a bunch of bullshit from Matt and the assholes. You can afford to just go through the next few years hoping they ignore you. You've got parents that don't fuck with you too much. You get along with people. Me? Aside from you, I don't really have anything."

Ryan looked away, unable to meet his gaze. Under normal circumstances, he would tease Hunter about being a pussy or a fag for a statement like that, but right now such a heartfelt expression was not deserving of such hazing.

"And you're hoping I'll change my mind and come with you, aren't you?" he asked, already knowing the answer.

Hunter raised one shoulder in a half-shrug. "You made yourself pretty clear yesterday, but yeah, I was hoping you'd change your mind."

It was blatantly clear that Hunter was trying to manipulate him, to use the black eye as a hammer against the formerly adamant refusal he'd been met with about this, but Ryan didn't care. Not much, at least. He and Hunter had been friends for as long as he could remember, and while what Hunter was doing right now was a bit questionable, his true loyalty had never come into doubt. If the situation had come about as a result of almost anything else, Ryan would have conceded easily, and used that fact at some point in the future to stop his friend from executing an even crazier plan. It was what they did.

The problem was the new wrinkle he'd discovered since Hunter first presented this particular idea. Somehow he just knew that taking Hunter to see the vampire would not end well for either of them. He didn't even need some kind of outside mental influence to know that. That his friend was in such a fragile state only cemented that surety in his mind. He simply couldn't do it.

Of course, they were talking about going during the day, not after dark. Ryan didn't know if that particular part of the vampire legend was true or just another thing the movies had gotten wrong, but it might not even have to come to that. As far as he knew, the vampire was still in the basement. Considering how weak it had claimed to be, it wasn't likely that it would be up and wandering around the upper levels of the asylum. It had, after all, said that when Ryan came back with something for it to feed on, he should bring it to the same storeroom where he'd first discovered it. As long as he kept Hunter away from there, he might be able to both help his friend feel better and keep him in the dark about what else lurked there, too.

"One condition," Ryan said. Hunter's face lit up with pleased shock, and he nodded eagerly. "We stay out of the basement. I had enough fun down there yesterday, what with falling and nearly breaking my damn neck and tripping over dead bodies and all."

Hunter hesitated, a flash of disappointment crossing his features. "I kinda wanted to see that for myself. Especially if it's as fucked up as you said it was."

"That's my price," Ryan insisted. "You want me to come with you, we stay the hell away from the basement. Besides, all the good shit's going to be on the upper floors anyway, in the old patient rooms or cells or whatever they were."

After a moment's consideration, Hunter nodded. "It's a deal."

Ryan sighed. He didn't really want to do this, not when he was going to have to go back later anyway, but a promise was a promise. If he didn't go, there was every chance Hunter would stumble across the vampire, and since he had no connection to it, he might not fare as well as Ryan had.

"Let me go tell my parents I'm going to hang out with you for a while," he said, turning toward the house. "Then we can get this over with."

CHAPTER SEVEN

He had to give credit where it was due: Hunter's idea about searching this place during daylight was actually smarter than he'd originally thought. There was enough sunlight streaming in through the windows to light their way without the need for flashlights, and when Ryan looked up he was able to see that there was actually a skylight of some sort set into the roof, making it easy to see whether or not the stairs were rotted or on the verge of collapse. A few were, but for the most part it looked like they would be able to go all the way to the top of the building without fear of injury. He couldn't speak to how the floors in the hallways off the stairwell were, but it was much, much better than trying to muck about in the dark like they had a couple of nights ago.

It was also abundantly clear that the former explorers of this place had limited themselves to the first or second floor, probably because they'd come in at night and didn't want to risk going any higher. As a result, many of the rooms were filled with signs of previous occupancy. Several of the beds still had sheets on them, and occasionally they would come across a nurse's station with charts, clipboards, and the other things the former employees needed to conduct their day to day business. Hunter managed to find an old stethoscope that was still in pretty decent condition, aside from the dry rot that had formed on the earpieces. He hung his prize around his neck, and for a brief moment Ryan thought he looked like some young intern hoping to make a name for himself.

Ryan saw other things that made him wonder about what had happened here before the place closed down, things he wouldn't have noticed except for what he knew was sitting down in the basement of this place. There were stains on some of the bedclothes, stains that looked suspiciously like blood that had sprayed across them. There were identical stains on some of the walls as well, a glaring indication that whatever had happened here, it hadn't been peaceful. Seeing them, Ryan had no problem with believing all those rumors about a patient uprising and a riot that left many members of the staff dead.

It suddenly occurred to him that he might have a source for the truth about what really happened here just a few floors beneath him. He didn't know how long the vampire had been around, and for that matter, he didn't know for certain that the place being closed wasn't a result of that thing. If the dream he'd had night before last had been the result of some kind of mental link, then all he really knew was that several people had hunted the thing down and put a wooden stake in its heart. Maybe, if things went well when he brought it something to feed on later tonight, he could ask it. He just hoped he wouldn't end up regretting it.

He looked up and saw Hunter staring at him with bemused impatience. He dimly remembered hearing his friend's voice but couldn't for the life of him think of what he'd said.

"Sorry," he said. "Kinda spaced out for a minute there."

Hunter chuckled and shook his head. "I asked if you wanted to try and find something for yourself, so we can both have something to give Matt tomorrow."

Ryan was still convinced that it was a waste of time to try and get Matt to honor the deal he'd made, but instead of saying so and possibly starting another argument, he chose to keep it to himself. He waited long enough that he thought it would seem he'd been considering the question and then shook his head.

"Nah, I think the one's fine. They never said anything about both of us having to come up with something, just that we had to come up with something together. We can always say how it took both of us to make it through the room to get ahold of that."

Hunter smiled, and Ryan could see him taking the story in his head and embellishing it to the edge of belief. "All they have to do is come in and see those warning signs, the holes in the floor, and they'll totally buy it. Nice one!"

Ryan gave him a half-hearted smile in return and checked his phone. It was just past eleven—still plenty of time to get back before anyone's suspicions were aroused. Well, at least in Hunter's case. His own parents knew he was out with Hunter, and so wouldn't be worried for a few more hours yet. He had no idea what kind of story Hunter had spun when he left, if any at all.

"So what now?" Ryan asked. He didn't want to go back home yet, wanted to wait and get back just after dark so he could go ahead and take care of his promise to the vampire beforehand. He also didn't want to stay here any longer than he had to. The longer they were here, the greater the chance that Hunter would sneak away and head into the basement and find what was living there. Maybe it wouldn't be a problem, but Ryan didn't want to risk it.

"I dunno," Hunter replied. "Maybe just hang at your place for a while?"

Ryan resisted the urge to swear at that. He should've expected it, considering what Hunter had apparently had to deal with last night at his own house, but it was the last thing Ryan wanted to do, and would make going back out again even harder.

"I really don't want to go home yet," he said. "I spent all day yesterday just sitting around. I was kind of thinking maybe we should do something, go somewhere."

Hunter shrugged. "What'd you have in mind?"

Ryan considered. This early on a Sunday morning, there really wasn't much for them to do. Living in a smallish town limited your options a good bit, adding a lazy day like Sunday into the mix nearly eliminated them entirely. Aside from church and the local grocery store, Ryan couldn't really think of anything that was open where they could go and kill a couple of hours. If they really wanted to, he supposed they could ride their bikes the few miles to the next town where the normal civilized places like Walmart and restaurants and the like were, but if they wanted to stick around here, and not be utterly exhausted when they got where they were going, they had to do some serious thinking.

"We could go hang at the park or something for a while," Ryan finally suggested.

Hunter rolled his eyes. "Wow, super exciting. You sure we can't just go to your place?"

Ryan shook his head. "Nah. Besides, maybe we can come up with a better idea once church lets out and there's more people wandering around. We might could even find Matt and show him our prize now, instead of waiting until tomorrow."

"Yeah, that would be good," Hunter said, squinting his eyes as he thought about it. "If he's legit, maybe we can show up already on our way to being cooler."

This time it was Ryan's turn to roll his eyes. He knew no such thing would happen, but again, he kept his mouth closed.

"And who knows, maybe there'll be some cute chicks out at the park already," Hunter said, tossing a wink in Ryan's direction. "We can figure out which of them we'll chase after once we're popular."

* * *

Hunter's hope couldn't have been further from reality. The place was all but deserted, only a couple of old-timers sitting on the benches scattered along the walking trails, tossing torn pieces of bread to the birds that hadn't begun their flight south for the upcoming winter yet. It was a little strange, actually. All the times Ryan had been here previously, except for when he'd come very late at night to meet Hunter before one of his insane schemes kicked off, he had been inundated with the sounds of children playing and adults engaged in casual conversation. To hear none of that now was almost disconcerting.

As he and Hunter strolled along the path that led across the top of a hill leading down to a decently-sized duck pond, he figured he'd better go ahead and enjoy this while he could. The weather was starting to change, the nights growing cooler, and it was only a matter of time before it would be too cold to be out here like this for any length of time. Halloween would be here in a couple of weeks, when the town held a party for the kids—billed as a "safe alternative" to traditional trick-or-treating—and after that, the park wouldn't see much use until the following spring. It was sad in some ways but considering that there was an almost constant stream of holidays to fill the time, it wasn't really that bad.

He glanced over and saw Hunter smiling mischievously. "What?"

Hunter shook his head. "I was just thinking. I really do appreciate you going out there with me today. I know you think it's bullshit, but I'm really glad you changed your mind."

Ryan kept his eyes locked on Hunter, waiting for the other shoe to drop. "No big deal. It actually was kind of interesting."

"I just want you to know it meant a lot to me, and that I will pay you back for it."

"You don't have to do that."

"Well, I'm going to anyway. And you might not understand at first, but you're going to thank me eventually."

Ryan frowned. "What the hell are you talking about?"

"This!"

Before Ryan knew what was happening, Hunter had planted his hands against Ryan's chest and shoved as hard as he could. One of his feet had snuck behind Ryan's ankle, so the final effect was that Ryan immediately lost his balance and fell off the side of the path, where he began skidding and rolling down the hill to the duck pond. He tried to catch himself, but by the time he was able to make himself start to act, he'd already picked up too much momentum. He was sure he was about to land in what was sure to be exceptionally cold water, and then he slammed into someone else's legs, knocking them over as well. The collision slowed him enough that he was able to stop himself from rolling any further, and the person he'd hit slammed into his gut ass-first before sliding up to his chest.. One flailing hand managed to catch him square in the balls, sending a wave of agony coursing through his body. He groaned and tried to curl up into a ball, but whoever it was had landed on him in such a way he could do nothing more than arch his back a bit.

Finally he was able to collect himself enough to look over at the person he'd knocked down, an apology already forming on his tongue. His words died as he found himself staring into a face that was familiar, but that he'd never been lucky enough to see this close before.

Incredibly, he found himself staring into the shocked but still painfully beautiful face of Kayla Monroe.

CHAPTER EIGHT

Time seemed to slow as Ryan disentangled himself from Kayla, his face burning, his throat clenched so tight that the apology he knew he should be offering simply would not come. He had no doubt that Hunter knew she was standing there, and that he knew exactly what was going to happen when he shoved Ryan down the hill. When Ryan looked back up to the path he'd been on just a few minutes before, he was surprised to see it empty. He'd expected to see Hunter staring back down at him, probably laughing his ass off at the situation he'd caused. Apparently his friend had some decency left and had vanished to give Ryan the chance to make amends for what happened in peace.

It ended up being Kayla who broke the silence, unselfconsciously brushing the dirt from her back and legs as she looked down at Ryan with something akin to sympathy on her face. He considered that a good sign. She could have very easily been staring at him with anger or irritation, both which would have been bad, or even disgust, which would have been worse..

"Are you okay?" she asked, and thankfully her voice sounded a bit concerned.

Ryan was only able to answer her when he closed his eyes, cutting off his view of her face. "I honestly don't know. Does pride count? Because that's a bit sore."

She let out a soft giggle that made his heart swell in his chest. He rolled over onto his hands and knees and pushed himself upright again, groaning a little as he felt a dull throb in his head and a twinge in his back from his tumble down the hill, and a lingering ache where he'd been whacked in the balls. When he finally got back to his feet, he looked over and saw that while the smile that crossed Kayla's face after his half-hearted attempt at a joke was still there, it was now a bit strained. She reached up and turned his head gently, causing another sharp wave of pain to radiate all the way down from his scalp to his neck.

"You're bleeding," she said.

Ryan touched the back of his head gently, wincing as his fingers brushed across a fairly small gash there. He pulled his hand back and glanced down at his fingers. Sure enough, there was blood. It wasn't much—nothing to get alarmed over—but it was there, and it was apparently visible if someone chose to look.

"Wonderful," he muttered, wiping his hand on his pants. He took a deep breath and tried to look at her again but couldn't quite meet her eyes. "Look, I'm so sorry about... well, running into you like that."

"Were you running?" she asked, and he could see the smile twitch her lips again. "I thought you must have been rolling."

His mind raced to come up with some way to correct himself without coming across as too much of an idiot, then he noticed that her smile was more of an amused smirk and realized she was just teasing him. "Well, then I'm sorry about rolling into you like that. Are you okay?"

"I'm not the one bleeding," she said. "Of course, even though you knocked me over, you were at least considerate enough to lie there and cushion my fall."

His stomach cramped slightly, as if reminding him that she'd landed butt-first right onto it. He forced his hand to remain still, to not drift across it and show he was in more pain than he was letting on. "All part of the service, I guess."

"So knocking me over was a service, was it?"

He knew she was still teasing him, trying to make light of the situation, but he wasn't able to tell if it was all in good fun, or if she was being politely mean about it. Better to not push his luck any further than he had already. He smiled at her as best he could, mumbled another apology, and turned to leave, already planning what he was going to do to Hunter once he found where his friend had wandered off to.

"You're Ryan, right?" Kayla asked. "Ryan Bradshaw?"

Ryan froze, his heart hammering, shocked that she knew his name at all, much less that she didn't seem willing to let him leave just yet. It could be a way for her to prolong his suffering, for he knew it must be plain on his face how embarrassed he was, but still, it was the first time he'd heard the girl of his dreams say his full name outside of his fantasies, and the effect was a little disorienting.

"That's me," he said, turning back to her, a weak grin on his face. "Now you know where to send the bill for any unforeseen damages."

She giggled again, and Ryan thought he might just pass out before this conversation was over.

"I've seen you around school," she said. "Mister Jernigan's English class, right? You had that freaky story for our creative writing assignment last month."

He was surprised that she remembered that silly little story. They'd been given a scene, a man standing atop a hill, looking out over some town somewhere, and were supposed to write a little story explaining who the man was and what he was doing there. Most of the results were bad, something Ryan had been forced to endure since they were all read aloud in front of the class, but there had been a few good ones, usually about how the man was either pining for the woman he loved—favored by many of the female students—or how he was coping with someone's death, or something along those lines. Ryan had gone for a more disturbing tale about a man who was being chased by someone who wanted to kill him, for reasons he didn't know.

Most of the guys in class had loved it, but most of the girls had given him looks like he'd taken a shit in their makeup bags. He had no idea how Kayla had felt about the story. He hadn't been able to look at her after he'd finished reading it.

"Yeah," he admitted, hoping this wasn't going to become a judgment on his character. "Sorry if it bothered you."

"No," she said, her face suddenly flashing alarm. "No, it's not that. I mean, it did bother me, but I kind of got the idea it was supposed to. Honestly, I thought it was really good. You did better than most of the idiots we're in class with."

He turned so he was facing her completely, pleased confusion playing across his face. "Really?"

"Well, yeah," she replied. "Actually, it made me wonder if the guy finally got away from whoever was chasing him."

Ryan shrugged, suddenly feeling self-conscious. "I don't know. I like to think he did, eventually, but I don't think it was easy for him."

Kayla cocked her head to one side, engrossed in the conversation now. "You don't know? But you wrote it, how can you not know?"

"I didn't think that far ahead," Ryan said. "I mean, I did, some, but we were only supposed to explain why he was on that hilltop, not everything that came after. I just never considered whether he managed to get away or not."

Kayla laughed. "That doesn't help me at all, you know. I'm really curious whether he made it or not. And if he didn't did he at least find out why he was being chased?"

"I could finish it for you, if you want," Ryan said, only realizing an instant after the words left his mouth exactly what he'd volunteered to do. While he enjoyed coming up with stories, reading that one aloud had been the first time he'd shared his work with anyone other than Hunter, and now he'd offered to just hand something he hadn't even done yet over to Kayla, of all people. He wanted to take it back, but it was too late for that now.

"Could you?" she asked, beaming. "That would be awesome!"

It took him a moment to regain his composure enough to speak again. "Give me a week or so? Better yet, how about I give it to you on Halloween? That way you get a spooky story for a spooky day."

Her face lit up with excitement. "Cool! I can't wait to read it!"

Ryan wanted to say more, to prolong this conversation as long as he possibly could, but he also didn't want to push his luck. She knew who he was and had been interested enough in the stupid story he'd cobbled together over a weekend to want to know what came next. He could hope that there was more to it than that, but aside from the fact that she wasn't as stuck-up as he'd feared, there was really nothing at all to indicate anything other than an interest in his writing. For now, it would have to be enough.

"Well, I'd better get going," he said, hating the words even as they left his mouth. "I need to go find a friend of mine and kick his ass."

Kayla laughed, a lilting sound that made him want to forgive Hunter completely for what he'd done. He still owed him some payback, but he had to admit the gambit had worked. He'd managed to have a pleasant conversation with Kayla. He'd have to make sure to point out that it hadn't had anything to do with Matt or his plan to become popular, either.

"Don't beat him too bad," she said. "It could've turned out much worse than it did."

The thought was so much a reflection of his own that for a brief moment Ryan wondered if Kayla could read his mind. If she could, though, she would probably be the one kicking his ass for all the weird fantasies he'd had about the two of them having a life together.

As he walked away, he couldn't resist a glance back over his shoulder, and found himself stunned to see that Kayla was still watching him leave. She held up a hand in farewell, and he replied in kind before turning around, face burning more than ever, wondering if they would talk again before he gave her that story on Halloween, and what that particular conversation might entail. Every road started somewhere, and while he wished he could run instead of walk at a steady pace, at least it seemed like he'd started on the road that included Kayla in his life in some way. He knew what he hoped for, but also knew that it might not play out that way.

Still, any chance was a chance, and if he could only have her as a friend, it would have to be enough for now.

* * *

Hunter was still nowhere to be found when Ryan made it back to the top of the hill, unable to resist one last look back toward the duck pond in the hopes of seeing Kayla still watching him, but she was gone as well. He looked around and saw her headed to the other side of the pond where a separate trail led up to the parking lot at the far end of the park from where he and Hunter had come in. She wasn't looking back, which was a disappointment, but at the same time it allowed him the opportunity to watch her without fear of being caught for a change.

He looked away when she started angling toward the path, knowing it would put him back in her eye line again. He turned around and looked both ways down the walking trail but saw no sign of Hunter anywhere. After a moment's debate, he shrugged, and then started back toward the smaller parking lot where they'd left their bikes.

The day had come off hot as the sun crept further into the sky, the clouds making it overcast but holding in the heat as effectively as a blanket held in a person's body temperature. There was a faint trace of moisture in the air, a sign that the weatherman's promise of rain would actually become reality this time around. Ryan didn't pay much attention to the news or the weather, but he thought he remembered hearing something about it coming in after dark tonight. He only hoped he would be able to make it to the asylum to fulfill his promise and then home again before it hit.

He frowned as the parking lot came into view. He'd expected that Hunter would either be waiting here for him or would've gone ahead and left once he saw that Kayla wasn't just screaming at Ryan or, worse, simply ignoring him after an apology, but his bike was chained in the same spot it had been when they first got here and there was still no sign of the boy anywhere. Ryan paused next to his own bike, eyes scanning the surrounding area to see if his friend had just wandered off in search of some place to take a piss or something, but the only other person he could see was an old man with a cane, making his slow walk to a car that looked like it had last seen a good wash sometime back in the previous century.

As much as he didn't want to just sit around, he didn't want to leave without at least letting Hunter know about it, either. He sighed and pulled out his cell phone, momentarily panicking until he saw that the fall from earlier hadn't cracked the screen or done any real damage to it. This was his third phone this year, and he knew if something happened to break this one, his parents either wouldn't get him a replacement, or they'd make sure it was so old that all he'd be able to do was make calls. Maybe that was what they were for, but Ryan didn't think he could survive without the ability to go on the internet from his phone so he could consult Encyclopedia Google whenever he felt the need.

He wished that Hunter had a phone as well so he could just call or shoot him a text or something, but since he didn't, there were no other options aside from bailing or waiting. Ryan figured he'd try waiting for a little while, and then if Hunter didn't show up within a reasonable amount of time, he'd just bail. He loaded the Facebook app on his phone and looked up Kayla's profile. He debated on whether or not to shoot her a friend request, but finally decided that it might come off as a little creepy this early in the game. Too much, too soon, maybe. He scrolled through a series of uninteresting posts and was about to close out of it when he heard the ding that signified he had a notification. He tapped on it and felt his breath catch when he saw that he had a new friend request, and it was from Kayla. He allowed his thumb to hover over the accept button, wondering if she might see his fast acceptance the same he worried she would've seen his sending a request to her, then went ahead and hit it anyway. It shouldn't matter how long it took him to respond. After all, more than half the school seemed to stay glued to their phones all day long, so it shouldn't seem that unusual.

Smiling to himself, he closed out of the app and looked around. The parking lot was now deserted, the old man long since gone along with his equally ancient car, leaving only Ryan and two bicycles. Hunter still hadn't shown up. Ryan sighed, considered going back down the walking trail to see if he could find his friend, but then dug the key out of his pocket and unlocked the bike's chain. He had no idea where Hunter might be, but he was tired of waiting for him to show up. After their jaunt to the asylum earlier in the day, Hunter should be in a good enough mood to forgive Ryan for not waiting on him any longer than he already had.

In the days and weeks to come, he would wonder about that decision, would wonder if things might have turned out differently had he gone looking for Hunter right then and there, but life only moves forward, not in reverse, so it was a question he would never have an answer to. He had no choice but to believe that things happened the way they were supposed to happen, and to live with that fact, no matter how much he wished he could change it.

CHAPTER NINE

It turned out that finding an animal suitable for the vampire was the easiest part of the plan for Ryan. He didn't even have to look that hard and still managed to find something that wouldn't make him feel overly guilty. As he was heading out after stopping at home for a quick nap following his adventures in the park, he found a dog that had been hit by a car lying alongside the street. It wasn't dead, but it only took one look for him to know that there was no way it was going to survive. Blood was trickling from its backside, and when Ryan glanced at the source, he saw a thick rope of something hanging beneath the pitiful thing's tail. He refused to look closer, not wanting to know exactly what it was, but he could make a good guess. He had never seen intestines with his own eyes, not in real life, but what little he could see matched every description for them he'd ever read. The dog was breathing—barely—and when he approached it didn't even lift its head to look at him, only rolled its eyes wildly, as if begging him to put it out of its misery. It was enough to make him feel a lump in his throat, and he had to fight the urge to break out in tears over the sight.

He hadn't thought to bring anything along with him other than a length of rope he had hoped to use as a leash, and even though it was on the verge of death, he just couldn't bring himself to tie the thing to the back of his bike and drag it down the middle of the road. There were just some lines he refused to cross. He stood along the side of the road and looked around, finally spotting several towels hanging on a clothesline behind a nearby house. He didn't see any vehicles in the driveway, nor did the house have a garage that might be hiding one, so he felt it safe to assume no one was home. He felt guilty about the thought of stealing from them, but since he was about to help feed a creature from hell, he figured that was the least of his worries.

Ryan didn't give himself time to think twice, simply hurried across the street and through the yard, eyes locked on the house to see if anyone stuck their head out to scream at him to get the hell off their lawn, but the doors remained closed, and no one appeared. As he darted past the edge of the house, he spotted a length of plywood propped up against a pair of sawhorses and suddenly had an idea how he could get the dog to the asylum without causing it any further undue agony.

First, he grabbed a sheet and a couple of larger towels from the line, snatching them so hard and fast that the clothespins actually twanged against the cord stretched between two metal poles. He barely paused, turning and darting back the way he'd come, angling so he could snag the plywood as he passed it, then made a beeline back across the street to the dog. Taking as much care as he could, he lifted the dog and transferred it to the length of plywood. It barely even whined as he moved it, already too far gone for the pain to really register anymore. Once he got it there, he gently tied the two towels around it, securing it, then lifted it onto the seat for his bike and balanced it with his knee while he wrapped the sheet around both the animal and his bicycle frame, hopefully securing it so it wouldn't fall off as he made the trip to the asylum. He somehow managed it and didn't tip the bike over and spill the poor thing back into the street in the process.

Navigating his bike down the road was a little trickier, the center of balance now wildly shifted by the added weight of the dog. Several times Ryan felt himself being pulled to the side as the bike threatened to tip, but he managed to keep it straight. By the time he finally made it to the bent section of fence that would allow him entry, he had sweat pouring from his face and running down his sides and back, and his arms and legs were trembling from the effort of keeping the bike upright. It took substantially more effort to get the dog unfastened and lowered back to the ground. For one terrifying, heartbreaking moment he was sure he was going to drop it with the plywood on top, crushing it into the crumbling pavement, but he managed to keep it somewhat righted until it was lying flat on the ground once more. After several deep breaths to try and regain the last bit of strength he was going to need, he picked up the plywood stretcher and began working his way through the fence and into the courtyard.

Getting the animal into the building was actually easier than he expected. Getting it down the stairs and into the basement was considerably harder. He stood at the top of the stairs, wondering how he was going to do this without banging the dog against every riser on the way down, before finally realizing that he was simply going to have to pick it up, carry it down, and hope that he didn't overbalance and fall the entire way down in the process. He took another brief break to catch his breath then picked it up and got to it.

He was surprised by the lights that had been set up along the hallway once he got to the basement landing, but he was grateful for them all the same. He'd brought a flashlight along with him, but it was impossible to carry it and the dog at the same time, so he'd been forced to leave it in his backpack along with a small lantern his dad kept in the garage for emergencies. It was just barely past dusk outside, but already the inside of the asylum was considerably darker than it had been when he'd been here with Hunter earlier, so the added illumination was welcomed, wherever it had come from.

Not that there were many real suspects for who'd put them up, that was. It had to have been the vampire, and the fact that he'd done so before the sun was fully down seemed to prove one more common thought about the creatures was either untrue or not entirely as he'd been led to believe.

The thing was sitting on an overturned bucket at the far side of the storeroom, flipping through what looked like an old medical manual of some sort. It glanced up as Ryan entered, grunting as he maneuvered the dog down the narrow aisles between the shelves. The vampire dropped the book to the floor casually and stood, watching Ryan approach. After he carefully put the dog on the floor at the thing's feet, it appeared to raise one eyebrow at him.

"Kind of small, isn't it?" the vampire asked. "And why'd you gift-wrap it for me?"

Ryan glowered at the thing as he tried to catch his breath and ignore then screaming of the muscles in his shoulders and back from carrying the animal all this way. The vampire chuckled and pulled the towels off the dog, then studied it for a moment before frowning over at him.

"What is this?"

"Your food," Ryan said. "It's alive, just like you wanted."

The vampire let out a weary sigh and shook its head. "Barely alive, and badly injured. It's lost a lot of blood already, so there's nowhere near as much as I was hoping for left."

"Will it work or not?" Ryan asked. "Because it's the best I'm going to be able to do for you."

The vampire glanced over to him, apparently curious at his sudden angry tone, and then nodded. "You've got too kind a heart for your own good, kid. I get it, and yes, I would've ended up killing it when I drained it, but you're wrong if you thought it would feel any pain from that. It would've gone peacefully. I may be what I am, but I'm not a monster by nature, no matter what the movies might have you believe. But to answer your question, yes, it will work. It'll be like having soup when you're starving for steak, but beggars can't be choosers, right? And maybe it's better that I ease into it, regain some of my control and composure. Hopefully there's enough blood left for me to do that, then I can go hunt on my own without having you bring it to me."

Ryan didn't know what to say to that, so he just remained silent. Finally the vampire turned and started to lean down to the wounded animal, then stopped when it realized Ryan was still watching him with morbid curiosity.

"You might not want to watch this," it said. "Considering how soft you are."

"Just get on with it."

The thing shrugged and turned back to the dog. "Wasn't meant as an insult, just stating a fact. But it's your mind, and your eyes, so what do I know?"

At that, the vampire ran a hand over the dog's head, causing it to shudder. Ryan didn't think it was from pain, since it seemed more relaxed than at any time since he'd found it, making him all the more fascinated at what was playing out before him. The vampire whispered something to the animal, and then used one long fingernail to cut a small slit in the dog's neck. The animal didn't even twitch. The vampire lowered its mouth to the wound, covering it before more than a trickle of blood could spill free, and began to feed.

While the process was slow, it was also silent, which was something of a surprise. Ryan had been expected at best a sound like someone drinking something through a straw, and at worst a sound like two people attempting to French kiss when they'd never done it before and had no idea what it was really like. He wondered if it was because the fur on the dog's neck prevented the creature's lips from making a complete seal over the wound, or maybe if the thing's lips were just too dry and cracked to do so, but while he was curious, he felt like it would be rude to ask. Maybe that shouldn't matter, since he doubted anyone would care about social norms when dealing with a creature feeding on the blood of another living thing, but he'd been raised to be polite, and couldn't stop the thought from coming even under such strange circumstances.

His only real clue that anything out of the ordinary was happening came when the dog's fur began to lose color, fading from a mottled brown to pure white before his very eyes. When the last of the pigment faded away, the vampire raised its head and let out a long, shuddering breath, apparently done with its "meal".

"How did you do that?" Ryan asked, pointing to the dog.

The vampire gave him a confused look, and Ryan saw that its features had filled out some, no longer looking quite as much like a corpse but more like a man who'd been sick for a long time and was finally starting to go on the mend. The vampire glanced back to the dog, and then seemed to understand what Ryan was talking about.

"The coloring," it said. "Just a side-effect. I never really thought too much about it, to tell you the truth. It's just one of those things that's always been. It probably has something to do with the fact I'm not just ingesting blood, but the dog's life force as well, but that's too philosophical for me to think about overmuch."

Ryan swallowed hard and asked the dreaded follow-up question that had suddenly sprung to mind. "Does it happen if you feed from... people?"

The vampire returned to his seat on the overturned bucket and considered the question. "Honestly, I'm not sure. I've never really paid that much attention. Of course, the few times I've actually drained a person dry over the years I didn't bother sticking around long enough to see how they fared after the process. People tend to frown on you being caught standing over a corpse with all its blood drained, you know."

"How many?" Ryan asked, his voice barely a whisper.

The vampire sighed. "How many people have I killed? In total, or just while I was a vampire?"

It seemed to realize how that must sound, because it held up a hand to forestall anything Ryan might say next. "I was a soldier in my old life, kid. During wartime. I wasn't the only one killing people."

Ryan nodded, feeling anything but reassured. "Just as a vampire, then."

"I don't know," it said after a moment. "Not for sure. I'm positive there were some I only thought I'd drained, but who were actually just on the edge. Let's say between five and eight, just to be on the safe side."

There must have been some expression of horror that crossed Ryan's face, because the vampire let out another long sigh. "If it helps, the only time I ever killed anyone as a vampire was when I was either threatened and defending my own life, or when I was on the edge of extreme starvation like when you found me. Not once have I gone out and decided that I was going to just slaughter someone for the fun of it."

It stood, stretched, and moved back to the now-dead animal lying on a plank. "I'm not telling you that to make you feel better. I know that's not going to happen. Your entire life you've been given two things you needed to know about vampires: one is that they're evil, damned creatures who kill for pleasure, and second is that they're not real. Well, you've already had one of those shattered for you, but that other one is so ingrained that there's not much hope of changing it."

"That's not true," Ryan replied. "Like you said, I've had to accept that you're real, even if you're nothing like I thought you'd be. Why couldn't the other be wrong, too? I'm not saying it is, especially since you just admitted to killing people, but what's the difference?"

"Think about it," the vampire said as it picked up the dog's corpse and carried it to the far side of the room. "You've just been slapped in the face with something incredible, and the only thing you care about it how many people I've killed, and whether or not I'm going to kill you before it's all said and done, too."

It turned and gave him a strange little grin that was disconcerting on its still somewhat shriveled face. "You don't see me any differently than you did that dog, truth be told. I can even prove it."

"How so?" Ryan asked.

"You never once asked my name, even when it became apparent that I wasn't going to consciously even try to hurt you."

Ryan wanted to feel outraged, but he was simply embarrassed that what the vampire was saying was true. He'd been so focused on what vampires were supposed to be, and how the creature before him might be affecting him personally, that he'd never even taken the time to consider that when he'd first seen it, there had been a stake in its heart, and that it had appeared to have been in great pain before it lost consciousness or whatever it was that had happened to it. He'd agreed to help bring it food, so he was capable of feeling some kind of compassion for it, but he'd still been trying to keep a substantial distance from it.

For that matter, he kept calling it "it", even in his own mind.

Worse, it suddenly occurred to him that the way he was treating this vampire was quite similar to how he felt Matt and his asshole buddies treated him and Hunter. He didn't want to think that he was similar to someone who'd apparently made it his goal in life to give him hell, but there it was, and now that he'd realized it, he couldn't get it out of his mind.

"You're right," Ryan said. "You're absolutely right. And I'm sorry."

The vampire stopped whatever it was doing with the dead dog and turned to look at him suspiciously. "That was fast. What changed?"

"This kid at my school..." Ryan started, then stopped himself and took a deep breath. "Let's just say I know what it feels like to be treated like you're less than you are, and I never meant to do the same thing to you."

He braced himself, then took a step toward the vampire and held out his hand. "I'm Ryan."

The vampire rose back to its full height, one eyebrow raised, and took a matching step toward him, hesitating briefly before extending his hand as well. "Francis. Francis Flynn."

Ryan shook hands with him, fighting the urge to pull away at the papery feel of the vampire's skin. It felt cold, though warmer than it had when he'd fallen on the corpse a couple of nights ago. Obviously feeding had done more than just smooth some of the withering that had occurred.

"Can I ask you something, Francis?"

"You just did," the vampire replied, smiling. "But you can ask something else, if you're so inclined. Just don't be offended if I choose not to answer."

"You said I've been conditioned to think of... vampires... a certain way," Ryan began. "So what's the truth? I don't see fangs, and that stake didn't turn you to dust, so what's it really like?"

Francis chuckled, and while his voice was still rough, at least the sounds of his mirth were no longer quite as unnerving as they had been. "I'll make a deal with you, Ryan.

You head home tonight, let me finish taking care of this body and then go do a little hunting so I can be more myself, then come back tomorrow and we'll talk more."

Ryan frowned. "I've got school. I doubt I'll be able to get out after dark."

"Lesson number one, then," Francis said, waving the comment away. "That whole sun thing? Not quite how it's been portrayed. I'm not going to the beach any time soon, but as long as I stay down here in the basement, I can tolerate it being in the sky. Come after your classes, then we can talk, then you can get home before your folks get too worried. Fair?"

"Fair," Ryan agreed. He nodded to where the dog's body lay in a heap near the wall. "Can I ask what you're doing?"

"Cleaning up," Francis replied, not turning back to look at him. "Best you don't know the details."

After thinking about it, Ryan figured he was probably right about that.

He spent the trip back home wondering about what he'd done, wondering if it was really a good idea to be hanging out with something that shouldn't exist but did, then tried to put it out of his mind. He was curious—more than ever, actually—and while he couldn't say the fear that he might be putting himself in danger was entirely gone, it had at least lessened from what it had been. More, he'd taken a step toward something that set him apart from everyone else he knew. If nothing else, he would always have that.

CHAPTER TEN

Because he'd overslept, Ryan got to school too late to discover whether or not Hunter had tried to get Matt and his idiot friends to accept the prize they'd discovered in the asylum. He didn't even see Hunter, not lounging around outside waiting for him like he sometimes did or even at his locker. Come to think of it, he couldn't remember whether or not he'd seen Hunter's bike in the rack near the side entrance to the school where they usually put them. Considering the size of that black eye, it was entirely possible that Hunter had elected to skip today, to wait until it healed a little more before he came in to face his peers and the potential mockery that could ensue from such an injury.

He did see Kayla though, as she walked through the hall with a couple of her friends. At first he thought she was just going to ignore him like she always did, but instead she actually met his eyes and offered him a slight but genuine smile as she passed him. Her friends didn't give any reaction to this, didn't even offer him the little scowls they normally did when they caught him staring at their friend whom he was certain they thought was much too good for the likes of him. It was another new development in a rapid-fire series of them over the last few days, and Ryan couldn't even begin to process what the meaning was behind it. Either way, being ignored was a definite step up from being ostracized, so he would take whatever he could get in that regard.

For a change, it was his pre-lunch classes that seemed to drag on forever, an endless parade of information that he knew he would barely retain. All he could think about was how he might be able to find out what was going on with Hunter and Matt and that whole plan at lunchtime, and then get the chance to see Kayla again during seventh period when they had English class together. He'd worked on the story for her a little bit last night before bed—one of the reasons why he'd overslept this morning, truth be told—and he was hoping that by simply being in her presence he would get the inspiration he needed to see it through. He'd written a few things before, mostly after finishing the latest paperback he'd picked up from the local used book store, but those always came out like he was trying to be the person who'd written the book he just read: if it was Stephen King, his own work came out flowing and detailed, while something from Brian Keene or Richard Laymon might yield something much more fast-paced and brutal. The story Kayla wanted him to finish, though, was one he thought sounded uniquely his own, and he was more than a little nervous to see how it turned out. If Hunter had skipped today, maybe he'd stick around after class and ask Mister Jernigan if he had any advice on how he could maintain that style and not devolve into the stuff he'd done before.

The lunch bell finally rang, and Ryan very nearly ran to the cafeteria after unceremoniously tossing his books into his locker and slamming the door shut. He didn't find Hunter—who he now assumed had skipped out today, despite his nearly obsessive desire to give Matt the stethoscope they'd discovered in the hopes of fulfilling their "deal"—but he did see the asshole himself, heading toward the vocational building with his buddies to grab a quick smoke behind the building before eating whatever junk they decided to either steal from whatever kid was unlucky enough to be their target for the day or pull out of the vending machines. He thought about going over to them and letting them know how shitty it was for them to bail Friday night, but doing so would be simply asking for a beating. They hadn't appeared to notice him yet, so it was probably best he keep it that way.

Ryan wasn't all that hungry himself, in spite of having missed breakfast after sleeping through his alarm, but he could definitely use some caffeine. He turned to head to the little nook where the vending machines were, one hand already slipping into his pocket to pull out a dollar, and very nearly ran headlong into Amber Thompson, one of Kayla's friends, and the one Hunter had labeled the Sergeant-at-Arms for the Bitch Brigade. She didn't flinch or recoil or do anything at all to try and avoid him, simply rolled her eyes as he was forced to slam himself painfully against the wall to both catch his balance again and avoid knocking her over.

She sighed and held out something to him before he had a chance to say anything, then gave him an impatient look when he hesitated before taking it.

"What's this?" he asked.

"Kayla asked me to give it to you," she said, her voice that of royalty speaking to an impetuous servant. "God knows why, but now I've done it, so now I can go talk to more important people."

She didn't even wait to make sure he had a hold on the folded-up paper before she turned away and walked quickly down the hall toward the doors leading into the cafeteria. He glanced down and saw his name written on the outside in a flowing, distinctly feminine script that he couldn't help but think of as "cute". He might be wrong, this might just be some kind of trick, but he was positive this really was from Kayla. After one quick glance around to make sure no one was waiting and watching him, readying themselves to drop the other shoe right on top of his head, he unfolded the letter and smiled as he started reading the brief note.

"Hey Ryan," it said. "Just thinking about you and hoping you're okay after you ran into me yesterday (ha, ha). You better have taken me seriously about that story, I really can't wait to read it. Hope you have a great day, and I'll see you in English."

She'd signed her name with a cutesy flourish that formed a smiley face underneath it.

The note meant nothing in the grand scheme of things, was exactly what it seemed to be at first, second, or even hundredth glance: a simple line to show there were no hard feelings about his rolling into her and knocking her down yesterday, and a reminder that she was waiting for him to finish that story for her. Still, Ryan couldn't help but imagine the possibilities the fact it had been written and delivered to him at all might create. Much of that came from that first line, those four simple words that indicated she'd been thinking about him today. Granted, she'd seen him in the hallway before first period, and for all he knew that was when she'd written it, but she had written it, and intended for him to actually get it, too. It was progress, an opening for something more down the line.

Realistically, he knew it might end up as nothing more than the two of them becoming friends, but even that was more than he had now, so why not dream before being forced to accept a harsh reality?

He re-read the note five or six more times after he'd snagged his Coke from the vending machine, leaning against the wall outside the building and enjoying the last vestiges of good weather before fall well and truly took over and cast a chill over the town. He was so lost in his daydreams that he didn't notice the shadow that fell across him at first, didn't hear the muffled sound of snickers behind someone's hand, didn't even know anyone else was within a thousand miles of him until he heard Matt's voice coming from above him.

"Well look at this shit," he said. "Looks like at least one of them made it out alive. Where's your boyfriend, asshole?"

Ryan didn't want to talk to him, wanted to just ignore him and hope he might give up and go away, but experience had taught him the unlikelihood of that happening. Ignoring him would just make him mad. Ryan refolded the note and looked up at Matt.

"I don't know where he is," he said. "Home sick, I guess."

Matt shook his head and cast a wicked smile back to his two ever-present companions. "Guess that's what happens when you suck too much dick. Maybe you got poison jizz or something. He needs to spit instead of swallow next time."

It was hard to resist the urge to roll his eyes at the pathetic attempts at an insult, but Ryan managed. Threat of bodily harm was a pretty good motivator. "Yeah, maybe."

"So what'd you find for me?" Matt asked, thumbs hooked into the front pockets of his jeans, fingers dangling casually in a frame around his crotch. Ryan noticed a large, pewter ring in the shape of a spiked skull on one finger, and morbidly wondered what it would feel like if that ring were to suddenly slam into his face.

"A stethoscope," Ryan answered. He wanted to get up, to deal with Matt face to face, but he didn't want to do anything the other boy might see as a sign of aggression. The last thing he wanted today was to get a black eye to match Hunter's.

"Really?" Matt said, and Ryan could've sworn he heard genuine curiosity in his voice. Probably just a trick of the mind. "You got it stored up your ass or something? Let's see it."

"Hunter's got it," Ryan replied. "When he comes back tomorrow, we can show it to you then."

"I call bullshit," Zach piped in. Matt turned to glance at him over his shoulder. "I bet the little fucks didn't find shit, and he's just trying to buy more time to come up with something. Ten to one that's where his butt-buddy's at, over at the asylum trying to come up with something cool."

Brandon snickered, but Matt was nodding when he turned back to Ryan. "Could be. You trying to weasel more time out of this deal, fucktard?"

He didn't give Ryan time to speak before he answered his own question. "Nah, you wouldn't do that. You're too much of a chickenshit to try to fuck me over, aren't you?"

Matt leaned down and for one insane instant Ryan thought he was about to kiss him. Instead, he leaned close to his face, the scent of stale cigarettes and the nasty chili they'd been serving for lunch today wafting across him.

"So here's the deal," Matt said. "I don't give two shits if your little fuckhead partner's got the clap or AIDS or even the fucking sniffles. You two are going to give me whatever you found in there by lunch tomorrow, or I'm going to beat both your asses to a fucking pulp. I don't like it when people go back on their agreements."

Again, Ryan had to fight the urge to point out that by leaving before the thirty minutes was up on Friday, Matt had done the very thing he was warning Ryan against, but somehow he managed to keep his tongue still. He nodded slowly, not looking away from Matt's grinning, psychotic face.

"Can't you fucking speak, asshole?" Matt asked.

Brandon chuckled. "Probably thinking about slipping you the tongue."

Matt raised one eyebrow. Ryan could see on his face that he didn't believe that for an instant, but he could also see that Matt intended to use it as an excuse to fuck with him a little longer. "Try it, you fucking fag. See what happens."

Ryan didn't move, simply held Matt's gaze until the other boy finally straightened back up and laughed. "Didn't fucking think so. Tell you what. You ever think about it again, though, here's a taste of what's in store for you."

The punch landed before Ryan even knew Matt was going to throw it. Knuckles slammed into his mouth, mashing his lips against his teeth and causing his head to bounce briskly off the brick wall behind him. Ryan groaned and slumped to the side, both hands rising to his face, already feeling the blood that ran from his split lip down across his chin. He saw spots in front of his eyes and could only think how lucky he'd been that Matt hadn't hit him with the hand wearing that massive skull ring.

"You know where to find me you ever want some more," Matt said, thankfully turning to walk away. "And you say shit about this, you know what happens."

He didn't wait for an answer, which was good. He was already back in the building by the time Ryan was able to pull himself back upright again and take his hands away from his bleeding mouth. He was going to need to clean himself up again before he went back to class, or at least before the wrong person saw him, or he would end up having to explain what happened without mentioning Matt, Brandon, or Zach's names unless he wanted to get a thousand times worse than this. He managed to get to his feet, only feeling slightly woozy, and somehow made it to the bathroom without anyone seeing him. He went straight to the mirror and looked at himself, wincing at how thick his bottom lip had grown, and at how much blood was drying on his teeth and chin.

The bell rang as he was studying himself, naturally, and he knew he was going to have to explain why he was late to his next class. The problem was coming up with an answer that wouldn't end up earning him a beating later on down the line. It might not come in the next day or two—especially if Matt and his asshole friends ended up getting suspended or even expelled by their actions—but it would come. Of that, there was no doubt. He could clean himself up as best he could and then try to explain that he'd been in the bathroom having stomach issues, but one look at his face would be all the teacher needed to call bullshit and start the train rolling.

Which left him with one alternative, and it was one he sincerely hated to use.

Ryan cleaned himself up as best he could, wincing as his fat lip continued oozing blood despite his best efforts, then slipped back out the door and around the school building. He unlocked his bike, hopped on, and started pedaling. He'd skipped class before, but this time he was doing it not because he wanted to, but because he didn't see a better way out. The worst part that was now he wouldn't get the chance to see Kayla during English class, or to ask Mister Jernigan for advice on writing, or even to write some reply to the note Kayla had sent him.

He couldn't go home; his mother was off work today for some reason or another. He thought about going to check on Hunter, but if his mom was home it would only be a matter of time before he got busted there as well. That left only one alternative. He turned his bike toward the asylum and hoped that Francis had been telling the truth about being able to stay up while the sun was out.

CHAPTER ELEVEN

While he didn't see Francis when he first came down into the basement, it was obvious that the vampire had been doing more than just hanging out down there. The lights he'd seen the night before were spread out a little more and now cast near-complete illumination on the hallway, from the stairs all the way to the doors at the other end of the corridor. The double doors to the storeroom were standing open, and more light shone into the hallway from within. When Ryan got close enough to look in, he could see that the shelving had also been moved around, creating a partition of sorts to separate the room out into smaller areas, almost as if they were being used as walls for building a little apartment down here.

He finally discovered the vampire in the largest of these partitioned areas, humming a song Ryan didn't recognize as he maneuvered an old and faded couch into place near one wall. Off to one side, he could see a couple of other chairs next to a table that looked like it had been pilfered from the asylum's cafeteria and then cleaned up for use here for whatever reason. Ryan couldn't help but wonder if Francis had brought one of the patient beds down and placed it in one of the other cubbies he'd made for himself.

Suddenly, Francis stopped what he was doing and stood up straight, head tilted upward like a dog that had caught a scent. He turned and gave Ryan an appraising look. With the additional light in the room, Ryan could clearly make out that the vampire's face no longer looked as withered as it had the night before and found himself wondering if that was simply a result of the blood he'd been able to get from the dog, or if he'd gone out at some point and found another food source as well. Truthfully, he wasn't sure he wanted to know.

"What happened to you?" Francis asked, one eyebrow raised quizzically. "You look like hell."

There was a part of Ryan that wanted to tell him what happened at school today, but a larger part was still much too embarrassed to speak those words yet. "I'd rather not talk about it. What are you doing?"

"Moving in," Francis said, smiling and gesturing to the furniture around him. "Or, well, maybe decorating would be a better way to put it, considering that all this stuff was already in the building and just needed to be dragged down here. Most of it was too wrecked to use, or was beyond any hope of cleaning up, but there were a few things I was able to scavenge."

"Why?" Ryan asked. It was only the first of what felt like a thousand questions that managed to bubble to the surface of his mind.

Francis shrugged and dropped onto the couch, arms outstretched and resting along the back of it, wrists bent slightly so his hands dangled loosely alongside himself. "Why not? I don't exactly know how long I'm going to be here, so I might as well be comfortable while I figure things out, wouldn't you say?"

"Makes sense," Ryan agreed, looking around the room again. "Where'd you get the lights? For that matter, how are they working?"

"Generator," Francis said, waving one hand in the direction of the doors. "There's an emergency supply room across the hall. It had a bunch of those lights on stands, and a generator to run them, too. There's one in every hall, from what I can tell, just in case something happened and the place lost power. Since it wasn't really for medical treatment, there were no life-support systems to worry about, but lights are always useful in an emergency. I don't know that a vampire taking up residence in the basement counts as one, but it wasn't like there was anyone around to complain about misuse, so here we are."

Ryan nodded and crossed to the table and chairs, debating on whether or not they were clean enough for him to chance sitting on.

"From the way my skin's itching," Francis commented. "I'd say it's still pretty early in the day. Afternoon, maybe? So shouldn't you still be in school right now, or is that also tied up in what you don't want to talk about?"

"I should and it is," Ryan said. He grabbed the least-dirty looking chair and pulled it into the same area where Francis lounged on the couch before sitting down on it gingerly, as if it had literally been his ass that was beaten instead of his mouth.

"Fair enough," Francis replied. "We've all got secrets. Of course, I've got a feeling you're about to try and get a bunch of mine out of me, aren't you?"

"Maybe," Ryan said, shrugging himself. "But you don't have to answer anything you don't want to."

"Goes without saying," Francis replied. "But you did bring me back from a fate worse than death, so I'll give you a little more leeway in that regard than I ordinarily would. So where would you like to start?"

Ryan thought for a moment and decided to start with the man rather than the "monster". "How old are you?"

Francis shrugged. "Depends. What year is it?"

"You don't even know what year it is?" Ryan asked, incredulous.

"All I know is that when I was so rudely assaulted, it was nineteen eighty-four. A fitting year for insanity, I suppose. At that time, I was pushing two hundred years old. So add whatever between then and now, and that's how old I am."

"You're nearly two hundred and thirty-five years old?" Ryan asked, shocked. He knew from the legends and books and movies and the like that vampires could live for hundreds, even thousands of years, but to find himself sitting across from someone who was nearly two and a half centuries old was mind-boggling.

"If that's how long it's been, then that's how old I am," Francis replied. "Don't happen to have any whiskey on you, do you? Apparently I've got some celebrating to catch up on."

Ryan shook his head, though even he wasn't sure if it was in response to the question or the revelation. "You said you were a soldier before you turned, so what war did you fight in? The Revolutionary War?"

Francis chuckled. "My pa was just a wee lad at that point, but you're not too far off. I believe you'd read about it as the War of 1812. Came over from Ireland to fight alongside the British fops along your Gulf Coast. Let me tell you, you've no idea how much I wish I'd taken my pa's advice and stayed home. If I hadn't come over here, I wouldn't be what I am today, if you catch my meaning."

"That's when you were turned?"

"You can call it that," Francis said, nodding. "I prefer to think of it as having my soul ripped out and replaced with boiling oil, but whatever sounds better to you."

"How?" Ryan asked, wanting to add more to the question but finding himself at a loss for words. Hopefully it would still be enough.

"We were barracked down in New Orleans," Francis said. "Me and some mates went out for a drink—completely against regulations, mind you—and found this beautiful negro woman who spoke this weird, bastard mix of English, French, and something I couldn't put my finger on at the time. Sorry to say, it was my curiosity got the better of me. My mates went on to some other place, anxious for a drink, while I sat and talked with the woman a while. The night wore on, and the more she talked, the more infatuated I became. Then she asked me if I'd like to spend the rest of eternity with her, or at least that was what my tired mind translated what she said to mean. I thought she meant she was willing to take me to bed, if I was willing to be with her forever or some such romantic nonsense, so I lied and said yes."

He laughed bitterly. "Had I known what she was really asking me, though, I think I would've put my dagger in her throat and run for the hills."

"She was a vampire," Ryan said. It wasn't a question.

"Aye, that she was," Francis replied. "She started nibbling away at my neck and I thought she was just being frisky. Then she bit in, and still I thought it was just something done in the throes of passion. Next thing I knew, I was waking up the next night on the floor of some horrid-smelling cellar and she was telling me I was damned. Not exactly what I thought I was signing up for."

Ryan nodded, and decided to shift to a slightly different topic, all in the hopes of getting Francis to tell him things he didn't realize he was telling. Hunter had a unique gift for doing it, and Ryan had been badgering him for tips on how it worked for years. Now he finally had the chance to try his luck at it.

"So you're British?"

"Bite your damned tongue," Francis said, scowling. "I hail from the beautiful isle of Ireland."

Ryan smirked at him. "Your accent seems a bit convenient."

Francis sighed. "Living around you Yanks and your bastardization of the King's and see if you can keep your native lilt. After two hundred years of indoctrination, so to speak, anybody's going to go native."

Ryan shrugged and chose to let the matter drop. His tactic had backfired a bit, in that Francis was already irritated with him over the slip about his heritage. Better to go back to what was expected for a bit.

"You're a vampire," Ryan began. "But what does that mean, exactly? I mean, I know what the movies tell me, and books, but you said they were wrong. So what's real?"

"No fangs, for one," Francis said, then opened his mouth so Ryan could see that his teeth looked straight and normal, like any other human's would. "That's all made-up. And obviously I don't need to sleep until the sun goes down. The sunlight won't exactly kill me, either, but it is painful to be out in it for any length of time. Like I said earlier, even just being awake while it's in the sky makes my skin itch like bugs crawling across it."

"Let's see, what else?" Francis continued, tapping one finger against his chin, eyes rolled up as he considered. "I'm not exactly immortal, but I am damned hard to kill. And before you ask, no, I won't be sharing what it takes to do me in, thank you very much."

"Obviously a stake to the heart won't do it," Ryan said.

"Not on its own, no," Francis admitted. "Think of it like this: when a vampire gets staked, it's like we go into a coma or a really deep sleep or something like that. The difference is, we're fully aware of the passage of time, of the hunger that's continually building in us, everything. You're lucky I was a hard-headed arse before I was 'turned', otherwise I might've not come back from that initial madness that made me attack you when you came in here after I woke up."

When he stopped to think what it must feel like to experience what Francis just described, Ryan thought that insanity was probably the best one could hope for. It was enough to cause him to shudder from the very concept.

"Crosses and holy water?" he asked, hoping to get to a less disturbing subject.

"They can be pretty and it's wet," Francis replied. "I won't say I'm not a creature of the devil, but that religious iconography stuff is stupid either way. Think about it: Satan himself was an angel once, why would symbols of faith have any real negative effect on him, or by extension, on creatures that are 'his'? I suppose if a person with genuine faith were using them they might have some kind of effect on me, but it's more the faith itself and not the objects they use that actually cause damage, if that makes sense."

"Not really," Ryan admitted.

"Sure it does," Francis said. "Think about it: Christ taught his disciples to cast out demons and such, but they didn't have to wave a crucifix at them or toss water that someone prayed over on them to do it. It was the power of their conviction that did the deed, not the fancy trappings they carried with them."

Ryan nodded, conceding the point. "Garlic?"

"Stinks."

"Can't cross running water?"

"I'm on the other side of the Mississippi River from where I started. That's a 'no', for clarification."

"Sleep in a coffin?"

"That's just creepy. Thank you, no."

Ryan sat back in his chair and let out an exasperated breath. "Well, at least I know the blood thing's accurate."

Francis shrugged. "Yes and no. Like I told you, I'm not really gaining the nourishment from the blood itself, but from the life force that's in the blood. Technically speaking, I could use anything that is a part of the prey to get that, blood's just the easiest."

"What does that mean?" Ryan asked, leaning forward.

"Exactly what it sounds like," Francis said. "I can use blood, but I could get the same thing from sweat or tears or even eating the flesh. I know one woman who has sex with her prey and collects their life force that way."

"Like a succubus."

"What the hell's a succubus?"

Ryan blinked. It never occurred to him that one demonic creature wouldn't know about others, even if for all he knew at the moment they were just legends. "A female demon that... has sex with men, usually while they're dreaming, to steal their souls."

Francis nodded appreciatively. "There some place I can sign up for that? They might not get much out of it, since I'm not too sure about the status of my soul these days, but I sure as hell wouldn't mind it."

Ryan felt his cheeks grow warm. "I don't think it works that way."

"Too bad," Francis said, shrugging. "I'd be first in line if they opened for applications."

"So if you can feed from any bodily fluid," Ryan began, a horrible thought suddenly coming to him. "Does that mean you could also use pee?"

Francis snorted a laugh. "Never gave it much thought, but I suppose you could. Then again, since that's a waste product, it probably wouldn't have the same effect. That said, would you want to test it?"

"Ewww, no!" Ryan exclaimed. "That's disgusting!"

"Then I guess we'll never know," Francis said, smiling. "Anything else?"

"So you live forever, and you can obviously heal yourself, but what else do you get out of this transformation?" Ryan asked. "I mean, can you turn into a bat, control animals with your mind... or other people?"

"I'm stronger than most humans," Francis said. "And can take more of a beating than most, too. I can run faster, leap further, that kind of thing. Let's just say my speed, strength, and agility are all considerably higher than normal, at least when I'm at my peak. For the record, in case you hadn't figured it out, I'm not quite there yet."

Ryan cast an appraising eye at the large couch that Francis had to have moved on his own and wondered just what he would be like at his peak. He wasn't entirely sure he wanted to be involved in any situation that caused him to find out.

"That shape-shifting bit is utter shite," Francis went on. "Though if there was one thing I wish I'd gotten that the stories say I should've, it's that. And I can't control animals any more than you could. Most of that's just training and patience, though I have noticed some animals don't particularly care for me. Cats are the worst. The little bastards'll either run like hell when they see me or try to claw my face off. Haven't really seen any in-between there."

"And the mind control?"

Francis narrowed his eyes and leaned a little closer to Ryan. "What's this mind control thing you're on about? You think I 'summoned' you to me or something?"

"I honestly don't know," Ryan admitted. He hadn't been planning on bringing this up, had actually been too afraid of the answer, but now that it was out there, he may as well find out the truth. "You did know I was the one who knocked the stake out of your chest, and that night I had a dream I was being chased by a bunch of people, I ran in here, and they managed to overpower me and ram that stake into me instead of you."

Francis shuddered visibly and was silent for a long moment. He was still facing Ryan, but he wasn't exactly looking at him. If anything, Ryan would almost swear the vampire was looking through him.

"If there is," Francis finally said. His voice was normal, but his cadence was slow and considering. "Then I was never really aware of it. You're right, I did know you were the one who un-staked me, and what you described is fairly close to what happened back when it first happened, so I'd have to say it's possible, but I've never tried to use it or do anything with it."

He hesitated, head cocked to one side as though he was suddenly remembering something. "Then again, I do seem to remember that Margeaux was able to find me, even when I was trying to hide from her, and when I finally came to kill her, she already knew what I was planning."

Ryan stared, shocked. Apparently his plan to get Francis to relax enough to give him information had worked, but now that he'd learned something extremely interesting, he didn't think it would be a good idea to question or pursue the topic. Beyond that, he now had something resembling confirmation that there was some kind of a connection between them, even if not even the supernatural creature that was causing it knew what it actually was.

"Tell you what," Francis said, snapping back out of whatever fugue state he'd been slipping into. "I'll leave it up to you. If you want to test that theory, to see if there is such a thing between us, we can. If you'd rather not, that's fine, too. To be quite honest with you, I still have a hard enough time dealing with what I am, much less adding the ability to control someone with my thoughts on top of that."

Ryan didn't even have to think about it. "I'll pass, if it's all the same to you."

He glanced down at his watch and saw it was time that school would just be letting out. He could go home without worrying that mom would catch him skipping class. If he was extremely lucky, he could get in without her seeing him and clean his face a little more thoroughly, too. He had a story about running into a door because he wasn't paying attention all ready to go, but it even sounded flimsy to him, so he really didn't want to use it if he didn't have to.

"I should get going," he said, getting to his feet. "School just let out, and I don't want to add to it if my parents find out I skipped the last couple of classes."

Francis nodded. "Look, we just met, and I can tell you're still not over the fact that I am what I am, but I do have some advice for you, if you'd care to hear it."

He'd left out that he was over two hundred years old and would most assuredly have considerable wisdom to impart after all that time, but Ryan thought of it anyway and knew he shouldn't pass up this kind of chance. "Okay, shoot."

"That thing you don't want to talk about," Francis said, nodding toward Ryan's chin as he did. "Don't hold it in forever. All you'll accomplish is having something gnaw away at you for the rest of your life. You don't have to tell me, or even your folks. Just talk to someone about it. I guarantee you'll feel better afterward."

Ryan stood staring at him for a long while, and then slowly nodded. "I know I've said it before, but you're not what I would've expected from a vampire."

Francis smiled and rose from the couch, turning to what Ryan thought of as the dining area based on the table and chairs sitting there. "I guess I'm just full of surprises, then. Take care, Ryan. Feel free to stop in again if you feel like having a proper chat instead of interrogating me."

Ryan started to protest that he hadn't been interrogating him but stopped when he realized the vampire was joking. As he walked back out into the hallway and toward the stairs, he couldn't help but think about how this had turned out to be one of the best and worst days of his life, all at the same time, and wondered what could possibly happen next to top it.

CHAPTER TWELVE

As if his day hadn't been strange enough already, when Ryan pedaled up in front of his house he saw Hunter's older sister Melanie sitting on the front steps staring down at her phone. She was dressed in her typical attire of torn and faded blue jean shorts and a t-shirt, what Hunter always called her white trash slut armor, and looked extremely uncomfortable as the cool October breeze drifted across her, eliciting a shudder. Ryan had always thought she was pretty, even if she did usually look a little trashy, but right now she looked like a shadow of her normal self. She was not wearing makeup for the first time he could remember since she'd entered middle school, and her face had a worn, pinched look that added a good ten years to it. She was only seventeen, not even old enough to legally buy the cigarettes she smoked, but right now Ryan thought she wouldn't even get carded buying hard liquor.

He coasted the bike to a stop next to the garage and dismounted, keeping his eyes locked on Melanie. She hadn't acted like she'd even noticed him arriving, still staring down at that phone, the worry lines next to her eyes getting deeper and deeper by the second. He glanced up when he saw movement at the living room window, and saw his mother's face appear briefly, casting a disdainful look over at the girl sitting on the steps, then letting the curtains fall back into place again. Melanie and Ryan's older brother Mike had dated for a little while before he graduated and went off to join the Army, and from what Ryan understood, things had not ended well. It seemed that Mom still held some hard feelings against the girl that had broken her oldest child's heart. Ryan had no idea if she knew more about the breakup than he did, but from that look it was obvious that she'd come to her own conclusions about it, even if they were only true in her mind and not reality.

And honestly, he couldn't think of any reason why Melanie would be sitting on his front steps to start with. Mike wouldn't be home on leave until near the end of November, and he doubted she cared much at all about getting to know him, so unless something bad had happened to Hunter, he couldn't come up with a good reason for her to be there.

She finally looked up when his shadow fell across her phone. Her expression was nearly enough to make Ryan forget about all the hurtful and hateful things he'd thought about her over the years. Her eyes were hollow, her cheeks gaunt. He'd read about people having a "haunted" look about them before, but he'd never expected to see it for himself, especially not on the face of his best friend's older sister.

"Is Hunter with you?" she asked without preamble, her voice shaking in a way that Ryan doubted had anything to do with the cool temperatures outside this afternoon. "Well, he's not here, so obviously not, but was he with you?"

Something was definitely going on here, something bad, and while Ryan didn't know what it was, he intended to find out. "No, I haven't seen him today. Why?"

"Not even at school?"

Ryan shook his head, his heart starting to beat a little faster as a weight settled into his stomach. Melanie sighed and shook her head.

"Look, I know you have every reason to hate me," she said. "Your brother and I didn't exactly part ways on a good note, and I've not really been that nice to you, either. I get it. But if you know where Hunter is, please tell me."

Ryan narrowed his eyes, and found he had to swallow the lump in his throat before he could answer her. "He wasn't at school today. The last time I saw him was yesterday afternoon."

Melanie dropped her eyes from his face and nodded, as if this was nothing more than what she'd expected to hear, even if she'd been hoping differently. Ryan had no idea what to say to her, but since it was looking more and more obvious that something bad had happened to Hunter, he knew he needed to find out everything he could.

"He said something about your mom's boyfriend punching him," Ryan offered. "I know he didn't seem all that anxious to get home, but we split up for a while at the park, then he apparently ditched me. His bike was still there when I left, but I didn't see him anywhere. Now what's going on?"

When she looked back to him, he was able to clearly see the ghost of a bruise along one of her cheeks. He hadn't noticed before because her hair had fallen across it, but now the breeze had blown it free, exposing the mark to any who cared to look. In an instant, he felt another large chunk of the ill will he'd borne against her dissipate, bouncing away on the wind with some of the fallen leaves that littered the front yard.

"Larry—that's mom's boyfriend—had too much to drink the other night," Melanie explained. "Hunter came into the room while he was bitching about there not being any more beer and accused him of stealing it. Hunter didn't much care for him anyway and told him to get a job and go buy more, so Larry knocked Hunter across the room and called him a disrespectful little shithead. Mom stepped in, Hunter went to his room, and when I went to go hide out in mine for a while, Larry was yelling at Mom about how she needed to control her brats. I snuck out after he'd passed out and didn't come home until yesterday morning. I just didn't want to deal with him. It was pretty shitty of me to leave Hunter all alone like that, but I just couldn't take anymore, you know? He'd already given me a shot last week when he caught me sneaking back in half-drunk, and I just couldn't take another argument. Hunter was leaving as I got there, and said he was going to hang out with you for a while. I told him I'd tell Mom I hadn't seen him, which I did.

"Everything seemed fine, until he didn't come home last night. I figured maybe he'd gone to crash with Mom's sister, since he and I have both done that when things got really bad, but she said the last time she saw him was a month ago. When I stopped by the house earlier, Mom was screaming at me because the school called and said Hunter hadn't shown up there, either. I thought—hoped really—that he crashed with you last night, but you're saying you haven't seen him all day, either?"

Ryan had to work the moisture back into his mouth before he could swallow again to clear his throat. "No, I haven't. Like I said, the last time I saw him was yesterday afternoon at the park. He was messing around and pushed me down a hill to make me talk to someone, but that was the last I saw of him. When I went looking a few minutes later, all I could find was his bike."

Melanie nodded again and chewed on her bottom lip, thinking. Finally she looked up at Ryan, tears starting to slip from her eyes. "I think something's happened to him."

As much as he didn't want to, Ryan had to admit it was starting to sound the same way to him, too. Worse, he was pretty sure he had a way to find out for sure one way or the other.

"I'll be right back," he said. "Don't go anywhere."

She nodded and he walked past her, up the short stairs and into the house. His mother was standing near the window, scowling at the curtains as though she could clearly see the girl outside through them. She glanced over at Ryan, acknowledging his presence, the turned and looked at him more fully when she saw the worry etched on his face.

"What's wrong?" she asked.

Ryan relayed the information he'd just gotten from Melanie and told her about possibly being the last person to see Hunter. When he was done filling her in and suggesting his plan, the annoyance on her face had turned to concern instead.

"I'll drive you," she said, turning to the closet where their jackets were hanging next to her purse. Ryan started to protest, but she cut him off with a look. "Tell Melanie I'll be right out."

* * *

The ride to the park was tense, to say the least. Ryan sat up front with Mom, who seemed to divide her time between watching the road ahead of her and giving alternating looks of annoyance and pity to the rear-view mirror and the girl sitting in the back seat. Melanie didn't comment if she noticed, which Ryan felt was no guarantee. Her attention was split between staring down at her phone as if hoping that Hunter had somehow gotten ahold of one and would be calling any minute to let her know he was okay and staring out the window while fighting to hold back her tears of worry.

Ryan knew how she felt. He was on the verge of tears as well, remembering how he'd debated on just leaving the park or going back down the trail to try and find Hunter the day before. For the first time, he wondered if it would've made a difference had had chosen to stay and look for his friend. Sadly, he knew even then that it probably wouldn't be the last time.

When they pulled into the parking lot where Ryan and Hunter had stashed their bikes the day before, all hope that things might actually turn out okay faded. Hunter's bike was still where it had been, lying on its side, chain looped through the spokes and the metal frame secured to the ground beside it. Beyond confirming to his mother that it was, in fact, Hunter's bike, Ryan was unable to speak. Melanie simply let out a low whine and covered her face.

Thankfully, Mom was able to keep it together, quickly pulling her own phone out of her purse and calling the police before rattling off everything she knew about what was going on and asking for an officer to come as soon as possible.

Within fifteen minutes, the park was swarming with cops. From Ryan's best guess, it looked like the entire local department was here, either stretching yellow caution tape across the entrance to the walking trail or kneeling next to Hunter's bike examining the area around it or heading out down the trail with flashlights in one hand and a radio in the other. He told three different officers the story about how they'd come here yesterday, and how Hunter had playfully pushed him down the hill to make him speak with Kayla, and how that had been the last he'd seen of his friend. He overheard Melanie relating the same things she'd already told him as well and was both horrified and thankful that she wasn't leaving out the bit about her mom's boyfriend punching on them. Mom stood off to one side, her attention bouncing between both Ryan and Melanie, apparently ready to step in should it look like either of them needed her. Ryan was actually happy to see that. No matter what he'd thought of Melanie before today, she was obviously in pain that her brother was missing and could use all the help and support she could get. It was painfully obvious that she wasn't getting it at home, so the fact that his own mother, a woman who acted like she hated her, was willing made his heart feel a little lighter.

If only they could find Hunter, it would make everything perfect.

He turned out to be the one who needed his mother's consoling first, though. After the fourth time relaying the information, it occurred to him that he might never see his best friend again, that the last time they'd been together had been when he'd been pushed down a hill, so he'd have no choice but to talk to the girl of his dreams for the first time. In a way, Hunter's disappearance could be his fault, if you wanted to look at it that way. He tried to fight the idea, tried to tell himself there was no way that could be true, but finally it overcame him, reducing him to tears. His mother was there at once, wrapping him in her arms and whispering consoling words to him, telling him it would be okay, and not to worry.

Amazingly, when he gently pulled away, he saw Melanie standing there watching him, tears in her eyes as well. She held out her arms and he entered them without hesitation, trying to comfort her even as she tried to comfort him, both of them knowing that no matter what happened from this point on, nothing would ever be the same again.

CHAPTER THIRTEEN

His parents were understanding enough to offer Ryan the chance to stay home from school, and after the sleepless night he'd spent he was sorely tempted to take that offer. He knew that if he stayed home, all he'd do was to wander aimlessly around the house worrying, so he elected to get dressed and give it a shot anyway. Even if he didn't manage to actually pay attention enough to learn anything, at least it was a chance to try and keep his mind off of everything.

The police had finally allowed Mom to bring him home after a couple hours of questioning, mostly rehashing the same things over and over and over again, mainly exactly what had transpired right after he'd last seen Hunter. They'd mentioned they would send someone out to talk to Kayla, just on the off-chance she saw something he'd missed, but they didn't really seem to think she would know much more than Ryan did. When they'd asked if he could think of anyone who might want to cause Hunter harm, he'd come close to selling Matt, Zach, and Brandon down the river, but held back, sure that if the cops looked into it and found nothing to warrant arresting them he would pay for bringing their names up in the first place. If the police spoke with anyone at school— which he was almost positive they'd do—the names would come up anyway, but he wanted to make sure he wasn't the one who mentioned them.

Not that it would matter. Whatever had happened to Hunter, Ryan was sure the asshole brigade had nothing to do with it. They were bullies, sure, but he doubted they'd go so far as to disappear someone like that. If nothing else, he doubted they had the smarts for it.

If the cops had questioned them already, they didn't let on. Ryan saw them not long after he got to school, but while they gave him looks every time they crossed paths, they never approached or said a word to him. For that matter, hardly anyone said anything to him all day, with the exception of Kayla, who stammered out something about how sorry she was but held the expression of someone who really didn't have any idea what to say. Ryan didn't mind. Had their roles been reversed, he wouldn't have known what to say, either.

When school finally let out, he immediately pulled out his cell phone and checked to see if there had been any word from Melanie about Hunter yet. There hadn't, the only notification on his phone a single text message from Mom saying she hoped he was handling things okay today, and that she loved him. He very nearly teared up at the simplicity of that statement, and the honesty he knew it held, which only served to prove to him how close to tears he'd been the entire day. His Mom told him she loved him all the time. For it to affect him so deeply today meant his emotions were very much at a razor's edge.

He got on his bike and rode away, noticing out of the corner of his eye that Kayla was standing on the steps leading down from the school's side entrance to the bike racks alongside the parking lot, watching as he passed. Her friends weren't anywhere around, and Ryan had a pretty good idea that maybe she'd been hoping to talk to him alone, but today he just wasn't in the mood for a full conversation with her. It was insane to think that only a day or so ago he'd have been over the moon to see her standing there like that, waiting for him, and now he only wanted to get as far away as he could.

A thought occurred to him as he slowed to a stop next to the stop sign at the end of the road. Hunter had mysteriously disappeared the same day Ryan was supposed to take food to Francis. All day he'd felt that taking Hunter to the asylum was a bad idea, but he'd ignored it. Francis didn't know if there was any mental bond between them, but he had been looking more alive when Ryan had next seen him. The dog hadn't done much for him, true, but what if he'd had Hunter there, waiting in reserve to top himself off because he knew Ryan wouldn't bring him exactly what he needed—or even in case Ryan didn't bring him anything at all?

It wasn't much, but it was all he had to go off of right now. Worse, it wasn't anything he could tell the cops. They'd think he was insane or something, or maybe even think he'd had something more to do with Hunter's disappearance than simply being there with him moments before it happened. All of which meant there was only one way to find out, and that was to confront a vampire and ask.

He turned his bike in the opposite direction from home and headed for the asylum as quick as his legs could carry him.

The place felt like he was walking into a tomb, whether because of his new suspicions or simply because it had always felt that way and he simply hadn't noticed before, he had no idea. The fact remained that this time it felt much, much creepier than it had the previous two times he'd been here. He was acutely aware of just how old the place was, and how much history was held within its walls, not to mention the vampire living in the place's basement.

Francis was not in the storeroom this time when he arrived, and Ryan didn't see any sign of him anywhere else in the basement area. The sun wasn't down, although it was starting its descent for another night, so he doubted the vampire had gone outside yet—while Francis said the sun wouldn't kill him, he did indicate that it wasn't exactly a pleasant experience for him to be out in it. If he ruled that out, then the vampire had to be in the building somewhere, though what he could be doing wasn't something Ryan even wanted to speculate about.

Unless....

If he was right, if Francis did have Hunter trapped in here somewhere, it was quite possible that the vampire was with him right now, maybe even feeding on his friend while he stood down here in the basement doing nothing. If it was true, Hunter could be dead before Ryan got the chance to talk to Francis, which would mean that it was his fault just as much as the vampire's that his best friend was killed. He couldn't let that happen.

He wished he'd brought a flashlight with him, but since he didn't he would have to do this fast, before it got too dark for him to see. He rushed out of the basement and took the stairs back to the main landing two at a time, hesitating only long enough to try and figure out where to go from there. While there was a chance the vampire might still be on the first floor, he doubted it. For one thing, it would be too easy for any cop who might happen to wander through to check things out to run across him on accident. Which meant he had to be on the second, third, or fourth floor instead. The fifth was possible, but from what Ryan had seen when he explored the place with Hunter a couple of days ago, more of the windows were open and exposed there than anywhere else in the building. So rule that one out too. Three floors to check, and very little time to do it.

Ryan decided to start at the top and work his way down, hoping that he would figure out where Francis was before it was too late. He ran up the steps, stumbling a couple of times when his toes would catch on the concrete, but somehow managing to not fall and bust his face open on the risers. He was breathing hard when he got to the fourth floor, but he pushed himself to keep going, darting through the open door and into the long corridor beyond. This floor was as silent as the basement had been, save for faint scurrying sounds Ryan was sure had to be mice nesting against the coming cold. He still looked into every open room he passed, only turning around and heading back when he reached the end of the hallway.

The third floor was much the same, only there were more closed doors which meant there was even less light than he'd had on the floor above. He was actually wheezing when he got to the end of that hallway and turned around, still failing to find either the vampire or his potential captive.

He forced himself to keep going, ignoring the black specks that had begun to dance at the edges of his field of vision. He barely paid attention as he passed the doors in the second-floor corridor, focusing only on remaining conscious and not passing out. His legs ached, his chest was screaming for more air, and his head had begun to feel muddied and light at the same time. His vision swam, his eyes un-focusing and refocusing in a steady rhythm. He screamed when he reached the end of the corridor, a cry of sheer frustration that echoed off the walls of the abandoned building, making it sound like there were hundreds just like him all crying out at once.

His vision tunneled in to a narrow pinprick as he charged through the door and back into the stairwell, intending on going back up and retracing his steps a little slower this time. His legs gave out and he felt himself starting to fall, not toward the stairs themselves, but toward the low railing that lined the landing. He slammed into it, barely noticing as the steel bars mashed his balls and drove into his stomach. He folded over it instinctively, trying to protect the injured areas on his torso, and ended up overbalancing, his feet going out from underneath him even as he tipped over the railing and started to fall into the open space that ended at the first-floor landing, a good ten feet below him.

Just as his feet left the ground and his mind began to comprehend what was about to happen, Ryan felt someone grab him by the back of his jeans and haul him backward, his stomach dragging painfully across the steel bar before he popped free and slammed to the floor of the landing on his back. He looked up, vision still a little hazy, and saw Francis standing there, staring down at him with confusion and wonder.

"What the hell are you doing, kid?" Francis asked. "Scream like a bloody banshee then try to jump off the damned stairs? Trying to break your fool neck, are you?"

Ryan wanted to scream at the vampire, lay his accusations out, but all he could do was gasp and croak as his lungs struggled to regain the air they'd lost during his mad dash up and down the stairs and corridors. He closed his eyes, laid his head back on the cool concrete, and tried to focus on breathing slowly, in and out, in and out. Finally, his chest began to loosen, and while his head still hurt, a dull ache almost directly between his eyes, he was at least able to think clearly again.

"Where is he?" he asked, his voice barely more than a whisper. "Where's Hunter?"

"I have no clue what you're on about," Francis replied. "Where's who?"

Ryan gave it a mental ten-count, and then pushed himself back to a sitting position. He glanced behind him and saw one of the larger patient beds sitting in the hallway, the mattress bound to the frame with strips of cloth tied along one side. When he turned back around, he saw Francis leaning against the same railing he'd very nearly fallen over, arms crossed over his chest, head cocked to one side as he studied him.

"Tell me the truth," Ryan said, deciding to take a gamble and bluff the vampire. "Lie and I'll know it. Did you take Hunter? Did you... feed from him? Kill him?"

A look of utter confusion crossed the vampire's face. "Who is Hunter? I haven't taken anyone, and aside from that dog you brought me, the only thing I've fed off of was a deer I spotted out in the woods behind here later that same night. Now what the hell is going on?"

Ryan groaned and lowered his head to his hands, resting them on his knees. He had no way to tell if Francis was lying to him or not, nor could he really do anything about it if he was. Even for all that, he couldn't think of any reason why the vampire would lie to him about this, and from the lack of comprehension on his face and in his voice, Ryan didn't think he was.

Which meant his only hope of figuring out what happened to his friend was gone. In all likelihood, he would never see Hunter alive again. He gave into the emotions that had been raging inside him all day and wept.

CHAPTER FOURTEEN

The lights were off, but it didn't matter. Francis didn't need them to see any more than he needed to breathe other than to keep up appearances or needed to eat real food except for fitting in with the rest of humankind. He could see just fine in the dark, his eyes cat-like in their ability to pierce the veil of night. It made him a more effective hunter, even if he didn't rely on those skills or choose to see himself in that way. His body might have changed, and to a lesser degree his mind, but he still saw himself as that scared young man from Waterford, seeing the larger world for the first time. Two hundred plus years and becoming damned hadn't altered that feeling. He hoped he never encountered anything that would.

He sat on the couch in his ramshackle "apartment", staring into the darkness at nothing in particular, the tingles across his skin beginning to calm as the sun dropped below the horizon and the moon rose to take its place. He marveled again at how becoming a vampire was in many ways like becoming a woman—both tied to the cycles of the moon, and both because of blood. True, he was required to ingest it rather than dispel it, and once you looked deeper the similarity wasn't all that close, but he couldn't help but think the way he thought.

It had taken him longer than he'd expected to calm the boy after finding and saving him from a nasty, possibly fatal fall. He'd known the boy was there, of course, and had even known something was bothering him—despite his insistence to the contrary, he was positive there was some kind of connection between them, though he couldn't begin to imagine how, why, or what the specifics of it were—but the sheer depth of the boy's emotional turmoil had been a surprise. It took a considerable amount of soothing words and gentle coaxing to get the story out of him, and now Francis found himself wondering what to do, or even whether or not he should get involved at all.

That the boy was being picked on at school was not that shocking. As Francis told him during one of their first conversations, he had too kind a heart, and unfortunately the predators of the world—both human and not—would see such a thing as a weakness. It was simply the way of nature to demean the kind and reward the mean. Francis considered himself proof of that. It wasn't even that surprising to hear that the boy had very few friends. To Francis, it was all part of the same. What he did find shocking was that the one person to whom the boy felt a true bond, something that went beyond simple friendship and into the realms of actual brotherhood, was now missing under suspicious circumstances.

What little humanity remained inside Francis felt for the boy, understood his pain and his plight. The monstrous part of him wondered why the boy didn't stand up for himself more, assert himself in a way that might improve his station in life, but perhaps this time did not view such things as beneficial. Certainly when he'd been captured and staked so long ago, it had been accepted, and even encouraged. Still, he could remember a time before that when it wasn't proper to act in such a manner. It appeared the cycle had come around again.

The boy suspected him of foul play when it came to his friend. Francis chastised him for this, but in truth, he didn't mind all that much. He knew what he was, knew how he was perceived by the normal populace. He supposed he should consider himself fortunate that the boy hadn't brought along a raving mob with him, intent on far worse than placing Francis back into that deep, near-death sleep again.

He felt some guilt at the harsh manner in which he'd attempted to prove his innocence in this matter. The look on the boy's face when Francis pointed out that he would not have hidden the fact he was feeding from the other one, should he have chosen to do so, had been heart-wrenching, even to one as hardened as his. He could have gone further, could have also pointed out to the boy that should he desire it, he could do whatever he chose and there was nothing the boy could do to stop it, but the combination of guilt and the surety that the point was already made stayed his tongue.

Now, the advice he'd given the boy before sending him on his way played back through his mind. It sounded hollower now, in retrospect, than it had when he spoke it. He'd advised allowing the local law enforcement to do their job, and to pray to whatever Higher Power the boy held dear that his friend would be found, but the more he considered it, the more fruitless he knew this course of action to be. Questions of God and faith aside—Francis had no illusions that while God did exist, He simply chose to be a passive bystander when it came to the troubles of the beings He'd created—the very concept that law enforcement would be able to accomplish anything of worth was laughable. They believed only in the facts before them, the things they could see with their own limited vision, and generally chose to act on the side of expedience rather than thoroughness. He'd met some who didn't fit the mold—one eager young detective who'd been assigned to a series of murders amongst London's prostitutes over a century ago came to mind—but they could hardly exact change when they were among the minority.

It was possible the police would find the missing boy, but Francis was certain it would be much too late to be of any real benefit. The boy was probably already dead, but he'd learned first-hand that only the recovery of his body could give any real sense of closure to those close to him. Until that happened, they would cling to the false hope that he would return to the same and sound, unchanged and unaffected by whatever he'd endured in the interim. His own Mum had gone down this rabbit hole when he was listed as missing amongst the troops returning to Britain following the war that brought him to this new country. When he finally managed to find his way home again, he'd found her a broken woman, so obsessed with his safe return that she'd lost her grip on reality. Even if he had presented himself to her—changed, but still enough of himself to soothe her mind—he doubted she would believe what she saw to be truth. His Pa branded him an abomination and took after him with a chunk of wood, so the decision to leave his own family behind had been a mixed one, but in the interest of allowing Mum to live out what little life she had in relative peace, he'd made it.

He'd never met the missing boy or his family, and therefore could care less about them, but he was connected to the boy who'd saved him—albeit inadvertently from the way the boy relayed the tale—and did not want to see him go down the same path as his own Mum. The boy was already weak enough. Such an experience would surely break him.

Francis felt something primal awaken within himself and knew the sun had finished its work for another day, leaving the world to those of his ilk, those who were born of and for the night. His abilities would be at their strongest for several hours now, until the day broke anew, so if he wanted to do something, now would be the time. He wasn't sure what he could accomplish—it had been many years since he'd applied himself to a hunt such as the one he now contemplated—but if there was anything he could do to ease the boy's suffering, reward him in a practical way for saving him from the Hell of eternal starvation and decay, he could at least try.

He stood and looked down at himself, sniffing as some foul odor penetrated his nostrils and assaulted his senses. He was filthy, his clothes torn and tattered and covered in dust from his work of moving things down here to his little hideaway beneath the former home of the mad. Of course he stank, why would he not? He'd spent nearly four decades unable to clean or groom himself. He supposed he should be thankful that he was beyond such mundane human issues as perspiration or the need to excrete waste, for he could only imagine his stench if those occurred while he lay in torment all those years. If he was going to be out in public among the humans, he needed to rectify this situation. He wanted to draw as little attention to himself as possible, not actively cause people to avoid him because of his appearance and hygiene. Otherwise, they might remember him, even if it was unfavorably, and that could result in dire consequences further down the line.

So a bath and a change of clothing first, then.

Which presented its own set of problems. The place he was in had no running water or electrical power, nor did he have any of his belongings with him. The hunters who had pursued him here would have taken those from his former lodgings, and even if they hadn't, after this long they would have surely been claimed and discarded by whomever took his former home for themselves after his departure. He would not be able to simply return there and resume his former life, which meant he needed money and a place to clean himself.

There was a pond across the fence at the back of the hospital's property, which would work for the latter, but he still needed clean clothes to change into. Robbery would be the easiest answer, though it meant he would run the risk of drawing too much attention to himself, yet he could think of no other way to get what he needed to rejoin society, even on a limited basis.

Unless....

He'd kept a stash of currency from various times and locales hidden at his former residence nearby. If the new owners hadn't found it, he could reclaim it and go about his business undisturbed. It was still a risk, but the potential for being captured was much smaller than if he simply broke into a clothing shop and stole what he needed from there. Worse come to worst, if the new owners accosted him, he could simply kill them to keep his secret safe. It wasn't something he particularly wanted to do, despite the sudden excitement at the prospect that filled that primal part of his mind, but he would and could do it if he had no other choice.

Either way, it meant he had to remember the skills he'd honed over the centuries of his reborn life. He let out a purely theatrical sigh in spite of there being no one there to witness it and headed for the stairs leading up out of this building, hoping that the boy was worth all the trouble he was about to go to for him.

* * *

Try as he might, Ryan could not make himself relax. Things had been fine—or at least as fine as they were going to get—when he got home from talking with Francis, but in the last little while he'd become more and more anxious, and he couldn't figure out any reason why. He'd tried lying on his bed staring at the ceiling, pacing the room, attempting to read, and even considered pulling up some of his secret porn stash on his laptop and masturbating before deciding that doing so while his parents were both still awake and active would be a potential recipe for sheer and utter embarrassment that he didn't want to chance.

He was staring out the window again, wondering why he had such a strange urge to go run around the yard like a maniac, when he heard the beeping sound from his laptop that said he had a message on Facebook. He'd been on there earlier, just killing time and browsing the feed, and apparently hadn't shut it down so it still indicated that he was online. He didn't really want to look at it, sure it was probably just Melanie telling him they hadn't heard anything new on Hunter yet. He'd already talked to her three times since he'd come home, and the last thing she'd said was that the police were considering it a runaway case, despite the fact that Hunter had left his bike behind and had taken nothing at all with him. While he felt sorry for Melanie and what she was going through, he simply couldn't deal with trying to be supportive for someone else when he just wanted someone to do the same for him.

Another beep sounded. Ryan sighed and cross the room. Apparently she wasn't going to give up until he replied, so he was going to tell her he wasn't feeling well and was going to bed early, then sign off and hope he could think of some way to make that statement a reality. When he clicked the messenger icon, though, he was shocked to see that it wasn't Melanie who'd been trying to reach him, but Kayla. Just two messages so far, but considering it was two more than she'd ever sent in the past, it was still notable.

"Just wanted to say I'm really sorry about Hunter," the first one read. "I know I didn't do such a good job of saying so at school, but it's true."

"I'm here if you want to talk," read the second. "About Hunter, or anything else if you need something to take your mind off it for a few minutes, if that's possible."

Ryan stared at the screen, heart racing, unsure whether to respond at all or just pretend that he hadn't seen them. Of course, he'd clicked the icon to bring them up, so he was pretty sure it would show on her end that he had seen them, but considering the way she'd phrased that second message, it was entirely possible that she wouldn't think anything of it, would just assume that he wasn't in the mood to talk right now. While that was partially true, it wasn't completely accurate—especially not with her. He'd just managed to get her into his life, even if only in small doses. The last thing he wanted was for her to think he wasn't interested in talking to her and have her go back to ignoring him.

Once he realized that he knew exactly what Hunter would want him to do, it made his decision a little easier, too.

"Thanks," he typed back. "I appreciate the offer, I'm just not sure I'd be much fun in a conversation right now."

He hit enter and then immediately began to worry that he'd said the wrong thing. Of course she wouldn't expect him to be a barrel of fun right now—she'd said as much in the first message. He thought she might not respond, then saw the little ellipsis that indicated she was typing something in reply and felt his hands break out in a cold sweat. He was practically bouncing when the next message finally popped up on his screen.

"If it helps, the only conversation we've had was after you knocked me down the other day, so I don't really have much to compare it to, so maybe it'll be more fun than you think?"

She'd finished it off with a series of emojis, a winky-face, followed by a smiley face, followed by a face with a tongue sticking out. He couldn't help but smile.

He couldn't figure out what to write back, so he decided to simply tell her that she'd managed to make him smile. It was true, and it was especially meaningful considering that he hadn't had much cause to smile over the last thirty-six hours or so. Again he waited, nervous about what would come back until the next message finally came across the screen.

"See, already off to a good start," it read. "Now let's really challenge you: what would you like to talk about? Fair warning, if you say me, I've been known to go for hours, just ask my sister."

He barked a laugh and bent over the keyboard. "That might not be such a bad thing. I know I'd love to hear more about you."

His nerves reached a fever pitch the second he sent the message. He hadn't intended on being so direct, had simply typed without thinking. It wasn't like him to be bold, even in something as minor as this. Perhaps it was a sign that writing was something he should pursue, if it was so easy to express himself by just typing without thinking about any repercussions until later.

Luckily, he didn't have to wait long for a response.

"Aw, that's sweet of you to say," it read. "So what do you want to know?"

Ryan leaned back in his chair and scratched his head. A thousand different questions flooded his mind, ranging from the innocent to the obscene. While he knew well enough not to even consider asking any of the latter end of that spectrum, he still had to wonder what might happen if he did ask them. Best not to take the chance though. He decided to start with something simple and as far to the innocent side of the scale as he could get.

"Ok," he typed. "You said you have a sister, any other siblings?"

"Younger brother," she replied. "Aidan's just starting middle school. Racheal is a senior this year. You?"

"Older brother. Mike graduated last year, he's in the Army now, down at Fort Benning."

"Cool. If he graduated last year, Racheal might know him. I'll have to ask. So what else you want to know?"

He was debating on his next question, something still firmly in the innocent realm, but found he was typing almost on autopilot, not even realizing what he asked until after he'd hit Enter and sent the question. When he saw it, he felt sweat break out on his palms, and wished for some way to delete or recall the message before she saw it. Unfortunately, no sooner than the thought came to his mind, he saw the little icon next to it change, indicating that she was reading it.

"Why do you hang out with that asshole Matt and his friends?" he'd asked.

He stood up and crossed back to the window again, positive that he'd managed to wreck things even faster than he'd feared he would. Not only was the question too blunt, it came off harsh and almost accusatory as well. The implication was, of course, that since she hung out with such assholes, she must be a raging bitch herself. He leaned forward until his forehead was resting against his window and began tapping it gently, making sure he didn't just slam into it and shatter the glass. He was trying to chastise himself, not slice his face to ribbons, after all.

When the computer beeped that he'd received a response, he jerked so hard in surprise that he nearly put his head through the window anyway. He raced back to his desk, heart racing, his body tensed in anticipation of the rebuke he was sure was coming his way. He felt a flash of increased nervousness when he saw the length of the message, but once he started to actually read it, he felt some of his tension ease away.

"Let me start by saying it's not entirely by choice," it read. "Believe me, all hanging around with them does is give me more chances to see exactly what kind of dicks they are. Since Amber and I have been friends since kindergarten, and since she's kind of dating Brandon, I just get pulled into the mix, even when I don't really want to. Granted, he's the least obnoxious of the bunch, but that's like saying dried dog poop is better than fresh elephant poop. It also doesn't help that

Matt keeps trying to hug me and put his hands on me and basically paw at me every time we're all together. I've told him I wasn't interested a thousand times, at least, but he just doesn't seem to take the hint. One of these days I'm going to end up kicking him square in the balls and see if that gets the point across clear enough. Are you asking because of how they treat you and Hunter all the time? If so, don't feel bad. Maybe it's not much help, but they spread it around plenty. You're not the only ones, believe me, even if it might feel like it sometimes. Come to think of it, is that why you left school early the other day? Did one of them do something?"

He still didn't want to say, not so much because of Matt's threats, but because of the embarrassment he still felt over the whole affair. Maybe it was because of her own experiences with him that he found himself responding the way he did, maybe it was something else. Either way, Francis had been right about how he shouldn't let it just fester.

"Yeah," he typed. "But that was nothing new. Just kind of wrecked what was turning into a pretty decent day."

He decided not to answer her question about why he'd asked about her hanging out with Matt and his group. He still wasn't sure why he'd asked it in the first place, even though it was something he was curious about.

"Really," came the fast response. "And what made it start out so good?"

He smiled, and to his credit, only hesitated for the briefest of instants before answering her.

"Maybe a note I got at lunch."

"Why would that make your day so good?"

Ryan couldn't tell if she was being coy, or playful, or what. The down side to a conversation like this was that emotion tended to be stripped away from the words once they formed on the screen. Either way, she was succeeding in making him smile, and that wasn't something he'd expected to be doing any time soon.

He blinked when he saw his response was already on the screen, too. This time, he hadn't even been aware he was typing it.

"Because you wrote it, naturally."

A couple of seconds later, her response showed up: the image of a cute little overweight cat with rosy red cheeks and a shy expression. He smiled again and started typing.

"So we both know I don't have a girlfriend, so what about you?"

"I don't have a girlfriend, either," came the reply. Ryan snorted a laugh.

"I meant, do you have a boyfriend?"

"No," she sent back. "Hadn't found the right guy yet, I suppose."

He started to type something back, and then stopped as it occurred to him there was something wrong with that sentence. He didn't have a lot of experience chatting with Kayla on Facebook or through text message or whatever, but he'd seen enough to know that she was pretty careful about what she typed. She didn't use a lot of those annoying acronyms, and she didn't come up with cutesy ways of spelling common words. He also knew from being in the same English class with her both this year and last year that she was extremely intelligent, so her use of the word "hadn't" as opposed to "haven't" was distinctly out of place. Maybe it meant nothing, but then again, maybe there was some meaning to it, something he wasn't ready to come back at head-on yet.

That didn't mean he couldn't brush up against it, though.

"Think you might change that soon?"

"Maybe," she replied. "I did start talking to this one guy, he seems pretty cool. Kinda cute, too. I'll let you know if it looks like anything's going to come of it."

"Make sure you do," he typed.

"Hate to cut this short," she sent. "Especially since we're finally starting to get into some interesting conversation, but my brother broke his computer and needs to use mine for some school thing, so I need to get off here. If you're up later, you can message me again, if you want. I know you probably need to get some sleep since I doubt you've had much of it the last couple days, but just know I'm here if you need or want to talk."

To his surprise, Ryan found that he actually felt somewhat at peace for the first time since he'd learned Hunter had gone missing. It was just one more thing to show that his feelings for Kayla weren't based solely on her looks, no matter what Hunter might've thought.

"Thanks," he typed back. "I may take you up on that, but if I don't, hope you have a good night, and hopefully I'll see you at school again either tomorrow or the next day."

"You, too," she sent back. "Sweet dreams!"

The little green dot next to her name disappeared, showing she'd gone offline. Ryan leaned back in his chair and felt that sweet dreams were definitely something that might happen tonight. He felt a little guilty for flirting with someone while Hunter could be out there somewhere, hurt or worse, but he knew his friend well enough to know that Hunter would want this for him, no matter what.

For tonight, at least, knowing that was enough.

CHAPTER FIFTEEN

For a change, Francis had a run of good luck. When he arrived at the old two-story farmhouse where he'd taken up residence nearly half a century ago, he was pleased to find that it was still in incredible condition, obviously well taken care of by its new owners, and better yet, they weren't home. It was encouraging, but he couldn't rely on his luck holding. He had no idea how long they'd be gone, or even how many people lived there, or if they'd come back at staggered times or what. He broke the lock on the cellar doors and hurried inside, thankful that unlike most other burglars, he didn't need a flashlight to find his way.

He was also pleased to see that the brick wall behind which he'd hidden his stash of money was still intact and undisturbed, meaning that everything behind it was probably still safe. He felt around until his fingers slipped into the groove near the top, then exercised his considerable strength and pulled the entire wall toward him. It didn't want to budge at first, but it finally broke free, scraping across the floor with a noise that sounded like the world's biggest hand scraping sharp fingernails down an equally large chalkboard. He stopped when there was just enough space for him to slip through, grabbed the valise of cash, and replaced the wall, gritting his teeth against that horrible noise.

His curiosity got the better of him, so he went upstairs to see what the old place looked like now. The kitchen was neat and tidy, with just enough knick-knacks scattered about for him to recognize a feminine touch. He passed through the dining room and into the larger living area, feeling a wave of unreality wash over him at the sight of all the modern electronics adorning the walls, the massive flat-screen television and the speakers in the corners of the room. Times had definitely changed, though it remained to be seen if it was for the better.

As he turned to head back into the kitchen and the cellar stairs beyond, he spied a calendar hanging on the wall with handwriting in the little boxes for the dates. He leaned closer, and easily deciphered the flowing script that he assumed came from the woman of the house. It seemed that the couple put their work and appointment schedules here, for easy reference. They also conveniently seemed to mark off each date as it passed, so there could be no mistake of what day it was and what was due to happen on it.

Based on what he read, it seemed the husband had to work until eight that night, and their child had some kind of school function that would keep them, and the wife occupied until seven. Francis glanced over to the clock hanging above the television, and saw it was not quite six yet. Factor in the time it would take for them to get from wherever they were to here, and he had plenty of time.

He changed course and wandered upstairs, checking through the rooms, and saw that the husband was apparently of a similar size and build to Francis. Shrugging, he pulled a shirt, some pants, socks, and a pair of shoes out of the closet and crossed to the master bathroom. He left the lights off and turned on the shower, setting the water to a temperature that would be too hot for most, but to him felt absolutely wonderful. He stripped off his old clothes and stepped in, scrubbed himself thoroughly, then rinsed. He took a moment to savor the steam and the feeling of the hot water pounding against his neck and scalp, then shut the water off and stepped out. He grabbed a towel from a nearby rack and dried himself, then dressed in his stolen clothes and left. He took his old clothing and the towel with him. No sense leaving them for the owners to wonder about, or to potentially lead hunters right to him again. He stuffed them into the valise with his money, then left the house the same way he'd come in. The owners might realize that someone had broken in, but when they saw nothing of value was missing, they probably wouldn't bother to report it. And if they did, what would the police really do about someone who broke in just to take a shower while no one was home, and then left again?

Instead of heading straight to the park where the kid—Ryan; if he was going to do something nice for him, the least he could do was remember his name—said his friend had disappeared, he stopped back by his basement apartment in the hospital to drop off his things. He didn't anticipate having to move fast tonight, but it was better to be prepared just in case, and he didn't want to chance losing all that money should he have to act quickly.

The park was deserted by the time he arrived, which was what he'd hoped for. The sun was going down much faster, resulting in an earlier onset of night, and while he wasn't bothered by the chill in the air tonight, he knew most humans would be. It was all for the best. He didn't want to be disturbed as he began his search.

He walked around without any particular idea of where he was going, trusting his instincts to guide his way. He finally stopped and found himself standing next to a fairly large duck pond in the middle of the park, just down the hill from a walking trail. He could sense Ryan's presence here, and for some strange reason found himself overcome with the feeling of mixed joy and terror. He turned and looked up toward the walking trail, noting the way the grass and fallen leaves had been disturbed by something's passage. He remembered Ryan saying he'd rolled down that hill and was reasonably certain he was in the right place.

Sure enough, the sense of the boy continued as he climbed the hill and looked both ways down the gravel pathway. He could feel Ryan leading back toward the parking lot and one of the park's exits. This matched what the boy had told him about his friend's disappearance. Francis considered going back that way, starting his search from there, but he had a feeling there wouldn't be any need for that. The other boy's bicycle had been left behind, so it was doubtful that whoever had taken him had done so that close to an open, public area.

Francis closed his eyes and knelt, resting his fingers lightly on the rough gravel, opening himself to the residue of events from days past that still lingered around the area. He was able to ascertain that dozens of people had passed by this way in the time since Ryan and his friend had stood here together, bringing a frown to his face. He could almost tell that some of those he felt were policemen, bored even as they searched for a missing child. It annoyed him that they could feel anything other than fear and worry, even if it was couched in businesslike detachment. Still, this was a different time and place from what he was used to, and it would do him no good to dwell on the modern excuse for law enforcement and their inadequacies.

He narrowed his focus, using the remnants of what he'd felt of Ryan as a guide, and managed to feel someone similar. He could tell they were young and male, and in this spot, at least, they were also amused and sad at the same time. They'd lingered here, a bittersweet melancholy rising up within them, then they'd gone on down the path, moving further away from the parking lot and the exit. Try as he might, Francis could not feel the person passing this way again, at least not at any time recently past, which meant he knew the direction he needed to go.

He opened his eyes and stood, turning his head to look down the long, winding walkway. The path disappeared into a copse of trees some distance away, the skeletal branches overhanging the gravel trail and lending an air of menace to the place. Francis supposed that was appropriate, considering the circumstances that had brought him here in the first place. Beyond the place where it entered the trees, the path was couched in shadow, a sharp curve just beyond the spot they began ensuring that once you went around it, you would be effectively cut off from the view of anyone else in this area who might happen to be looking.

Francis headed toward that curve, holding onto the feel of the missing boy, sure that whatever answers this place held would be found somewhere over there. As he neared the overhanging trees, the feeling intensified, the others who'd been here more recently fading into the background. The police had done a cursory check at best, another reason for him to be irritated at them.

He was a little surprised that he was able to feel as much as he did. Whatever low-level psychic ability that had been granted to him with his conversion had always been spotty at best, though it had also been useful on occasion. He'd learned over the years that if the person he was tracking felt strong enough emotions, he was able to feel them more easily, but for one as young as the missing boy to leave such a trace was almost unheard of. This was someone who'd been in significant emotional pain, to a degree that Francis found staggering. He'd met full-grown adults who hadn't experienced enough from life to even come close to matching it. Whatever had been going on in this boy's life had obviously affected him more deeply that Ryan probably knew about. Francis could feel the boy's joy for his friend, but everything self-reflective was tinged with sadness, heartache, and torment. He'd begun this search to help Ryan, but now he intended to see it through to honor this kid's memory. He deserved that much, even if he wasn't going to be around to see it.

After turning the corner, Francis found that both sides of the trail were flanked by thick foliage, bushes and the like that would probably stay leafy even in the depth of winter. His predator's mind told him this was the perfect spot to lie in wait for easy prey, and if his suspicions were correct, he could bet his quarry would've felt much the same.

He stopped as a feeling of alarm overwhelmed him to the point he was bracing for an ambush before he realized it hadn't come from within himself, but from the boy he was tracking. He turned a slow circle, taking note of the disturbed bushes on one side of the trail right next to him, as well as another trampled area a bit further down. He took one more slow step toward that second break, and felt the boy's residual energy wane considerably, becoming more diffuse in the span of barely two feet. Whatever had happened to him, this was where it started.

Francis knelt again, his eyes searching the packed gravel, but he could find nothing of interest or use. He closed his eyes and leaned down, as if he was bowing before some all-powerful god, and sniffed heartily.

There it was. Faint, but instantly recognizable. Blood.

He reached out with his finger, trying madly to touch the smell, and then opened his eyes again. He gently moved some of the small stones aside and saw what he was looking for on the rocks beneath. The hint of a stain that would appear almost black to anyone who happened to notice it, but which carried a dull glow to his supernatural sight. Blood had been spilled here. It was minimal, quite possibly the result of a quick, powerful blow that had dazed the boy, if not knocking him completely unconscious. Francis still couldn't discern his final fate, but he did have verification that whatever happened had definitely been bad.

He concentrated again, focusing on the blood to try and narrow his search, but he could not feel any trace of another person who seemed likely to have just assaulted a child. He frowned. He knew the psychic ability wasn't absolute, and he was sorely out of practice, but to find such absence where there should have been a rush of adrenaline at the very least was disorienting. Trying to focus on the boy was no help, either. His thoughts had been driven into the background noise of the world, hidden even from otherworldly sight. If he was to continue this, he would have to do it the old-fashioned way, at least for a time.

He made his way through the trampled area in the bushes and found himself nearing the edge of the tree line overlooking a wide, open field. He'd noticed another curve in the path before he ducked through the foliage, and figured that where he was standing now would put him with his back to the direction the walking path continued in. If his guess was right, this would lead further away from the areas of the park that might be populated at any given time, allowing the attacker more privacy to do whatever he wished with the boy he'd taken. It was another bad sign in a series of them, and he was growing more and more certain than he already was that he would not find the boy alive at the end of this.

It only took a brief glance to see the broken stems on the high grass that had grown up in this area, a trail that could've been made by some random person, but which Francis felt sure would lead him in the same direction as the mysterious assailant. He followed the trail, taking care to tread in the same approximate places the man he was tracking had in case the police came out here to investigate at the end of all this. He had little faith they would find anything, if their previous lackadaisical attitude was anything to go by, but it was better to make sure they were only looking for one person, not two.

At least he thought it was only one. The inability to pick up any emotional traces of the person was growing more and more annoying by the second.

The trail led him across the field and into another grouping of trees. Francis could hear water trickling ahead of him, a creek judging from the resonance, and noted with no real surprise that the trail headed right for it. He obligingly followed along, eyes scanning the surrounding area for any other clues as to what the boy's condition had been up to this point, or even more fruitlessly, in the hopes the attacker might have made a mistake and left something behind that could be used to find him. As expected, he found nothing of use.

Until he got to the creek.

Francis had always felt that the vast improvement to his night vision, and to his vision in general, had been one of the biggest boons to come from his transformation. Now, however, being able to see the still form laying half in and half out of that creek made him curse that improved vision. He approached slowly, reaching out with his senses, and was nearly driven to his knees by a burst of fear and pain so great it was almost more than he could stand. He'd felt death before, and even had caused it. He'd been present and aware and immersed in this extended way of sensing things when some fairly violent deaths had occurred, but he had never felt anything as terrible as this. It wasn't so much the pain, or the fear, or even the combination of the two that did it. It was the undercurrent of hopelessness mixed with acceptance. That anyone could feel such a thing, much less someone so young, was humbling and frightening all at once.

Thankfully, it only took a brief glance to confirm what he suspected: the body was that of a young man, and they were quite dead. He forced himself to look closer, needing to verify as much as he was able that this was the boy he was looking for. They were naked from the waist down, a smattering of hair on their legs and buttocks indicating they were past the beginning stages of puberty and well on their way to true manhood when they had been killed. There was a thick pool of blood staining the back of their thighs and even the ground beneath them, and while he had no intention of checking to be sure, Francis was almost positive they'd been sexually abused before they'd been killed. Their face was turned slightly so he could only see a part of it, with the rest hidden by the flowing water of the creek, but it was enough to see a wide-open, staring eye that was filled with fear. A ragged wound worked its way down from the boy's ear and across his neck before disappearing beneath the dark surface of the water as well.

Francis sighed and stood, looking away. His gaze landed on the boy's pants and underclothes lying in a small pile not too far away. He used some rocks sticking out of the creek to hop his way across, and approached the discarded clothing, then poked them with his toe. The pants had been cut away in part, the underclothes ripped down the sides, further proof if any was needed of the violent nature of this attack.

In a way, it was ironic. People thought he was a monster, but what he found here was proof positive that the real monsters were somewhere else, doing things much worse than he would ever even imagine, much less consider.

He closed his eyes and opened himself to the feelings around him once more, but felt nothing, only the gentle breeze that washed over him. He felt a throbbing sensation behind his eyes. While he wasn't susceptible to things like migraine headaches any longer, it still felt very similar to what people said the onset of one was like. That last blast from the boy had pushed his long-dormant skills to their breaking point. There was nothing more to be gained from them tonight and probably not until he had the chance to feed again.

Francis opened his eyes and shook his head slowly. He couldn't just leave the boy here like this, but he also couldn't just take him out of here himself unless he wanted to chance someone accusing him of being the one responsible. To do right by this dead child, he needed to report his find to the authorities, even though it meant they would come here and destroy any possible clues he could pick up when he was fully rested to resume his search for the boy's assailant. As much as he hated it, there was no other possible choice to make.

He carefully made his way back across the creek and field, not stopping when he got back to the walking trail but continuing down it, headed for the parking lot on the other side of the pond from where he'd entered the park. He'd noticed that pay phones were practically non-existent, but he sincerely hoped he could find one to make an anonymous call to the police. Something told him that simply walking into the station to report his find would only be the start of a series of events that would not end well for anyone.

One way or another, he would make that report. Then, he would do his best to help Ryan deal with the reality of his friend's brutal murder, out of respect for the admittedly inadvertent help he'd given Francis. And then, once the boy was stabilized, Francis intended to feed, and resume his search for whoever had done this.

And when he finally found them, they would discover what it was like to truly feel pain and fear.

CHAPTER SIXTEEN

T he house phone rang an instant before his cell phone did, jerking Ryan from the light doze he'd drifted into and sending his heart rate into overdrive. It could just be a coincidence, but for both phones to being ringing at once, he doubted anything good was going to come of it. He heard his father's muffled voice as he picked up downstairs, so Ryan grabbed his cell phone and looked at the screen. It was Melanie. He hesitated with his thumb over the answer button, dread creeping up his spine, wanting to believe she was just calling for more worried commiseration but knowing it was so much more than that this time.

Just before it rolled over to his voicemail, he forced himself to hit the button, then took a deep breath and brought the phone to his ear. He could hear her sobs before he even had the chance to offer any greeting and knew what she was about to say.

"Melanie," he said, dispensing with the pleasantries in favor of expedience. "What's wrong?"

At first he couldn't understand her—she was crying too hard. Finally she took a deep, hitching breath, and practically yelled it in his ear.

"He's dead!"

He didn't need to ask who she was talking about, even though he didn't want to believe it, didn't want to accept it. But hadn't he known? Deep down, hadn't he known this was the way it was going to play out? Again, he didn't want to accept it, but he knew without any doubt that what she was saying was no prank, no accident of misidentification, but the actual, harsh truth of reality: Hunter was dead, and he wasn't coming back.

He found himself trying to listen to Melanie, trying to decipher what she was saying through her anguished wailing, and trying to stop the light-headed feeling that had come over him, rendering everything in a dream-like haze that couldn't touch him, couldn't affect him. He'd known even when it first came out that Hunter was missing that this was the likely outcome, but since he hadn't been found, he held onto the slim thread of hope that his friend would turn up safe and sound. Now, that thread had snapped, and he found himself falling into a deep chasm from which he knew it would be a hard journey to escape.

There was a knock at his door, and then Dad stuck his face in, his expression that of a man who had a thousand things on his mind but was determined to see his present task through to completion. Ryan lowered his phone, Melanie still talking and screaming loud enough that he could almost make out what she was saying with it at his waist, and absently hit the button to end the call. Her voice cut off at once, leaving an eerie silence in its wake.

Dad glanced down at the phone and back up to Ryan's face, a hint of relief in his eyes that he wouldn't have to be the one to break the news.

"I take it you heard already."

Ryan nodded. "Who was on the home phone?"

"That was the police," Dad replied, coming into the room and closing the door behind him. "They want me or your mom to bring you down to the station tomorrow so they can talk to you again. You're not in any trouble, but it looks like you're the last one to see Hunter...."

He trailed off, but Ryan knew how that sentence was going to end anyway. He'd seen enough cop shows to know the routine. "You were the last one to see Hunter alive."

"Okay," he said simply. There was no need to say anything about going to school tomorrow. It was apparently taken for granted that he wouldn't be.

"How are you holding up?" Dad asked, laying a hand on his shoulder. Ryan was sure it was supposed to be comforting, but right now all he felt was the weight and heat of it.

"I don't know," he replied, and knew it was the truth. "It...."

"Hasn't sunk in yet?"

Ryan shook his head. Dad nodded.

"Look, I know this can't be easy for you, but try and get some rest, and if you need us, Mom and I are right downstairs."

"Thanks," Ryan said. He turned and headed to his window, staring out at the calm evening deepening into night. He faintly heard the click of his door opening and closing again and knew Dad had left him to think and perhaps mourn in peace.

He tried a few times to focus his thoughts, but he couldn't get his racing mind to stop for more than a couple of seconds here and there. He couldn't even focus on good memories of him and Hunter and the things they'd done over the years. It was as if being told that his best friend was dead had wiped his mind clean, leaving only scraps of memory and thought behind. He wasn't even crying, which was a little surprising until he remembered how he'd broken down in front of Francis. Maybe he'd just cried himself out for a while.

Suddenly, thoughts began to clarify in his mind. Francis seemed normal, even though he most assuredly wasn't. He also seemed to have come to terms with seeing people die, if the way he talked was any indication. And while he knew the vampire felt pain, it seemed to be limited to the physical level and not the emotional one. With the storm he could feel rising up inside himself, that was something he needed right about now.

He sighed and moved to his bed, lying on top of his covers with his hands folded over his belly. His thoughts began to drift again, allowing him to doze once more, even though he hadn't expected that sleep would be forthcoming any time soon. When he awoke, his clock showed it was nearly two in the morning. He left his room to use the toilet, and saw the lights were off all through the house as well.

Sleep was appealing, but he didn't think he could feel more awake than if he'd slept for a year before now. He left the bathroom and went downstairs, hoping to find something to snack on or drink before trying to go back to bed. His hand landed on the fridge door, then stopped when he heard something moving in the garage next to him. He held his breath, waiting to see if the sound was repeated, and was rewarded with another soft clattering sound.

Ryan didn't hesitate, simply turned and rushed down the hall to Dad's study. He grabbed the pistol from the center desk drawer, made sure it was loaded, and made his way slowly back to the kitchen, halfway expecting to see the door to the garage standing wide open, the shape of whatever intruder had come to rob or kill them silhouetted there, but the door remained closed, and the house continued to feel as empty as it had before. He crept closer and closer to the door, listening for some sign of movement beyond it, gun at the ready. He'd never had to fire it in a situation like this before, but Dad had made sure to take him to the range a few times, and he knew how to use it and not blow his own foot off in the process. He only hoped if it came down to it, that he'd be able to act when time came.

When he heard a familiar, whispered "shit" through the door, he relaxed and lowered the gun before opening the door, stepping out into the garage and turning on the lights.

Francis flinched at the sudden brightness, and then gave Ryan a shame-faced look that seemed incredibly out of place coming from a creature as old as he was. His foot was tangled in the long extension cord Dad used with their electric weed-eater, and he was balancing a box of something that had been stored on a shelf over the workbench on one hand.

"Little help?" Francis asked, nodding in the direction of the precariously balanced box.

Ryan rolled his eyes and helped Francis shove the box back onto the shelf it had fallen from, and then held onto the extension cord so the vampire could step out of it.

"What are you doing here?" he asked. "For that matter, how'd you know where I lived?"

"It would take too long to explain the second question," Francis said, leaning against the bench. "As to the first, I found out something about your friend."

"He's dead," Ryan said, impressed that he was able to keep his voice calm and relatively emotionless. "You're the third person to tell me that tonight. How did you know?"

Francis regarded him evenly. "I'm the one who found him."

Ryan started at that, suddenly more interested in what the vampire had to say.

"I went to that park you mentioned," Francis said. "Did a little looking around."

He hesitated. "You sure you want to hear this?"

Ryan didn't even have to think about it. "Yes."

Francis shrugged and went on. "I found a spot in the path where whoever grabbed him ducked through. Followed the trail they left back through the field into some more woods, found him lying in the creek back there. His throat had been slit."

"Did he suffer?"

The hesitation was all the answer Ryan needed. He closed his eyes and ran a hand over his face, willing himself not to think about it. Finally he looked up and met Francis's eyes.

"Can you turn me into what you are?"

A look of confusion crossed Francis's face. "What are you talking about?"

"Make me a vampire."

Francis jerked so hard he nearly fell over. "Hell, no! Why in the bloody hell would you want something like that?"

"You wouldn't understand."

"You're bleedin' right about that! You touched in the head?"

Ryan glared at him. "No, I'm just sick of hurting so fucking much!"

It came out louder and harsher then he'd intended, but it succeeded in shocking Francis so badly that all the vampire could do was open and close his mouth dumbly.

"My best friend is dead," Ryan went on, taking care to lower his voice lest he chance waking his parents. The last thing he wanted to do tonight was explain why a two-hundred plus year-old vampire was standing in their garage in the middle of the night. "Which has pretty much demolished my life. To make it worse, he disappeared on the day I finally talked to a girl I've had a crush on for years, and she didn't just tell me to go away. Kids at school don't understand, or care. Most of them just look at me like I'm a freak, or something they stepped in and can't get rid of. So why wouldn't I want to be like you? Live forever, do whatever I want, and not feel a damn thing anymore?"

Francis was silent for a long moment, and then he took a step closer to Ryan, still holding his gaze. "Is that what you think? That I don't feel anything?"

"Don't you?"

"As a matter of fact, I do," Francis replied. Ryan narrowed his eyes. "Maybe not as deeply as you, but I haven't lost all my humanity yet. I've worked very hard to keep as much of it as I could. If I'm being completely honest, you were the reason I ended up out there looking for your friend in the first place. After that meltdown you had, I felt like I had to do something. I wish I could've found the bastard that did it, but finding your friend was the best I could do.

"For the rest of it, I told you before, I'm not immortal. Long-lived, but I can still be killed, just like anything else. And in case you hadn't noticed, I've been living in the basement of an abandoned mental hospital. Does that sound like 'doing whatever I want' to you?"

"It's still worth it," Ryan said. "Anything has to be better than this."

Francis nodded, and then gave Ryan a look of bitter sadness. "You ever been hungry and know it's going to be a while before you get food? Sure you have, everyone has. Imagine that feeling, then imagine it a thousand-fold, but the only thing that will sate your hunger is the life force of another living being. Imagine drinking blood, that salty, coppery taste so heavy in your mouth that you can't taste anything else. Imagine having to fight your own impulse to kill, even if the person you want to kill is pure and innocent and doesn't deserve what you want to do to them. Imagine looking over your shoulder every day for a hundred years, wondering if today's the day the hunters find you. Maybe they'll kill you, at least you hope they do. The alternative is staking you, leaving you frozen and helpless, feeling your body rot day by day until fate lets you wake up again, feeling every second of your trapped existence, hungry, aching with no way to relieve it, and the knowledge that you're not going to die, so there's not even a chance for peace there.

"I don't know if you're religious or not, but if you are, imagine wondering if after you die, that final death, I mean, that God's going to tell you you're an abomination and that there's no place for you in His Heaven. That's my existence, Ryan, that's what I've dealt with every single day for the last two hundred and some-odd years. That is what you're asking me to give you. Do I feel? Yes. Enough that I can't give you what you're asking for. There is no way I'm going to be responsible for damning you the way I was damned. Beg, plead, do whatever you want. The answer will always be no."

Ryan stared at Francis, suddenly aware that his mouth was hanging open and his eyes were wide. It was the most the vampire had confessed about the truth of his existence, and with only fiction to base things on, the realization of that truth was a little disorienting. Ryan had always believed that while vampires didn't particularly care for being undead or whatever they were, they had come to a point where they almost reveled in it. Francis, by comparison, sounded like he actually despised what he'd become, and welcomed the day it finally ended, even if that meant he was damned to Hell just by nature of his existence.

"I'm sorry," he said, not sure what else to say.

"Don't be," Francis replied. "Just understand. That's all I ask."

He stepped back and stretched. "And now, I should get back. You need time to process all this."

Ryan nodded. "I'm supposed to go talk to the cops tomorrow."

He paused, considering. "You found Hunter, so how'd the police find out?"

"There's a pay phone in the park's parking lot," Francis said. "Surprised me, since I hadn't really seen any anywhere after you woke me up. I guess something else came along to replace them since the eighties. Anyway, I made an anonymous call, then watched from the top of a tree while they did their business. When I saw a couple of guys in suits ordering everyone around then leaving, I figured it was time to come let you know. I was hoping I'd find you first, but I guess they said something before I got here."

"Hunter's sister called, too," Ryan said. "About the same time the cops did, actually."

Francis nodded. "For what it's worth, I am sorry about your friend. I never met him, but you seem a decent enough lad, so I assume he was, too. You know where to find me if you need me."

The vampire was crouching down to leave under the garage door when Ryan called out to him.

"Do you know who did it?" he asked. "I know you said you didn't find him, but do you know?"

"No," Francis said. "But I aim to find out."

With that, he was gone.

CHAPTER SEVENTEEN

There wasn't anything new for Ryan to tell the police that he hadn't already told them the night Hunter was reported missing. As much as he wanted to give them something, anything to help them find whoever was responsible for his murder, he'd simply been so focused on talking to Kayla that he hadn't noticed what was going on back up at the walking path. He didn't break down in tears over it, but he'd come close. The only thing that even made the whole experience worthwhile was seeing Kayla coming into the station as he was leaving. She'd taken his hand briefly and given it a comforting squeeze before disappearing down the corridor where the interview rooms were located. The encounter hadn't lasted long, but it had done more to ease his aching heart than anything else since Hunter's disappearance.

He returned to school the next day, despite his parents' assurances that he could take the rest of the week off if he wanted to, to give himself time to come to terms with everything that had happened. He couldn't come up with the words to explain that sitting in his room actually made things worse, his disconnect from the rest of the world giving him nothing to think about beyond a life without his best friend at his side. And truthfully, it wasn't so bad. He managed to avoid Matt, Zach, and Brandon by basically keeping to himself and moving through the halls like a ghost. The only person he spoke with aside from his teachers was Kayla, who was at his side every time the opportunity arose. She even started waiting for him outside the doors, the way Hunter used to, and would spend the fifteen to twenty minutes before the first bell rang talking with him, and generally just being there for him. He didn't know if he was comfortable saying the two of them were going steady or anything like that, but things felt like they were headed that direction. It was the only bright spot in an otherwise miserable couple of weeks.

He also spent a good portion of time talking to Francis, wondering if he was subconsciously trying to replace Hunter's friendship with that of a vampire, of all things. Francis was cordial, perhaps the only person who didn't coddle Ryan or treat him like he was fragile. The vampire seemed to be of a mind that the only thing Ryan could do was suck it up and deal with the situation, and while it was strange to think so, Ryan was grateful for it.

Hunter's funeral was on the following Sunday, held at the little Methodist church where his family was apparently still considered members. Ryan didn't know anything about that, couldn't even remember the last time he'd seen Hunter, Melanie or their mother wake up on Sunday morning and head to services, but they were recognized and welcomed all the same. It was strange seeing them both there, not so much because they were wearing much nicer clothes than he'd ever seen them wear, but because their roles appeared to be reversed. It was Melanie who was trying to hold it together and thank people for coming and accept their condolences, while her mother sat halfway passed out nearby, so drunk you could smell the stale liquor on her from across the room.

It began to spit rain as they were all leaving the church, and by the time they made it to the little graveyard just up the road, it was pouring. Since he and Hunter had been so close, Ryan got to stand underneath the canopy that was erected at graveside for family. Kayla stood beside him, holding onto his hand tightly while Hunter's coffin was lowered into the ground and the minister spoke on how fragile life is, and how he was now in Christ's loving arms, and many other things that Ryan barely heard. His thoughts were too consumed by the memory of his friend.

Four days later, the second child went missing.

Her name was Maddie Prince, she was twelve, and in the seventh grade. She went missing while walking home from the middle school one afternoon. Her body was found three days after that, lying naked in a corn field on the edge of town. From what Ryan heard, there were tire tracks cutting through the field, stopping a little way away from where her body was found. Her clothing was never recovered, and rumors abounded that she'd been sexually assaulted, though the police would never confirm nor deny that particular bit of information. Ryan couldn't help but wonder if it was the same person who'd killed Hunter and felt that it probably was.

After the second victim showed up, Francis all but disappeared as well. Ryan was sure he was still living in the basement of the asylum, since all of his meager belongings were there, but often when he visited there was no sign of the vampire anywhere to be seen. Once or twice Ryan thought he heard a sound, a soft shuffling of feet on the floor nearby, but when he looked, there was nothing there. On the rare occasions he found Francis there, the vampire was even more distant than normal, refusing to say where he'd been or what he was doing. He did assure Ryan that he wasn't avoiding him, but that he had a lot going on, and left it at that.

Naturally, the second murder in less than two weeks' time sent the town into a fervor. While the police didn't come right out and institute a curfew, they did suggest that anyone under eighteen should not go out on their own, and should remain in well-lit, well-populated areas until they managed to track down the person or persons responsible for the—as they put it—untimely deaths of two young people. While Ryan was a little annoyed that they hadn't taken Hunter's disappearance seriously at first, at least they were paying attention now and doing all they could to stop it from happening again. He just wished they were doing more. He just wanted it to be over.

He was sitting up in his room on the Saturday before Halloween, playing some mindless video game when the doorbell rang. He frowned and glanced over to his window, as if there was some mirror to let him see who was standing at his door downstairs. His parents had gone out for an afternoon visit with friends and weren't due back until later this evening. As far as he knew, no one was supposed to be stopping by. He thought for a moment it might be Francis, but the day was unusually bright and sunny for this far into October, so it wasn't likely that the vampire would be out wandering around in the daylight. It looked like there was only one way to find out who it was, and that was to go and see. Ryan stood, stretched, and started downstairs just as the doorbell rang again.

"Yeah, yeah, I'm coming," he muttered, absently scratching his wild mop of hair. He was getting to the point where he was in serious need of a haircut, but with everything else going on lately, it had slipped by the wayside. Honestly, he didn't really care. He was at home in a torn pair of sweatpants and an old rock t-shirt he'd inherited from his brother, and if someone wanted to stop by unannounced, they could just deal with his unkempt appearance.

His attitude did an abrupt about-face when he opened the door and found Kayla and Amber standing on his front porch. His face went red at once, and he wished he'd actually changed clothes when he got out of bed this morning.

Amber was wearing a scowl, which was nothing unusual for her, but she wasn't what drew Ryan's attention. Kayla was wearing a black skirt that showed off her toned legs, and a fuzzy sweater that looked so comfortable Ryan wanted to lay his head on it, a feeling that only increased the heat in his cheeks considering that he kind of wanted her to be wearing it at the time, too. Her hair was pulled back into a ponytail, giving him a clear view of her slim neck. He could just make out the beating of her pulse in the early afternoon sun. He finally focused on her face, and saw a bemused expression highlighted by sparkling eyes.

"Hi," she said.

"Um, hi," he said back, trying to think of something else to say, but failing miserably.

"This is thrilling," Amber said, impatience clear in her voice. "Can I go now?"

Kayla shot her a withering look and then returned her attention to Ryan. "I was wondering if you might want to hang out or go do something."

She smirked as she took in his disheveled clothing. "You might want to change first, though. I can't say I'd be willing to go out in public with anybody dressed like that."

He recognized her teasing tone, but apparently Amber thought it was an actual insult based on the snort she let out. Kayla's eyes shifted in her direction briefly, her face darkening, but then she was back to her bemused self again.

"Yeah, that sounds fun," he stammered. "Um, you want to come in for a minute while I get ready?"

"Sure," Kayla replied. She took a step forward and stopped when Amber put a hand on her arm.

"I got you here, now I'm going," Amber said. "Brandon's supposed to come get me at home in an hour."

"Then wait here for him," Kayla said, turning to face her friend. "You know you're not supposed to be out on your own, and I'm not leaving until Ryan's ready, too."

Ryan felt his face flush again and was thankful for the solidarity, even against someone she'd been friends with for years.

"Oh, fuck that noise," Amber said. "It's early afternoon. That pedophile asshole's not going to do shit until it starts getting dark. Too many people are watching for him now."

"You're sure of that?"

"Sure enough," Amber replied. "Look, you're the one that wants to hang with him, not me. I don't get it, but I guess I don't have to. I'm leaving. You want to stay, fine. That was the plan. But you're not dragging me into it."

With that, she turned on her heel and quickly stomped down the steps, her eyes locked on the sidewalk at the end of the yard. Kayla called out for her a couple of times, but Amber refused to look back. She turned and headed down the sidewalk, and then was gone. Kayla watched after her for a long moment, then let out a heavy sigh and turned to face Ryan again.

"I am so sorry about that," she said. "She's not normally like that."

Ryan shrugged. "She doesn't like me. I get it. She doesn't even know me, but that hasn't exactly stopped anyone else."

"It's not just that," Kayla said. "In fact, she's been telling Brandon that they should lay off you for a while. I didn't even have to prompt her to, either. I think she just doesn't know how to act around you."

Ryan doubted that was the case, but he didn't want to belabor the point. "It's okay. Um, if you want to go after her, I'd totally understand...."

"Nope," Kayla said, pushing past him and into the house. "I said we were going to go do something, so we are. She can be a bitch all she wants, my mind's made up."

"I'll try and remember that," Ryan said, unable to help smiling at the surety in her voice. He closed the door and followed her into the house.

She was standing in the living room, her eyes taking everything in. When she noticed the wall filled with DVD and BluRay disks that comprised Dad's movie collection, her face lit up. She crossed the room and began poring over the titles arranged alphabetically in neat, even rows.

"Wow," she said, occasionally pulling out a movie and glancing at the description on the back. "The only place I've ever seen this many movies in one place was at the store. Are they all yours, or...?"

"They're my Dad's," he said, coming up beside her. "He's been collecting them since he was a teenager, from what he says. He's been slowly replacing the DVDs with BluRay, in addition to buying more. Every Tuesday he stops at Target and picks up almost everything on their 'New Release' rack."

She squealed when she found one particular movie in the shelf. Ryan noted it was the original Friday the 13th, and suddenly knew what was coming next.

"Would you believe I've never seen this?" she asked, turning to him, her face alight with glee. "My parents aren't big on horror movies anyway, and my sister thinks they're stupid, but I watch everything I get a chance to. Do you think we could watch it now?"

Ryan felt heat rising up within himself, along with a case of nerves that threatened to buckle his knees. Kayla showing up on his doorstep to suggest they go out and do something was one thing—one wonderful, glorious thing—but now she was suggesting that they not go out. She was suggesting that they sit here in his house watching a horror movie. Alone. While his parents were out.

While it was something he definitely wanted, it also scared the living shit out of him.

"I thought you already had something lined up for us to do," he said, mentally kicking himself for attempting to sabotage what could turn out to be an incredible day.

She shrugged. "Not really. I wanted us to go do something, maybe something we could even consider our first date, but I hadn't really made any plans."

He forced down the lump that had risen in his throat. Had she really just said she wanted this to be their first date? He opened his mouth, unsure how he was going to respond to that, and found himself pleasantly surprised by what came out.

"We could pretend we've gone to the movies, even if we're just staying here, I guess."

Her smile was enough to make him light-headed. "You have popcorn?"

"And cokes," he replied. "They're in cans, but I guess I could put too much ice in a glass then pour a trickle of it over them, then toss ten bucks in the garbage so it would feel like we'd bought them at a concession stand."

She giggled, a high, girlish sound so unlike her normal persona that Ryan had to wonder if she was just as nervous about the suggestion she'd made as he was. "Sounds good to me. Don't trash the money, though. Maybe we can go out somewhere after the movie and get something to eat."

"Should I go change anyway?" he asked, gesturing to his messy clothes.

"Why bother?" she replied. "It's your house, and if we do decide to go anywhere you can always change clothes then."

"I'll just go get the snacks ready, then," he said, smiling back at her as he turned toward the kitchen. "Just make yourself at home, and I'll be right back."

"Is that really something you should be saying since we're about to watch a horror movie? I thought that was code for 'go ahead and come get me' to the monsters."

Despite the joke, Ryan felt a flash of fear run up his back at the knowledge that there really was a monster out there somewhere, one who was raping and killing kids just about their age. He forced the thoughts away. They were in his house, safe and secure, and even more than that, for the first time since his life had gone to shit a couple weeks ago, he was starting to feel somewhat normal again. He didn't want anything to ruin that or his first "date" with Kayla. He made himself laugh, and hoped it came out sounding natural.

"Dad loves these movies," he said. "I'm pretty sure he's monster-proofed the house, so I should be okay."

His mind quickly ran through the number of steps it would take him to reach the study and the gun if he had to, then he headed to the kitchen, determined to make the most of the opportunity that had so suddenly presented itself to him this afternoon.

When he returned with a huge bowl of popcorn that he'd doused in a half a stick of butter and two glasses of Pepsi balanced in one hand, he was a little surprised to see that while he was gone Kayla had closed all the blinds and turned off the overhead light, leaving only a small lamp next to the table and what diffused sunlight crept through the cracks in the blinds to illuminate the room. She must have noticed the confusion on his face, because she laughed that nervous laugh again as she crossed the room to help him with the drinks.

"Set the mood," she explained. "This way, it feels more like we're in a theater. With the size of that television, it should help even more."

He glanced over to Dad's biggest splurge, a massive seventy-inch flat screen that took up nearly one entire wall on its own, not to mention the surround sound system and BluRay player on the stand beneath it. When he'd first brought it home, Mom had given him holy Hell over it, but Ryan heard her comment not that long ago that after watching shows and movies on it for so long, she didn't think she could go back to having a smaller screen anymore. Dad had thoughtfully kept the "I told you so" to himself.

Kayla grabbed a pair of coasters from the little stand on the coffee table and set them down before transferring the one drink she held as well as the one he still had to them. He positioned the bowl of popcorn between them and grabbed the universal remote so he could get the movie set up and running.

"Where's your bathroom?" Kayla asked. "Better get it out of the way before we get started. Don't want you to have to pause it in the middle of one of the good scenes."

"Down the hall, first door on the right," he said, pointing to the hallway next to the stairs. She went that way immediately, and Ryan found himself captivated by the way her ponytail bounced across her shoulders, and the way her legs lifted the skirt ever so slightly with each stride. He was sure she was going to turn around at any second and catch him staring, but she didn't. He finally tore his gaze away when she angled toward the bathroom door.

He was sitting on the sofa with the menu screen up and running through its repetitive animation when she returned a couple of minutes later. She plopped down beside him, close enough that her hip brushed against his thigh, took a sip of her drink, then leaned back.

"Ready?" he asked.

"Let's do this," she said.

He hit play, tossed the remote onto the coffee table, and leaned back himself. As the prologue began to play, showing a couple of camp counselors sneaking off for some sex before getting slaughtered for it, he felt Kayla tug gently at his arm. He let her move it where she wanted, shocked when she wrapped it around her shoulders. She kicked off her shoes and tucked her feet up beside her, snuggling against his side as she made sure his arm was holding her securely.

"In case I get scared," she whispered, and was that a slight shake he heard in her voice?

He had no complaints, finding himself extremely conscious of her gentle weight against him, the heat of her along his side, and the way his hand dangled slightly off her opposite shoulder. It would be nothing to "accidentally" brush his palm against her burgeoning breast, so he moved it so he was cupping her shoulder, more to remove the temptation than for any other practical reason. She seemed to approve, wriggling slightly as she settled into place against him.

It had been a rough few weeks, but for right now, none of that existed. At this very moment, Ryan was positive he was having the best day of his life.

CHAPTER EIGHTEEN

The shadow Francis crouched in was on the verge of disappearing completely as the sun finished its journey over the top of the house behind him. He shuffled his feet back, trying to keep every little bit of himself possible hidden for as long as he could. The sunlight wouldn't kill him, but it would be so distracting he wouldn't be able to keep his ability to hide at the level it needed to be at. The last thing he wanted was to be spotted while watching a kid's house while there was a child predator on the loose.

He'd come to finally tell Ryan about what he'd been doing the last few days, how he'd been scouring the crime scenes for clues the cops might have missed, in the hopes that he would be able to track down the killer. It was frustrating that he hadn't been able to pick up any trail yet, had found nothing of the man's emotional residue. Such ability was indicative of the supernatural, and he knew he still wasn't at the level of strength he'd need to be in order to face such a thing.

Francis watched as Ryan's parents left, then waited a little longer to make sure they weren't just making a quick trip somewhere. Just as he'd been about to approach the house, the two girls had shown up. He'd felt Ryan's pleased shock at seeing them, watching with interest as the one girl went inside and the other one left. Ryan hadn't mentioned a girlfriend during their previous conversations, but Francis had gathered there was someone he had feelings for. He wondered if that was the girl who'd gone inside the house with him. If so, good for him. After the shite luck he'd had, it was about time something went his way for once.

When the girl didn't come out after several minutes, Francis actually chuckled. He could feel nervousness and joy radiating down whatever bond connected them. He also felt something else, something that he didn't think Ryan was even aware of himself: arousal. That the boy was inexperienced was a given, that all of that might change this afternoon was both amusing and concerning at the same time. Francis knew how far Ryan might fall over this girl, and knew that with the heartache he'd already endured, there was no telling what might happen to the boy's fragile psyche should things end badly.

For now, though, it was enough to let him have his moment.

While he could just find another hiding place and wait it out, the thought that he might be as good as spying on Ryan while the kid was in the middle of his first sexual encounter was too creepy for even a centuries-old thing such as himself to handle. Instead, he made his way to the back of the house and headed off in the direction the other girl had gone. Francis knew there was some kind of warning in place for kids to not go out alone, and while he didn't know specifics, he did understand the nature of predator and prey. Were he the one doing the hunting, that lone girl would make an excellent target. She acted tough, carrying herself with an assurance that on the surface seemed to validate that, but Francis knew better. She was terrified, and weak, and would fall easily, without much effort at all. The least he could do while he was out and about was to make sure she got to wherever it was she was going without incident.

At least the sunlight didn't affect his speed. If anything, it enhanced it, as though his body was determined to get away from that bright ball of fire and into blissful darkness once more. She had a bit of a head start on him, but he managed to catch up with her soon enough. She was walking down the sidewalk, hands tucked into the pockets of her pull-over sweatshirt—"hoodie", he thought they were calling them now—with her head down and a scowl across her face. She only seemed to be paying the loosest attention to where she was going, not appearing to watch her surroundings at all. As he'd predicted, she looked like exceptionally easy prey as she made her way down the street.

She stopped at an intersection, checked both ways, then turned and started off toward a less populated area of town.

They were still among the nearly-identical houses that made up the city's residential section, but the distance between them was growing. Francis had no idea where she could be heading—from what little he could remember, the only thing out this way was a factory that provided the main source of income for a great many of the town's populace—but he didn't much care for the fact that she was leaving what little relative safety she'd had behind. It actually made him glad he'd decided to follow her. He might be the only thing that stood a chance of keeping her safe.

He frowned as she passed the last house on the street and left the sidewalk, now walking along the side of the road near a forested area he thought was the buffer between the factory and the residential area. While on the one hand he had a little more cover here, more places to hide, the trees were relatively sparse, so he would have to hang back further than he would've liked to avoid the chance of her seeing him. He struggled to come up with where a girl her age would be going way out here. To meet her own boyfriend, maybe? Francis supposed it was possible he was freshly graduated from high school and had gone straight to work instead of heading to university. She could also be going to see her father, or mother, he supposed. Why they would be okay with her wandering around alone right now was a bit on the weird side, but who was he to judge? It wasn't like he had any kids of his own and therefore a leg to stand on when it came to parenting advice.

A car sped past, coming from the direction of the old factory and heading toward the residential section. Francis started to duck down behind a tree, but noticed it was moving much too fast to have had time to see him there. Doubly annoying was that the woman driving wasn't even watching the road, but had her head turned toward the passenger side and appeared to be leaning over slightly, as if she was trying to pick up something that was in the floorboard. Had she been just a few more feet to the side, she might very well have slammed into the girl he'd been following, turning her into a red paste across the highway. He watched until she was out of sight, then turned back and froze in place.

The girl was gone. He'd been so fixated on the idiot driver that he'd lost track of his reason for being out here in the first place.

"Ah, Francis," he muttered under his breath. "May the lamb of God stir his hoof through the roof of heaven and kick you in the arse down to hell."

He looked around but saw no sign of the girl anywhere. He waited, hoping that maybe she'd just popped off into the woods for a bit of a wee—not something it would be good for him to walk up on—and would resume her journey any moment. He didn't have a watch to be sure, but after it seemed she'd been gone long enough to turn her bladder inside out and shake the damned thing dry, he began to creep forward again, already opening his senses to try and catch a feel for her. Finally he caught something faint, a hint of surprise mixed with a flash of pain, and then that diffuse feeling he'd picked up from Ryan's friend when he'd first been taken.

Francis felt his heart lurch in his chest. This was exactly what he'd been hoping to prevent, and now the shit had not only hit the fan but slammed into it and splattered. He could almost imagine the girl turning to watch the idiot in the car drive past, then she'd felt the blast of pain on the back of her head as whoever else had been watching took their chance. It was disturbing to think that there had been someone else in the woods and Francis hadn't known about it, but it wasn't all that surprising considering it had been the case on both of the other missing kids so far.

The difference was that this time there still might be a chance to save her.

He narrowed his focus and forced it to the forefront of his mind, pushing his skills far enough against their limit that he began to feel a throbbing in his temples and across the front of his head. He turned and raced through the woods, angling himself to the source of that faint trail left during the girl's involuntary passage, hoping that he could catch up to her before it faded completely, or worse, before he began to feel it in real-time, as it was happening, when it turned from diffusion to pain and agony and terror.

As he neared the trail formed by her emotional residue, he finally felt it: a second presence intermingling with the girl's. Trying to make out anything about it was like trying to catch running water in a fish net. The thoughts and emotions were all over the place, never settling on any one thing for long enough to identify. The only thing concrete that he could identify was the primal need that radiated from the other individual, the sheer force of will to do whatever it intended to do.

Strangely, that feeling was vaguely familiar, and if it had been projected with more consistency, maybe he could reason out exactly why that was. He'd felt something like this before, but he couldn't think of when or where that had been. Perhaps when he caught up with them, he'd take the time to ask some questions before he tore the assailant to shreds. Then again, the answers weren't that important. Only the need to prevent more kids from being killed for no good reason mattered.

Francis broke through the woods and found himself standing in the middle of a gravel access road. Up ahead, he could just make out a large form tossing the girl into the back of a pickup truck that was so dented and rusted it was impossible to tell how old it was or even what color it used to be. Something about the entire scene felt surreal, even the way the man deposited the girl's limp form into the bed of the truck. He put her back there carelessly, but at the same time there was a reverence in his movements that made little sense in context.

Suddenly, the man stood up straight and turned, staring at Francis with eyes that practically glowed red in the sunlight, a surprised yet pleased grin spreading across his almost ageless face. He nodded once in Francis's direction, then turned and started walking down the side of the truck to where the driver's side door stood open.

Francis started to run, to tap into the reserves of power that helped enhance his speed, but they didn't help. It had been too long since last he fed, and the intensity with which he'd followed the emotional trails left by both the girl and the man who took her had sapped the last of his reserves. Even the sunlight seemed twice as hot as it had when he first started out after her.

The man, if he truly was a man, got into the truck and slammed the door as he started the engine. Francis gave chase as best he was able, closing the gap until the man floored the accelerator and threw gravel in all directions as he tore off down the road. Francis gritted his teeth and tried to prepare himself for an extended chase, then suddenly stopped and cried out, hands grabbing his temples as something exploded in his mind, a distinct rebuke that felt of slime and ooze and a festering corpse, tinged with the feel of the man he now knew was his quarry. It was a psychic assault the likes of which he'd not experienced in nearly a hundred years, and one with enough potency to have killed a normal human. He was able to briefly wonder whether or not the man had recognized him for what he was and then the pain intensified, a final aftershock should the first blast not be enough.

Francis dropped to his knees and then fell forward onto his face, hands still clutched to his head. He felt his nose break with a snap, but the pain barely registered in the wake of that assault. He tried to force himself back up but failed. His vision began to swim, then to tunnel, and then he finally slipped into a merciful unconsciousness that was so deep for a brief moment he thought he'd somehow managed to stake himself when he fell.

He wasn't out for long, but it was long enough. When he awoke, the truck was long since gone, and even the faint resonance the girl left behind had dissipated on the winds. He cursed himself and sat staring in the direction he'd last seen the truck flee.

He had his chance, but he'd failed, and now there was going to be another child killed because of it. At first, he'd intended to capture the man, to turn him over to the police to face human justice, but now that changed. Now, once he caught that bastard, he was going to exact his own brand of justice. What he had in mind might cost him what little remained of his humanity, but he was at peace with that. If ever there was anything worth such a price, it was this.

CHAPTER NINETEEN

There was no question that snuggling with Kayla and watching an old horror movie was just the therapy Ryan needed to deal with the real-life terrors of the last couple of weeks. He didn't care that she'd somehow managed to tuck herself right against one of the blood vessels in his shoulder, causing his right arm to go almost completely numb. Moving it meant disturbing her, and he refused to do that. He wasn't even paying that much attention to the movie, was instead spending his time studying her as she sat engrossed in it, watching as the so-far-unidentified killer made short work of the counselors who dared try to reopen Camp Crystal Lake.

Several times she'd jumped at whatever scare was playing out on the screen, clutching him tighter and occasionally even burying her face in his chest when one of the gorier moments came. He couldn't help but smile as he rubbed her back and waited for her to laugh once the initial terror had passed. Like as not, she'd pull back, a sheepish grin on her face, and apologize for acting like a scaredy-cat. He'd tell her it was fine, she'd go back to watching the movie, and then the whole process would repeat itself a few minutes later.

It was absolutely wonderful.

When she eventually leaned forward, breaking their contact, Ryan felt a moment of disappointment that their time together might be coming to an end. Instead of getting up to leave, however, she took a drink of her Pepsi, not seeming to care that the ice had long since melted, turning it into so much colored water, then scooted over slightly and laid her head in his lap before pulling his hand back down to continue caressing her arm through her sweater.

The sweater was every bit as soft as he'd imagined it would be, now that he was finally able to feel it properly instead of through half-numbed fingers. The problem was that the gentle heat from her head and the softness of her hair was almost directly over his crotch, stirring feelings within him that he'd experienced during one of his fantasies before now. He felt himself responding, and tried to will his body to stop, but to no avail. Now that it had begun, there was nothing he could do to reverse it. He gritted his teeth and tried to think about anything else, but he couldn't get the reality of their closeness out of his thoughts. The best he could hope for was that she wouldn't notice.

Her body went rigid for a moment, and her head came up and turned toward him, a smile twitching at the corner of her mouth. He tried not to look at her, to focus on anything but her, but knowing what kind of expression had to be on his face, he figured that would make him look all the more foolish. He couldn't quite meet her eyes, focusing instead on her lips, which only served to make the problem worse.

"I take it you're enjoying our time together?" she asked, her voice playful and a little hesitant as well.

He had to clear his throat before he was able to speak. "Sorry."

"Don't be," she said. "I suppose I should take it as a compliment, right?"

Ryan was sure his cheeks would burst into flame at any moment. "Yeah, definitely."

She didn't lay her head back down, but she didn't get up, either. When Ryan forced himself to look at her, really look at her, he found her studying his face in the flickering light of the television and the dim sunlight that was coming through the closed blinds. Her eyes were considering, flicking across his own, then down to his mouth, and back again in a slow, languid circuit. Finally she seemed to decide something and her eyes drifted closed as she lifted her face toward his, tilting her chin slightly to better the angle.

Not quite able to believe it was happening, Ryan lowered his own face to hers, fighting the shaking in his body as he gently pressed his lips against hers. He was so nervous that at first he succeeded only in kissing her chin, prompting a slight smile from her, and then he adjusted and managed to get his mouth against hers, top lip on top and bottom lip on bottom. He wasn't sure what he was supposed to do next—what he'd seen in movies and on television just didn't feel right, for some reason—so he remained that way for a long while, holding his breath so he didn't blow buttered popcorn and cola all over her face. He could feel her own hesitancy in the way she responded, also holding the awkward kiss for what felt like a very long while, then her lips parted slightly and her mouth moved so that his bottom lip was trapped between both of hers and suddenly he knew they'd gotten it right, or at least right for them in this particular moment.

Time seemed to stop, the dialogue and music from the movie fading into the background as they experienced their first kiss, one that drew out and gradually got better and better the longer they went about it. Kayla shifted so she was half sitting, half lying against his chest, and he found this only served to improve the angle of their mouths' connection, making it even better than it had been. He could taste her lipstick, something with a faint berry flavor, and could also taste the sweetness of her breath despite the fact that she'd been eating the same greasy junk that he had. Her tongue gently lapped against his upper lip, tentative and probing, and he responded on instinct, opening his own lips slightly and allowing her tongue to dart into his mouth, brushing against his own.

She made a low groaning sound and pushed herself against him, her tongue reaching further and further until he thought he was going to suffocate. He found he could breathe slightly through his nose, which helped, so he took advantage of the improvement to mirror her motions, slipping his tongue across hers, entwining with it on occasion. His hands came up to caress her back through her sweater, his palms gliding across the soft material, feeling the smoothness of her back broken only by the brief strip of fabric that comprised her bra. She responded by brushing a hand across his swollen crotch, and the sensation was enough to make him feel like he was going to explode.

He pulled back, breaking the kiss and let out a low, guttural moan before panting for breath. His eyes finally opened and stared into hers, which were now filled with something he'd never seen before, something that made his stomach tingle and his heart race even harder than it already was. Her hand was still covering his crotch, not moving, but emitting a heat that was nearly maddening.

"Are you okay?" she whispered.

He nodded, not trusting his voice enough to respond.

"Should we stop?"

Intellectually, he knew they should, but it was obvious from the question that while he didn't know how far she intended to take this, it was further than they'd already gone. It suddenly occurred to him that she was sitting on second base while he was still stuck on first, and while he didn't mind that at all, he desperately wanted to even things out. Before he knew what he was doing, he shook his head.

She smiled and bit her bottom lip, then pulled her hand away from his groin. The disappointment was almost instantaneous, replaced before it could fully form by confusion and anticipation as he noticed she'd pulled her arms into her sweater and was doing something he couldn't see. After a moment of awkward fumbling, she pushed her arms back out the sleeves and pulled something from beneath the bottom of the sweater.

He felt himself trembling harder when he saw it was her bra.

Kayla moved closer, straddling him, the heat from her thighs trapping his legs in place. She took his hands and placed them against her breasts, leaning into them so he had no choice but to support her with his palms. He could feel her small nipples hardening against his hands, and wished that this day would never end, that this moment would just continue to replay itself forever.

Her hand brushed against his crotch again briefly, then rose, lingering at the waistband of his sweatpants. He could feel her entire body trembling, as though she were a live electric wire that he'd suddenly grabbed onto, and then her fingers slid beneath his sweats, sending little tendrils of tingling fire in their wake.

Something slammed against the front door hard enough to rattle the pictures hanging next to it in their frames. Kayla let out a startled squeak and jerked away from him so hard that she very nearly went toppling over onto the coffee table, dragging one long fingernail painfully across the sensitive skin of his lower abdomen. The doorbell rang, followed in quick succession by a series of rapid but firm knocks on the door itself.

Kayla stood and hopped on one foot awkwardly, trying to disentangle herself from Ryan's legs. As soon as she was clear, he leapt to his feet as well, wincing at the dull ache that was starting to form in his testicles, which also felt swollen and tender. Thankfully, his erection was gone, startled into submission by the sudden, furious burst of noise. From the way his underpants felt like they were sticking to his thighs, he thought that maybe more had happened down there than he originally thought.

"Who is that?" Kayla hissed, leaning past him to snatch her bra from the couch before trying to hide it in the waistband of her skirt. It created a little lump at the front of her sweater that Ryan doubted would fool anyone with half a brain but was still better than the alternative.

"I have no idea," he replied. "You think it's Amber or Brandon or somebody, looking for you?"

The pounding started anew, along with a near constant ding-dong noise from the doorbell.

"I don't know," she said. "But I think you'd better answer it."

Ryan felt a flash of fear at the thought that maybe it was the killer, come to take them both because of what they'd been about to do, just like one of the maniac slashers in the movies, but he knew Kayla was right. It was obvious that whoever it was wasn't planning to go away unless he answered the door and dealt with them.

He stumbled toward it, pausing long enough to slap the light switch before he opened the door. He flinched and squinted at the sudden blast of light, then turned the knob and threw the door open before he allowed himself time to consider what he was doing.

Francis practically fell into the house, looking far worse than at any time since Ryan had discovered him up and moving around. He wasn't withered and grotesque, thankfully, but that was the best Ryan could say for him. The vampire caught his balance, and then seemed to notice Kayla standing in the middle of the living room with a decidedly guilty look on her face.

"Hello there, lassie," he said, his voice heavy with his native accent. "So sorry to be bustin' in like this, but I need to get some help from my nephew here. Could I trouble ye to grab me a glass of water, help dilute this damnable whiskey a bit?"

"Uh...," she began, glancing to Ryan for some idea of what to do. He wasn't much help was just as confused as she was, though at least he wasn't running or trying to fight the man who'd almost literally dropped in on them. "Yeah, I'll be right back."

She turned and hurried from the room, disappearing into the kitchen. Ryan thought she was just grateful for the chance to get herself straightened back out in the presence of sudden adult supervision rather than being overly willing to do as the stranger asked.

As soon as she was gone, Francis's expression lost the gleeful humor it had taken on, and he looked at Ryan with eyes so serious it was unnerving.

"Sorry to ruin your little dalliance there," Francis said, his voice suddenly back to normal again. "But you need to get rid of her. Walk her home then get back here, whatever you have to do."

"Okay," Ryan replied, still trying to adjust from a moment of passion to this sudden intrusion. "Why?"

"I saw the one who's killing the kids," Francis said. "And it seems we've got a bigger problem than we thought."

CHAPTER TWENTY

etting Kayla home again became an ordeal that was beyond Ryan's worst imaginations. First, he hadn't wanted her to go home yet at all, had actually wanted Francis to go away and come back later, but the vampire insisted that he had to speak with him, and refused to do so until Kayla was home and safe. Ryan supposed that considering what Francis needed to talk to him about, it was for the best. He explained to Kayla that his "uncle" had been drinking a bit too much, so he was going to have to cut their afternoon short. Thankfully, she understood. Ryan was sure that a large part of that understanding came from her being embarrassed beyond words at what they'd nearly been caught doing and that she wanted to get as far away from anything resembling a responsible adult as possible.

Ryan changed quickly, wincing as he yanked his sweats off and saw the small dark stain that had formed on the front of his undershorts. He peeled them off as well and pulled on fresh clothes, then stuffed his old ones down in the bottom of his hamper. He raced back downstairs, terrified to think what Francis might have told Kayla while he'd been out of the room, and found the vampire leaning against the wall, talking non-stop with that thick Irish accent that made it almost impossible to understand what he was saying. Kayla had the look of someone who was trying their best to be part of a conversation, but who also had no idea what the topic of said conversation was. She gave Ryan a look of intense gratefulness as soon as she saw him come down the stairs.

The next part of the whole process started as they were leaving, when Francis insisted on accompanying them to make sure they were both safe. Ryan pointed out that they would be together, which was what the police suggested, and Francis destroyed the argument by mentioning that after he'd dropped Kayla off, he'd be alone again. Ryan was forced to concede that point. Still, it seemed that the vampire understood how awkward he'd made things because he stayed a good ten to twenty paces behind them as they made their way down the sidewalk to Kayla's house. He even tipped Ryan a quick salute before sitting down at the edge of the street with his back to them while Ryan walked Kayla to her front door.

"I'm so sorry about this," Ryan said. "I had no idea he was coming over today, much less like... that."

Kayla smiled and took both of his hands in hers. "It's okay. As fun as it was, we probably needed to stop. No telling what might have happened if he hadn't shown up."

Ryan had a damned good idea what might have happened, but he kept the thought to himself and simply nodded. "Can I call you later?"

"I think you'd better," Kayla replied, her smile shifting into a smirk. She poked him firmly but gently in the chest with one finger. "Don't think I've done anything like that with anyone else before. It meant something to me, and it better have meant something to you, too."

"Oh, it did," Ryan said. "Dear, God, it did. Believe me."

"Good."

She lifted herself up on her tiptoes and brushed a kiss across his lips. He wanted to pull her against him, extend that chaste farewell into something closer to what they'd been doing earlier, but he knew this was not the right time or place for such a thing. He only hoped there would be a right time and place for it again, and soon.

"Oh! With the other stuff, I almost forgot," Kayla exclaimed, pulling back from him slightly, but holding onto his hands again. "There's a Halloween party this Saturday night at the old asylum. I wanted to see if you'd maybe want to go with me?"

Ryan felt a flash of nervousness at the proposal, both because of his knowledge of who—or what, more accurately— was living in the basement of the old place, but also because he'd never been to a party the likes of which he was sure she was proposing. This wouldn't be some simple kids' party with punch and cookies and bobbing for apples. There would most likely be alcohol there, and maybe even drugs. While he'd only sipped beer before, stolen from dad's stash when he was tipping a few in front of the game on Thursday nights, he'd never even been around drugs—at least not that he knew of.

Then again, if he were being honest with himself, he knew it wasn't the thought of illegal "refreshments" being there so much as who might be on the attendance list.

"You think that's a good idea?" he asked. "I mean, I've managed to avoid Matt and his gang so far, but you said Amber's dating Brandon, and if he's there...."

"Don't worry about it so much," Kayla replied, her face turning serious as her grip on his hands tightened. "To Hell with those three. Just stay with me and you'll be fine. Besides, it's about time some of those other assholes got to know what a great guy you are, too."

He was far from convinced, but he also didn't want to let her think he was a "chickenshit," as Matt put it so crudely a couple of weeks ago, so he forced a smile and nodded. "That sounds great."

"Good," she said, smiling again as she brushed another gentle kiss across his lips. "I'll give you the details when you call me tonight."

"Okay," he said. His smile faded as it started to sink in exactly what was happening to him. He wanted so badly to call Hunter and tell him, to share in the wonderful news, but he couldn't do that. Not anymore.

Kayla pulled away again and turned toward her door, but Ryan held on for another moment, stopping her. She looked at him over her shoulder, one eyebrow raised in question.

"Today was...," he began. He swallowed, and then forced himself to meet her eyes. "Today was incredible. It really did mean something to me. I just wanted you to know that."

"Good, I'm glad," she said. "Maybe next time...."

She stopped, a slight blush rising in her cheeks, and shook her head. "I'll talk to you tonight, okay?"

"Can't wait."

He stood there for another few seconds, watching the door even after she'd closed it behind her, and then turned and walked back down through the yard to where Francis sat on the curb, absently tossing pebbles into the street. The vampire glanced up when Ryan stopped beside him, then dropped his handful of rocks, brushed his hands off, and stood.

"Okay, she's home," Ryan said. "Now what's going on?"

Francis raised his chin back the way they'd come and started walking. Ryan shook his head and then fell into step alongside him.

"Like I said, I saw the killer," Francis said. Ryan noted that the harsh accent was gone, and wondered if it had simply been an affectation, or if that was his real way of speaking and what he was hearing now was the disguise. "He snatched your lady's friend."

"What?" Ryan said, stopping and staring at the vampire. "Why didn't you say anything sooner? We could've called the police, or...."

"They can't help her now," Francis said. He grabbed Ryan by the arm and pulled him along after him. "She's as good as dead. Don't you think I'd have stopped him if I could?"

"I don't know," Ryan shot back. "Seems awfully funny that you apparently saw it happen but didn't do anything about it. For all I know...."

"The guy's a vampire, too."

Ryan's mouth shut so hard and fast that his teeth clicked together audibly. If Francis hadn't practically been dragging him along, he would've possibly fallen over from how shocked he felt.

"Are you sure about that?"

"Reasonably," Francis said. "He hit me with a psychic attack. Since I haven't been awake that long, and I haven't really been eating all that well since I did wake up, it hit like a ton of bricks falling on my head. If I'd been human, it probably would've killed me. Beyond that... let's just say we know our own and let it go at that."

"Did you know him? Like, personally, I mean?"

Francis gave him an incredulous look. "It's not like we're some super-secret club that meets every Tuesday or something. I haven't seen another of my kind in probably seventy, eighty years. And I was basically unconscious for forty or so of those, I might add. No, I didn't know him."

"So what do we do?"

The look Francis gave him this time was enough to nearly make Ryan ruin a second pair of underwear. "I have no idea."

The vampire shook his head. "I take that back. I do have an idea, it's just not a very good one. In fact, it's a bloody mad one. And it's also one I have no idea how to pull off."

"Well, what is it?"

When Francis didn't answer, Ryan pulled free of his grip, rushed to get in front of him, and then stopped, staring into the vampire's face.

"What's the idea?"

Francis wouldn't meet his eyes, just stood there shaking his head. Finally he let out a long, slow breath that Ryan suspected was just theatrical, and rubbed a hand over his face.

"Find some hunters."

It took a moment for Ryan to understand exactly what he was saying. "Vampire hunters. You, a vampire, want to figure out how to call in vampire hunters to take down the vampire that's raping and killing kids."

He paused as the unreality of what he'd just said out loud finally sank in. "For that matter, how is that possible? I thought you guys just took our blood, drained us dry, you know, killed us? How is it even possible that you could rape anyone?"

Francis barked out a humorless laugh. "It's not like impotence is a side-effect of being turned, you know. Nor is castration, though considering what I've seen today, maybe it should be. We're still perfectly capable of having sex with someone. We can't reproduce, not that way, but the mechanics still work. There's no practical benefit to it, not for men. We can't feed that way like women could, but it still feels pretty damned good, so we bloody well take advantage when the opportunity presents itself, just like any human man would."

Ryan shook his head, trying to wrap his mind around this new discovery about vampires that while close to the way it was presented in fiction, wasn't exactly what he'd expected to hear. "Okay, so you can have sex. Fine. Isn't that neck... necro... ah, what's the word for doing it with dead people?"

"Necrophilia," Francis said. "And we're not exactly dead. We're not exactly alive, either, but no, it's not disgusting. Well, no more than sex normally is, if you look at it objectively."

"We're getting off track," Ryan said, raising a hand and closing his eyes, fighting the image of a corpse having passionate sex with another corpse. "How do you plan on getting vampire hunters to show up? And wouldn't they be after you, too?"

"Now you see why I said the plan was bloody mad," Francis replied. "Beyond the fact they'd want to kill me on sight, it's not like I can just pick up a telephone and make a call, say 'hi, this is the bloke you lot jammed a chunk of wood through a couple of decades or so ago. I'm awake now, and I need you bloody bastards to come back here and finish the real monster off before he kills anymore kids.'"

"They were chasing you, though, right?" Ryan asked. "How'd they find you?"

Francis shrugged. "No clue, mate. I thought I was covering my tracks fairly well, then one night I find a bleedin' mob after me. You've seen how well that turned out for me. Maybe they had connections somewhere, or I slipped up and a cop took notice or something. Best I could tell, those bell-ends were tight knit, even if they stayed in the shadows just as much as my lot did. No idea their techniques, though."

Ryan nodded, distracted as an idea came to him. "The internet."

"The what's-it?"

"The internet," Ryan repeated. Francis shrugged again, an uncomprehending look on his face. "It's a global network of computers that people use to find information, shop, look at porn, that kind of thing."

"I've been out of touch since that actor was president over here," Francis said. "So I've no bloody clue what you're on about."

Ryan shook his head, realizing that it would be almost impossible to explain computers and the internet to Francis without something to show him what he was talking about. "It doesn't matter. What if I posted something online, something about thinking there was a vampire in town? You think they'd see it and come check it out?"

"No idea," Francis said. "I might have one if I knew what you were talking about, but as it stands, I can't answer that."

"Well, you said they acted like private detectives or something, right? Hear rumors, come check on them, get occasional calls from the police, that kind of thing?"

"Best I could figure out, yeah."

"Then it stands to reason they changed with the times," Ryan said. "Instead of making phone calls, or subscribing to a bunch of big newspapers, they can just go on the internet and look for clues. I bet they've even got a way to search for any posts that mention vampires."

"Could be."

"So I make one," Ryan finished. "I put something online about thinking a vampire's killing kids in town. You can give me enough details about how vampires really act that it will seem real to them, so they come and check it out."

Francis nodded, considering. "You might be on the hook with it, too, though. If you're the one what makes that report, they'll come to you first, might find out about me instead of our psychotic friend who's really doing the killing."

"I won't mention you," Ryan insisted. "I'll just focus on the murders, using whatever you give me to say."

Francis laughed bitterly. "They're good, these blokes. They'll see through you like a freshly-washed window. Still, it's the best option we've got, I suppose, unless I want to start feeding off humans to build my strength so I can face this bastard, and I'm not really looking to become a murderer myself."

Ryan looked behind himself and saw they'd managed to make it back to his house. "Then I'll go in and make the post. Hopefully they contact me in the next day or so, and maybe we can save Amber, still."

"I'd give up on that if I was you," Francis said. "But what do I know? Maybe I'm wrong. It's worth the chance, I suppose. You start putting it together, come find me if you need specifics to make it sound real. Then you put it out there on that internet thing you're so keen on, and we can see what happens. Better than sitting around doing shit-all to try and stop the bastard, I can tell you that for free."

"It's a plan, then," Ryan said. He gave Francis one more confident smile, then turned and headed back to his house. The plan would work; it had to. There was simply no other choice. And, he had to admit, it felt pretty good to think he was going to play a part in catching the monster that had killed his best friend.

He thought Hunter would've approved.

CHAPTER TWENTY-ONE

The rabbit sniffed at the ground beneath where Francis sat on a thick tree branch, and then, finding nothing that appealed to its particular appetite at that moment, turned and hopped off, looking for something more interesting. Francis watched it go, then leaned his back against the trunk of the tree and stretched out his legs across the branch, waiting for something more useful to his own purposes to wander by. He'd hated doing this back home, before his existence had changed so dramatically, and to find himself once again relegated to hunting for his meal was disheartening. He could always just go and find a willing human to feed from—not fully, just enough to help recharge himself—but that was a slippery slope. It would be more potent than anything he could get from an animal, even one as large as he hoped to bag tonight, but there was too much of a chance for someone to remember and tell the wrong people later on down the line.

It wouldn't be that hard to do. The way he understood it, his supernatural appearance kept him looking younger than he was even when he'd first been changed, also gifting him with unnatural charisma. He could just go to one of the local bars, find an attractive woman, convince her to take him home with her, and satisfy two desires at once. He'd fed during sex before, despite his intimations to Ryan of the contrary, and so long as he was careful, his partners wouldn't notice anything amiss other than feeling a little more tired than normal the next day. The problem, beyond not knowing if he'd be able to stop himself from going too far, was that there was a killer on the loose in this town, and one he knew without a doubt was another vampire. That made any such dalliances a terrible risk.

An even more intense risk considering that there might well be vampire hunters swarming this town soon.

He despised the idea of reaching out to the same type of people who'd staked him and left him for dead, but he knew his limits, and knew that he was nowhere near as strong as he needed to be to face the killer alone. His extended torpor had weakened him more than he would've believed possible, and his almost sedentary lifestyle—for one of his kind, at least—had only made matters worse. His abilities were severely out of practice, and like any other muscle one didn't use often, they had weakened greatly before the hunters caught him. Perhaps that was how they'd been able to do so as easily as they had. He'd seen his own maker take on a group twice as large as the one that came for him, and defeat them handily, all while being half the age he was now.

Of course, she had reveled in her supernatural existence, while he merely saw it as one more hardship he had to endure. It was the Irish in him, and in typical fashion, he sought to console himself with whiskey and fights that inevitably drew the attention of more hunters to his locale.

He snorted with amusement. He'd known several members of his own family who would have taken him to task for thinking such a thing, but stereotypes came into existence for a reason. While it might not be true of every Irishman who'd ever walked the earth, it had most assuredly been the case with those same family members that would've been upset by his narrow-minded view of his heritage. Hypocrisy, thy name was Flynn.

Francis glanced toward the sleeping town and hoped that Ryan proved to be as smart as he seemed to be. Despite his admonitions against it, he'd come to the hospital earlier to ask for the specific details he should put in his "online post," whatever that was. Francis had cautioned him many times to try and keep it anonymous, to draw the hunters to the town, while trying not to lead them directly to either Ryan or him. The boy had given him a look similar to what he'd seen on the face of his old da when he was a wee lad himself and would ask something that should be blatantly obvious, even to the dullest of individuals. He'd shaken off the strange, sudden nostalgia and escorted the boy home as quickly as he could.

He liked Ryan's company, had come to look forward to his visits, even, but right then, he was so far into his own past that he just needed to find a way to set himself straight again.

Which put him up in this tree, waiting for some animal large enough to do him some good to wander into his chosen kill zone directly below his perch.

He was hoping for a deer, hence his increased elevation. He'd found over the centuries that his scent immediately registered to less-intelligent beings as that of a predator, causing them to run the second they caught wind of him. This way, even if the breeze shifted, his scent would be carried over them, or would seem to be coming from further away than he was. Once upon a time, he could run down a fleeing animal with ease. In his current, diminished state, he would be lucky to drop right on top of them and still manage to succeed in feeding from them.

Francis head a rustling of leaves from somewhere below him, drawing his attention back to the matter at hand. He looked down, waiting with anticipation for his quarry to arrive, and then frowned as a mangy-looking dog appeared. It sniffed around the area the rabbit had been, and as it moved, Francis noticed that it seemed to be favoring one of its front paws. He focused and smelled the blood from whatever injury it had sustained, already well on its way to clotting so it could heal. If it had the chance, that was. The animal was emaciated, its ribs showing along its sides. The poor creature was as hungry as he was.

He considered dropping down from his hiding spot and putting the thing out of its misery but chose to remain where he was. It deserved a chance at survival, so he would allow it that. Perhaps if he managed to find prey of his own, he would take some of it and find the dog so it could share his bounty.

A low chuckle escaped his throat, spooking the dog and sending it limping off into the underbrush. He'd accused Ryan of having a soft heart, and here he was, planning on trying to share his kill with a stray dog. Maybe the boy was rubbing off on him.

The truth was, he'd once been as soft as Ryan. Things had been different, then, life harder in many ways, and that had killed off much of that softness. It was somewhat refreshing to see that a bit of it remained. He had to wonder if his desire to stop this child killer and his desire to help that stray dog were both one and the same in that regard. Granted, a vampire killing kids was much more of a direct threat, so stopping him was an act of self-preservation as much as it was doing a service to a community he wasn't really a part of, but he still had to wonder.

His eyes drifted again, this time turning toward the thick trees near the abandoned factory where he'd encountered the other vampire. He had been strong, stronger even that Francis could remember his maker being. That meant he was probably old, if not ancient. It was also obvious he was in full control of his abilities, as evidenced by the attack that had stopped Francis in his tracks. And while he'd told Ryan that he didn't know who the vampire was—which was essentially true—there had been something vaguely familiar about him, and about the way he felt that Francis couldn't figure out. He was probably overthinking it, and the connection he felt was probably nothing more than the fact they were both supernatural creatures, but it still nagged at him like a sore on his tongue he kept tapping against his teeth.

Another rustling of leaves made him glance down, fully expecting to see another rabbit, or dog, or even a bloody cat wandering by, teasing and taunting him. Instead, he saw a deer—a doe, by the lack of antlers—casually making its way past his hiding spot, maybe on its way home after an evening doing whatever the hell it was deer did when they weren't asleep or being carved up by hunters. Francis pulled the knife from his belt and slowly pushed away from the tree trunk, creeping along the branch until the animal was almost directly beneath him.

He dropped, knife held before him as he fell, and landed with the blade squarely in the creature's neck. It dropped at once, the connection between its body and brain severed, a strange little squealing sound escaping its throat. Francis rolled off the animal, withdrawing the blade, and then plunged it into the deer's neck, severing its jugular and sending a spray of blood directly into his face. He closed his lips around the wound, drinking deeply of the animal's life energy, feeling his own mind and body responding as it flowed through him the same way the coppery blood flowed down his throat and into his stomach.

In seconds, the deer was dead, its fur now a pure white instead of a light brownish hue, all of its energy absorbed by his modified metabolism. Francis staggered backward, drunk with the transfer of whatever energy was actually there, the headache that had persisted since that other vampire's attack finally fading away. Once that was done, he could almost feel himself growing stronger, feel the few remaining lines in his face smoothing out, leaving behind his normal, youthful appearance. His scalp tingled as his hair grew back to the length it had been on the night he'd been changed, a bit shaggy and in need of a trim, but full and thick and healthy once more.

He smiled. He'd thought himself nearly recovered after doing this the night Ryan brought him the dying dog, but now he knew he'd truly replenished himself. He almost felt as though he could face that other vampire again and not fall so easily this time. He would still fail—despite his hopes that he could handle this on his own, he knew his limitations and could face reality when he had to—but this time it would take more than a simple mental punch to take him down.

The clarity of thought brought another idea to mind: the length of time between when the vampire had taken the children, and when they'd been discovered dead. True, the first—Ryan's friend—had been killed the same day, but the other one, the girl, had been discovered a couple of days later in a completely different spot from where she'd disappeared. It was possible, if unlikely, that the one taken earlier in the day was still alive. She could very well be his prisoner, right this moment, being subjected to degradations of the flesh that would make even the most hardened human serial killer wince in sympathy.

The night was young, and Francis felt rejuvenated. The least he could do was explore the possibility. He might fail, and if he had to face the other vampire one on one he might well meet his true death, but even if all he managed was to learn something useful, it would be beneficial. Maybe he could even figure out a way to take the thing down without involving the infernal hunters who might come for him instead.

So thinking, he turned and rushed through the woods, toward the area where the girl had been taken. At least he could feel like he was doing something.

For now, it would have to be enough.

CHAPTER TWENTY-TWO

The gravel access road where he'd watched the other vampire take the girl looked much the same at night as it had during the day. If anything, the scant moonlight that penetrated the overhanging trees made it look even more desolate and isolated than it had at the time. Francis shuddered as he stood in the middle of the road, studying the place where the other vampire's truck had been parked, feeling the ghost of that mental blast lingering at the periphery of his senses, threatening to make him turn and run and forget this whole mad plan he'd concocted. The rush from feeding had worn off, leaving him his normal cynical self, so he knew what he was doing was probably pointless, but he was here, so he may as well see it through to the inevitable end.

He forced himself to walk forward, closer to where the truck had been, ignoring the feeling of dread that settled in the pit of his stomach. He was sure that was just more of the lingering residue from the attack earlier, and not a sign that the other had left some kind of trap for him. They'd never gotten that close to one another, and he doubted the other even knew that Francis was also a vampire, so he had no way of knowing that his intended victim would have survived the attack in the first place.

Unless he'd come back after stashing the girl somewhere and found Francis gone, of course.

After mentally bracing himself, Francis opened his senses, reaching out in search of some remnant from the other vampire and not the girl's diffuse pain and fear, or the remnants of the psychic blast. There wasn't much here, on any of those three fronts, even though at least the girl should have come through clearly, even if he couldn't follow the emotional threads due to how scattered they would be. He'd heard that some could purge an area of emotional resonance, though he'd never learned the trick himself. It was how his own maker claimed to cover her tracks, due to her propensity toward killing her food sources rather than taking only what she needed from them. Maybe he should have waited another decade or so before killing her.

If only she hadn't forced his hand.

With no resonance to guide him, that meant he had to rely on old-fashioned detective work. He shook his head and continued down the road, following the direction the vampire had gone when he drove away.

It became immediately apparent why the vampire had chosen this spot for one of his hunting grounds. There were several other dirt roads and narrower trails branching off from the access road, some barely large enough for a person to walk down, others large enough to fit a truck twice the size of the other vampire's down. He considered checking out a few of these larger ones—after all, they were there and would be a perfect hiding spot, a true "needle in a haystack" situation—but hesitated. He'd heard the phrase for most of his very long life, in one form or another, but it all amounted to the same thing: "don't shit where you eat." Vampires were predators by nature, true, but they were also blessed with the intelligence and cunning of humanity. If the vampire he was looking for was old—and he had every reason to believe he was—then he would've learned a long time ago how to survive, and how to hunt without fear of being caught. That he was choosing kids and killing them afterward meant that he would've been hunted himself, much more than any other vampire would be had they prayed solely on adults. Since he hadn't been caught, he obviously knew a thing or two about what he was doing. There was no way he would chance making his home, or even his feeding area, this close to where the girl had been taken. Francis ignored the side trails and continued on.

He swore as the gravel road began to widen further, then fought the urge to kick himself in the arse when it ended at a normal, paved road that led either back toward town or out of it, depending on which direction you went. He could try and apply logic and reason to the problem all night, but it still boiled down to a fifty-fifty chance. Even if he picked the right one, there was no way to know where amongst the thousands of potential places the other vampire might be hiding out. He had truly reached a dead end.

Francis considered following the road back into town, but the route it would make him take to get home again would be through several well-populated areas. With a killer on the loose, it wouldn't be a good idea for a stranger to be seen wandering the streets so late at night. He was trying to keep a low profile. The last thing he needed was to draw any kind of attention to himself that might alert the cops. He could keep them from taking him, but that would get messy and wasn't anything he wanted to take part in, anyway. Better to go back the way he'd come and stick to the shadows, even if it meant taking a longer trip home again.

He was about halfway back to where he'd started his search when something slammed into the ground right in front of his feet, making him stop. He crouched and pulled the object from the gravel, eyebrows rising as he realized what it was: a crossbow bolt, thick, and made of solid wood from tip to tail.

The way hunters preferred them, back in the older days when they used such weapons more commonly.

He stood slowly, eyes scanning the area around him. He wasn't too worried that any future shots might be intended to stake him from a distance; hunters typically didn't issue warning shots. But he had no desire to have to exert energy healing a wound if he could prevent getting it in the first place.

"I was right. I'll be damned."

The voice came from almost directly in front of him, the hint of a Slavic accent making the words come out harsher than they would from any other mouth. Finally, he saw the owner of that voice, standing some distance away, barely visible in the thick shadows. From the size of the figure he was looking at, Francis was fairly confident he'd found his quarry.

"About what, mate?"

The hint of laughter drifted over to him on the breeze, but the figure remained where it was standing.

"You're not human, are you?" it asked.

"And what gives you that idea?"

"You're standing there," the man replied. "That hit should have killed you, yet here you are, up and moving around like nothing happened. Who did you feed from, may I ask? Must have been a powerful person, I would think. You would have needed much energy to recover this well."

"I'm just full of surprises," Francis replied. "And whoever I fed from, at least they weren't a child, and I didn't bugger them first."

"You should try it," the man said. "Is the best of all worlds. Fear, pain, sexual awakening; all things that make the energy released equal to that of a man who's lived four times as long."

"And morally reprehensible," Francis added. "You forgot that bit."

"Whose morals? Humankind's? You know as well as I that we are beyond such things. We answer to no one save ourselves. Which is as it should be."

"Yeah, you keep thinking that," Francis said. A part of him wanted to rush the figure, attempt to take him down quickly in the hopes that he could gain the upper hand and defeat him, but he still held that damned crossbow, and it wasn't likely that sharing a common damnation would be cause for the man to hold his fire should he feel threatened. "You do know how stupid you're being? What you're doing, it's liable to draw hunters here. Maybe you take down the first batch, but they'll just send more. I think there's liable to be more of them than there are of us."

"Another argument in favor of my methods," the man said. "Humanity is filled with their own monsters. What I do, it is viewed as man's cruelty, nothing more. Nothing that points to anything other than that. I don't even take enough to lighten their hair. Only sips, nothing more. That is why I make the meals potent, first. So I need no more than that.

"Did you know," the man went on. "There are some humans who eat others of their kind? Not in the way we feed, but those who actually cook and consume them? And not for nourishment, not to stay alive, but because they get a thrill from such an act? Yet we are the monsters. What I do is no different from some humans across the world. These cattle have become so accustomed to it, they never think there may be more than what they see. We are in the age of death, my friend, and by our heritage, were made to rule it."

"Then why hide?" Francis asked. "I've never heard of a ruler who doesn't want anyone to know who he is."

"All things in time."

Francis shook his head. "I'm going to find a way to stop you, you understand. What you're doing? It cannot be allowed to continue."

"So you say," the man said, chuckling. "But as I recall, you fared not so well the last time we met. If not for my curiosity about you, I would have already ended you now."

"My pasty arse," Francis replied. "You just like to talk."

"I admit it has been some time since I had the ability to converse with another of our kind," the man said. "But it is clear you and I are nothing alike. You seek to hide, I plan to rule. While you cower in the shadow, I will stand triumphant before my herd."

"You will shove your own head up your arse and call yourself a bloody Christmas wreath," Francis said. "Why tell me all this, then? Don't believe I can stop you?"

"No, I do not," the man said. "And I tell you this to give you a choice: either accept the truth, or whimper while I continue my hunt here. This place is not of enough consequence for me to concern myself with for much longer. Once I have taken my fill, I will move on. You can stay out of my way, or you can die trying to stop me. And save that threat you are about to use. I defeated you easily before, I can do so again just as easily. I am strong, a lion in the jungle. You are a rabbit, weak and frightened. There is no contest."

"It's not a threat," Francis said. "I will stop you."

"I do not wish to harm one of the brethren," the man said. "But persist in this, and I will have no other choice. This is your only opportunity to walk away. Seek me again, and I will grant you the true death you seem to crave."

The shape moved, and Francis tensed, preparing to try and avoid the bolt he knew was coming his way, but nothing happened. The other vampire had gone, leaving him standing in the middle of the road, holding onto a wooden bolt like a fool, screaming insults at the darkness.

He had come to find the girl and had failed. What he had found was proof that she was either dead, or soon to be, and that the creature who had killed her planned to do so again. As much as he hated to admit it, his original plan had been the right one, no matter how mad.

He hoped that Ryan had some luck in contacting the hunters. They were going to be sorely needed.

CHAPTER TWENTY-THREE

I f not for the fact his parents had made it abundantly clear that if he broke his laptop, he would only get another one when he paid for it, Ryan might well have thrown the computer across the room. He'd made anonymous postings on every "true vampire" website he could find, and even a few that were so obscure and badly designed that he was afraid his parents might walk in on him and think he was looking at porn—a concept made all the more frightening by the fact he basically was. The sites were filled with images of vampires and their half-naked slaves, and while their message boards were filled with what he, even at his relatively young age, recognized as nothing more than fantasies and wish fulfillment, it also had a few stories posted that seemed to mesh with what Francis had told him, so he took the chance.

Only it had apparently all been for nothing. The past three mornings he'd logged into the email address he created specifically for this purpose, only to see that he had no messages asking about the stories he'd told. Actually, that wasn't true. He'd found fifteen offers for him to come enslave himself to a "vampire king" in exchange for great power, wealth, and immortality, two offering the same from "vampire queens," six requests to join a live-action vampire-themed roleplaying game, and six hundred and fifteen penis-related offers ranging from pills that would keep him hard all weekend to an assortment of ways to increase his length and girth with minimal effort, genetics be damned. Either the people he was trying to reach didn't believe him or they weren't monitoring those forums. He supposed both were viable options, but it was still frustrating to be no closer to getting them here than he was when he first sat down to write his posts.

He leaned back in his chair and ground the balls of his hands into his eyes, trying to rub away the headache that threatened to burst forth from behind them. He'd taken a couple of ibuprofens earlier, and while they'd helped, they hadn't gotten rid of it completely. What he needed to do was give up and go to bed, hoping that maybe tomorrow would bring something different. He doubted it would, but at least it didn't bother him while he was sleeping.

Instead, he picked up his phone and scrolled down his meager list of contacts before stopping with his thumb hovering over Kayla's name. She'd reacted better to Amber's disappearance than he had to Hunter's and was honestly more freaked out that twice she'd been the last one to see someone who'd gone missing. She insisted she was fine, and that she hadn't even really liked Amber all that much, but Ryan thought she was just trying to put on a brave face. He knew he was a little freaked out, and he'd almost hated the girl.

He tapped the icon to call her and put the phone to his ear. It rang once, twice, three times.... Ryan disconnected the call before it could roll over to voicemail. He'd had an idea of what to say—asking if the party was still on for tomorrow night, along with the specific details he would need to meet up with her—but he'd also intended to press her a bit, try to get her talking and dealing with the situation instead of burying it deep down inside. That wouldn't be an easy thing to do through voicemail, so he would just have to try again later.

Ryan tossed his phone over onto his bed then plopped down next to it. As much as he wanted to go to sleep and forget the world, his mind was racing, and showed no signs of slowing any time soon. He rolled over onto his back and crossed his hands behind his head. To anyone who came in, it would look like he was staring up at the ceiling. In reality, though, he was staring into the past. For a change, it wasn't Hunter he was thinking about this time, but Kayla. He'd been so busy with getting information from Francis and making the posts online, and then dealing with the cops yet again after Amber's disappearance was reported that he hadn't had the chance to think back on their encounter this past Saturday.

He couldn't help but wonder where it would've ended up had Francis not interrupted them, nor could he decide if that interruption had been a good or bad thing. Kayla said it was, but he'd seen something totally different in her eyes as she said it. He also had believed her when she claimed that she'd never gone that far with anyone, either, and wondered why she'd chosen him for that particular honor.

The way she'd felt leaning against him during the movie, and how hot her thighs had been against his own, even through his pants, caused him to stir at the memory. He shifted position on the bed, but it didn't help. He was awake down there as well, and since his mind was determined to replay the events of that afternoon over and over, there would be no getting rid of it now.

Unless....

He rolled off the bed and locked his door, then returned to it and settled back down again. His eyes fluttered closed as one hand began undoing his jeans, and then his phone rang, making him jump and deflating him at once despite his surety that nothing would be able to accomplish such a feat. He grabbed the phone and looked at the screen, unsurprised to see it was Kayla, returning his earlier call. He hit the icon to answer it and was chuckling as he put the phone to his ear.

"I was just thinking about you," he said.

There was a slight pause, and then she replied. "I'm assuming you mean for reasons other than just having called me. Should I call back in a little bit, or would you rather I come over and gave you a hand with that?"

He coughed, face going red at the comment. "I think you know the answer to that."

Kayla sighed. "Well, I doubt I can get out of the house this late, so you'll just have to imagine I'm there. But, since you called me, I guess you'll have to wait for that."

"That's mean," he replied, laughing.

"You'll live," she said, a smile in her own voice. "So what's up, besides you?"

Ryan shook his head, even though he knew she couldn't see it. "I wanted to ask about tomorrow night, actually. With everything going on, and... another disappearance, I didn't know if it had been called off, or what."

She was quiet for a long moment. When she finally replied, her voice was hesitant. "I was going to talk to you about this at school, but I don't know if you're going to want to go now."

"Why would you think that?" Ryan asked, his forehead creasing. "Of course I want to go."

"That was before," she explained. "Matt heard you're planning to be there. I think he's going to try something."

Ryan felt a flash of ice run across his back. "Oh."

"Look, we can always go do something else," Kayla said. "We could go see a movie or something, just the two of us. Maybe grab something to eat, too. I'll even treat you, be an independent woman and all."

He knew she was just trying to keep the peace, spare him a potentially embarrassing encounter, and he could appreciate that. If this had been a few weeks ago, even, he might've taken her up on that offer. But he'd been through a lot since his last encounter with Matt and his asshole friends, and he was determined not to ever bow and scrape for a dickhead like that again.

"We can still go," he said. "We'll try to avoid him, but if we can't, well... fuck him."

It was the first time he'd used that kind of language around a girl, the first time he'd used it when speaking with anyone other than Hunter or maybe Francis, and he felt an immediate flash of guilt for it. Then Kayla began to chuckle, and he knew it had been the right call, this time.

"You've definitely changed, did you know that?" she asked. "That's a good thing, by the way. Okay, so we'll go. Any idea what you're going as?"

His expression froze. "I have to go in costume?"

"No," she said, dragging the word out playfully. "But I will be. Just thought you might want to as well."

He sighed. "Then what are you going as?"

"It's a surprise," she said. "But I think you'll like it."

Visions of her dressed as a slutty witch, or a slutty pirate, or something along those lines danced through his mind, renewing his earlier enthusiasm. "That's intriguing."

"It was meant to be."

"Okay, I'll figure something out then."

"Good. Should I let you get back to your other matter?"

He hesitated, and then took a deep breath. "Actually, I did want to ask how you were doing. With the whole Amber thing, I mean."

"I told you before, I'm fine," she said, but there was a slight hitch to her voice as she said it.

"I was just thinking," he went on. "I mean, it freaked me out, and I barely knew her. I know you said you guys weren't close friends, but you still knew her better than I did."

There was a long pause, and for a moment Ryan thought he'd gone too far and made her hang up. Finally, she sighed, letting him know she was still on the line.

"Look, when I said I was more freaked out that I was one of the last ones to see both her and Hunter, I wasn't just blowing it off. That's the truth. And yeah, Amber being taken bothers me, mainly because if I hadn't been so determined to stay there with you, it might not have happened. But you said that you felt the same way about talking to me the day Hunter went missing. So I have to remember what I told you then, too. If we'd have been with them, maybe we would've gone missing and been killed, too. Or maybe they would have been taken at a different time. Until we know why this asshole's doing it, we don't know whether or not we should feel guilty."

Ryan shuddered. From what Francis told him, he had a pretty good idea of why the asshole was taking kids, and there was no reasonable explanation for it. He didn't seem to have any particular affinity for boys or girls, which meant it was complete, random chance. But he took Kayla's meaning, and while he hadn't really heeded her words at the time she'd said them, he had come to believe the truth of them as the days passed. Francis had told him much the same thing the day he'd broken down at the asylum when he'd been thinking the vampire had been the one responsible.

"Okay," he said. "That makes sense, and you're right, that is what you told me. Just do me a favor. If you do start to feel bad, or freaked out, or whatever about it, talk to somebody. Me or whoever. I've been through it, and believe me, I know how much it sucks when it finally does come out."

"Thanks, I will," she said. "You know, you're a really sweet guy, Ryan. A really good guy. I hope I don't turn out to be something less than you think I am."

"That'll never happen," he replied, the words coming on instinct. "You're perfect, no matter what."

"No, I'm not," she replied softly. "But thank you for thinking that I am. I really do need to get off here. I'm not supposed to be on the phone this late, and I've got some homework to finish up for Biology. We can work out where to meet before the party at school tomorrow, okay?"

"Sounds great," he said.

"Sweet dreams," she said. "Hope they're of me."

She hung up before he could say anything else. Ryan shook his head, dropped his phone beside him, and then leaned back on his bed, trying to figure out what he could possibly do for a Halloween costume in less than twenty-four hours.

He did well; he made it almost thirty minutes before the realization of what he'd agreed to, and the real possibility that he was going to end up in a fight with Matt at that party sank in and gave him a case of the shakes that kept all thoughts of Kayla and anything resembling sleep away for a long time.

CHAPTER TWENTY-FOUR

Naturally, there were problems with the idea of going to the Halloween party that Ryan hadn't considered, chief among them that his parents were totally against the idea. The very concept that he would be out somewhere running the risk of being kidnapped and killed was more than enough for them to shut the idea down completely. The solution came, strangely enough, from Hunter—or at least, from his legacy. Since his death, Melanie had taken a "big sister" approach where Ryan was concerned, mothering and protecting him in a way he was sure she wished that she had with Hunter. As a result, once she caught wind of the problem, and heard there was a girl involved, she came to the rescue. She sat down with his parents, insisted she was going to be there, and that she wanted Ryan to come with her, so she could feel closer to Hunter by proxy, since he would've gone, had he been alive to do so.

It was a stretch. Hunter wouldn't have dreamed of going to this particular party under normal circumstances. True, he probably would've agreed to go because Ryan would be there with Kayla, but he wouldn't have enjoyed it, and would only have been there to support his friend. In the end, it didn't matter. While it was a little far-fetched, it was believable, and that was the important part.

Mom had thawed toward Melanie in the wake of her brother's untimely death, but apparently she still held some internalized anger at the way the girl had broken her oldest son's heart. Melanie had barely gotten the words out before Mom was shooting it down as a bad idea, using the reasonable logic that Melanie wouldn't be much protection if the killer chose to strike either one of them. Incredibly, Dad had been the voice of reason to win her over. He pointed out that it was unlikely the killer would strike a place that was full of kids, and that Melanie deserved the opportunity to heal after everything that happened, and if that required helping Ryan meet new friends and have some fun, well, so be it.

He gave Melanie the usual speech about how she was offering to be responsible, so that was the expectation, and how Ryan better not come home drunk or high or anything like that, to which Melanie readily agreed. Ryan thought that had to be exceptionally easy for her—she had to work tonight, the only one in the family who was doing so after Hunter's death, apparently—and would only be acting as transportation for him and Kayla.

"That doesn't mean I'm abandoning you, though," she'd said. "If you need me, you call me. I'll drop whatever I'm doing and come help you however I can. If it gets me fired, oh well. My boss is a fucking asshole anyway."

She also spent a great deal of the ride to Kayla's house offering advice and hints on how to make this a great night for both of them. Ryan suspected the offerings were culled from the things she'd wished guys had done for her, but he didn't ask or point this out. She was trying to make something of her life, to make something good come from a tragedy, and he wasn't about to do anything to disrupt that. Honestly, he appreciated the effort, even if some of it—primarily the parts about taking things slow—contradicted things that had already happened. Sisterly attitude or no, there were some things he wasn't about to confess to her.

He waited in the car while Melanie went to collect Kayla. She knew Kayla's sister, so she already had an in with the family, and had wisely pointed out that with a killer on the loose, specifically one who was sexually assaulting his victims first, it would look better for a girl they knew to pick Kayla up instead of a guy they'd never met before. While she was gone, he looked down at the torn clothes he wore, the fake blood streaked across them, and at the creepy clown mask in his hands. It wasn't the costume he would've picked if he'd given it much thought, but there weren't too many options at the local dollar store when he'd stopped after school. Trying to find a decent costume on Halloween was like trying to squeeze water from a log; you might could pull it off, but not without a lot of effort and probably some pain.

When he saw Kayla emerge from the house behind Melanie, he burst out laughing. She'd said he would like it, and she was right, but not for the reasons he'd assumed. The costume looked to be made of polyester and nylon rather than reinforced spandex, and she carried the mask part of it in one hand, but the way her hair was tied into a ponytail atop her head and the red and black logo on the plastic belt were all-too familiar to a nerd like him.

She saw him looking and paused for a brief curtsey, the effect thrown off a bit by the plastic guns strapped to her thighs and the fake sword handles crossed over her back. He turned to face her when she opened the door behind him and climbed in, still laughing, pleased beyond all measure.

"Lady Deadpool!" he exclaimed. "I don't believe it. I didn't even know you knew she existed!"

Kayla gave him an amused but confused look. "Wait... I just saw the movie, liked it, and thought this would be something you were into. You mean there actually is a female version? Did I accidentally make a real geek reference here?"

Ryan laughed all the harder. "Yeah, you did!"

His laughter trailed off as his door was pulled open. He turned to see Melanie standing beside the car, shaking her head at him.

"What is wrong with you?" she asked in a stage whisper. "I'm not your date, she is, so get back there with her. Jesus, do I have to draw you a roadmap?"

He rolled his eyes and got out of the car, ignoring her chuckles as he moved past her and got in the back. Kayla slid over a bit to make room for him, but stayed close by his side, her leg touching his as the door shut. He couldn't help but wonder what she was wearing underneath that tight suit. He stopped thinking about it before his imagination created what could be a potentially embarrassing situation with Melanie in the front seat and easily able to glance back and see if he was trying to hide his crotch.

The ride to the asylum wasn't what Ryan thought it would be. He figured he and Kayla would get so lost in each other that they forgot where they were, but instead, they simply remained silent. He hoped it was simply because Melanie was in the car, too, and was given some verification of that when Kayla put a hand on his thigh before leaning against his side, but it was still nothing like he'd imagined or hoped it would be. It wasn't bad, just different. Enough so that when Melanie finally pulled up at the mouth of the short access road that led to the hole in the fence where everyone normally entered, he was grateful beyond words that the ride was over.

Melanie motioned for him after he got out, and Kayla nodded, so he approached alone and leaned down so he could hear through the partially opened window.

"I'm leaving it to you to get home safe," Melanie said. "Don't do anything stupid, but if you do, use this."

She pressed something into his hand. He looked down and felt his cheeks go red when he saw the foil wrapper with the familiar Roman guy on it.

"Thanks," he mumbled, too embarrassed to say much more than that.

Melanie gave him a pointed look, then smiled and hit the button to close the window again. He stepped away and waited for her to back up so she could get turned around, then went back over to Kayla, stuffing the condom into his pants pocket and hoping she hadn't seen it. He held out a hand in the direction of the asylum.

"Right this way."

She gave him a look of mild curiosity but didn't say anything. She smiled and gave that odd little curtsey again before heading down the path.

The first thing to cross Ryan's mind when he saw the courtyard beyond the trampled down fence was that the cops would be busting this party soon. Kids milled about every-where, some with red plastic cups in hand, others with open beer bottles. One kid that Ryan thought he recognized from his gym class was on his hands and knees just past the fence, apparently puking up everything he'd eaten in the last week. The eye-watering stench of alcohol and vomit was nearly enough to make Ryan want to join him.

Kayla lightly punched his arm, drawing his attention back to her. She'd pulled on the mask for her costume, and he was amused to see that her hair stuck out a hole in the top, just like the character she didn't know she was portraying. She gestured to the clown mask still clutched in one of his hands.

"Get your game face on."

He laughed and pulled the mask over his face. Thankfully, the scent of cheap rubber was enough to drown out the worst of the pool of sick beneath the other boy's heaving mouth. Once he had the eyeholes situated so he wasn't trying to walk around blind, Kayla nodded, then took him by the hand and led him into the thick of the debauchery.

Two pickup trucks were parked near one side of the throng of people, their tailgates down to serve as makeshift bars. One held a pair of kegs sitting in buckets of ice, while the other contained an assortment of soda and liquor bottles, and a large stack of those red cups. How the trucks had gotten into the courtyard was a mystery all its own. Ryan was sure they had to have cut the lock off the main gates at the other end of the building, so he wasn't sure exactly how they were expecting to keep this in the least bit subtle.

Then again, the sheer number of people milling about had already demolished that possibility, so it was doubtful anyone was thinking about such things. The single goal here was to have fun and forget about everything else for a while, and to that end, it already looked like a raging success.

"You want to grab a drink?" Kayla asked, pointing to the trucks and their stockpiles of libations.

He considered it, and then shook his head. He'd tasted booze before, and wasn't completely opposed to the idea of drinking, but Matt was supposed to be around someplace, and would probably be looking for him to start something. He wanted to remain clear-headed for such a confrontation. As if that would do any real good.

"Maybe later," he said.

Kayla didn't seem to mind, which was something of a relief to Ryan. He was afraid she might want something and would only abstain because he did, but she seemed to be more apathetic about the prospect than he was. They moved off into the crowd together, mingling, stopping occasionally so that Kayla could say hello to people she knew who were there.

Surprisingly, she also made it a point to introduce him on these occasions. Incredibly, he wasn't met with blank stares or looks of barely-restrained disgust. Everyone seemed to be genuinely happy to meet him, and a few even asked how he was holding up. They didn't quite go so far as to mention Hunter by name, but it was obvious from the way they presented the question that was what they were referring to.

Ryan thought his friend would have found it hilarious that one of them was finally starting to break through the near-impenetrable wall of "cool" high school cliques, and it had only taken the other being brutally murdered to pull it off.

Well, that, and to land Kayla as a girlfriend, but that was so surreal he still couldn't completely wrap his mind around it.

Near one of the trucks, someone had set up a speaker system blaring dance music in between creepy sound effects that would've been better suited for a primary school haunted house than a party for a bunch of high school kids, but for some reason it struck the perfect balance between serious and playful. Ryan found the bizarre soundtrack actually helped to relax his mind.

Despite his initial concerns, he was actually having fun.

Kayla finally pulled him away from the crowd after a while and led him over near the front doors to the asylum. From what he'd seen there was an almost unspoken rule that no one would go in there, though whether for the sake of practicality or because so many people believed the place was really haunted, he couldn't say. He did find it funny that of everyone here, he alone knew the secret of what lurked beneath the ruined hospital.

They stopped near the doors, and Kayla let go of his hand long enough to pull her mask off and smile over at him. A few strands of her hair were stuck to her sweaty face, which to Ryan only served to make her cuter than ever. He followed her lead and pulled off his own mask, eliciting a laugh from her.

"What?" he asked, suddenly a bit self-conscious. "What's wrong?"

She reached over and carefully plucked his own matted hair away from his face, then kissed him lightly on the cheek. "Nothing at all. You just look like you've been trapped in an oven for the last hour or so."

"Kind of feels that way, now that you mention it," he replied.

Her eyes locked on his, and he noticed the hint of something in them, as if she was waiting for something. He wasn't sure if it was what she had in mind, but he leaned forward and kissed her gently. When he felt her arms go around his neck and her lips part slightly, he knew it had been the right call.

She finally pulled away and glanced around. "Think they'd miss us if we went inside?"

"No idea," Ryan said, shrugging. "You sure you want to?"

"You made it in and back out, right?" she asked. "Twice, if I remember correctly."

"Yeah, so?"

"So let's make it three for you and a first for me," she said. "You can show me the way, be my guide."

Feeling the sweat on his forehead break out again, he wondered if they were talking about the same thing anymore.

"Okay," he said, stopping himself from saying more and possibly coming off as unconfident as he felt. "Let's see what we can find. But we don't have lights, so it might be...."

He trailed off when she pulled a pair of glow sticks from one of the pouches on her belt and snapped them to life. The light they gave off wasn't the brightest, but it would be more than enough for them to find their way once they were in the dark building. It suddenly occurred to him that for her to have brought them tonight meant this had more than likely been her plan all along, which made him laugh a little.

"You thought of everything, didn't you?"

"You have no idea," she said. "I'm full of surprises."

She turned and walked backward toward the door, almost daring him to follow. He'd already done so many, many times, so he didn't even make her wait before he went after her.

They hadn't gone very far into the reception area when a shadow leapt from the darkness, grabbing Kayla and dragging her toward the hallway door. It took a second for Ryan to realize what had happened, and another second for him to understand that by the way she was screaming, this wasn't part of some joke she'd planned to mess with him. He started after her, and felt his shins slam up against something, tripping him up. He hit the ground hard and slid a couple of feet, then rolled over and saw Zach standing over him, a wicked grin on his face.

Zach reached down and grabbed him, and then hauled him back up to his feet. Ryan tried to swing at him, but the bigger boy easily dodged the blow before slamming a fist into Ryan's nose. It didn't break—at least he didn't think it did—but it began to gush blood over his lips and chin. Zach wasted no time in wrapping an arm around Ryan's throat, getting him in a chokehold that was nearly tight enough to cut off his air completely, and then dragged him along in the direction the other shape had taken Kayla.

After what felt like forever, the hold loosened. Ryan had half a second to gasp for air, and then he was shoved backward roughly. His feet tangled together, and he hit the ground hard, knocking what little wind he'd been able to gain back out again. His head bounced briskly off the floor, further dazing him and making the world spin for a moment.

"Well hi there, fuckface."

Ryan turned and saw Matt leaning with one foot flat against the wall behind him, a cigarette dangling limply from his lips. He had a pint bottle of something in his hand, and there was just enough light from Kayla's confiscated glow stick to see that it was three-quarters of the way empty already.

He turned his head and saw Brandon holding onto Kayla, one hand clamped over her mouth to keep her screams from getting too loud. He needn't have bothered. From what Ryan could hear, it was so loud outside that no one would've noticed them anyway. She had a panicked look in her eye, and it was clear she wasn't so much afraid for herself, as she was for whatever they planned to do to him.

"What do you want, Matt?" he asked, turning his attention back to the leader of this motley bunch.

"To fuck you up," Matt said, as if it was the most obvious answer in the world. "What else?"

"Why?"

Matt blinked, as if he hadn't given that particular question much thought. Ryan thought he probably hadn't. Matt was never going to be one of the all-time great intellects in the world.

"Well, tonight, it's because of the shit you started."

Ryan blinked. Under normal circumstances he wouldn't have even made it this far, would have simply cowed and let them do whatever they wanted to do. This time—maybe because Kayla was right there watching it all unfold—he refused to take their shit lying down. He forced himself back to his knees, and then waited. If he could keep Matt talking, maybe he could find a way to make a quick strike and get him and Kayla out of this mess.

"And what shit did I start?"

"Lippy little fucker tonight, ain't he?" Zach asked, laughing. "I'm going to knock his fucking teeth out, maybe that'll shut him up."

"You're not doing jack shit," Matt said, his eyes never leaving Ryan. "You're going to stick to the plan, and that's it. If there's anything left of the shit-stain once I'm done with him, then you can get a few licks in. Until then, shut up and do what I told you to."

From the way he grumbled, Ryan could tell Zach wasn't happy about this rebuke, but he apparently knew his place well enough to let it go.

"You know what you did," Matt said, addressing Ryan again. "You and your faggot buddy. He caught that pedophile asshole's attention, now Brandon's girl got taken, too. If he hadn't been wiggle-assing around, none of this would be happening, and you might even be left alone tonight. I'm drunk enough it could've gone either way."

Ryan doubted that, but what he was hearing was so ludicrous that he didn't have the chance to focus on the tail end of it. "Wait.... Are you seriously telling me that since Hunter was the first to get killed, it's his fault the others are, too?"

Matt said nothing, just stared hateful daggers at him.

If he'd been asked to imagine this exact scenario, and how he would react to it, Ryan would've been able to give at least a dozen answers, ranging from the fantastic where he fought back and beat all three of their asses, to the hyper-real where they put him in the hospital for a week or two. What he never would've thought of was how he really reacted to it.

He laughed.

Not just a chuckle, or a quick snort, either. He let out a long, loud, braying, hysterical stream of laughter that actually doubled him over for a moment so he could try and catch his breath.

It was the worst thing he could've done.

Matt's foot caught him square in the jaw, knocking him onto his back again and bouncing his head off the ground much harder than before. Matt followed the kick up by stomping down into his stomach hard. Ryan gagged, and would've vomited if he'd eaten anything in the last few hours. As it was, he rolled into a ball, groaning and holding his stomach, hoping nothing important had burst from that stomp.

No one moved or spoke. The only sound Ryan could hear were Kayla's frantic, muffled protests. He finally managed to straighten out enough to look up, determined to see the next punch before it landed.

But Matt wasn't looking at him anymore. He was looking to the side, his gaze intent. Ryan followed it, feeling his heart lurch when he realized Matt was staring at Kayla. After several moments of silence, Matt looked back to him.

"You know, I've got an idea," he said. "Something that'll fuck you up but good, and something way more fun than just kicking your ass for the hundredth time. If I'm reading this right, you and this little bitch are a thing now, right?"

Ryan didn't answer. Not only was he confused by the sudden change in the conversation's direction, he still couldn't get enough air to speak.

Matt nodded as though Ryan had confirmed things for him anyway. "Yeah, this'll be much better. You, come here!"

He grabbed Kayla by the wrist and yanked her toward him. Brandon held on for another moment, stretching her between them, and then he finally let go, causing her to snap toward Matt like a rubber band that was suddenly let loose. Her mouth opened, probably to scream, but she never got the chance. Matt planted his forearm across her chin, clothes-lining her as neatly as any professional wrestler. She didn't fall, but it was only because he caught her. There was nothing altruistic about this, however, since he immediately punched her once more in the face then let go of her. She crumpled to the floor, barely conscious.

Matt looked from Brandon to Zach, and then pointed at Ryan. "Hold him. You let him up, I'm fucking you up next."

To their credit, Brandon and Zach looked just as confused as Ryan felt, although without the impotent rage to add to things. Ryan forced himself back to his hands and knees, not sure what Matt had in mind, but with every intention of stopping him. He'd hit Kayla, and while he didn't know how badly she was hurt, he didn't intend to give the asshole the chance to do anything worse to her.

"I said fucking hold him!" Matt screamed.

That was enough to get the other two moving. They each grabbed one of Ryan's arms and jerked him roughly to his knees again. The pain in his stomach was nearly overwhelming, and despite his desire to show a strong front, he could feel tears starting to run down his cheeks.

Matt leered at him. "You have any idea how many times this stuck-up little bitch has shot me down? Then what does she do? Goes after the biggest pussy on the planet. Guess that makes her a dyke or something. That's okay. I'm about to fix that."

Suddenly, Ryan understood. He went wild in Zach and Brandon's grip, and for one delirious moment, he almost slipped free. Then they tightened down and held him fast again, locking him in place.

"No!" he screamed, fear and anger twisting together in his voice. "Leave her alone you motherfucking piece of shit!"

Matt smiled and looked to his asshole friends. "He looks away, he misses any of this, you two have fucking had it."

"I don't know about this Matt," Brandon said. "You sure this is such a good idea?"

"You shut the fuck up," Matt said. "Amber's gone because of these little shits, remember? Think what she must be going through right now, if she's even still alive. Don't you think it's fair they get to feel even a little of that?"

Brandon said nothing else, but Ryan could feel the trembling in his arms, even though he didn't loosen his hold at all. Matt leaned down, staring into Ryan's eyes.

"Watch and see how a real man does this," he said.

Ryan screamed again, and this time it must have been enough to cause Kayla to stir. He heard her groan, and then Matt was on her, ripping at her costume. She came fully awake at once, thrashing about, prompting Matt to punch her twice more—*BAM! BAM!*—before returning to his furious attempt at removing her clothes. Ryan screamed at him to stop, incoherently, but filled with rage and pain and fear. Matt simply laughed, then unfastened his pants.

And then the floor exploded.

CHAPTER TWENTY-FIVE

The first thought that went through Ryan's head was that it had finally happened: the building was collapsing around them. It was going to suck to be killed, but at least he and Kayla could be spared the pain and humiliation of what had been about to happen to them. And, he supposed, at least he would get to see Hunter again, soon. He just hoped his parents were able to recover from his loss.

Then he realized the building hadn't collapsed, despite the fine dust that was raining down on them. He also wasn't being held anymore. He blinked and looked around, and discovered his former captors holding their arms over their heads, trying to shield themselves from any potentially dangerous debris. Matt had paused in the midst of undoing his pants, holding one hand up keep the dust from his eyes as he stared at something not too far away from them. Ryan turned to see what had captured his attention, and felt his breath catch in his throat.

Francis stood there, legs bent, arms loose at his side, appearing to pant despite not needing to breathe. His eyes were locked onto Matt. They actually looked like they were glowing faintly—not red, the way Ryan would've expected from all the movies, but simply brighter than normal. His face had changed subtly as well, no longer that of his normal carefree-but-world-worn self, but of the monster he claimed to be the opposite of.

All in all, he looked absolutely terrifying.

It suddenly occurred to Ryan that Francis said he wasn't at his peak, was in fact still recovering from his time lying dormant with a stake in his chest. Yet, for all of that, he'd just burst through a concrete floor and looked none the worse for wear because of it. It didn't look like the floor was all that thick, not from this angle, but it was still concrete, and bits of it were settling on Ryan's shoulders.

Not that this realization did anything to calm Ryan's nerves. If anything, it put them more on edge.

"Tell me, laddie," Francis said. His voice was harsh, clipped, as though everything he'd learned about how to be civil had been wiped away. "What in the hell do you think ye be doin'?"

"What the fuck?" Matt whispered. His eyes were wide, locked onto Francis's terrifying face, and Ryan thought he could see the older boy starting to tremble a bit. The trembling got worse when Francis took a step toward him.

"Nah, shan't just tell you," Francis said, and that playful tone only served to scare Ryan even more than he already was. "Let me show you."

Ryan's mind wanted to think that Francis had closed the distance to Matt, or ran at him, or anything along those lines, but such thoughts would imply that he'd actually seen the vampire move. He must have, but it had been too fast for Ryan's brain to register. One moment he was standing next to the edge of the hole in the floor, and the next he was standing beside where Matt was kneeling, holding the bully aloft with one slim hand wrapped around his throat.

Francis growled, a low, primal sound that made the hair on the back of Ryan's neck stand up. He drew Matt close, so close it crazily looked like they were about to kiss, and then thrust his hand back out, letting go at the last instant. Matt sailed down the hallway before slamming into the doorframe and bouncing off again. He hit the floor and rolled, disappearing back into the reception area.

Someone yelled behind Ryan, startling him. He turned to see Zach rush past him, apparently intent on defending his friend. How he thought he was going to fare any better after this skinny little man had just tossed his burly best friend away like a kid tossing a stone into the river, Ryan couldn't imagine, but he had to give the boy points for loyalty, if not for intelligence.

As soon as he got close enough, Francis rammed out one fist, not even looking away from the spot where Matt had disappeared and drove Zach backward like a fastball knocked for a home run. Zach staggered backward, blood and broken teeth spewing out of his ruined mouth in equal measure, turned, tripped over his own feet, and then fell to the floor next to Ryan where he lay still. Ryan stared at him, hoping the vampire hadn't killed him, concerned only because of what it might mean for Francis if he had. He looked back up and saw Francis had stopped and was staring over at Brandon.

"You going to take a try, too?"

Brandon held up both hands and backed away until he hit the wall. "I didn't even want to be a part of this to start with, man. We're cool."

Francis smiled. Ryan heard a soft pattering sound and noticed liquid dripping from Brandon's pants leg onto the concrete floor.

"No, laddie, we are worlds from that," Francis said. "But you get a chance. Run. Don't look back."

Brandon needed no further prompting. He turned and raced down the hallway. Ryan had no idea where he thought he was going, since he was headed deeper into the hospital, but that thought obviously hadn't crossed the older boy's mind yet.

Francis laughed and returned to stalking Matt.

Once he was gone, Ryan seemed to regain control of his body and scrambled over to where Kayla lay shaking on the other side of the hallway, her back to him. He knelt beside her and placed a tentative hand on her shoulder. She jerked away from him, then turned and saw his face and practically leapt into his arms. Tears had turned her face into a blotchy, sodden mess, and her costume was ripped and torn in several places, exposing a red bra and the traces of a pair of black panties, but none of this interested Ryan at the moment. The only thing he cared about was that she hadn't been seriously hurt, aside from the punches Matt had landed on her, and that she didn't appear to hate him for what had nearly happened to her.

He held her, stroking her hair and her back as she wept into his shoulder. Little by little she got herself back under control. He felt her pull away and while he didn't want to let her go, not yet, he also didn't want to keep her from doing what she apparently wanted, either. She'd had enough of that for one night.

She wiped her face with both hands and offered him a weak smile before glancing off down the hallway to where Ryan could faintly hear Francis mockingly calling out for Matt. When she looked back to him, stark fear was playing across her eyes.

"What was that?" she asked.

Ryan sighed. "You know how some people have guardian angels?"

She gave him a look of such utter confusion that he very nearly laughed. Thankfully, the situation was still much too tense for that.

"Well," he continued. "It seems we have a guardian vampire."

By the way she started staring at him, Ryan knew she was about to ask if he was really trying to make jokes right now. When she turned and looked from the hole in the floor, to Zach's unconscious—or dead, he still wasn't sure about that—body, to the puddle left by Brandon before his flight, and then back to Ryan, though, there was enough doubt and belief mixing on her face for him to know she didn't think he was completely insane.

Before he could explain, they heard a scream from the reception area. It had to be either Matt or Francis and from the high-pitched terror that filled it, Ryan was fairly certain it wasn't the vampire. This was followed by a massive crashing sound, and then glass tinkling onto the floor. Then, a series of heavy steps followed by crunching as someone—Francis, presumably—stepped through the broken window and out into the courtyard beyond.

And then, most alarmingly, many, many more screams.

Ryan looked over at Kayla, panic rising in his chest. "Can you walk?"

"Yeah," she replied. "I'm still shaken up, but I'm okay. Why?"

"Because we need to get out there, or someone's going to end up dead."

Her face took on a mask of anger. "Fuck Matt. He deserves whatever he's going to get."

"He's not the reason I want to stop this," Ryan said. He got to his feet and held out a hand to help her do the same. Once he was sure she wasn't just telling him what she thought he wanted to hear, and truly was able to walk, he pulled her after him as he rushed back outside, hoping he made it before Francis did something irreversible.

They made it outside just in time to see the vampire had caught up with Matt. He was holding the bully upside down by one ankle, laughing as the boy screamed and flailed. He seemed to grow tired of this, so he jerked his arm quickly, flicking his wrist. Ryan could hear the snap as Matt's bones broke from all the way across the courtyard. Matt's frantic screams somehow got even louder and shriller, his thrashing coming to a halt as he reached for his demolished ankle.

Francis tossed him casually to one side, watching as he sailed across the ground before slamming against the tailgate of one of the trucks, sending half-empty liquor bottles and red plastic cups flying in all directions. The vampire glanced down, noticing something on his hand. Ryan tentatively moved closer, feeling resistance as Kayla tried to keep him from doing so. He saw with no surprise that it was Zach's blood.

The vampire lifted his hand to his mouth and sucked the blood from his knuckles, his eyes rolling up slightly as he savored it. After another couple of licks to make sure he'd gotten everything he could, he started toward the truck where Matt lay groaning in the bed.

"Francis!" Ryan yelled. He could barely hear himself over the pounding in his ears from his increased heartbeat. "He's had enough! Don't do this!"

Francis paused and glanced over to him. Ryan recoiled when he met the vampire's gaze. There was nothing of the man he'd come to know in his eyes, only a wild hunger. There was no question the thing before him was a beast, a predator.

And now it had the scent of weak prey. Francis looked away and continued stalking toward the truck. Ryan jerked free of Kayla's grasp and ran across the courtyard, putting himself directly in front of the vampire, cutting him off from his intended victim.

"Move," Francis said.

"You said you weren't the monster," Ryan replied. He could feel tears starting to sting at his eyes, more terrified than he'd been in his entire life, but he stood his ground. "You do this, what you're about to do, you're no better than him."

Francis laughed, but it was the furthest thing from humorous laughter that Ryan had ever heard. "You think I'm no better than this pathetic cow? I've had potato soup with more backbone."

"Not him," Ryan said, shaking his head. "He's a piece of shit, but he's done. He's beaten. If you do this, you're no better than the other one. You'll be just like him. You'll be a child killer."

Francis snarled and raised his hand. Ryan closed his eyes, waiting for the blow to land, to break his jaw, or even his neck, but it never did. When he finally chanced opening his eyes again, he saw Francis staring at him, arms at his sides. His face had lost its ferocity, had reverted back to the mask of humanity he normally wore; and Ryan knew now it was a mask, knew without any shadow of doubt.

After a long, tense moment, he could see in Francis's eyes that the vampire knew it as well. He shook his head and turned back toward the asylum.

"Go home, kid," Francis said. His voice was tired, but it was back to normal as well. "I'm here if you need me, but it's probably best you try to forget about me."

Ryan watched him go, and then turned back to the crowd milling about, watching the horrific drama play out. He saw their faces, shocked, frightened, and amazed. He saw their eyes, many filled with tears. Then he froze when he saw their hands, all holding phones.

All recording everything that just happened.

He stumbled back over to Kayla, who was watching him with a mixture of fear, worry, and admiration. He nearly fell into her arms. Thankfully, she held him, the way he'd held her only minutes before, stroking his back, soothing him.

He couldn't even explain that Francis wasn't the bad guy—she'd seen proof otherwise. He couldn't explain that he only wanted to help the vampire, the way Francis had done for him. He couldn't explain that all of that was ruined now, ruined by those phones and their all-seeing lenses. Even if he somehow managed to convince the few people who'd been closest to the action to keep it to themselves, it wouldn't matter. Enough had filmed the gory details to undo all his attempts at protecting Francis.

By morning, those videos would be online, and would have already been seen by hundreds, if not thousands, of people.

Including the vampire hunters.

The plan was going to work, but not at all like he'd hoped.

Ryan did the only thing left for him to do. He began to cry.

CHAPTER TWENTY-SIX

Ryan spent the next week in a state of near-constant panic, waiting to see the full impact of the fallout from the party. The video was online by the time he got home—admittedly delayed since he'd had to deal with the cops who had showed up not long after Francis had disappeared back into the hospital once more. There was no denying his involvement, since all the officers had to do was look at that video from one of a dozen different angles to see that he was the one who finally got Francis to stop. He also had no other choice but to tell what happened the way he'd seen it; too many people were able to contradict any lies he told. He did leave out the fact that Francis was a vampire, as well as leaving out his name, but he had to give his description, which was bad enough.

Kayla was more than willing to keep her story as rooted in the world of the normal as he was. After making Ryan swear he would explain everything, she'd tried to protect Francis the same way he had. To her mind, the vampire had saved her from a fate worse than death, and supernatural creature or not, she was grateful for his interference.

Matt and Zach were the only ones to maintain that the man who'd attacked them wasn't human—once they both regained consciousness and were given enough painkillers to be able to speak at all, that was. Brandon was the surprise that proved them wrong, however. He had confessed to everything, lending credence to Kayla's former insistence that he wasn't all that bad on his own, and when pressed about the superhuman abilities their attacker had possessed, he insisted that he'd been so freaked out he couldn't be sure what he saw and let it go at that.

It was two days before Ryan got the chance to tell Kayla about Francis. He could've done it at any time before then, really, but he'd wanted to make sure he was able to take her to the asylum to find the vampire, so he could prove what he was saying was true. When they arrived, though, Francis was nowhere to be seen, and his makeshift apartment in the basement was mostly disassembled as well. Ryan had no idea where he'd gone, but he was sure the vampire was hiding out, most likely waiting until the hunters had been and gone before revealing himself again.

If he ever would. There was every possibility that Francis had left town and had no intention of coming back. Some part of Ryan hoped the vampire would just show up at his house some night, the way he'd done when he almost caught him and Kayla in the middle of something, but that didn't happen, either.

Thankfully, Kayla believed his story without the need for additional proof. She'd seen what happened at the party just like everyone else had.

The police briefly considered Francis as a suspect in the other killings, but as the week wore on with no sign they were actively looking for him, Ryan assumed they'd realized that someone who was killing kids after molesting them wouldn't have saved Kayla from being raped to start with.

But when Ryan checked the number of views on the videos people had posted to YouTube and Facebook and everywhere else on the internet they could broadcast such things, he knew it was only a matter of time before someone better equipped to find both Francis and the killer showed up in town. As the view count rose, so did the likelihood of the hunters arriving. For the same reasons he hadn't been able to make up a story for the cops, he knew they would be coming to find him, first. He'd faced off against a vampire, and the vampire had listened to him. Worse, one of the videos clearly caught the brief conversation between them, including Francis's admonition for him to go home. The police didn't think anything much about that, but the hunters most assuredly would.

Or so he thought, at least. He knew less about vampire hunters than he did about vampires themselves at this point.

On the plus side, the fact that he'd stood up to a potential killer in front of everyone at the party had earned him notoriety of sorts. Kids at school that he'd never so much as shared a passing glance with went out of their way to stop him in the hallway and say hello. He even started to wonder if he should just walk from class to class with one hand held up in a fist to receive all the bumps that were sent his way. He knew he'd be lying if he said he didn't enjoy it, but he still didn't trust it. Kayla said it was because they finally got the chance to see the genuinely cool guy he was. He knew he was just the hero of the moment, wandering confused through his fifteen minutes of fame.

This was why he didn't pay too much attention to the old muscle car that pulled up alongside him as he and Kayla walked home from school on the Friday after the party. He could see two people inside, and while he couldn't make out anything about the man behind the wheel, he could see the passenger was a young girl, not much older than him. When the car slowed enough to match his and Kayla's pace and the window began to slide down, he sighed, bracing himself for another round of insincere "you're awesome."

When the girl in the passenger seat leaned her head out and turned her sunglass-covered eyes his direction, he saw that his initial guess had been a bit off the mark. She looked older than he'd first assumed, maybe college-age instead of high school. Her shortish, bleached hair stood up in little spikes atop her head, mixing with those big aviator-style glasses and the leather coat zipped all the way to her neck to make her look more like a punk-rock reject from the eighties as opposed to the kind of person you'd see on a college campus in this day and time. If not for that obvious youthful quality to her skin, he might have re-thought even his second assessment and put her as an aging middle-aged woman who was trying her hardest to look young again.

"Hey, man," she said, her voice sounding a little harsh but still much too young for her attire. "Can you give us some directions? We're kind of new here."

He started to angle toward the car, and then felt Kayla's grip on his hand tighten, holding him back. He glanced to her, saw the slight shake of her head, and remained where he was.

"Maybe," he said. "Where are you going?"

She pulled the glasses down her nose, staring at him with eyes so blue they didn't look real. "We hear there's some old abandoned insane asylum around here still got one patient left. Know anything about that?"

Ryan went stone still, his back tightening and forcing him to stand a little straighter than he had been. It took him a minute to work moisture back into his mouth so he could answer. He shook his head slowly, trying to look confused. "No, that doesn't sound familiar."

A hand appeared from the back seat, handing the girl a tablet computer. Ryan realized for the first time that there was someone lying down back there. He doubted they were hiding—otherwise why give themselves away by something as casual as that handoff?—but it was still unnerving that he couldn't see them.

The girl turned the tablet so he could see the screen. Ryan winced when he saw the video cued up, his face frozen in an expression of pleading, his hands held out toward the lithe man who stood before him, nearly towering over him.

"You sure about that?" the girl asked, arching one eyebrow.

"Who are you?" he asked, already knowing the general answer if not the specific ones.

"Look, we don't want to hurt you, man," she said, pushing the glasses back into place with her free hand. "We just want to talk. You might be in more danger than you can imagine."

Ryan's mouth worked, but he could come up with no response that would make them go away and leave him alone. Thankfully, Kayla came to his rescue.

"You said you're new around here," she said. "So maybe you don't know there's somebody killing kids in town. Not really a good idea to just pull up to a couple of them and start talking like this."

The girl glanced over to the driver, who shrugged but remained silent. She turned back to Ryan and Kayla.

"Actually, we do know that," she said. "Which is why we need to talk."

"If you know that already," Ryan said, finally finding his voice again. "Then do you know he's a vampire?"

The girl's lips twitched like she wanted to smile but didn't quite dare. Not yet. "I thought you didn't know anything."

A muffled voice said something Ryan couldn't make out, drawing the girl back into the car once more. He considered grabbing Kayla and running but knew they would only chase after him and catch him. Even if they let him go today, they'd find him again eventually. Better to get this over now than wait and wonder and look over his shoulder until it happened.

After a brief conversation, the girl's face reappeared at the window.

"All right, let's make a deal, here," she began. "You don't know us, and you don't want to talk to us. At the same time, you want this killer stopped. Am I right so far?"

"I'm listening," Ryan said.

"You also know what this guy really is, which is damned interesting in and of itself," she went on. "Which makes me and my friends curious. So let's do this: you set the terms. What's it going to take to get you to help us find out what we need to find out?"

"What if I ask for money?" Ryan asked. Kayla gave him a strange look but didn't contradict him.

"Are you?" the girl replied.

"Maybe."

The girl laughed and for a moment, Ryan saw her as the young woman she really was beyond the tough guy act. It was a genuine expression, which strangely did much to help him relax.

"Do you see this beast we're in?" the girl asked. "Does it look like we've got money?"

Ryan opened his mouth to answer, and then stopped. The obvious answer was that they didn't, but he thought that was part of the act, just like the hair style and the sunglasses and the leather jacket. Something to make people think one thing when another was actually true.

"Here's what I think," he finally answered. "Gas isn't cheap, and from what my dad has said, those old cars drink it like water. Plus, that coat's easily a hundred and fifty bucks, and since all we have to do is scream to get the police here, the fact that you don't seem worried about that means you probably didn't steal it. So, to answer your question, no, it doesn't look like you have money, but that's just what you want me to think. The truth is that you probably have some fairly deep pockets."

This time, the girl took the sunglasses off completely and tossed them casually onto the dashboard of the car. "I'm impressed, brother. You are most definitely smarter than I gave you credit for, and I truly apologize for that. But that brings us back to the original question: are you asking us for money?"

"No," Ryan said. He had no idea where the feeling he suddenly had was coming from, but he knew that he needed to somehow take control of this situation if he ever hoped to point them in the direction he wanted them to go. "What I'm asking for is respect."

A hint of a smile played at the girl's lips again. "Fair enough."

He chewed on his bottom lip, and then gestured in the direction of the little downtown business strip. "About two miles back that way, there's a diner. We're in between the lunch and dinner rushes, so there shouldn't be many people there. You buy me and my girlfriend dinner, and I'll talk to you."

The girl started to smile again, and Ryan held up his hand.

"But if I don't want to answer something you ask me, I don't have to. Respect, like I said."

The girl glanced back into the car again, and Ryan saw the driver give another of those noncommittal shrugs. She turned back to him. "Deal. Need a lift?"

"Thanks," Ryan said. "But I think we'll walk. We'll be there in a few minutes."

The smile finally came to her lips as she narrowed her eyes at him. "And how do we know you're not just going to run off and turn us in to the cops for messing with you?"

Ryan smiled back. "Because respect works both ways."

The girl nodded, grabbed her sunglasses, and put them back on. "See you in a few."

The car pulled away, then made a U-turn in the middle of the street and headed back the way Ryan had indicated. He watched it go, and then turned to find Kayla giving him an appraising look.

"I hope you know what you're doing," she said.

He turned back to watch the car's tail lights disappear around a corner. "So do I."

CHAPTER TWENTY-SEVEN

Much to his surprise, the trio from the car was apparently willing to take the "giving respect" angle as far as they could. When Ryan and Kayla walked up the sidewalk to the diner, they saw the car was parked in one of the available spots right near the doors, and while the three occupants had gotten out, they hadn't yet entered the diner, apparently willing to concede even something as simple as which table they picked to him. He supposed it was possible they were doing it out of spite, just to mess with him, but he hadn't expected it at all, so he was going to take it as a sign of possible cooperation.

As if he had much of a choice. He wasn't positive that these three were the vampire hunters he'd been expecting to show up, but it made sense. Seeing them all together now only proved that they were cut from the same basic cloth. The girl was leaning against the car, still wearing her sunglasses despite the fact the sun was already dipping below the horizon. Her posture was that of someone who was completely relaxed, but Ryan could feel those eyes watching him and Kayla approaching, and he knew she was probably ready to leap into action if there was a reason to. Some part of him had been expecting the leather tough-chick look to continue all the way to her feet, but instead of biker gear she wore a simple pair of jeans and scuffed sneakers.

And older man was leaning against the other side of the car, bald head resting on the roof as he stared up at the sky. Ryan couldn't make out much more than his profile, but his cheeks were dotted with salt-and-pepper stubble, putting him around the age that he could be the girl's father.

A younger man, somewhere around the girl's age, sat on the hood of the car idly smoking a cigarette. He was the only one of the three not wearing a coat from what Ryan could see, but the cold wind didn't seem to bother him. He was wearing a t-shirt with some obscure band's logo emblazoned across the front, black cargo pants, and black work boots. Of the three, he was the closest to what Ryan imagined a vampire hunter would look like, though it was still something of a stretch.

"So, I've got to ask," Kayla said, once they'd come closer. "Who finances you guys, Buffy or the Winchesters?"

"Jesus fucking Christ," the younger guy muttered, tossing his cigarette onto the pavement and stomping a foot down on it to make sure it was extinguished. "Here we go. Can we get this over with, for fuck's sake?"

The girl actually smiled. "I asked the same thing, hon. Got the same response. I take it this was the place you had in mind?"

"It is," Ryan answered. There were several reasons he'd picked this diner to meet, not the least of which being that he really was getting hungry. The two biggest, though, were that the entire front of the building was glass, meaning there wasn't a more public place where they could get any sort of privacy in town. The second, and the one that could end up working against him as much as it helped him, was that the owners knew him, and knew his parents. They'd attended the same church, and although Ryan himself didn't usually go anymore, his parents still did. If anything untoward were to happen to him, he could rest assured that descriptions of these three would be in the hands of the cops before he even finished yelling for help.

The girl nodded, took off her sunglasses, and stashed them in one of the pockets of her jacket before gesturing toward the door. "Then let's eat."

"Shouldn't we introduce ourselves, first?" Ryan asked. "Since you're going to pry into my life, I think that much is fair before we start, right?"

Her hand dropped as she shook her head, chuckling. "You're something else, man, you know that? Fine."

She pointed to the older guy on the other side of the car, who had turned and was watching them suspiciously over the roof. Ryan's guess about his age had been pretty close judging by the lines in his face to go along with the graying hair on his cheeks. "That's Joe. I guess if I'm the spokesperson for our little group, you can call him the brains. And, in case that wasn't clear enough, he's the boss. So that respect thing you're so keen on? Keep it in mind."

She jerked a thumb in the direction of the younger guy, who was watching them just like Joe was, only with a scowl instead of suspicion. "That's Mario. Call him the muscle. Definitely not the brains. You'll figure it out."

"Real fucking nice," Mario muttered again.

"I'm Carrie," the girl finished. "Like I said, I'm the talker. Call me public relations, if you want. Your turn."

"You don't already know?" Ryan asked.

"We've seen both your faces on grainy cellphone videos uploaded to the internet, kid," Joe said. His voice was gravelly, as if he'd smoked five packs a day for most of his life. "They didn't exactly come with subtitles or identification panels."

If they'd been doing any research on him, they were good about not giving that fact away. Ryan would just have to wait and see how much they knew. In a way, it was a good sign. It meant he could spin the story some, and possibly still manage to keep Francis out of their direct line of fire. "This is Kayla, and I'm Ryan."

"And you've been... do they still call it 'going steady' now?" Carrie asked. She waved a hand. "Whatever it is, you've been doing it... a month, give or take?"

Ryan thought it, but it was Kayla who said it. "How could you possibly know that?"

Carrie laughed. "Body language, hon. You two have been holding hands every time we've seen you, and from how tight your grips are, I'm surprised you've got any circulation left in your fingers."

Ryan and Kayla both looked down at the same time and were almost comically surprised to see that the girl was right. Carrie laughed harder.

"I'll admit, we've been watching you since we got into town," she said. "It's not hard to see new puppy love when it's on full display for you."

He bristled at hearing it demeaned like that, but Kayla laughed, which helped him to relax as well. "Cute."

"It is at that," Carrie agreed. "Now that we're all introduced, can we get to this? I wasn't before, but now that we're here, I'm a little hungry myself."

Ryan shrugged. Joe pushed away from the car and moved to the diner's main door, opened it, and held it for the rest of them. As he passed, Ryan saw the source of that raspy voice: a long, puckered pink scar that ran across one side of Joe's throat. It was thin, which meant it wasn't from a rope—though he could only blame Quentin Tarantino and Brad Pitt's character in Inglorious Bastards for that particular thought—and looked to have been made cleanly whenever it happened. He glanced up and saw that Joe had caught him staring, but instead of being angry or self-conscious about it, he actually seemed to be grinning slightly. Ryan quickly looked away and pulled Kayla with him into the diner.

He didn't see Mister or Missus Richards, the couple who owned the place, but their oldest daughter Molly was leaning against the counter, talking to the grizzled old short-order cook whose name Ryan could never remember. It wasn't exactly what he'd been hoping for, since he didn't know Molly nearly as well as he did her parents, but at least they were acquainted, so she would be able to identify the three with him should anything happen.

She turned and smiled at him and Kayla as they entered. The smile froze when she noticed the other three filing in behind them, her eyes narrowing as she sized them up. Finally, she turned her eyes back to Ryan.

"Hey guys, you doing all right today?"

"Doing fine," Ryan answered. "Can we get a table for five, Molly?"

Her eyes narrowed again, marginally, then went back to normal as she tried to hide her suspicion. "Sure thing. Who's your friends? I don't think I've seen them around before."

Maybe she wasn't hiding that suspicion as well as Ryan thought she would. Naturally, it was Carrie who took over at that point, stepping forward with a hand outstretched.

"Hi, I'm Carrie Tempest," she said. "I'm Kayla's cousin. This is my dad and my brother. Kayla and Ryan here agreed to show us around town, but we insisted they find us a good place to eat first."

Molly tentatively shook Carrie's hand, glancing from her to Ryan to Kayla, who simply smiled back at her. Ryan tried to adopt a similar nonchalant smile as well, hoping it didn't look anywhere near as fake as it felt. From the way Molly's posture relaxed, he thought it had done the trick.

"It's such a pleasure to meet you," she said. "And they definitely brought you to the right place. There's a table over there in the corner, right next to the window. Should be perfect for you. Head on over and I'll bring some menus."

"Can't wait!" Carrie replied.

The group moved over to the table and sat down, Ryan making sure he and Kayla were in the best position to run if they needed to. Joe snorted as they took their seats, making Ryan wonder if he'd figured them out that easily, and decided that he probably had. He had a feeling the man didn't miss much at all. Molly appeared a moment later, passing out the familiar one-page menu for the diner, took their drink orders, then left to go prepare them. Ryan sat his menu on the table, as did Kayla. They'd both eaten here enough over the years that they didn't need them to order anymore. Carrie glanced over hers briefly, but Joe and Mario both set theirs aside as well.

"Okay," Kayla said. "I've got to tell you, 'cousin Carrie,' you've got the fakest sounding name I've ever heard."

Carrie glanced at her over the top of her menu, her lips twitching. "What makes you say that?"

Kayla shrugged. "I don't know, just sounds... off."

Carrie chuckled and went back to looking at the menu, not bothering to respond further. Kayla blew out an exasperated breath and crossed her arms across her chest as she leaned back in her chair.

Molly chose that moment to reappear, a tray of drinks balanced on one hand. She transferred them to the table—coke for Ryan and Kayla, coffee for Joe, tea for Carrie, and water, no lemon for Mario—then took their orders. Ryan got his usual, a basic cheeseburger and fries, and Kayla ordered pork chops. Joe, surprisingly, opted for the same thing Ryan got. Carrie went for the house salad, a strange choice, Ryan thought, for the amount of time she'd spent studying the menu, and Mario continued his stand-offish behavior by ordering nothing. Molly smiled, gave them one last appraising glance, then left to put the orders in.

"Okay, kid," Joe said, after sipping his coffee. "Start talking."

"Not so fast," Ryan said. "Fair is fair, right? And isn't respect earned by giving and receiving? So I'll answer your questions as long as you answer mine."

"Listen, you little shit," Mario hissed, leaning toward him. "You have no idea who you're fucking with here, so why don't you...?"

He stopped as Joe laid a hand on his shoulder and pulled him back into his chair. After giving him a stern look, Joe turned back to Ryan and smiled.

"One condition," he said. "Am I safe in assuming you're only going to answer the questions you want to the way you want to?"

Ryan mulled the question over, and then shrugged. "Guess you'll have to ask and see."

"Then the same goes both ways," Joe agreed. "Ask whatever you want, but we're under no obligation to actually answer you. See, respect is also allowing someone you just met to keep their secrets, wouldn't you agree?"

It wasn't what he wanted, but Ryan had to concede that point. He had been the one to hammer the respect bit, so it would hardly give him any benefit to back out of it now. Dad had told him many times that respect could only be given to a certain point. To truly have someone's respect, you had to earn it. And that began by granting them the same courtesies you wanted them to grant you.

"Deal," he said. "So, while Kayla was joking earlier, I'm betting you do work for someone else, so who is it? Is it a single person, or an organization, or what?"

Carrie glanced over at Joe, who gave her a brief nod. "We're not the only ones involved in this crusade, you're right about that. But that's all I can say about it, for now. So looks like it's your turn, man. What happened at that asylum?"

"No," Joe said. "I've got a better question."

For the first time, Carrie's good-natured façade slipped. She turned and stared at the older man, but he wasn't paying her any attention. Instead, his eyes were locked on Ryan's face, that strange little smile still set on his lips.

"A better question," she repeated. "Better than the reason we're here in the first place?"

"Much better," he said. He moved his cup of coffee to the side and crossed his arms on the table, leaning over it slightly, his gaze never wavering. "Why are you so damned defensive?"

"I..." Ryan started, suddenly feeling the force of will behind those eyes. "I don't know what you mean."

"Sure you do," Joe replied. "Make a deal to talk to us at all, then make another one to guarantee you can evade whatever you don't want to answer. Sit in the perfect power position at this table, and by the same turn, the easiest to get away without making us look like we've got something other than your best intentions at heart. So I genuinely want to know: why are you so defensive?"

Ryan swallowed, and looked over at Kayla. She sighed, and then gave him a slight nod.

"The guy you're here for," he said. "He's not the one you should be after."

"He's not?"

"No," Ryan said, shaking his head. "He's one of the good guys."

Mario brayed laughter so loud it made Molly snap her head around to stare at them. Carrie gave Ryan a look of stark disbelief. Joe's expression, however, never changed. He simply nodded once to acknowledge he'd heard what Ryan said.

"One of the good guys," he repeated slowly. "You do know what that 'guy' really is, don't you?"

Ryan decided that he wasn't about to be cowed by the man, if that was indeed what he was attempting to do. He met Joe's eyes and nodded. "He's a...."

Joe held up a hand, cutting him off. "Don't say it out loud. You start talking like that in public and people are going to think you've lost your mind. You've got enough attention on you right now, kid. That's not the kind you want added onto it."

He studied Ryan carefully, then nodded once more and took another sip of his coffee. "You think it's your friend, don't you?"

"He."

"Pardon?"

"He, not it," Ryan insisted. "And yes, he's my friend."

Mario let out another burst of laughter. Carrie actually winced and lowered her head, shaking it slowly.

"I'm going to tell you something you're not going to want to hear," Joe said. "That thing is nobody's friend. Friendship requires an emotional bond, and I haven't met one of those things capable of that. You might think that he's your friend, but the truth is that best case, you're serving a purpose. Worst case, he's just waiting for the right time to strike, once you've exhausted whatever sick amusement you're providing for him."

"What makes you so sure?"

"Because I've seen it happen. More times than I care to remember. And every single time, it's ended badly for the person who put their trust in one of those things. You seem like a nice enough kid, and you're actually a lot smarter than your age indicates. You don't know me from Adam, but I'm betting you can tell I'm being sincere, so believe me when I say I do not want your death on my conscience, if I can prevent it.

"So let me tell you how things have gone so far, and you tell me afterward if I was wrong about anything. If I'm wrong, correct me. I'll listen to you, so long as you do the same for me. Deal?"

The man was right about Ryan not wanting to hear this, but at the same time, he felt like he needed to. "Deal."

Joe leaned back, sipped his coffee, and then glanced toward the kitchen, gauging how much time they had before the food arrived. When it seemed they weren't about to be interrupted in the next minute or so, he turned back to Ryan.

"You met on accident," he began. "How doesn't really matter. You were lonely, or afraid. Maybe he even attacked you, then stopped himself. That part always has similar highlights, but the specifics vary. Anyway, you did what any normal person would do when faced with something like that, something you thought was a fairy tale suddenly coming to life right in front of you: you ran. But you couldn't stop thinking about it, about what a chance this could be. So, against your better judgment, you went back. He talked to you, like an equal. He told you about his hopes and dreams before he changed. Told you who he was before. Insisted that he wasn't like the rest, that he was no monster. And you believed him. How am I doing so far?"

Ryan kept his hands under the table so they couldn't see how badly they were shaking. He hoped he could keep that shake out of his voice. "Go on."

"You kept going back, and everything you saw proved he was right," Joe continued. "He maybe even did things for you without you having to ask, things that helped prove what he was telling you was true. Things seemed fine, until that one time, when something happened that showed you who he really is. Something that even though you tried to justify it to yourself, you felt that first tingle of doubt. You walked away from it, sure, but for that brief moment, you doubted."

He leaned forward again. "Now I'm betting that event happened, and I'm betting it's what we've already seen on video. That being the case, let me tell you what happens next, if you don't help us stop it. That doubt won't go away. It's going to grow. You've probably already tried to find him, get him to explain, but it either wasn't successful or wasn't good enough. One day, though, you will see him. He'll beg forgiveness, insist it was a moment of weakness, and because you're a good kid who tries to see the good in him, you'll overlook that doubt and give him a second chance."

He held up a finger. "When that happens, it's too late. You've let him in too far. The time for it to all come crashing down is never consistent, but the day will come when you and he are together, and everything seems fine, and then the next thing you know, he's on you, and you realize you're nothing more than food to him, nothing more than a plaything. Of course, by the time you understand, it's too late. Because within seconds of understanding, you're too dead to do anything about it."

As if proving that wait staff are trained to look for the most inopportune moments, Molly appeared with their food. Joe leaned back, smiled at her, and complimented her on the coffee. Her cheeks reddened a bit, and he became the first to be served. He didn't bother to wait for the others to get their food before he popped a fry into his mouth and made exaggerated noises of enjoyment.

Once the food was in front of them and Molly was gone again, blushing furiously for no real reason Ryan could see, Carrie reached over and laid a hand gently on his arm.

"Was he wrong?"

He turned to Kayla, who was alternately looking at him with concern and shooting daggers at Carrie, then dropped his eyes and sighed.

"He's wrong."

"About what?"

Ryan looked up, ignoring Carrie, focusing his gaze back on Joe. "If he's so bad, why is he helping to try and find this guy who's killing kids? Why did he refuse when I asked him to make me like him?"

Carrie recoiled from him at that. Mario stared at him in amazement, and while he didn't see her expression, he could hear Kayla's shocked gasp beside him. Joe's face took on a contemplative expression.

"You asked him to turn you?"

"He said the real killer was like him," Ryan said, ignoring the question. "Or, more like what you're describing, anyway."

"He told you that."

"Yeah," Ryan said, feeling anger start to bubble up from inside him. "He did. He went after the other one, tried to fight him. Got beaten pretty badly because he didn't expect him to be... one of them."

"How did he get beaten?"

Ryan shook his head. "I don't know. Something about a psychic attack."

"You saw it?"

"No," Ryan replied. "He told me about it after."

"I see. Did this attack leave any physical signs?"

"Well, no," Ryan said. "It was a psychic attack. Mental?"

"Of course, my mistake."

Ryan shook his head, his anger barely held in check. "He was trying to find out who killed my best friend."

Joe nodded, and then scratched idly at the scar on his neck. "Did you know that many times a serial killer will try to interject themselves into the investigation somehow? That way they know where the cops stand on such things. It's even one of the things profilers look for when building their assessment of the possible suspect."

"F.... He didn't kill Hunter."

"Did he tell you that, too?"

"This is bullshit!" Ryan screamed, standing up so fast his chair fell over with a loud crash. "You're looking in the wrong place! You want the one that's doing this? There's an access road near the abandoned factory on Friar's Mill Road. That's where my friend saw this other one, and where that attack happened. He said one of the kids who's been taken was taken there, too, so why don't you go check that out and stop trying to pawn it off on someone else just because you can't see past your own racism?"

Mario was the first to respond, blinking and then looking over to Joe. "Did he seriously just call us racists?"

"Fuck you!" Ryan screamed, then turned and stormed off toward the exit. He heard Kayla calling to him, and heard her own chair moving as she got up to quickly chase after him, but he was beyond caring. He'd been trying to call these people here to help, but they weren't willing to listen to him—and why should they? He was just a kid, one who'd lost his best friend, and now was starting to think he was about to lose another, all because of some asshole vampire who'd chosen his hometown to mess with.

The last thing he heard before he pushed through the door and into the early evening was Carrie's stunned voice coming from the table he'd just made an ass of himself leaving.

"That went well," she said.

CHAPTER TWENTY-EIGHT

Carrie stood up, ready to chase after the kid, a little surprised at the vehemence of his outburst. She'd seen there was some steel in him that she never would've expected, but violence wasn't even in her mind until she'd seen how his eyes flashed when he knocked his chair over. She made it two steps toward the door before Joe's voice stopped her.

"Pick that chair up and sit down."

She turned and stared at him. "You do realize our only chance at finding this thing is currently heading across the parking lot with a look on his face like he's ready to tear something in half, right?"

"He's not our only chance," Joe replied, his voice calm. "Hell, he's not any chance. Or did you miss the fact he's not going to give anything up?"

Carrie stared at him another couple of seconds, then picked up Ryan's chair and put it back into place at the table before sitting back down. "You're just going to let him go, then?"

"For now," Joe agreed, finishing his coffee and setting the empty mug down next to his plate. "He's pissed, but he's thinking about what I told him. Either he'll realize I'm right and come find us, or he won't in which case we can only hope to save him in spite of himself. There's no middle ground."

Despite the fact that Carrie thought he was wrong about that, she held her tongue. Joe had been through more than her and Mario combined, and had been dealing with vampires since before either of them had been born. He was their leader for a reason, and she respected that, even if she didn't always think he was right in his assessments.

"I'll give the kid credit," Mario said, sipping his water. "He's got more balls than I thought he did."

"It's not all him," Joe replied, staring off in the direction the kid had gone. "That thing's got its hooks in him, augmenting him, triggering his emotions in ways the kid never would on his own. I've seen it before."

"Can we help him?" Carrie asked. "Will killing the thing release him?"

Joe gave her a look and she sighed. There was no way to be sure stopping the creature would free its thralls, not without knowing the full extent of their connection. If the kid's anger was enhanced by his connection to the thing, it was very possible killing it would send the kid into an emotional downward spiral.

This was the part of the job she hated. Too many people got hurt that didn't deserve it, their lives irrevocably altered the first time they let one of these semi-immortal monsters talk to them, get in their heads. To see it happening to someone so young was heartbreaking. It didn't help that it brought up some painful memories about her own introduction into this life, either.

"So what now?" she asked. "He never did tell us where that hospital or whatever it was is at."

"I'm sure we can find it," Joe said. "Though the 'killer-on-the-loose' aspect does make it harder to get information from people. Maybe if the bastard wasn't singling out kids for his sick fun."

"You believe that shit about a second one?" Mario asked.

Joe considered it for a moment, and then slowly nodded. "I don't think the kid was lying about that. It wouldn't be the first time we've seen rivals after one another. Even if that is the creature's way of covering its tracks, we can't risk dismissing it until we've checked it out. When we roll out of here, we're going to do it knowing the town's safe from these things for the foreseeable future."

"So what's the plan?"

"Find a hotel," Joe said. "Get checked in. Mario, you're going to take the car and go see if you can't find this hospital or whatever it is. Give it a quick once-over, but don't get stupid about it. That thing's probably hightailed it from there, but you never know. No sense risking your ass unnecessarily without backup. Carrie, you're going to see if you can't track the kid down. Don't approach him, we don't want to push him any more than we already have for right now, but make sure he's safe, if you can."

She nodded. It was what she'd been planning to do all along. "And what are you going to do?"

"This town, the hospital... there's something familiar about it," he said. "I'm going to make some calls, talk to some of the others, see if this rings any bells. It's probably nothing, but anything we can get that might help us, we need to try for."

"What about the factory or whatever the kid mentioned?" Mario asked.

"We'll check it out tomorrow," Joe said. "If that part is true, I'm not about to go hunting anything that powerful after dark. Not until I have a much better idea what I'm going up against."

He nodded to the counter. "Carrie, go settle up, apologize for the ruckus, and leave a big tip. Family squabbles or whatever."

"I can always say you didn't approve of Ryan," she offered. "Tie it into the cover story I gave the waitress."

"Whatever works," Joe said. "Just smooth it over as best you can. I think we've made a big enough scene for one night."

She shrugged and got up, digging a wad of crumpled bills from her jacket pocket as she made her way to the counter. What little good nature the waitress had built up toward them was gone, replaced by a look of deep suspicion that made Carrie wince inwardly. It was hard enough doing something that kept you on the fringes of society for most of your life, but to always get looked at the way the waitress was looking at her now wore you down over time. It wasn't hard to understand why Joe had such hard times making connections beyond the surface ones. She had only been doing it five or six years, and she could already feel the disconnect with the rest of the world setting in.

Thankfully, for moments like this, she'd perfected the art of faking it. She gave the waitress a smile that was both warm and apologetic, expressing with a single look that she knew they'd been a problem, and how sorry she was for that.

"Dad never was good at first impressions," she said, taking on a tone of commiseration to try and win her way back into the woman's good graces. "He sometimes doesn't have an internal filter. Can we just settle up so we can get out of your hair?"

The woman's expression never changed. Carrie should've known. People who lived in towns this small usually all knew each other, at least by sight. The waitress's connection to Ryan probably wasn't as tight as it could be, but it was definitely strong. They would need to watch their step later on, depending how long they ended up being here.

"Forty-five and a quarter," the woman said.

Carrie handed her three twenties and told her to keep it, then turned around and saw Joe and Mario standing just outside the front door. Mario was talking, occasionally gesturing her way, so it didn't take much to figure out who he was talking about. She sighed. Since she'd shot him down about the two of them going out, claiming it wouldn't be good because they worked together in a very high-stress, dangerous job, he'd gone out of his way to make her life hell. Joe saw through the bullshit, at least, and had never said anything to her aside from telling her she'd made the right choice by avoiding romantic entanglements, but it was still annoying. While she knew Mario had her back when the chips were down, it would be nice for them to all get along, too.

As soon as she stepped outside, Mario went silent, further confirming that she'd been the topic of conversation. Joe looked over to her, and then glanced behind her at the waitress. Carrie didn't need to turn to know the woman was still watching them. She could feel her eyes on her back.

"We good?" Joe asked.

"Not really," Carrie admitted. "Small town."

"Damn," he muttered. "Think she's going to sic the cops on us?"

Carrie shook her head slowly. "I don't think so, but she's a tough one to read. I'm not sure if she doesn't buy the story, or if she's just upset we pissed off someone she knew."

"Better assume the worst," he said. "We'll circle the block and drop you back where we first saw the kid. I'm betting it'll take you to the girl's house, but we might get lucky and find out they're neighbors or something."

"Fair enough. What hotel can I find you at later?"

He thought for a minute, and then pointed a little further down the road. "There's a shithole on the edge of town, back the way we drove in. Looks like the perfect place to lay low."

She nodded, fighting back the look of disgust she felt trying to break free. "I remember it."

Joe nodded, slipping back into the contemplative silence that was his normal mode of being, and headed toward the car. Mario gave her one last annoyed glance, and then followed after him. Carrie sighed, and then headed in that direction as well, reminding herself that no matter how annoyed she got, what she was doing was worthwhile.

The car ride was tense and silent, but it was also mercifully short. Carrie was out before Joe even had the vehicle completely stopped, already walking off in the direction Ryan and Kayla had been headed earlier. She heard Joe call out for her to be careful and held a hand up to indicate she'd heard him, not bothering to looking back. She heard the engine rev, then saw the car pull into a nearby driveway and turn around, leaving her alone on the streets of yet another place she didn't know.

She stretched, and then stuck her hands deep into her coat pockets. She should've grabbed a pair of gloves since the air had gone chilly now that the sun was down, but those were packed away in her bag which was locked in the trunk of the car. Mario was obviously in one of his moods, his annoyance at her very nearly a physical thing, so cold fingers were a small price to pay to be free from that for a little while.

It was doubtful that she was going to find Ryan or Kayla just standing outside, making it easy for her to figure out where they were going, so she ran back through her memories, looking over the pictures they'd found on the internet during their initial research of this place. Ryan had actually been named in one of the postings of that video they'd seen, which gave them a good starting place. It had been easy for the organization to find his social media profiles after that. There wasn't much there, but Carrie thought she could remember a few pictures that showed what could well be his house in the background.

The problem, of course, was that most of the houses looked the same in these small-town suburbs. It was going to take a fair bit of luck to find it, especially now that night was coming on.

Maybe she would luck out and find Kayla's house first. She might could even stop and ask the girl where Ryan lived. Then again, judging by those looks the girl was giving her as the aborted dinner wore on, she would be more likely to slam the door in Carrie's face. Ryan seemed like a sweet enough guy, and he obviously cared for the girl, but Carrie had to wonder what could inspire that level of jealousy in someone that young.

But that could be answering her own question. She remembered being young and "in love" herself. She'd said and done some pretty stupid things, too. This was probably nothing more than the exuberance of youth.

Still, it would be nice to find a guy who inspired such feelings in her now. If Ryan had been a few years older, or if she had been a few years younger, maybe she'd have even stolen him from Kayla and seen for herself. But time was what it was, so there was no point in thinking about it.

She looked up and frowned at the sight of a man wandering up the sidewalk in front of her. The way he walked was off somehow, a bit stiff. The long coat with the collar pulled up against the wind wasn't all that out of place, but for some reason she got the sense that the man wasn't doing it to stay warm, but to keep anyone from getting a clear view of his face. It was that style of walking and movement that gave him away. He didn't act cold, just determined.

She froze in place when the man stopped walking, his head tilting as though he heard something he was straining to identify. She turned and started up the sidewalk to one of the nearby houses that didn't look like anyone was home, hoping that if the man turned around, he would think she'd arrived at where she'd been heading. She watched out of the corner of her eye as the man did turn slightly, allowing her to catch a brief flash of reddish hair. He finally resumed his stride, appearing to ignore her completely.

Instincts took over, causing her to dart into the shadows where she could keep an eye on the guy without him being able to see her easily. If it turned out the way she was suddenly expecting it to, the shadows wouldn't really do much good, but at least they could help if this was just some normal guy out for a stroll.

She trailed after him as he made his way down the sidewalk, darting shadow to shadow when she could, doing everything within her power to stay out of sight. She also did the best she could to stay downwind of her quarry. If it was the creature—one of the creatures, she supposed—the last thing she needed was for it to catch a whiff of her. Joe had always claimed they could sense hunters on their trail, and Carrie had seen enough over the years to believe that. She was consciously aware that she was alone, and without the benefit of any of her normal weapons. She reached for her pocket and bit back a cry of irritation when she realized that she'd also left her phone in the car. If something happened, she would have no way to call for backup.

After turning another corner, she stopped, frowning, scanning the empty street before her. She hadn't been that far behind the guy in the coat, so there was no way he should've disappeared this completely this fast, but the fact remained that he apparently had. She blew out a long breath, and then noticed a familiar house a little ways down the street. Added to the man's sudden disappearance, this new discovery was more than a little disconcerting. She glanced behind her to make sure no one was trying to slip up and grab her or anything, and then slowly made her way down the street toward the house.

The downstairs lights were out, but she could see a lamp burning in an upstairs window. Carrie crossed the street, darting into the long shadows next to the house, and looked up at the window. A few minutes later, she was rewarded when a form appeared in the window, staring out at the darkened street. The shape was right, at least from what she could remember. It looked like she'd followed the man in the coat straight to Ryan's house.

She debated for a moment, wanting to try and talk to him, to make amends for the harsh way Joe had pushed him, but not sure how he was going to take it. Still, it would be easier for them to do what they had to with the kid's help than going it all alone, so she should at least try. She sighed, stood up straight, and started to leave her hiding place. She would go over there, ring the bell, tell him she was sorry how Joe acted, maybe run a hand down his arm to use physical connection to help sell her story, and then ask if they could please talk about it as long as she was willing to consider what he had to say. If things went well, she could filter through his words and hopefully find some little nugget of useful information.

Before she could leave the shadow, she heard something heavy hit the ground behind her. She started to spin around, her fists coming up as she settled into a defensive posture, but strong hands grabbed her by the collar of her coat and then threw her sideways. She slammed into the side of another house hard enough to make her bite her tongue, but aside from that and a probable bruise, she didn't think she'd been seriously injured. Rolling over, she started to get back to her feet, but something slammed against her back, knocking her flat. Those same hands grabbed her and flipped her like a burger on a grill, then a knee dropped into her stomach—not enough to hurt, but enough to knock some of her wind out.

Carrie looked up and saw the glowing eyes of the creature staring back at her, a sick grin playing across its face. It wasn't the first time she'd faced a vampire, but it was the first time in nearly a decade that she'd done so completely unarmed and without any backup coming.

"Hello, there, lassie," the thing said. "Why do I think you've been looking for me?"

The thing's weight was impossible, nearly crushing her beneath it. Carrie tried to lift her hands, to try somehow to keep the vampire from tearing her apart, but her arms were held to the ground by its knees, her fingers starting to tingle from the way the circulation had been cut off. She could move them forward and backward a little, but not enough to do any good. Her legs were free, so she planted her feet flat against the ground and pushed as hard as she could, trying to buck the creature off, but it held fast, riding her like a child on a toy horse, laughing as she struggled.

She cursed under her breath. She had no one to blame for this but herself. She'd let her guard down, and now she was going to die for it unless she did something to break free. Embarrassing as it would be, there was only one choice left. She drew in as much breath as she could and prepared to scream for help at the top of her lungs.

The thing seemed to sense what she was doing and clamped a hand over her mouth and nose. Her eyes went wide, and her lungs started to burn at once, aching to release the breath she'd taken in. This was more torturous than if she'd been struggling for air in the first place. She could feel her swollen lungs trying to clamp down and release the now-useless air, but she just. Couldn't.

As her vision began to tunnel down, the thing finally removed its hand, letting her breathe again. The wind rushed out of her as though he'd punched her in the gut, and she started gasping for more at once, fighting to stay conscious. When she finally regained enough composure to look back up at her assailant, his smile was gone, replaced by a serious, considering expression that sent chill bumps running across her skin.

"I know what you are," the thing said. "But you're after the wrong beastie here, lass. Not to mention you're skulking about in the wrong place for my liking. As much as I'd like to rid myself of you permanently, it's not something I care to do, so I'll give you a chance. A choice. Ready to listen?"

Carrie nodded, not trusting that she'd be able to speak if she tried.

"Good. I'm going to let you up. You'll get to your feet, walk past me, down this street the way you came, and you're not going to tell the others with you that I was ever here. You do that, I let you live. You try to cross to that house across the street, you'll wish I was going to kill you. You go get your friends and come back after me, you die first. So, leave me along and you live. Come after me and you die. Go after that boy, you will become intimately acquainted with pain. Nod if you agree."

She had no intention of agreeing any more than it took to get her back to her feet and on a somewhat even playing field again, but she nodded anyway. The thing studied her eyes, looking for some sign of duplicity, then nodded itself and moved quickly, leaping backward off of her and landing on its feet as lightly as a cat leaping from a table. She'd seen how agile these creatures could be, but it was still an incredible sight.

She sat up slowly, fighting an unexpected wave of dizziness at the motion. She wondered if the thing was somehow altering her thoughts, but her plan was still firmly formed and hadn't wavered, so that wasn't likely. She made sure to stand just as slowly, and then brushed the dirt from her pants and turned to face the thing. It was watching her warily, and she could see how tense its muscles still were. She was going to have to be very careful with this next bit.

"Can I ask you something?" she asked.

The wariness in its eyes didn't go away, but surprisingly, it laughed. "Why does everyone start off that way? Don't you realize you're asking me something by asking if you can ask me something?"

It was the first time she'd seen humor that wasn't part of some sadistic game from a vampire, and she had to admit it was a little off-putting. She didn't think they were capable of such things, and here one was, proving her wrong.

"You're right," she said. She pointed toward her inside coat pocket. "Can I grab a smoke, then ask you a question about something you just told me?"

"I thought I was pretty clear," it said.

"You were," she confirmed. "I don't need clarification, I'm just curious about something."

The thing shrugged. "I see anything other than a cigarette and lighter come out of your coat, I make both your knees bend the wrong way."

The tremble as she moved her hand into her jacket wasn't faked. "You seem protective of the kid over there. You afraid we're going to convince him you're just using him?"

She felt around in her pocket, finally managing to get her finger slipped into the metal ring she was looking for. She hesitated, making it look like she was just nervous and trying to get a cigarette from a pack, and hoped the thing was buying it.

"I could care less what kind of shite you try to feed him," the thing replied, shaking its head. "He's smart enough to figure out the truth for himself, without either of us trying to feed him our biased perspectives. I want you to leave him alone because he's been through enough before you idiots showed up acting like you're not just as evil as I am."

She paused, genuinely confused. That sounded like an honest expression of concern for the kid's well-being. Like the laughter earlier, it wasn't something she expected from a vampire.

"What?" she asked, not sure how best to clarify what she wanted to know.

The thing laughed again, this time mockingly, which put her back on familiar ground. "It doesn't matter. What does matter is that Ryan has already had to deal with his best friend getting killed, me fucking the sheep trying to help catch the right bastard that done it, wading into the waters of romance for the first time, and then the bloody arse what swore he wasn't a monster nearly beating another right bastard to death for trying to rape his girl."

Again, she hesitated. This conversation was going nothing at all like she expected it to, nor was the creature behaving the way she'd been taught it would. The way it talked, especially the self-depreciating nature of its words, seemed almost... human.

She also noticed that she'd been stalling with her hand unmoving in her pocket for some time, and the thing hadn't even tried to attack her, or do anything else to scare her. It occurred to her that she had a chance that no other member of the organization had ever experienced—at least not that they'd mentioned or admitted to. Besides that, strange as it seemed, the possibility was there that the kid hadn't been duped, and that he'd been telling the absolute truth.

"I've got a counter-proposal for you," she said.

The thing's smile dropped at once, and its head cocked to one side. She could see it preparing to attack now, knew that she needed to choose her next words very, very carefully.

"I don't recall opening things up for discussion," it said. "I told, you agreed. You back out now, you know the consequences."

"I'm standing here listening to you," she insisted. "When's the last time one of my kind did that? Can't you at least hear me out, too?"

The thing sighed; yet another surprise in a night filled with them. It didn't breathe that she knew of, so why sigh other than for effect?

"Fine," it said. "What's your 'counter-proposal'?"

"We talk," she said. "And I actually keep an open mind and listen. You, me, and Ryan."

"No!" the thing bellowed as it took a step toward her. "I told you what happens if you try to drag him back into this...."

"No, you told me what happens if I cross the street to his house," she replied. "I'm not going to do that. I'm saying we call him over here."

"You're not doing that, either."

"Yes, I am."

The thing moved, leaping the distance between them, teeth bared in a snarl. As its hands clamped onto her shoulders, driving her down onto her back again, she jerked her hand from inside the coat. The thing looked confused for a moment at the sight of the metal ring on her finger, the long cord trailing down to a stainless-steel pin. Then the rape alarm in her pocket started wailing and the vampire rolled off of her, hands clasped over its ears to try and block out the sound.

Carrie scrambled to her feet and pulled the alarm from her pocket, glancing across the street and nearly laughing in triumph as she saw Ryan staring out of his upstairs window for a moment before disappearing back into his room. Her triumph was short-lived. She felt the powerful hand land atop hers and the alarm, then felt it clench. She screamed, trying to let go of the alarm and pull away, sure she was about to feel her hand being crushed to powder in the force of that grip, but it let go instead, snatching the alarm before it could even hit the ground. The vampire crushed it in one quick motion, silencing the wail and sending tiny shards of plastic in all directions. She looked up and saw it was staring at her, the meaning in its eyes crystal clear: the only reason that wasn't her hand was because he knew Ryan was on the way, and he didn't want to have to explain himself.

It snarled at her again, and then shoved her shoulder, spinning her around. The vampire grabbed the back of her coat and nearly lifted her off her feet before striding across the street toward Ryan's house. The front door was opening just as they started up the steps to the porch. Ryan stepped out, his face growing more confused when he saw who was there.

"Francis?" he asked. "Carrie? What's...?"

"We need to get out of the open," the vampire said, pushing Carrie past Ryan and into the house. "And it looks like we need to talk, too."

CHAPTER TWENTY-NINE

Something scurried along the wall, too low and fast to be anything other than a rat. Mario didn't bother to check. If he was wrong, it would give him something to do other than wander aimlessly through a deserted mental asylum, looking for signs of some bloodsucking asshole. True, it was his job, but he was more suited for action, not for skulking around in the dark trying not to get into trouble.

He peered into the next room he came to, the beam from his flashlight dancing across collapsed shelves and scattered debris that once had a purpose other than nesting materials for the vermin that lived here now. He could tell it had been picked over at some point, too much regularity to a couple of the nearby piles to be anything else, but that was easily chalked up to adventurous kids. If they were having a party outside in the courtyard, it stood to reason that they'd been inside as well.

Something reflected his light back at him, and he saw a rat the same approximate size as a small dog glaring at him, upset that he'd dared to disturb its foraging. Mario moved the light away and continued down the hall, ignoring the thing. When he'd first started with the organization, he'd been convinced vampires could control the little bastards, and would send them out as scouts and weapons. Now that he'd gained some experience and learned the truth, they were just a disgusting aggravation in the places he found himself checking out.

He came to a t-intersection at the end of the hall and shined the light both directions down the corridor. There was nothing of interest either way, only a scattering of broken glass where someone had thrown rocks through the windows overlooking the field behind the building. He imagined the corridors led to more areas along the sides of the hospital, offices in all likelihood, though it was possible there were some exam rooms scattered there as well. He considered going to check them out, make a thorough sweep of this floor, but he'd promised not to get too deep in the place until Joe and Carrie were able to check it out along with him.

It was annoying, but it was procedure. When you didn't know what you were up against, you didn't go into it alone. He was here to scout and that was it. Actual confrontation would come only after they'd determined the best plan for success. He would much prefer to find where they thought the bastard was hiding out, then storm the place, or burn it to the ground and wait for the fucker to emerge, but he wasn't the one in charge, so he had to do it the way he was told.

For now.

A grin blossomed on his face as he thought about the day he finally got to lead his own hunting party. The first thing he would do would be to ditch the bullshit that came along with having people like Carrie around. The girl was hot, but she was absolutely worthless when it came to getting her hands dirty. Sure, she could scrap, but Mario had serious doubts about her ability to fight if it came to that. So far she'd only been around for two kills, and both times she'd done more in the role of playing bait than in actually taking the bloodsucker down. The first time they'd finished one off, she'd even puked. Admittedly, not everyone was okay with seeing a head hacked from a body, even if that body belonged to something evil, but there were better ways to handle it than blowing chunks all over the place. If they hadn't thoroughly scrubbed the place before taking the body to dispose of it, that kind of carelessness could even bring them unwanted attention.

He'd offered to show her the ropes, but she'd turned him down cold. Maybe he should've left off the bit about showing her his rope as well but fuck her if she couldn't take a joke. He couldn't believe she still hadn't gotten over it, either. That had been over a year ago, but she still acted like she held it against him.

The flashlight beam landed on the massive hole in the floor he'd passed on his way through. He stopped and studied it again, shaking his head at the force it must have taken to punch it out. He looked around at the chunks of concrete lying about this section of the hallway, and the thin patina of grey dust that covered the floor. Whatever had made this hole had done so from below, slamming through it to emerge up here.

Curious, he knelt beside it and shined his light down into it. He could see what looked like shelves lined up, and if he wasn't mistaken, assorted furniture pushed into one corner of the room below him. He'd been sent here to find the thing's lair, and if his guess was correct, he was now staring into it.

He looked back down the hall, and thought he remembered seeing a stairwell off to one side of the reception area. Joe wouldn't be happy that he did this, but it was better that when he reported back, he could do so sure in the knowledge he'd found the right place.

His fingers tapped against the phone tucked into his back pocket. He could always just give Joe a call, have him come out here and check it out with him, but he would probably go and grab Carrie first, and Mario didn't want to deal with her dead weight along for the ride. He stood and headed for the stairs. Joe could yell at him later. Right now, he was going to do his job the way he saw it needed to be done.

The light barely cut through the darkness of the basement, which was a little strange. Normally when he explored the underground areas of places, there was enough dust floating around in the air to reflect and refract the beam, making it brighter while cutting its range, but for some reason it seemed to be doing the opposite here. A pinprick of light danced far off down the corridor, but the beam didn't illuminate shit. He held one hand out in front of the flashlight and shook his head. Even that seemed darker than it should have, being in the direct line of the light's glow. The batteries were probably starting to go. He'd meant to change them before he got out of the car but had been too anxious to get going. The light had come on, it had seemed reasonably bright, so that had been enough. Now, he wished he'd taken more time to prepare. It was an amateur mistake, and one he hoped didn't come back to bite him on the ass.

Mario worked his way down the hall, occasionally glancing up at the ceiling to try and reorient himself to where he thought that hole was. He stopped next to an open door that appeared to lead into a storeroom of sorts. The lines of shelving looked similar to what he'd seen from the floor above, so he felt safe in assuming this was the right room. He moved into it slowly, feeling the tension in his shoulders build as he looked around for any potential dangers.

At the far end of the room, he found an area where the dust on the floor was heavily disturbed, along with a few dark splotches that looked suspiciously like dried blood. He knelt and started to reach for one to test it, then stopped himself. It was possible this was only animal blood. He had seen that most vampires chose not to kill their prey in their own lairs for whatever reason. If it wasn't though, and especially if the kid had been right about there being someone killing kids in town, then this could well be a crime scene. While the organization did allow for circumvention of local law enforcement during an active removal operation such as this, they also encouraged cooperation where it was evident human laws had been violated. Dead kids would certainly qualify as that. He would need to investigate with his eyes only, not his hands.

Something slammed into his back, knocking him to the floor and driving the breath from him. His nose clipped the concrete floor, and Mario felt blood begin to gush from his nostrils. It wasn't the first time it had been broken, but that didn't make it hurt any less, nor did it stop his eyes from watering up. He bucked, throwing whatever hit him off, and then rolled onto his back, amazed he'd managed to hold onto the flashlight through the ambush.

The light landed on an unfamiliar face. The man was smiling at him, his eyes aglow. Mario frowned. He'd expected to see the thing from the video, but it wasn't this guy. The kid's assertion that there was a second vampire ran through his head, and he realized he might be in a little more trouble than he'd anticipated here.

"Hello, hunter," the thing said. "Seems we're looking for the same prey."

"What the fuck are you talking about?" Mario asked. He turned his head and spat a long stream of phlegm and blood onto the concrete. "What's a hunter?"

"Don't play with me, human," the thing replied. "I can smell the blood of my brethren on you. Tell me, how many of my kind have you killed in their sleep? How many have you sent to Hell? And of those, how many did you have the balls to face alone?"

Mario bristled at that. True, every kill he'd been a part of was a team effort, but only because that was what the organization demanded. It didn't mean he wasn't fully capable of handling things on his own if he had to. Which he was now going to demonstrate.

He kicked out, the heel of his boot connecting squarely on the thing's kneecap. Its face took on a mask of surprise just before it stumbled backward, tripping over a fallen shelf to land on its back a few feet away. Mario didn't give himself time to hesitate. He shoved himself to his feet and rushed the creature, swinging the flashlight in a wide arc as he leapt over the shelf, intent on crushing the thing's head, wondering if that would be as effective as cutting it off.

The creature was impossibly fast, already rolling away before Mario had time to alter his trajectory. The flashlight slammed against the concrete floor hard enough to bend the metal shaft. The light flickered and went out. Mario realized his mistake at once. He'd destroyed the only source of light he had, and now he was at a severe disadvantage.

The point was proven seconds later when a pair of strong hands grabbed him by the shirt and hauled him to his feet. He swung out again with the broken flashlight but hit only air. Then what felt like a stone fist landed against his chin, lifting him off his feet and sending him flying backward. He landed in one of the still-standing shelves, knocking it over as he fell. He could feel the metal edges digging into his back, just above his kidneys, and hoped the hit hadn't affected his spine.

He groaned as he rolled off the shelf and onto the floor. His legs were tingling slightly, but still appeared to be working. His head spun, but he could still focus enough to think. He remained on his hands and knees, waiting, his ears straining to hear the thing's approach. Finally he heard it, the soft tapping of footsteps on concrete as the vampire stepped closer, ready for the next strike. Mario asked whatever higher power might be listening for help, then linked his hands together and turned, swinging with as much of his weight behind it as he could.

Mario nearly screamed with joy when he felt the blow land, his exaltation growing as he realized he'd connected right between the thing's legs. Human or vampire, that was going to hurt. The thing groaned and backed away, and then Mario heard the soft thump as it dropped to its knees somewhere ahead of him. He got to his feet and ran to where he'd heard the sound, screaming in rage the whole time, the flashlight barrel held out before him. He felt it connect, heard the wet and sickly smacking sound and the lighter click of the thing's nose breaking as well, and felt satisfied that he'd managed to issue a little payback.

Then he felt the hand grab his ankle, yanking him off-balance, and he realized he'd just been played. The hand held his foot in place even as he fell, and there was a sharp snap that sent waves of paid radiating up his leg to blend with the other bursts from his back and his face. He threw his hands up to try and break his fall, losing the flashlight in the process, and felt another snap in his wrist as he hit at the wrong angle.

No two ways around it. He was officially fucked.

The thing landed on his back again, driving him fully to the floor. This time, he managed to keep his head up to spare himself any further pain to his already throbbing nose, but when he felt the long, thin blade slip into his throat, he knew that he'd played right into the thing's hands again.

"You tried," the thing whispered into his ear. "You're to be commended for that. Had you been one of us, we might have been evenly matched. But you are simply human, and I am a god."

"Fuck you," Mario replied. He could feel the blood bubbling over his lips and wondered if it was coming from his broken nose or the injury to his throat.

Then he felt the blade slip away, replaced by the creature's cold lips, and he found he no longer had it in him to care.

CHAPTER THIRTY

H e had the surreal feeling that if his life were to get any weirder, his brain would shut down and leave him babbling to his Mom's potted plant sitting in the corner of the living room. It was strange enough to see a vampire and a vampire hunter in the same room as one another when neither was trying to actively kill the other, stranger still that the room was his own living room. Francis stood to one side, looking miserable and annoyed, while Carrie used a damp cloth she'd procured from Ryan to clean the mud stains off the back of her leather coat. While her expression was casual, Ryan could almost feel the tension coming off of her from where he sat on the stairs.

Topping things off, Carrie had been the only one of that trio he'd felt had been remotely nice to him, and Francis had been avoiding him since the Halloween party, so he wasn't a hundred percent sure which of them he would be rooting for if a fight did break out.

Most likely, he'd just be rooting for the house to survive intact.

"Damn," Carrie said. She stopped rubbing at her coat, brought it closer to her face, and then began running a finger across it slowly. "I think there was a rock under me. Gouged it pretty good here."

"That's what you want to discuss?" Francis asked. "My lack of manners when I was trying to prevent you from coming after an innocent kid?"

Carrie glanced over at him. "First, you were the one who wanted to make sure the cops weren't about to pound the door down before we started talking. Second, the kid's not that innocent if he's tangled up with you."

Francis threw his hands up and shook his head as he turned and began studying the pictures hanging on the wall behind him. He cocked his head, and then looked over at Ryan.

"Your mum and pop aren't about to come wandering in on us are they?" he asked. "Something tells me that would be worse than the cops."

Ryan shook his head. "My grandmother had her gall bladder removed today, so they went to see her in the hospital. Said they'd be back late tonight."

"They left you here alone with a child killer on the loose?" Carrie asked, raising an eyebrow at him.

"I can take care of myself," he said. He couldn't tell if that was genuine concern in her voice, or if she was mocking him. Considering the way her friends acted earlier, it could go either way.

He fully expected her to press him on that answer, but she simply shrugged and went back to trying to clean her coat.

"Okay, since no one's telling me anything, I'll ask," Ryan said. "What the hell's going on? I see something outside, then the next thing I know there's an alarm going off so loud I thought it was going to shatter the windows, then I open the door to see you two."

"That reminds me," Francis said, turning to face him. "What's wrong with you, anyway? You hear an alarm, so you go to the door and open it?"

Ryan sighed, got up, and retrieved Dad's pistol from where he'd dropped it into the potted plant he thought he might soon be conversing with. He hadn't put it there on purpose, had actually dropped it in surprise when he saw who was on his front porch, but he wasn't about to tell them that.

The sight of the gun caught Carrie's attention. She raised her eyebrows again, this time in what Ryan thought was actual surprise, and studied the weapon. He could tell she wanted to grab it from him but didn't quite dare.

"That's not some shitty nine-millimeter, is it?" she asked. "Looks like a good, old-fashioned nineteen-eleven."

"I have no idea," Ryan admitted. "I know Dad said it's a forty-five caliber, but I don't know anything beyond that."

"Decent piece," she said, hanging her coat over the side of the sofa. "Good stopping power. Even against something like that."

The look of fury that flashed across Francis's face when she pointed at him was nearly enough to make Ryan think he would have to test her theory. The vampire closed his eyes and appeared to get himself back under control again. "Okay, lassie, we're all here, nobody's going to crash the party, and I'm sick of the smell of you, so what did you want?"

There was another taunt there, Ryan could almost feel it, but Carrie didn't rise to the bait. "Fine. Let's start with this. You say you're no danger to the kid here, and from the way you acted outside I'm willing to believe that, even if I still think you've got some ulterior motive for it. So convince me."

"Of what?" Francis asked.

"That you don't intend to hurt Ryan in any way, now or in the future."

"You just said the way I acted left you inclined to believe it," Francis said. "What bloody more do you need? Should I pinch his cheeks like I'm his old 'ma?"

"No!" Ryan said before Carrie could respond. She jumped a bit at the vehemence of the response. Francis only chuckled. "I'm standing right here, and in case you forgot, I'm the one with the gun, so why not treat me like I'm not five years old?"

"Sorry," Carrie said, holding up a hand. She gave Francis a dirty look when the vampire chuckled harder.

"That goes for you, too," Ryan told him. "Just because you've got more than two hundred years on me is no excuse to patronize me."

The rebuke cut the laughter off fast. Ryan couldn't help but notice the way Carrie's brow furrowed at that.

"Sorry," Francis muttered. "You're right. We shouldn't talk about you like you're not here, nor should I treat you like an infant, even though in many ways, to me, you are."

Ryan shook his head and looked to Carrie. "What makes you think he's going to hurt me? I told you and your friends that he wasn't going to do anything to me, and now he's apparently done something to make you question that more. By the way, what was that?"

"Threatened to let her know what pain really was if she didn't leave you the hell alone," Francis answered for her. "Still considering it."

"You've done enough," Ryan said. "Or do you not remember what you did to Matt at that party?"

"He deserved worse."

"Maybe, but it wasn't your call to decide how much he needed. The cops could've done that. All you had to do was take him down, keep him from doing... what he was trying to do to Kayla. You didn't have to nearly kill him."

"Oh, Christ," Carrie muttered, rubbing a hand over her eyes. "That's what prompted the fight, isn't it? Some bully trying to hurt your girlfriend."

"Trying to rape his girlfriend," Francis said, eyes still locked on Ryan. "Don't whitewash it."

"That explains some things," Carrie said. She looked up, locking eyes with Ryan. "You were being forced to watch or listen or something, weren't you?"

Ryan nodded, not wanting to break her train of thought.

"And I imagine you were furious, terrified, and probably feeling some emotions you couldn't even name, right?"

"They wanted me to watch before they kicked my ass, too," Ryan said, shuddering as the memory of that moment flashed through his mind. He was dimly aware of Francis doing the same thing, but he didn't pay any attention to it. "That matters?"

"Like I said, it explains things," Carrie said. She looked over to Francis. "You felt it, didn't you? Everything he felt. That's what sent you into the rage that gave you the strength to do what I saw on that video."

Francis flinched. "What?"

He glanced to Ryan for clarification.

"Those people holding their phones up," Ryan explained. "They were recording everything. The video was on the internet within hours."

"I have no idea what that means," Francis said. "But I feel safe in assuming it's bad, right?"

"Yeah," Ryan said, nodding. "It's also how these guys knew to come here. But what about what she said, about the emotions? Is that true?"

Francis shrugged. "All I remember is sitting there in the quiet, resting, and then I suddenly felt more furious than I had in probably a hundred years. I felt you were in some kind of danger, so I acted. I don't remember much about it until I realized I was standing there with you begging me to stop."

"Is it possible though?" Carrie asked.

"It could be," Francis said. "I honestly don't know. But I do know this kid is convinced there's some sort of mind control going on, but to me, it seems like that would be working in reverse from what he was afraid of."

"Not mind control," Carrie said, shaking her head in wonder. "That would manifest differently, and from what I was taught, it never travels both ways. An attachment, yes. Apparently an emotional one. Now how the hell did that happen?"

Francis grunted in surprise, but the expression on his face was one of sudden understanding. "Because I was staked when he found me, and he removed it."

Carrie gave Ryan a look of confusion and reproach. "What on earth possessed you to...."

Ryan held up both hands, making it look like he was a crook who'd been caught and was surrendering. "I didn't exactly do it on purpose! It was dark, I tripped, fell, and landed on him, which knocked the stake out."

"Dumb luck," Carrie muttered, shaking her head. "All of this because of sheer dumb luck."

Francis started to say something, but she held up a hand to stop him. "Okay, I'm not going to say I trust you, but in this, at least, I believe what you're telling me. No one else in the organization would, mind you, but I do.

"So," she went on, forcing Francis to meet her eyes. "Why kill the other kids?"

"As me old pappy would say," Francis said, snarling a little. "May the devil cut the head off you and make a day's work of your neck. I haven't been killing no kiddies, lass. Best watch your tongue lest I give old scratch a clean hole to use first."

"Colorful," Carrie said. "I only followed enough of that to know you want the devil to do bad things to my tongue-less mouth and neck stump, but you're both claiming a vampire's killing kids, and there hasn't been a report putting two of you in the same place for a very long time, so forgive me if I have trouble believing you."

"And because a thing doesn't happen often it can't happen at all?"

"I never said that."

"He didn't kill the kids," Ryan said. "Use logic. He attacked Matt at the party because you say he felt what I was feeling. Aside from that, he's only even hunted from animals, so why kill other kids?"

"I would point out that you only have his word that he's been feeding on animals," Carrie said, still watching Francis warily. "But you'd just ignore me. So I'll ask him: you have any proof of that?"

"I just woke up from a fifty-year nap," Francis said, still holding her gaze. "Courtesy of you paranoid knobs, I might add. If I was feeding off anything more than critters, where's the trail of bodies? Or, to put it in terms you'll understand, how could I hold myself back when I was that hungry? I didn't fare so well when I met the other one, in large part because I'm still not back up to full strength yet. And look at me. You got any worthwhile training from your merry band of arseholes, you'd see I'm not exactly steady on my feet after exerting myself at that party you saw in the video thing got you so interested."

Carrie nodded, conceding the point. "So tell me about this 'other one'."

"I never got a really good look at him," Francis said. "A little from a distance, then later we were both in the dark and he was using the shadows to hide himself."

Something about the way he said that made it sound supernatural, which meant it was the first time Ryan was hearing about this potential new ability. "You can do that?"

Francis ignored him. "Like most of us, he was pretty average. Dark hair, pale complexion, medium build. Slavic accent of some sort. I'm guessing he's old, older than me, at least. And in full control of his abilities. I was tracking him psychically, and when I confronted him, he swatted me down like a damn baby. If I'd been human, I'd most likely be in the hospital right now, drooling over my chin for the rest of my pathetic life. If I hadn't hemorrhaged out every one of my orifices, that is."

"You and he are alike, for the most part," Carrie said. "So why would he be killing kids?"

"Who knows?" Francis said. "Easy prey? Sweeten their life force with fear before he feeds on them? I do know he's being careful. I didn't see any sign one of us had fed on the one I found."

Carrie sat up a little straighter. "You found one of the dead kids?"

Francis gave Ryan a sympathetic look. Ryan swallowed and nodded, knowing what the unspoken question in that look was. He vividly remembered questioning Francis relentlessly about Hunter once he knew the vampire had discovered his friend's body and he knew what was liable to be coming next.

"The first one," Francis said. "Hunter. Ryan's friend."

Carrie winced. "I'm sorry."

Ryan gave her a half-hearted smile. "Thanks."

"Let's just say he didn't meet a quick end," Francis said. "If you need more details than that, I'll give them one-on-one. Unless you plan to stake me, or something should we end up alone together."

"Maybe one day," Carrie replied. "But for now, it looks like you've got information I need."

"I've got more than that," Francis said. "At least, I do if you're operating like you used to. How many of you are there?"

"What's that got to do with anything?" Carrie asked.

"Everything," Francis replied. "From what I remember, you and the other murderous assholes used to run around in little groups, usually between two and five. Unless you've decided to up your numbers, it's not going to be enough. This guy can probably take on more humans than that and walk away from it, if the attack he hit me with is any indication."

Carrie chewed on her lip, watching him, and then sighed. "Three. There's three of us."

Francis chuckled. "You'd barely be able to handle me. You need to seriously think about...."

He suddenly doubled over, hands clutching his head as his voice trailed off into a long, sustained groan. His entire body began to shake, and Ryan thought for one crazy moment that he was about to transform into a wolf or something, despite his insistence that vampires couldn't do such things. The strange fit passed as quickly as it had begun, and Francis stumbled backward against the wall hard enough to rattle the pictures in their frames.

"What the hell was that, man?" Carrie said. She'd come to her feet and had crept closer to Ryan during the episode, even though he'd been too distracted by Francis to notice at the time.

Francis waved one hand weakly, still trying to collect himself. Finally he was able to stand up straight again, though he still trembled slightly.

"I have no idea," he said. "But I get the sense I've just been called out into the street for a fight."

Though she made it look natural, Ryan couldn't help but notice as Carrie angled herself away from the front door. "This street?"

"Figure of speech," Francis said. "No, I think our mystery killer wants me to come to him. He tried to get me to join him before, but somehow I don't think he's going to be as pleasant this time."

Ryan could see Carrie wanted to explore that particular statement further, but he didn't give her the time. "So where is he?"

Francis shook his head. "I don't know for sure. There was a sense of familiarity there, but it was mostly just... noise, I guess you could say."

"The asylum, then," Ryan said. "It's the only place you've spent any real time around here. And if he tracked you the same way you were tracking him...."

"Shit," Carrie said. "I need a phone."

Ryan gave her a confused look as he retrieved the cordless phone from the kitchen and handed it to her. She dialed, pacing as she put the phone to her ear, waited, and then swore as she hung up and started dialing again. This time it seemed that someone picked up, but she wandered out of the room, preventing Ryan from being able to hear what was said. When she returned to the room a couple of minutes later, her face had lost some of its color and the phone was held loosely in one hand, arm dangling loosely at her side.

"It's the asylum, all right," she confirmed. "One of my team went to check it out, and hasn't reported in. He's also not answering his phone."

"Maybe he doesn't have cell service," Ryan offered. "It can get spotty out there."

Carrie shook her head. "We have satellite phones to use when we're on the job. It gets worse, though. He had the car, so we don't even have a way to get us and our gear out there."

"You also don't have a workable plan for when you do show up," Francis said. "I wasn't a soldier that long, but I remember that was key to accomplishing anything."

Ryan sighed and met Carrie's eyes. "I might can get you a ride, but we're going to have to make a deal, first."

That actually got a smile out of her. "If you don't go into politics when you're older, then buddy, it's a waste of your talents."

While he smiled back, Ryan was more concerned with how he was going to convince everyone else involved to go along with what he had in mind. He knew they would argue—and with good reason—but he'd seen this through so far, and he would be damned if he was going to hear second-hand how it all played out now.

CHAPTER THIRTY-ONE

With the way Melanie kept shifting her eyes to Carrie sitting in the passenger seat, and then across the rear-view mirror to Ryan and Francis, only occasionally looking at the road in front of them, Ryan was sure they were going to end up dying in a wreck before they even made it to the hotel to pick up Joe. She'd rushed over when Ryan called, knowing nothing more than it was an emergency. When she walked in and found Carrie and Francis lounging in the living room, giving each other occasional wary glances, she immediately turned to Ryan and demanded he tell her what was going on, and what he'd gotten himself involved in.

They'd given her a truncated run-down of what was happening, and a slightly deeper explanation in the car on the way here. So far, she was handling it much better than Ryan would have were he in her shoes. She'd only swerved slightly when they told her what Francis was. She hadn't asked for proof, but Ryan didn't know if that meant she simply believed them, or if she was convinced they were pulling some sick prank on her and was just playing along.

The car slowed as she turned onto the main road through town, then slowed further as she neared the little collection of motels scattered along the sides. Obviously she was paying some attention to the road to be able to make that turn, which allowed Ryan to relax somewhat.

"Last one on the left," Carrie said. "Joe should be in room 110."

Melanie nodded and eased into the median turn lane, then swung into the parking lot. The room was on the far end, just before you circled the building. Ryan wondered if that had been done by design or accident. Everything these hunters did seemed like it was premeditated, and it also seemed like they wanted to distance themselves from the town as much as possible. Considering the kind of thing they were here to do, he supposed that made sense, but it was still weird if they carried it so far as to choose the furthest hotel room away from town without actually leaving town.

Carrie was starting to open her door before the car was even parked. "Thanks for the ride, I think we can take it from here."

"No," Melanie said simply.

Carrie stopped, half in and half out of the car, and looked back at her. "No, what?"

"No, you're not going to 'take it from here'," Melanie replied. "I'm coming with you."

Francis grumbled something unintelligible and shifted in his seat. Ryan had to bite back a laugh, despite the seriousness of the situation. He'd made this same demand before he was willing to call Melanie. He wondered if she was going to meet the same resistance he had.

"Why are all you people around here so dead-set on getting yourselves hurt or killed?" Carrie asked. She hung her head, leaning on the door for support. "Fine, but can we just get on with this?"

"It took longer than that for me to convince you," Ryan said, feeling a bit put out by how fast she'd relented.

"You're fifteen!" Carrie shot back. "She's not. And I'm too damned tired to argue anymore."

She pushed herself away from the door, and then slammed it behind her. The car rocked on its wheels from the force of that slam. Ryan looked over to Francis, who simply rolled his eyes and got out as well. Ryan reached for the door handle, and then noticed that Melanie was staring at him intently.

"What?" he asked.

"You're coming on this insane thing, too?"

He sat back in the seat and sighed. "I am."

She looked back to watch as Carrie disappeared through the door to the hotel room, leaving Francis leaning against the wall outside, waiting. "I should try to stop you. You know that, right?"

"You're welcome to try," he replied. "But I'm still going. Hunter was my best friend."

"And he was my brother," Melanie said, turning to face him again. "How much sense does it make if we both end up dead trying to bring his killer to justice?"

He gave her a slight smile. "Asking yourself that, too?"

She sighed. "Maybe. That's assuming I actually believe what you've told me."

She turned and looked back over to Francis again. "He's really a vampire. An immortal, drink-your-blood vampire."

"He is," Ryan confirmed.

"And the motherfucker that killed Hunter is, too."

"Yes."

"And that girl, along with whoever's in that room, are vampire hunters. And we're about to join up with them to go get the bad vampire all while hoping the good one doesn't turn on us."

"Sounds like you picked up more of Carrie's version of things than mine or Francis's, but that's the basic idea, yes."

Melanie shook her head, and then looked back to him again. "This sounds insane, you get that? Are you sure you haven't just landed with a bunch of people trying to take advantage of you?"

She held up a hand, forestalling his answer before he could give it. "Never mind. It doesn't matter, I guess. We're here now, so we might as well see the next part of this through."

With that, she opened her own door and got out, and waited for Ryan before leading the way over to the hotel room. The door was partially open, kept from closing all the way by the security lock turned the wrong way. Ryan could hear the raised voices emanating from inside, but he couldn't quite make out what was being said. He was able to make a pretty good guess, though. He glanced over to find Francis smiling back at him.

"I do believe our young huntress is still fairly new to all this," he said. "Her self-righteous arse of a boss has finished emphatically detailing how she messed up by even talking to a creature of evil such as me and has moved on to chastising her for bringing me along. I think you're going to have an interesting time trying to plead your own cases as well, though they haven't gotten to that bit yet."

Ryan didn't bother to knock. He just pulled the door open and strode inside. Carrie was standing on one side of a small table just inside the room, staring across at Joe, who stood on the other side. Both were yelling at each other, their words overlapping and tangling, making it impossible even for them to know what was being said.

It was Joe who first noticed him standing there. He broke off what he was saying, lowered his head slightly, exposing the rock-hard tendons in his neck, and then glared at him and Melanie standing just behind him.

"And then there's this," he said, pointing a finger.

Carrie looked over her shoulder, eyes blazing, and then turned back. "They're coming."

"No, they most certainly are not," Joe said. "If there's one thing I absolutely will not do, it's put innocent civilians at risk. Especially when one of them probably doesn't even have hair on his balls, yet!"

Ryan started to feel the hold on his temper slip, the way it had back in the diner, but it was Melanie who spoke up first.

"In case you forgot, asshole," she said. "You don't have a car right now. I do. If I'm driving, I'm going."

Joe nodded, then turned and dug through a satchel on the floor next to him before tossing a stack of bills onto the table. Ryan felt his eyebrows go up. From what he could see, it looked like it was mostly hundreds and fifties. At a guess, there was a couple thousand dollars lying there in front of him.

"I'm renting your car for a few hours," he said. "There's your deposit, and a rental fee. Actually, forget it. I'll just buy the damn thing from you. Let me know if that's not enough."

Ryan had to admit, despite how badly he wanted to be there when this other vampire met his end, all that money was sorely tempting. If it was up to him, he'd take it and run.

But it wasn't his call, it was Melanie's. From the look on her face, she wasn't about to budge.

"You can shove that stack of bills right up your ass," she said. "I'm going, period. With or without you. If just me, Ryan, and...."

She turned to Ryan, one eyebrow raised.

"Francis."

"If just me, Ryan and Francis have to face this thing, then we will."

"And me," Carrie put in. "I'm coming, too. The way I understood my job, it was to stop the threat, no matter what it took to accomplish that."

"Even if it means getting someone killed," Joe grumbled.

"If these two have to die in order for us to stop that thing," she said, locking eyes with him. "Then yes. And don't try throwing age back into it. I've already used that argument and felt shitty about it. I wasn't much older than Ryan when you found me and took me in."

"No," Joe agreed. "But considering the bloodbath you were in the middle of, and that you didn't have anything to lose or a family to mourn you anymore, it was a different situation."

He blew out a long breath that ruffled the bills on the table. "But, I take your point. Fine. If they want to die, I'm not going to stop it. That said, if you do come along, you do exactly what I tell you to, and you don't question my orders. There's more than likely a reason for them, so don't argue when you should be doing something more important. If you can agree to that, then we have a deal."

"Done," Melanie replied. Ryan nodded his agreement as well.

Joe bowed his head, staring at the table. "I know you can hear me, bloodsucker. Give me one reason why I shouldn't just take you out right now before we even get started."

Francis appeared in the open doorway and started to step inside. Joe glared at him.

"I'm not inviting you in," Joe said.

Francis shrugged and walked through the door. "Good to see you don't know everything. That needing to be invited in thing is utter shite. Most times, it only comes about as a part of proper manners. Oh, and because my kind likes to feed you arseholes false information from time to time. Amuses us no end. At least it does me."

For a moment, Ryan thought Joe was going to launch himself over the table at Francis. If that happened, he was positive Melanie would get the proof she needed that all of this was real. It would also probably end their chances at stopping the other one, so he felt a flash of relief when Joe closed his eyes for a ten-count, then opened them and sat down.

"As for why you shouldn't kill me," Francis said, pulling out the other chair and sitting down as well. "I can give you several, but let's start with us being in a public place."

Joe's lips twitched. "And why should that matter? I've killed your kind in public before."

"Maybe you have," Francis said. "But you lot also have a thing about not shitting where you eat. You set me on fire, this whole place will end up in flames. That's going to displace and possibly harm those innocents you're so concerned about. So, cut my head off, then. It's quieter, less flashy, but it would make quite the mess. Even with all your training I don't think you'd manage to get the blood off every surface in this room. Stumps tend to spray, you know. And then you'd have to kill or kidnap Ryan and his friend here, which—while I wouldn't put either of those things past you—I don't think you especially want to do. Is that good enough, or should I continue?"

"You've made your point," Joe replied. "I assume you have some grand plan in mind, some way to take out your partner? What happened, he double-cross you or something?"

"Watch your bloody mouth," Francis said. "Or I may just see how far down your throat I can reach before ripping your tongue out. That monster is no friend to me, and the only thing I have ever wanted from him was his end."

"Can you stop swinging your dicks at each other?" Melanie asked. "If we're going to do this, then let's hear how we're going to do it."

"I made some calls," Joe said, ignoring her, his eyes still focused on Francis. "Found out a few interesting things about that old asylum. Seems there were a rash of killings there back in the mid-eighties. Inmates got loose, started killing doctors. Turned into a real shit-show. That's what the press found out. What they didn't learn was that the organization Carrie and I work for tracked a vampire to this town before losing him. A team was sent out to do a more detailed search. While they were here, that revolt started. They investigated, and found that those inmates weren't just insane, they'd been turned."

"What kind of maniac would think turning spastics was a good idea?" Francis grumbled under his breath.

"Lucky for us," Joe went on. "There was a bigger team here for that one, just because the bloodsucker we'd been tracking had proven to be especially brutal. The full team went to the asylum to try and contain the threat. While working their way through the inmates, they found a vampire who wasn't wearing a hospital gown, right there in the middle of the killing."

Francis had gone more and more still as Joe went on, and now his face had taken on an almost haunted look as well. Just from his posture, Ryan could already guess what was about to come next.

"Half the team chased him down," Joe said. "Cornered him in the basement and staked him until they could finish dealing with the situation upstairs. The end result? Two hundred dead, including over three-fourths of the hunter team on site. They cleaned it up, spun it to the media, and got the hell out of there. Only they were in such a rush, they forgot something."

"They forgot about him," Ryan said, pointing at Francis. "They forgot he was down there."

Joe nodded, still watching Francis. "You want me to trust you, to believe you're not a monster, tell me how I'm supposed to do that when you were in the middle of a goddamned slaughter."

Ryan found himself fascinated by the question, even more so by what the answer might be. This was something he'd never thought to ask Francis about: what happened to really close the asylum? Of course, he'd just assumed that either Francis came after that happened, or he'd already been staked, but never once had it occurred to him that he might have been present for it, or even somehow involved in it.

"You sanctimonious fools," Francis said. Instead of anger, his words actually sounded like they were tinged in sorrow. "You've so convinced yourself that aberration and abomination are all one and the same, you never stop to truly assess a situation once you've entered it. You see a vampire in the middle of a warzone—which is more apt than 'slaughter', mind you—and don't bother paying attention to anything else. Like the fact I was killing turned inmates, not innocent doctors or human patients. And here's something for you to puzzle out while I explain: if you idiots hadn't come after me with such force, if you'd actually seen what I was doing and let me continue, what're the odds more of your men would've made it out? How many more doctors and normal patients? How much of that slaughter could've been avoided?"

Joe continued holding the vampire's gaze, but Carrie actually bowed her head and stared intently at the filthy carpet.

"I guess it doesn't matter. You just want me to say something so you can tell me it's a lie. Well, it won't be a lie, but far be it for me to remind you of your prejudice by disagreeing after the fact.

"It's going to offend your hard little head to hear this, but humans and vampires share a good many things in common. In fact, we're more alike than we are different. I don't need to breathe anymore, though I still do it from instinct. I can go out in the sun, even if it isn't the most comfortable thing in the world. I'm stronger, and faster. I have limited innate psychic ability. I can only gain nourishment and sustenance from the life force of another living creature, even though I can eat whatever I want. My health remains constant unless I go long periods without feeding, meaning I don't get sick, I don't age, and there's no such thing as 'natural' death in the cards for me. I can't reproduce the same way humans can, though everything down there is in fine working order, let me add. Aside from that, we're basically the same.

"There are those of us who also refuse to accept that, though. They see us as better, worthier than you. My maker was one of those. The one here killing kids is another. The one who started that bloody mess at the hospital? She was a third, and I will take responsibility only so far that she was in some ways my fault."

He closed his eyes and sighed. "I killed my maker in 1843. She was always disappointed in me, always annoyed that I wouldn't 'let my true self free' as she put it. We lived in New Orleans at the time, and I had developed something of a friendship with a negro man who played the piano in one of the bars there. He didn't know what I was, at least he never said if he did, but surely he noticed I never aged and never seemed to become inebriated no matter how much I drank. He was the closest thing to a friend I had during those early years, and to my mind, my one remaining connection to the human life that had been taken from me.

"My maker thought that same thing, and so to prove her point to me, she set out intending to kill him. I refused to let her do that, so I killed her. I drained her dry, absorbing her life energy. It made me stronger, and I didn't feel the urge to feed for nearly three months, but more importantly, it set me free. But we weren't the only vampires in New Orleans, and what I'd done was tantamount to treason in their eyes. They wanted me dead. So I ran.

"I met people here and there, but I never really remained in one place long enough to forge real connections with them. I think I was afraid to. I'd seen the monster I could become, seen it first in my maker and then in how I'd dispatched her. I didn't want to be that way, so I never let anyone, human or vampire, get too close.

"Until I met Christine.

"We met in New York, where I was looking for a change in scenery and she was trying to find her way, being only a decade or so on this side of her turn. Her master had been the opposite of mine. He'd changed her, then pushed her away to figure things out for herself. Maybe because of that, she, like me, wanted to retain more of her human side for as long as she could.

"You can guess what happened next. We fell in love. We talked many long nights about the possibility of living a normal life somewhere. We both agreed that somewhere sparsely populated would be best, which brought us here. We took jobs at the hospital—she had nursing training before her change, and I made a passable orderly—and settled into the same routine most couples do. We knew it couldn't last forever—the not aging thing would eventually give us away—but we were determined to enjoy it as long as we could.

"Then she started to change. Maybe it was being around all those lunatics every night, maybe it was some latent desire her maker instilled in her. The cause doesn't really matter. The result, though, was her asking what I thought about changing a child, so we could have an offspring of sorts. Something that could make us more like a real family.

"I was horrified by the idea. What bloody loon would want to subject a child to this insanity? And what did she think would happen? That the child would grow up like a human? It was asinine, and I told her so.

"A week later, she comes up to me in the hallway and tells me she's found our child. I reminded her that such a thing couldn't happen, and she laughed, and told me that it was too late. She'd already turned them. Worse, she refused to tell me who they were, so I could go and kill them before the change took full effect. When you're changed, one of the first effects is that you enter an extremely deep sleep while your mind and body are altered. Well, we were in a place where nearly everyone was in a deep sleep. If I was to try and keep things from going so horribly sideways, I had no choice but to wait and watch.

"The thing she hadn't told me, the thing that started that whole downward spiral, was that she'd realized how I might react, and so she'd changed a couple of others as well to act as guards for her 'child'. Then a couple more, knowing how old I was and therefore how strong I was. Then two more. Seven, all total.

"Seven patients in an insane asylum, now with my kind's strength and skills."

"Sweet Christ," Carrie whispered.

"Things didn't make it until nightfall," Francis continued. "Those seven awoke, raving and hungry, and began to lay waste to the hospital. I begged Christine to help me stop them, already knowing it was so out of hand there was nothing I could feasibly do, but she attacked me instead. I had to kill her to stop her, and then I had to try and right what she'd done. Which is where your story picks up, hunter. That is when your idiot brethren found me."

"Found you," Joe pointed out. "No other vampires in the mix outside the patients, just you."

"Because I killed her the same way I killed my maker," Francis said. "I drained her of her life force. Once that happens, whatever magic that makes us what we are is gone, and so time catches up. Age, disease, and the damage we'd done to ourselves through exertion, all returning at once. She wasn't old enough to wither and die, but she'd apparently been a whore before her change, and riddled with enough disease to destroy her body in a hurry. From dust we came, and to the dust we return, if you catch my meaning."

"Convenient," Joe said. He let out a weary breath and rubbed a hand over his face. "But since the vampire that hunter team tracked here was supposed to have been female, it does line up. So let's say I'm inclined to believe that part of your story. I'm not quite buying that one juvenile vampire could do the kind of damage you're claiming she did, but let's set that aside for a moment. None of that does a damn thing toward making me think I should trust you enough to work with you."

"Two things," Francis said, folding his hands and resting them on the table. "First, you don't have enough of a force to defeat the foe you're after, and there's no time to call for reinforcements. You knew only of fire or beheading before I told you a third way, and that one requires someone like me to accomplish."

"What are you suggesting?" Joe asked, his eyes narrowing.

Francis shrugged. "You will distract him, engage him, keep his attention on you. While that happens, I'll strike from the shadows, so to speak, and consume him. You won't even have a mess to clean up, aside from your other friend who is most likely already dead."

Joe let out a humorless laugh. "Didn't you just say that would make you stronger? We're headed to the right place for this, since you are definitely crazy if you think I'm going to let that happen."

"Which brings me to the second reason," Francis said, a sad smile playing across his lips. "When I killed my maker, because she was older and more powerful, there was a brief moment where my body went into a sort of shock as it tried to process her life force. During that time, I will be helpless."

Joe grunted and jerked a little in his seat. He nodded, the hint of a grin coming to his own lips. Carrie looked from him to Francis, obviously confused.

"What does that mean?" she asked.

"It means, lassie," Francis said. "That when the sun rises tomorrow, you can brag to the other idiot hunters that you killed two vampires tonight."

CHAPTER THIRTY-TWO

Ryan knew he should be back in the room with the rest of them, helping or at least listening as they all worked out the details for the impending attack, but his mind was racing too much to be able to focus on that right now. Francis had dropped a bombshell by offering to sacrifice himself, and the fact he hadn't given any indication he would ever suggest such a thing only made it worse. Ryan wanted to argue the point right then and there, but he was smart enough to realize that he stood no chance of changing the vampire's mind about this. He wanted to, but he knew he couldn't. And so he'd stood up, fighting to hold back tears, and walked out the door, stopping at Melanie's car and then turning to sit on the hood and stare aimlessly back at the motel room.

He wasn't thinking about anything in particular, though there were a thousand different things flitting through his head that he could try and grab onto. Instead, he simply felt, raw emotion racing through him, threatening to drag him down into a deep, deep darkness. Somehow he knew that if he let himself make that slide, he'd never be able to find his way back out again. Still, it was tempting.

The door to the room opened, and Francis stepped outside to join him. Ryan couldn't even bring himself to look at the vampire, simply continued staring down at the cracked concrete of the sidewalk in front of the motel. Out of the corner of his eye, he saw Francis move to join him, felt the car sink as he settled onto the hood next to him. For a long moment, no one said anything. Ryan could feel Francis watching him, trying to gauge his mood, and wondered if he was using some of that low-level psychic ability he'd mentioned to do it.

"I'm sorry this upsets you," Francis finally said. "But it's for the best."

Ryan snorted derisively. "Right. Losing one friend isn't enough, I have to lose another one, too."

Francis sighed, and Ryan felt his temper flare at the sound of it.

"Stop that," he said. "Why do you do that, anyway? You're not breathing, so stop acting like you are."

A shudder ran through Francis, and Ryan had the distinct impression he was trying not to let out another of those theatrical sighs. Finally he shook his head.

"It's a way to hold onto my humanity," he said. "A sigh is a distinctly human expression, even if other animals do it, too. But maybe you're right. Maybe it's pointless."

He turned and faced Ryan, though Ryan refused to look back up at him.

"I'm touched you think of me as a friend," he said. "It's been a bloody long time since anyone's done that, human or otherwise. But the reality is that I'm not your friend. I can't have friends. Because if I did, they'd always be in danger. The fact these hunters listened to you is a bleeding miracle. Most would assume you to be under my control and kill you outright for it. You don't deserve that, to be always looking over your shoulder. You deserve as much of a normal life as you can get after all this.

"I never wanted this existence," he continued. "I had it forced on me, and then had no choice but to live with it. If I'm being honest, and I think I owe you that much, there are times I wish you hadn't woken me up from that long sleep. The world's changed so much since then, and even more than before, I have no place in it. I should've died when those hunters caught up to me, and it's only a cruelty that I didn't."

"But you fought back," Ryan said. "You tried to stay alive."

Francis shrugged. "Instinct. For me, it's stronger even than it is for you. That's why this is the only way I can finally find some peace."

Ryan shook his head. "I don't buy that. You've done everything you could to stay alive since I woke you. If you really wanted to die, you could've found a way. Why heal yourself if you didn't even want to live?"

The vampire was silent for a long moment, long enough that Ryan thought he wasn't going to get an answer. He looked over to see Francis with an unusually contemplative look on his face. Finally, Francis sighed and then cast a reproachful look to Ryan.

"Sorry, habit," he said. "And it's because of that night, the one that made me so popular, it seems. I realized that the monster was in there, no matter how much I tried to fight it. I started to wonder if maybe there was nothing I could do to stop it. If the older I got, the more the monster would emerge. My maker was nearly half a millennium old when I killed her, and she was every bit the horror fiction makes vampires out to be. What if that's what lies ahead for me, no matter what I do? What if that monster is just sleeping beneath the surface, waiting for me to relax my guard and let it out?"

He shook his head. "I refuse to let that happen. If that means I sacrifice myself to bring down another monster, so be it. At least my death will mean something. My life certainly hasn't."

"It has to me," Ryan said softly. As much as he didn't want to, not after chastising Francis for it, he couldn't help but sigh himself. "But I get it. I think it's complete and utter bullshit, but I get it. Just don't expect me to like it, or ever forgive you for it."

"Fair enough," Francis said. "And I'll make a deal with you: you come up with some way for us to pull this off, to make the hunters think I'm dead so they stay off my trail, and to make sure the monster never finds his way out, and I'll listen. I just don't think you're going to be able to manage both parts of that."

Ryan nodded. "I guess it's better than nothing. A small hope is still a hope, right?"

Francis smiled. "Now you're learning, laddie."

The motel room door opened, and Melanie stuck her head out. She looked as though she'd aged ten years in the last ten minutes or so, wearing an expression of such conflict that Ryan was sure she was about to back out of the whole thing. Instead, she nodded in his direction and motioned for him to come back inside.

"They've got about everything worked out other than how you fit into it all," she said. "You're going to need to hammer that Joe guy on this, I think. He's all for kicking you out of the car before we even get there."

"I hope you talked him out of that, at least," Ryan said as he slid off the hood and started toward her.

"Me and Carrie did," Melanie said. "I think it was telling him he'd be riding in the back and you'd be up front with me that finally did it, though. Still, might want to make sure your seat belt's fastened pretty tight."

"I'll sit between him and the lovely lass," Francis said, also getting to his feet. "Might give him something else to focus on instead of our fearless leader, here."

Melanie raised an eyebrow, and Ryan looked over at him, both amused and confused. "What makes you think I'm the leader here and not Joe?"

Francis clapped him on the shoulder as he moved past Melanie and back into the room. "Everything."

Melanie shrugged and waited for Ryan to enter before closing the door again. Carrie was sitting on the edge of the bed, her legs crossed, a calm look on her face. It was the most demure and ladylike Ryan had seen her appear since he'd met her, and he wondered if he was catching a glimpse of the real person beneath her tough-guy façade. She glanced over as he entered and nodded to him, and then went back to looking pensive.

Joe was still seated behind the table where he'd been when Ryan first got here, but now instead of looking around with barely restrained ferocity, he sat with his head in his hands, fingers rubbing his temples like he had a headache he just couldn't get rid of. For some strange reason, Ryan thought he was one of the main sources of that particular pain. He also looked up when Ryan came in, but he only glowered at him.

"Well, kid, since it seems I can't get rid of you because no one else here has any goddamn brains, do you at least have any athletic ability?" he asked. "Any hunting in your past? Anything that might actually help me think I'm not going to have to fight a damn bloodsucker and babysit you?"

"I played some little league a few years ago," Ryan said. He knew it wasn't what the man was hoping to hear, but it was about all he really had. "Shortstop. I always thought I was pretty good at it."

Joe stared at him, and then ran a hand slowly down his face. "Jesus Christ. Little league. Fine, I might be able to work with that. Here's how this is going to work: you and your friend—the human one, I guess I should be clear about that— are going to hang back and let me and Carrie do the bulk of the work. If we need to reload, or step out to catch our bearings or something, that's when you'll come in, and only until we're back in the fight, at which point you get the hell away again. If you can live with that, we'll go ahead with this crazy fucking plan. If you can't, then have a nice damned life, and we'll figure it out on our own."

Ryan looked over to Melanie, who nodded. "I'm going, and if this is what it takes, that's what I'll do. If you want to be there, to see this fucker that killed Hunter taken out, I'd suggest you do the same."

"Not a total idiot," Joe mumbled. "Just mostly."

Melanie rolled her eyes, and Ryan had to fight the urge to laugh. This was definitely not the time for humor, and he actually didn't feel all that amused, but something about that particular reaction was so familiar, so much like Hunter that he couldn't help but revert to the way things had been, when Hunter was alive, and when it seemed like there was nothing that would ever stop them. The nostalgia was immediately followed by a wave of sorrow and grief so strong it nearly buckled his knees. He nodded, swallowed the lump that had suddenly risen in his throat, and looked back to Joe.

"Agreed."

"Then let's get on with this," the man said, getting up so fast his chair actually squeaked as it slid across the tile floor. "Before I realize how stupid I'm being and change my mind."

Ryan turned to the door and felt Melanie's hand on his arm. He looked up and saw there were tears standing in her eyes. "This is for Hunter."

He felt his own eyes go warm as tears threatened to fill them as well. "For Hunter."

And as they piled into the car, Ryan thought he could feel one other presence there as well, the presence of someone whose death had started this whole insane path he was on. Someone who was just as eager to see them succeed as they were.

CHAPTER THIRTY-THREE

I t was like a scene from a movie. As Ryan watched Joe and Carrie pulling gear from the trunk of their car and strapping on assault vests and loading what looked like machine guns, he felt like he was watching some big action film getting ready to shoot its climactic fight scene. Then Joe secured a samurai sword in its sheath onto his back and suddenly everything descended into B-movie territory. At least there were no crucifixes or little vials of holy water to make it look even more stereotypical. Francis had disappeared almost as soon as they'd parked the car, off to prepare for his role in the confrontation to come, but Melanie stood nearby, the expression on her face making it clear that she felt the same way Ryan did about this strange display.

Joe turned toward them as he attached a pair of metal plates over his gloves. They gleamed in the rising moonlight, and Ryan found himself wondering if they were made out of silver or if they were just well-polished. When he finished tightening the plate down, he lifted the gun hanging from a sling over his shoulder.

"When we get in there," he said. "It's imperative that both of you stay behind us. These are loaded with tracer rounds, which means not only will they do what normal bullets will, they're also going to be flammable. So unless you want to get yourself truly fucked up, don't get in the line of fire."

While he didn't know everything there was to know about guns, his brother had taught him a few things both before and after he'd left for the Army. Most of it was trivial, or exceptionally technical, but something about Joe's statement clicked with all that random knowledge.

"Won't that cause the barrel to heat up, soften, deform, and then jam?" he asked. "I thought tracer rounds burned hotter than normal ones."

Carrie chuckled as she tightened the straps on her vest. Melanie gave him a shocked look, and Joe's expression became one of appraisal, as if he was truly seeing Ryan for the first time. Ryan shrugged. "What? My brother's in the military."

"Normally, you'd be correct," Joe said. He pointed to the gun's barrel. "These have been customized. The barrel is made from titanium, so we can fire longer than we normally would. And before you ask, yes, tracer rounds are normally used only to verify you're firing at the right spot in the dark, every third or fifth round, but when you're dealing with creatures that are able to basically ignore normal bullets but are extremely susceptible to fire, it doesn't hurt to hedge your bets."

"Okay, whatever," Ryan said. "So where's our guns?"

"Not a hope in hell, kid," Joe said. He turned back to the trunk, pulled out a pistol, and handed it to Melanie. "You know how to use this?"

"Point and pull the trigger, right?" she asked.

"Basically," Joe replied, and then resumed digging through the trunk. "Just do me a favor. If you end up shooting me, make sure it's in the head so I can be guaranteed to not have to worry about this shit anymore."

He pulled out a baseball bat wrapped in barbed wire and handed it to Ryan. "Here you go, slugger. Let's see how that little league practice works out for you."

Ryan rolled his eyes as he took the bat, feeling like a wrestler getting ready for one of those "hardcore" matches he'd seen a few times, or maybe that guy from Walking Dead who liked to bash people's heads in with his own barbed-wire bat. "I thought you didn't want me getting close enough to use this."

"I don't," Joe replied. "I'm also not stupid enough to leave you completely defenseless."

"I do know how to use a gun, you know."

"Hooray for you. I'm still not giving you one. Tell you what, though. I die, you can grab mine off my corpse."

"Anyone ever tell you you're an asshole?"

Joe actually smiled at him. "All the time, kid. All the time."

Ryan shook his head as Joe turned and looked to Carrie, who nodded at him and slammed the trunk closed. Joe clicked on the flashlight affixed to the side of his gun and started toward the building. Carrie gave Ryan and Melanie a quick reassuring smile, then turned on her own light and followed after him.

"If this goes bad," Melanie said softly. "You run like hell. Get out of there. I'm not going to have your death on my conscience, too."

"Only if you're running beside me," Ryan replied. "Otherwise I'm not going anywhere."

She smiled and gave him a quick but furious hug. After planting a kiss on his cheek, she pulled away and started after the other two. Ryan swallowed hard, trying to force down the bout of nerves that had been trying to overtake him since they got in the car to come out here, hefted his bat, and brought up the rear.

Francis had already told Joe and Carrie that he'd spent most of his time in the basement, so Joe had elected to start the search there and work their way up. Once they entered the reception area, he and Carrie quickly searched the room and then turned their attention to the stairwell. It was strange to watch how efficiently they moved, their lights dancing in complement to one another, and the positions they took to descend the stairs was tight enough that Ryan thought any SWAT team would be jealous.

At the bottom of the stairs, they split up, one creeping down the left side of the hall while the other took the right. Instead of ignoring the closed doors they came upon, whichever of them found it would click their tongue, alerting the other, then both would open the door and make sure the room beyond was empty before resuming their former positions. They bypassed the pair of doors leading into the storeroom, the room Francis had told them had been his little makeshift home, saving it for last. Carrie remained behind to guard those doors while Joe continued to the laundry room.

Ryan could feel his nervousness increasing the longer the man was gone. He breathed a sigh of relief when he saw the first traces of a flashlight beam dancing off the floor as he returned. He made his way to the second door into the storeroom, looked over to Carrie, and then raised one hand, fingers extended. He lowered them one by one, a silent countdown, before finally pointing at her and then ducking through the open door. Carrie followed, equally silent and equally fast.

They didn't find the other vampire in the storeroom, but it wasn't empty either. Ryan heard Carrie's soft exhalation of breath and saw both lights shining down at the floor as he and Melanie entered behind them. When he finally caught a glimpse of what those lights illuminated, he had to fight to keep his meager dinner in his stomach where it belonged. He held one hand over his mouth to silence it if he did vomit, but luckily, everything stayed down.

A body lay on the floor, streaks of red radiating outward from it in every direction. Ryan assumed this was the other hunter he'd met at the diner—Mario, he thought the name was—but there was no way to be sure based on what he could see of the man now. His skin had turned from dark to light gray, giving him an albino appearance that was broken by the blood that coated him. His arms and legs were twisted into unnatural angles, his plain t-shirt shredded and dipping into the hollow cavity that used to be his abdomen. Ryan let his eyes trail up from there and felt a moment of disorientation when he saw nothing above the man's neck. Suddenly, he realized what this meant and turned away before he lost the tenuous control he'd managed over his gorge.

It didn't help; he could see a shadow just outside the circle of light the two hunters made, and realized he'd found Mario's head. It had been either cut or torn off, and lay cast aside like a basketball in the driveway after a pick-up game had to be cut short because of a storm. His stomach rebelled again, and this time there was no stopping it. He doubled over, vomit already streaming from his mouth, trying unsuccessfully to be sick as quietly as possible. He felt a gentle hand on his back, rubbing soothingly, and was grateful for it. He managed to get himself back under control, wiped his mouth with the back of one hand, and then looked up, expecting to see Melanie standing beside him.

He was wrong. Carrie stood there, hand on his back, her weapon pointed so the light still shone in the direction of the body. She had a sympathetic smile on her face, and her eyes were filled with such care and understanding that it was nearly enough to bring tears to his own eyes. In that moment, highlighted by the scant traces of light, she was quite possibly the most beautiful woman he'd ever seen. The thought made him feel immediately guilty, like he was cheating on Kayla despite the fact he was too young for Carrie to have that kind of an interest in, and his cheeks burned from the embarrassment of it.

"I'm sorry," he whispered, even though he wasn't sure if he was apologizing for being sick or for the momentary feeling of inappropriate lust that had overwhelmed him.

"Don't be," Carrie whispered back. "I'd be more worried if you took seeing that in stride."

"How are you doing it? Taking it in stride, I mean."

Her eyes took on a sad, almost haunted look. "It's not the first time I've seen something like that, and I've learned to hold it in until the job's done. Believe me, if we all walk out of here, I'll have my own tears and puke to get rid of soon enough."

He barked out as quiet a laugh as he could manage, and then winced at the taste of bile and regurgitated food that filled his mouth. Another light danced at the edge of his vision, and he looked over to see Joe and Melanie approaching. Melanie gave him a half-smile, and Ryan wondered if she'd been sick, too. Joe's face, on the other hand, had gone even harder than it was when they first started out.

"Whoever this bastard is, he's a vicious son of a bitch," the man said softly. "He obviously got his fill, but he wasted as much blood as he took in. That doesn't happen often. Much as I hate to say it, I think your bloodsucking friend was right: we're dealing with a true monster, here."

"Looks like this floor's clear," Carrie said. Her hand moved away from Ryan's back as she renewed the grip on her weapon, and he felt a flash of sadness at its absence.

Joe nodded, and then looked from Melanie to Ryan. "You both sure I can't convince you to get the hell out of here, now? We can escort you back to your car, then report back once we've finished up...."

"No," Ryan said. His throat burned from the stomach acid, giving his voice a harshness it didn't normally possess. "We're here, so we're in this until it's over."

Melanie reached over, took his hand, and gave it a gentle squeeze. "We'll leave when that thing's dead."

"Your funerals," Joe said. He glanced back to where Mario's body lay, once more hidden by the shadows in the room. "I hate to just leave him there like that, but there's no time to get him out and come back. I guess I'll have to settle for making that monster pay for what he did to him."

He nodded to Carrie. "Back up the stairs, then clear the first floor. Maybe we can luck out and find some fire stairs near the end, so we don't have to double back."

Carrie started moving without bothering to acknowledge him, weapon snapping as if by rote into a ready position in front of her. Joe fell into place behind and a little to one side of her. As Ryan and Melanie once more took up the rear guard, he found himself unable to stop seeing that headless, mangled body that he knew was right behind him, and for the first time, truly began to wonder if he was ever going to walk out of this place again.

CHAPTER THIRTY-FOUR

A s he worked his way up the chipped and broken wall to the roof and the access door he knew would grant him entry to the building, Francis realized that he felt something he hadn't felt in a very long time, perhaps not since those horrible and bloody first nights after his turn. His stomach ached, even though he was long beyond food or illness causing such a reaction. There was a slight tremble in his hands that he wanted to credit to the chill that was in the air, but since temperature changes also didn't affect him, he knew that couldn't be the case either. His heart sat still in his chest, but he could feel the phantom sensation of it pounding away, threatening to burst free of his ribs like that alien creature in some movie he'd seen so long ago.

Unfamiliar as it was anymore, that collection of feelings all added up to one thing, surprising as it might be: fear.

He wasn't afraid of facing the other vampire, that much he knew. Both of them had more in common with animals than with humans when it came to things like territoriality or establishing dominance. This confrontation was nothing more than an extension of that. No, it was something deeper that disturbed him. He paused when he made it to the roof, looking out over the field leading to thick woods at the back of the hospital's property, and tried to put his finger on exactly what it was.

It didn't take long to conclude that he was afraid of his own impending death.

No matter how this night went, he would not survive it. If the other vampire didn't send him off to that final death and whatever tortures lay beyond for something like him, one of those hunters would. Worse, he'd asked them to. He had his reasons, of course, far beyond what he'd confessed to Ryan. While that had been true, there was so much more to it than simply a desire to die with his humanity mostly intact.

Since he'd awakened from his sleep, his thoughts had been filled with memories of his long-departed family, of sweet Fiona, also long since gone to whatever life lay across the border of mortality, even of Christine, and the look of fear in her eyes in the final moments before he drained the artificial life from her and put an end to the horror-show of an existence she'd forged for herself. He missed them, all of them, and yearned to join them. He knew better than to think he'd be given such a gift as reuniting with them after he was dead and gone. More likely God or whatever force was running things would condemn him as a monster and send him to whatever deep, dark, hellish pit existed for those of his ilk, but not being allowed to live in the world with them in it as well had become more of a burden than he would've thought possible.

He shook his head, turned, and started toward the little enclosure over the stairs leading down into the hospital itself. There was no time to allow himself to be distracted by such thoughts. He had a job to do and needed to use as much mental power as he could to block his presence from the other vampire. The entire plan hinged on his ability to attack by surprise. In a fair, one-on-one fight, there was no way he would be able to prevail, and even this sneak attack stood an unreasonably high chance of failing. If there was any chance to succeed, he had to concentrate, had to block the emotions and thoughts he projected. He had to focus on the task at hand. He would make his peace and prepare to die once the other was defeated, in those scant moments while he would be lying helpless on the floor.

Francis paused in front of the door and closed his eyes. He imagined himself building walls around everything in his mind, blocking them even from his own view. As he slid the final mental brick into place, he felt calmness overtake him, settling him, steeling him for the confrontation ahead. He couldn't stop the deeper, low-level thoughts, but at least those didn't project far. The other might sense him as he was attacking, but if the rest of the group did their job, he'd be too distracted to do anything about it.

The door was locked and nearly rusted shut by age and the elements. He reached out, took hold of the handle, and yanked the door completely off its hinges. He winced and lowered it slowly to the ground, trying not to make any more noise than he already had. All that effort to silence his thoughts and emotions, and he never stopped to consider he needed to silence his physical self as well. If it wouldn't be counter-productive, he would have a good, long laugh at that one.

He waited at the now-open doorway, ears straining, waiting for the other vampire to come rushing up the stairs and attack him instead of the other way around. Nothing happened. Either it hadn't heard or hadn't cared about the noise from the roof. Unfortunately, that meant Francis had no way of knowing whether or not an ambush would be waiting for him once he got down those stairs or not. He started to sigh, remembered Ryan's admonition against it, and simply crooked a half-smile instead as he started down the steps.

He chanced one quick mental search of the floor but came up with nothing. He wanted to extend that emotional sensor to include as much of the rest of the building as he could, but he didn't dare. If that other felt it, and retaliated, he would be helpless when the rest of the group started their attack and would arrive too late to save them. The hunters he could care less about, but the sister of the first boy killed didn't deserve such a death, and Ryan most definitely had suffered enough for one lifetime. If he was going to find this thing, he was going to have to do it the old-fashioned way.

Francis crept down the darkened hallway, trying to avoid the occasional pools of faint light from the moon shining in through the dusty windows. He discovered this was one of the rare times he was grateful for his enhanced senses. With no need of a flashlight to see clearly, there was no risk of alerting his quarry that he was here by bouncing some random beam of light across the walls and floor ahead of him. Unfortunately, even with his superhuman senses, this particular prey emitted no normal human sounds to make him easier to track, no breath, no heartbeat, not even the faint sloshing of whatever meal he'd last eaten digesting in his stomach. The entire place smelled of dust and mold and mildew, so there was no tracking him by scent, either. Francis had to rely on sight and instinct, and while there was something refreshing about that, something that appealed to the soldier he used to be, it was also unnerving to the point of irritation.

He searched quickly but thoroughly, entering the rooms only to ensure there was no one hiding just beyond the doorway with their back pressed up against the wall, and then moved on to the next. It was tedious, and Francis could feel time slipping away from him, but it was the only way. He hoped the group downstairs was being as cautious as he was. Otherwise, they might well find the other vampire and engage him before Francis was even on the floor directly above them. He didn't know how he would react if he found them only to discover that the other vampire had already killed them all. Acting on emotion tended to cause mistakes, and that was something he could not afford. Not tonight.

When he reached the main stairwell in the opposite corner of the floor from where he'd started, he looked down into the spiraling landings below and fought the urge to sigh again. There were four stories below this one, not counting the basement which he was fairly confident the hunter group would have already cleared or would soon clear if they hadn't already. By a rough estimate, it had taken him nearly half an hour to deal with this floor, and he knew he was moving faster than they would be. If he wasn't careful, there was every chance he'd find his prey before the others had a chance to distract him, and the entire plan would fall apart. Still, he couldn't slow down too much, or he would risk them getting seriously injured before he was able to join the fray. Some part of him wished that he'd simply embraced what he was, thereby allowing himself to amass the strength he needed to do this on his own. Of course, had he done that, the odds were that he wouldn't care enough to be doing it in the first place.

He put his feet on the first step, and then felt a hand slam into his back with the force of a tree being felled in the woods. His body lurched forward, thrown off-balance, and before he had the chance to try and catch himself, he was falling. He hit the stairs about halfway down to the next landing, then rolled, feeling his bones crack from every hard impact. While they didn't break, they would require some of his energy reserves to heal—reserves he could scarcely afford to expend now.

When he finally slammed onto the final landing, he managed to grab ahold of the railing to stop himself. He felt his shoulder lurch but managed to hold fast. He looked up and saw nothing, but he didn't need to. He'd been tricked somehow. He let loose with a string of his favorite curses, and let his head drop back to the landing. On the one hand, he knew where his prey was. On the other, he also knew he would have to heal before he could even think about launching his part of the attack.

He only hoped the group could survive long enough for him to get there.

CHAPTER THIRTY-FIVE

By the time they'd discovered that the first floor was as deserted as the basement, Ryan was sure he'd given himself whiplash. Every little noise behind him, or beside him, or even at an angle in front of him had prompted an immediate head-jerk in that direction, his eyes searching for whatever had made it. Not that he'd seen anything to either alleviate his concerns or validate them. The few times he had seen the source of the noises, it had been mice. Once it was a rat easily as large as a small dog scurrying along the wall, racing back to whatever nest it had made for itself. Seeing that thing had been bad enough, remembering how many stories he'd heard about people having sex in here only made it worse.

After the first few times he'd anxiously whispered, "What was that?", the rest of the group had grown tired of his interruptions, so he'd stopped asking. Thankfully, the one time he nearly lost what scant control he had, they'd heard it as well. It was something heavy and meaty, a thud that echoed through the empty hallways. Joe and Carrie split up, Carrie crouching down to cover the front while Joe raced back past Ryan and Melanie, his flashlight scanning the corridor they'd just come down. They saw nothing, the sound wasn't repeated, and when nothing jumped out at them even after standing there with the light off for what felt like forever, they resumed their search.

Thankfully, there were emergency stairs at each of the far corners of the building, so they wouldn't have to double back in order to head up to the second floor. They just had to move diagonally across the floor they were on, then up, then diagonal again until they'd covered all the ground. The process would still take all night, but at least it was faster than retracing their steps the whole time.

Where the first floor had been mostly examination rooms and offices, the second floor was obviously one of the patient wards. The rooms seemed eerie cast only in the small beams of the flashlights, and in every one of them, Ryan had the distinct sensation that the occupant was only out for a brief excursion and would return at any minute. Knowing the true fate that had befallen the former patients here only made it worse. Until a few weeks ago, he would have said he didn't believe in ghosts. Since then, he'd learned that vampires were real, and whenever he thought about the violent ends the former inhabitants of this building met, he had to wonder if vampires could become ghosts, and if they'd be just as violent in the afterlife.

Silly, maybe. But right now, in this place, at this moment, it seemed all too plausible.

He was grateful when they finally emerged into the second-floor foyer off the main stairwell but was also tenser than ever that they still hadn't found the other vampire yet. Francis had been positive this was where he was, and while Ryan didn't know much about visions or psychic ability, he'd seen the near-seizure the "calling" had caused. He believed Francis, and more importantly, Joe and Carrie—who he assumed did have at least a working knowledge of the paranormal—seemed to believe him as well. They'd found Mario's body downstairs, which also added to the likelihood that this was where the vampire was hiding, so where was he?

They made their way up the stairs to the third floor, and then began working their way through the labyrinthine corridors, searching what appeared to be more patient rooms. This floor differed from the one below it, though, as the main hallway led to a large, open room in what Ryan thought was the center of the building. They'd seen the cafeteria on the first floor, along with the kitchen, so Ryan had no idea at first what this room would have been used for. Then the lights played across several toppled bookshelves, their contents scattered on the floor, and he understood. This was a patient lounge, where they would gather for games, or arts and crafts, or just socialization. A boxy old television was mounted in one corner, its screen shattered, part of what he thought was one of those metal stands to mount IV bags on still stuck deep in its innards. He found himself wondering if that had been done during the fighting, or if it was done by the previous hunters who'd cleaned the place afterward, a hopefully tell-tale sign of a patient riot.

He knelt to pick up a tiny bent metal pipe that he thought belonged to a Clue board game, and then heard a soft thump behind him. He fought the urge to turn and look, telling himself it was just something disturbed by their passage, repeating what Joe had told him so many times during his paranoia on the first floor. He focused on that little game piece, his fingertips brushing against the little threads the makers had etched into the end of it, all the while trying to get his racing heart back under control.

Then he heard Melanie scream.

He looked up in time to see her flying across the room before her legs hit one of the overturned bookcases, causing her to flip and disappear behind it. He saw a blurred shape racing toward him, and felt his crotch go warm as his bladder let go. He first thought he was only screaming in his own head, and then he realized how much his throat was hurting and knew he was doing it out loud as well. He dropped the game piece, clumsily wrapped his hand around the narrow end of the baseball bat propped on his shoulder and swung it as hard as he could.

His grip was terrible, and his aim was worse. He succeeded only in clipping himself in the side of the head with the end just below his hands, knocking himself off balance. He sprawled to the floor, bit and pieces from assorted games digging into his ribs. His head began to throb at once, and the fat end of the bat rapped hard against the floor, the wrapped barbed wire around it making a strange little *sproing* sound as it bounced off the chipped tile. He started to curse himself for managing to hit nothing other than himself, and then realized that his mistake may well have saved his life. The blurred form overshot him, and he was able to make out a hand that had been reaching for where his head had been only seconds before. He felt the air displaced above him, and then lights nearly blinded him an instant before gunshots rang out as the hunters opened fire.

Ryan had seen war movies before, had seen the images of soldiers hunkered down in foxholes while the enemy fired wildly over their heads, but the reality was immensely more terrifying than the movies made it out to be. Worse, since the hunters were firing tracer rounds instead of normal bullets. The space above him looked as though it was being inundated with little bolts of flame that left streaking afterimages on his retinas. He could feel the heat from them—doubly concerning since that had to mean they were actually pretty damned close to him—and covered his head with his hands, praying to God for this to be over quickly, one way or the other.

One of those rounds must have found its mark, because suddenly the air was split by a scream so loud and ferocious that it managed to even drown out the non-stop roar of the hunter's machine guns. Curiosity being the persistent bitch that she is, Ryan couldn't help but roll over and stare, his mind demanding to know what could have possibly made a sound like that.

A man stood not two feet away from him, one arm across his chest so he could hold the opposite shoulder. Only Ryan knew at once that this was not a man, at least not in the way he normally applied that term. He looked not that much older than Francis, but the blood that covered his chin and the look of anger and madness in his eyes made him considerably more terrifying. Despite having all his flesh intact—aside from the shoulder wound, Ryan supposed—this man had a cadaverous look about him that reeked of death and the grave. When Ryan saw vampires in the movies, or imagined them when he read books featuring them, this was the image that came to his mind's eye. All the monster was missing were the fangs.

Even Joe and Carrie seemed surprised by the thing's scream of pain and frustration, because they stopped firing for the briefest of instants. Ryan could make out the shock on Joe's face immediately revert to resolve, but the thing was moving before his finger could even twitch against his weapon's trigger. They'd given it an opening, and it was determined to take it.

It rushed them, moving faster than the eye could register. Carrie started to fire again, and then her weapon was knocked from her hands. The light didn't break when it hit the floor. Instead, it spun away, the beam casting a dizzying pattern across the tile as it slid to the other side of the room and hit something, stopping its momentum with the light pointed at the far corner. Ryan heard a grunt, followed by a thud, and knew that Carrie was down as well.

Joe never got the chance to get a bead on the thing. The blur weaved as it streaked toward him before finally blocking out the light as it slammed into him. Ryan could make out just enough to see that it had driven the hunter to the floor and was now sitting atop his chest like some sick and twisted adornment. The gun popped free, skidding a couple of feet away, the flashlight beam acting like a makeshift spotlight for the struggle now occurring between vampire and hunter.

The thing shook Joe, bouncing his head off the tile floor once, twice, a third time. To his credit, Joe remained conscious, and continued to fight for all he was worth, but it simply wasn't enough. His punches did as much to move the thing as a cat batting at a car's bumper would move the car. The thing reared back, dragging Joe's upper body along with it. It bent so far that for one crazy moment Ryan thought it was going to tap its own head on the tile, and then it shoved itself forward again, hammering the floor with Joe's head as hard as it possibly could. The sound of shattering tile mixed with what Ryan could only describe as a rotten pumpkin being dropped onto the ground. There was just enough light for Ryan to see the blood that shot across the floor. Joe's arms dropped limply to his sides even as his feet began to kick about wildly before they, too, went still.

Ryan fought back the urge to scream. He wanted to think it was because he was being brave, but he knew it was purely because he didn't want to remind the thing that he was there and possibly make himself its next target. He'd missed with his bat and couldn't bring himself to move to try again even if he wanted to. Melanie had yet to reappear from behind the bookcase where she'd landed after the thing threw her. Carrie was down, and quite possibly unconscious. Francis was nowhere to be seen.

In a word, they were fucked. The best Ryan could hope for now was that the monster was so pissed off that it killed them quickly.

The vampire stood slowly, head down, arms held out before it. Ryan thought he could detect a slight tremble as well, but that could have been a trick of the light. He had no idea whether or not a vampire could experience an adrenaline rush, and under the circumstances, he had no real desire to find out.

"Is this the best you can do?" the thing roared. Ryan clapped his hands to his ears, his head throbbing worse than it already was from the sheer volume of it. "A couple of pups and a pair of incompetent hunters? Did you really think they were going to surprise me? I've been watching this pathetic excuse for a hunting party since you got here!"

It turned, still standing over Joe's still form, and raised its head to stare at the ceiling. Apparently, it knew Francis was here somewhere, too, and was taunting him. Ryan wished he could do it quieter.

"Here's what's about to happen," it roared. "I'm going to feast on the littlest whelp, and then I'm going to turn the bitches into brides. Once that's done, the three of us are going to send you to the final death your maker should have given you your first night out of the womb!"

A gunshot rang out, eliciting a decidedly unmanly squeak from Ryan and a grunt of surprise from the vampire. Its face, once a terrifying mask of fury, adopted a look of complete and utter confusion as blood began to trickle down its nose before dripping off the end and onto the floor.

Ryan turned to see Melanie standing on the other side of the bookcase in the classic shooter's stance his brother taught him—feet spread shoulder-width apart, gun held firmly in one hand with the other cupping the bottom of the grip, head level, eyes staring straight down the barrel at her target. He looked back to the vampire and realized his brother's lessons had done her a world of good—she'd hit him almost directly between his eyes.

"You talk too fucking much," she said.

Impossibly, the thing smiled. Ryan expected more rage, or even a wordless, expressionless attack, but somehow that smile was so much more unnerving and horrifying. It locked its eyes on her, then stuck out its tongue suggestively, allowing some of the blood to drip onto it before sucking it back into its mouth.

"You're going to make a wonderful bride," it said. "And I'm thrilled you need to be broken, first. That makes it so much more fun."

When the thing took a step toward her, Ryan felt something inside his mind snap. A protective instinct he hadn't even known he possessed suddenly flared to life, solidifying his resolve. He reached over and grabbed the bat again, clenching it so tightly that his fingers ached. He wanted to get up and start swinging, but he knew that would be tantamount to suicide right now. Instead, he watched, the anger growing inside him, as the thing stalked toward Melanie. He heard the gun bark twice more, saw the vampire twitch as the bullets slammed into him, but still it moved. When he thought—hoped—it was close enough, Ryan screamed, pushing himself to his knees and swinging the bat in a low arc.

This time, he hit his mark.

The head of the bat, along with the barbed wire wrapped around it, buried itself directly in the vampire's crotch.

This time, it didn't scream; it screeched. Ryan thought for sure his eardrums were going to explode from the force of that sound. His hands dropped away to cover his ears, but crazily, the bat stayed in place, secured to the thing's genitals by the barbs. The veins on the sides of its neck stood out as it stood there, legs splayed, hands slowly moving to grasp the improvised weapon. It took hold of it and yanked, causing another of those earth-shattering shrieks to tear loose from its throat. It threw the bat across the room as easily as a man tossing a wadded-up piece of paper at a trash can, and then turned to stare at Ryan with a mix of agony and disbelief.

There were no taunts this time, no grand speeches. It just leapt at him.

And fell flat on its face as something slammed into it from behind.

Francis snarled and clamped his teeth down on the other vampire's neck, then jerked his head back. Ryan felt something warm splatter against his face and had just enough time to realize it was blood before Francis dove in again, locking his lips over the wound he'd made and began to suck.

The other vampire went wild beneath him, but Francis wrapped his arms and legs around it and held on for all he was worth. Ryan gaped as the other vampire's hair began to lighten, before finally streaking through with a white that nearly glowed in the dim light. Its face began to change as well, becoming sunken, lips stretching away from its teeth in a rictus grin. Its mouth opened wide, like a snake about to devour its prey, and Ryan heard himself screaming as its tongue withered to dust in front of his eyes.

He scrambled away, turning from that awful sight, unable to bear it any longer. He felt tears streaming down his cheeks even as a strange exultation rose within him from knowing that the monster who'd killed Hunter and those other kids was finally feeling some of the same fear it had given them. He felt as well as heard a final gasping exhalation, and then there was a soft pattering sound that was unlike anything he'd ever heard before. His mind recalled his mother accidentally knocking an open bag of sugar onto the kitchen floor, the closest comparison he could make.

And then, silence.

Finally, he forced himself to turn and see the end result. Francis lay nearby on his side, eyes glowing, staring up at nothing in particular. His mouth was hanging open, and his fingers were tracing the contours of his lips. A wide swath of some strange powdery dust lay between them, and Ryan knew it was all that remained of the other vampire. A light breeze and even that would be gone, as if the thing had never existed to start with.

Francis turned his head slightly, and his eyes focused on Ryan's face. His mouth snapped closed, and a faint grin spread across his lips.

"It's time," Francis whispered. "Can I ask a favor?"

Ryan nodded, unable to speak.

"Can you do it? I think I'll feel better knowing it was someone who actually cared, maybe cared for the first time in my entire existence."

Ryan's mouth trembled as he fought for words. "There's got to be another way."

Francis closed his eyes, still smiling slightly. "As long as the hunters know I exist, they'll come for me. Believe me, this is better."

Ryan nodded again and forced himself to his feet. He looked over and saw Melanie, tears of her own streaming from her eyes, staring at the spot where the other vampire had once been. He stumbled past Francis and approached Joe's body, thankful that the light kept him from seeing the mess that had been made of the man's head. He knelt and reached for the sword still strapped to the man's back, not even caring that it was now coated in blood and brains. With an effort, he finally managed to slide it free from its sheath. He stared down at it, the polished blade glimmering even in the near-darkness. He looked over and saw Carrie, still lying on the ground, her hands moving slowly toward her head.

There was no more putting things off. Francis was right. As long as the hunters knew he existed, they would chase him to the ends of the earth. A part of him wished he could convince Carrie to let him alone, but he'd heard her back at the motel. She would do her duty, no matter what.

He staggered back over to Francis and stared down at him. The vampire's eyes were still closed, the smile still on his face. Somehow, that made things worse.

"Thank you," Ryan croaked. "For everything. You changed my life."

The smile widened. "And you mine. Thank you. For this, and everything else as well. I lay my head to rest, and in doing so, lay at your feet the faces I have seen, the voices I have heard, the words I have spoken, the hands I have shaken, the service I have given, the joys I have shared, the sorrows revealed, I lay them at your feet, and in doing so lay my head to rest."

Ryan lowered his head and fought to clear the tears from his vision. He traced one thumb along the edge of the sword's blade, felt it part the skin, and knew it was sharp enough to do the job. He took a deep breath, gripped the handle in both hands, and raised it over his head.

"Goodbye, Francis," he whispered.

And brought the sword down.

EPILOGUE

It was hard to imagine the town without the abandoned asylum there, but as Ryan stood looking over the backhoes, cranes, and dump trucks clearing the burned-out husk of the building from the lot where it once stood, he knew it was something he was going to have to get used to. His eyes strained to see into the hole that had been opened up, hoping to see some small sign of Francis's old apartment, but he knew that even if he could, there would be nothing to see. It had burned, along with the rest of the building, the night he'd helped stop the child killer from ever killing again.

Not that he'd been present for the actual fire, of course. Once she'd come to a bit more, Carrie had gotten in contact with what she refused to call anything other than "The Organization" to arrange a clean-up crew. With Joe dead, the duty fell to her, whether she wanted it or not. From what Ryan understood, they'd arrived shortly after midday, done what they had to do, and were gone before anyone of any importance in town even knew they were there. When he and Kayla had come to see what happened later that evening, the place had been surrounded by emergency crews, including trucks from fire departments two towns over. They'd been ordered to leave, so they did. When they went back the next day, there was nothing left of the place but a burned-out husk.

That hadn't stopped him from coming here almost every day since. He never went past the fence, just stood outside it and looked out over the place. He could never explain it, but somehow he felt connected here. To Hunter, and to Francis, and those insane few weeks where his life had changed.

And to Melanie and Carrie, too, though he still heard from them on occasion. Carrie less often, even with Melanie's mail being checked before she could send it to him. He never expected that in all of the insanity that followed that long, tense night, she would find her calling doing a job no one else would ever believe actually existed in the real world. Yet there she was, in some place she couldn't tell him about, learning how to be a vampire hunter. She promised to come and see him once she was able, but he knew better. Her life was going to be devoted to a higher calling now, and that would leave precious little time for friends.

Carrie had insisted that she was pushing for changes in the way the organization did things, but he held little hope they would see much traction. Her last email had indicated that she was apt to face some pretty severe consequences if she didn't drop it, and while he hadn't learned of her final decision yet, he knew what it would be. She was smart and wouldn't push things too far. She was a survivor, just like him.

She'd even confided in him, explaining how she'd come to be a hunter in the first place after the death of her parents and her sister. He could feel the emotion in that email, even with untold miles between them. He'd almost told her what really happened that night, but he just couldn't bring himself to. He trusted her, he just didn't know if he trusted her that much.

It had taken time for the town to relax and stop being fearful that the child killer was going to strike again any time, but it finally had. Well, to some degree. Nothing was ever the same after that, and he'd heard adults mentioning how they now locked their doors at night when they never had before. And kids from school still tended to stay in pairs or small groups when they went anywhere, but that was probably a smart precaution, no matter what. Even taking vampires out of the equation, there were still plenty of monsters out there who enjoyed preying on kids.

Kayla squeezed his hand, drawing him back from his thoughts. He turned and saw her smiling at him.

"You about ready?"

He smiled back, and then leaned over and kissed her. He still felt a tingle run through him as their lips touched and hoped that would stay forever. He knew better—life was all about change, after all, and that meant there had to be loss as well. He knew that the day would come when their love would fade into a fond memory they could share ten or twenty years down the line, when they were married and had kids of their own with other people, but for now, he could hope.

She pulled back, still smiling, and then turned and began to lead him back to the road, and whatever might lay further along it. He cast one final glance back to the place where he'd learned a portion of the real truth beneath the surface of the world, and then followed after her. It was only a building, only a construct, but it was where he gained this strange wisdom, the product of a connection he still couldn't hope to understand, and knew it would live on in his memories, and the story he'd started writing just last week as well.

He paused briefly as he thought he caught a familiar flash of red hair, and then put it out of his mind. He knew it wasn't Francis. He was gone forever. If he wasn't, the hunters never would have left this place, would still be here, searching for him. Would have chased him all the way back to Ireland, if what he felt was anything to go by.

He smiled as he let Kayla lead him away from the old asylum. Somewhere, he was sure Hunter was smiling, too.

THE END

ABOUT THE AUTHOR

If you ask his wife, John Quick is compelled to tell stories because he's full of baloney. He prefers to think he simply has an affinity for things that are strange, disturbing, and terrifying. As proof, he will explain how he suffered **Consequences**, transcribed **The Journal of Jeremy Todd**, and regaled the tale of **Mudcat**. He lives in Middle Tennessee with his aforementioned long-suffering wife, two exceptionally patient kids, four dogs that could care less so long as he keeps scratching that perfect spot on their noses, and a cat who barely acknowledges his existence.

ALSO FROM
BLOODSHOT BOOKS

From a crater lake on an island off the coast of Bronze Age Estonia...

To a crippled Viking warrior's conquest of England ...

To the bloody temple of an Aztec god of death and resurrection...

Their presence has shaped our world. They are the Riders.

One month ago, an urban explorer was drawn to an abandoned asylum in the mountains of northern Massachusetts. There he discovered a large specimen jar, containing something organic, unnatural and possibly alive.

Now, he and a group of unsuspecting individuals have discovered one of history's most horrific secrets. Whether they want to or not, they are caught in the middle of a millennia-old war and the latest battle is about to begin.

Available in paperback or Kindle on Amazon.com

FINALLY IN PRINT AFTER MORE THAN THREE DECADES, THE NOVEL MARK MORRIS WROTE BEFORE *TOADY*

EVIL NEEDS ONLY A SEED

Limefield has had more than its fair share of tragedy. Barely six years ago, a disturbed young boy named Russell Swaney died beneath the wheels of a passenger train mere moments after committing a heinous act of unthinkable sadism. Now, a forest fire caused by the thoughtless actions of two teens has laid waste to hundreds of acres of the surrounding woodlands and unleashed a demonic entity

EVIL TAKES ROOT

Now, a series of murders plague the area and numerous local residents have been reported missing, including the entire population of the nearby prison. But none of this compares to the appearance of the Winter Tree, a twisted wooden spire which seems to leech the warmth from the surrounding land.

EVIL FLOURISHES

Horrified by what they have caused, the two young men team up with a former teacher and the local police constabulary to find the killer, but it may already be too late. Once planted, evil is voracious. Like a weed, it strangles all life, and the roots of the Winter Tree are already around their necks.

Available in paperback or Kindle on Amazon.com

http://bit.ly/TreeKindle

There's a monster coming to the small town of Pikeburn. In half an hour, it will begin feeding on the citizens, but no one will call the authorities for help. They are the ones who sent it to Pikeburn. They are the ones who are broadcasting the massacre live to the world. Every year, Red Diamond unleashes a new creation in a different town as a display of savage terror that is part warning and part celebration. Only no one is celebrating in Pikeburn now. No one feels honored or patriotic. They feel like prey.

Local Sheriff Yan Corban refuses to succumb to the fear, paranoia, and violence that suddenly grips his town. Stepping forward to battle this year's lab-grown monster, Sheriff Corban must organize a defense against the impossible. His allies include an old art teacher, a shell-shocked mechanic, a hateful millionaire, a fearless sharpshooter, a local meth kingpin, and a monster groupie. Old grudges, distrust, and terror will be the monster's allies in a game of wits and savagery, ambushes and treachery. As the conflict escalates and the bodies pile up, it becomes clear this creature is unlike anything Red Diamond has unleashed before.

No mercy will be asked for or given in this battle of man vs monster. It's time to run, hide, or fight. It's time for Red Diamond.

Available in paperback or Kindle on Amazon.com

http://bit.ly/DiamondUS

January 12, 1888

When a day dawns warm and mild in the middle of a long cold winter, it's greeted as a blessing, a reprieve. A chance for those who've been cooped up indoors to get out, do chores, run errands, send the children to school... little knowing that they're only seeing the calm before the storm.

The blizzard hits out of nowhere, screaming across the Great Plains like a runaway train. It brings slicing winds, blinding snow, plummeting temperatures. Livestock will be found frozen in the fields, their heads encased in blocks of ice formed from their own steaming breath. Frostbite and hypothermia wait for anyone caught without shelter.

For the hardy settlers of Far Enough, in the Montana Territory, it's about to get worse. Something else has arrived with the blizzard. Something sleek and savage and hungry. Wild animal or vengeful spirit from native legend, it blends into the snow and bites with sharper teeth than the wind.

It is called the *wanageeska*.

It is the White Death

http://bit.ly/WDKindle

ON THE HORIZON FROM
BLOODSHOT BOOKS
2019-20

The Cryptids – Elana Gomel

Clownflesh – Tim Curran

Midnight Solitaire – Greg F. Gifune

Jimmy the Freak – Charles Colyott & Mark Steensland

Dead Branches – Benjamin Langley

Dead Sea Chronicles – Tim Curran

The October Boys – Adam Millard

Behemoth – H.P. Newquist

Blood Mother: A Novel of Terror – Pete Kahle

Not Your Average Monster – World Tour

The Abomination (The Riders Saga #2) – Pete Kahle

The Horsemen (The Riders Saga #3) – Pete Kahle

other titles to be added when confirmed

BLOODSHOT BOOKS

READ UNTIL YOU BLEED!

Printed in Great Britain
by Amazon